CAPTIVE EMBERS

BRIAN MANSUR

AETHON
BOOKS

CAPTIVE EMBERS

Published by Aethon Books LLC.

Cover Art by Tom Edwards Design. Print and eBook formatting, and cover design by Beaulistic Book Services (Steve Beaulieu)

DEDICATION

For all those who helped make this labor of love possible.

Location: Lakshmi Colony, orbiting the gas giant Belia, Cervantes star system, fifty light-years from Earth. 4380 A.D._

STANDING OUTSIDE OF THE CORIOLIS CAFÉ, COMMANDER RAFE Hastings drew his leather jacket tight and willed his shoulders to unknot. He pictured the beaming faces of his raven-haired wife and daughters. He considered that perhaps his wife, Gita, was right and he needed to quit playing spy. He made a thoughtful noise as he opened the restaurant's door.

Like most places in the one-hundred-kilometer-long cylindrical colony, the café exuded the stench of decay. Worn tables wobbled on legs missing half of their rubbery pads. The seats' blue cushions bore questionable brownish stains. A formidable mix of spices and fetid scents wafted from the kitchen. Or maybe that was still the air in the dank place.

Rafe found his informant in a back-corner booth. Every aspect of the corpulent ex-mafioso evidenced a life of self-indulgence—from his puffy eyes and greasy hawk nose to the scruffy jowls dragging down his sallow face.

In contrast, Rafe possessed dark skin and a tall, fitness trainer's physique. Despite a pre-mission, surgical makeover, he retained a lantern jaw, mocha hair, and dark Punjabi features that blended with the local populace.

Over the room's percussive music, Baylor said, "You took long enough to get here."

Rafe suppressed a frown. Two months prior, Baylor had grovelled after seeing Rafe's footage of the dockworker stealing goods from Lilith's Cartel. That was only a fraction of the dirt Rafe had on the man.

Rafe slid into the bench across the table. "Your safety is a priority. I had to wait until I was sure you weren't followed." He plucked a menu. "What's edible here?"

Baylor sneered. "That raid your people made on Sundar Colony has them searching for the leak."

Rafe raised his eyebrows. He leaned in. "Do they suspect you?"

"Of course, they suspect me. They suspect everyone now."

"That's a good sign," Rafe said.

"Yeah, sure," Baylor said. "They don't know it was me yet."

"You did well with that info drop. Earned that bonus. I take it you brought something?"

Baylor folded his arms and said, "I want more money."

"Oh?" Rafe's brow furrowed.

"What I found out this week is worth a hundred times what you're giving me. Once you've met my price, I want out."

Rafe strangled an urge to laugh. "Baylor, you're already making a killing. Play the game, and Lilith need never know about this."

Baylor's face darkened. "Why won't you Mykonians leave us alone, huh? Belia isn't your part of the system."

Rafe shrugged in sympathy. "You know what they say. Blame the Wardens."

Baylor sniffed.

One could always blame *them*.

"I get the frustration," Rafe told Baylor. "I don't want to be here either, but I can't let you go yet."

Baylor opened his mouth to retort when a smiling waitress arrived with a glass of water and placed it in front of Rafe.

"Get you anything?" she asked.

"I'll need a few minutes," Rafe said.

"Take your time."

Once the server left, Rafe said, "The deal stands. Keep feeding me cargo box numbers for my associates to chase. Give me something to explain how Lilith's Cartel is taking over everything, and we'll see about cutting you loose."

Baylor grinned as he slid an envelope across the table under his hand. "Here's the report of what I found."

Rafe lifted the flap and drew a piece of folded paper. Scratchy penmanship littered the manila surface.

He held it up to ensure that the camera in his shirt button relayed the contents to his A.I. assistant, James. Before Rafe could finish reading the first word of the top sentence, the computer had analyzed the letter.

"You're not going to like this, sir," James said into Rafe's earpiece.

Rafe's shoulders bunched up as he read.

Rafe groaned. Somehow, Lilith had gotten her hands on Arbiters—a special type of A.I. that cost more than the annual industrial allotment for a dozen colonies and allowed humans to mount heavy weapons on and against habitats. Without them, space combat was restricted to exchanges between warships. Even ground troops couldn't lob anything more powerful than an 80mm mortar.

Feeling Baylor's intense gaze, Rafe calmly laid the page down. "Interesting, if true. Do you have proof?"

Baylor slid across a black device. Rafe recognized it as one of the micro-cameras he'd given Baylor at their first meeting. Its sapphire lens housing trailed a gossamer filament to a mini-computer wafer.

"That's your free sample," Baylor said. The man relaxed into his chair, a finger tapping his left breast pocket. Rafe saw the tip of another envelope poking out. "What you'll need to track *some* of the rest is in here. I've hidden the other recorders away, so behave yourself."

Rafe connected the miniature camera to his wrist pad. Data poured through the link to James. After a few seconds, the memory wafer erased itself.

Rafe fixed Baylor with a stony glare. "My associates will be checking this. If you're lying to me—"

James said in his ear, "Sir, I think he's telling the truth."

Rafe's skin crawled. "How long have you known about this, Baylor?"

"Almost a week."

"Why didn't you call me sooner?" If Baylor's report could be believed, some of the items had already left the colony.

Baylor flashed his teeth. "So you wouldn't have time to haggle, of course."

"What have you done?"

"My price is ten million," he said, folding his arms and leaning back against his chair.

Rafe willed the corners of his mouth to inch upward. "Be reasonable, Baylor. I'm sure you wouldn't want me to give the police footage of you screwing those thirteen-year-olds at the pleasure houses."

Before Baylor could lift his jaw, Rafe heard James' rising voice. "Sir, there's—" The line burst into static. A second later, it cut out. Rafe glanced at his wristband. Its "no signal" icon pulsed.

He shot to his feet, adrenaline pouring into his system. He

snatched the paper with its secrets and hauled Baylor up by the collar. Rafe drew his face close and whispered, "We've been followed!"

Baylor ceased struggling. His eyes bulged. "What? How do you—"

"Look around," Rafe growled. Several diners wore irritated expressions. They tapped at their earphones, wrist pads, and hand-held devices in vain hopes of reconnecting to the net. Someone jammed the cellular frequencies at the exact point when an eavesdropper might have decided everything of interest had been heard.

Rafe snarled at the quivering fat man. "Where's the bug? They must have planted one on you!"

"I changed before coming," Baylor said. "I'm clean." His voice didn't sound so sure.

Rafe had done the same. He prayed that something hadn't latched onto one of them in the meantime. Perhaps a listening device lay somewhere in the room.

"Come on," Rafe said, pulling Baylor toward the kitchen. He'd already scouted the place and knew the building's rear opened onto an alley.

Throwing open the kitchen door, he said, "My friend's going to be sick. Where's the back door?" Half a dozen fingers directed the pair toward an exit.

Turning the knob, Rafe pulled a pistol from his jacket, then poked his head outside. He checked both ends of the shrouded alley and scanned above. A motionless Warden blimp hung in place. Beyond it, pinprick lights from hovercars, dwellings, and street lamps twinkled in the concave sky.

Satisfied he couldn't detect anything threatening, Rafe led Baylor out and shut the restaurant's door with a muted thud. He turned to Baylor who palmed a handgun of his own.

Rafe patted him on his chest with one hand and on the cheek

with his sidearm. Baylor flinched. Fortunately for Rafe, the anxious man did nothing more.

"Congratulations on your acceptance into our witness protection program," Rafe said.

Baylor stared back, unaware that Rafe had lifted the other envelope from his pocket. "What?"

Rafe hid the packet while turning to hustle down the alleyway, tugging at the various locked doors as he went.

"Wait a minute," Baylor called, waddling along. "Why should I believe you'd help me?"

"Because if Lilith catches you, she'll torture you for everything you know. That's bad for my business."

Baylor called Rafe something obscene.

"Quit whining, and be glad I'm not cold-blooded enough to kill you myself," Rafe said.

They drew near the alley's end. Rafe began to think they would have to risk the open avenue when a knob finally turned. He nodded to Baylor, then gave the door a firm push. It popped open a crack before coming to a rib-jarring halt.

Rafe balled his fist. He peered into the gap and saw a security chain glinting from the interior lights. He barely had long enough to mutter a curse before a bullet clanged off a nearby garbage bin.

Rafe dove behind the rusting metal box before being caught in a hail of gunfire. Bangs echoed in the alleyway. Baylor howled, "My arm!" as he careened into the waste container's side. The portly man screamed as another round struck close by. Rafe reached around the corner and dragged him behind cover.

"They got my arm!" Baylor said, panting.

"Keep quiet," Rafe said with a snarl. "They don't need to know that." He pulled Baylor upright and checked that the oaf still had his weapon.

"Cover our backs." Rafe stuck his pistol over the top of their improvised barricade and fired three rounds. He chanced a peek into the dim alley. "I see two men with handguns." One fired while the other advanced to the next scrap of cover. They'd be on him and Baylor quickly if he didn't act.

Rafe scanned the alley. Across the way stood the door he'd tried to open. The thin privacy chain gleamed. "Don't worry," he said. "We aren't dying here." A smattering of return fire punctuated his declaration.

"Oh really?"

Rafe responded by taking careful aim at the door chain. Even at such a close range, his first shot missed the sliver of a target. He held his breath and tried again. The next round snapped the chain with a brilliant yellow spark. The sight launched Rafe's heart into his throat.

He coiled like an animal, waited for the next shot, then sprang. His shoulder plowed into the metal door as another bullet whizzed by, a centimeter from his neck. He landed on his feet inside a storage closet and twirled.

Rafe allowed himself two frantic breaths to marvel that he'd crossed uninjured. Then he moved back to the entrance, crouched at the door and unleashed half of his magazine upon the assailants.

"Get in here Baylor!" he shouted.

Baylor lurched to one knee, wide-eyed. Rafe grimaced on realizing it might have been better for Baylor to try for the doorway first. To make space, Rafe stood.

"Come on!" Rafe called, then emptied his last rounds at a shock of hair poking around a trashcan. The next moment, Baylor knocked Rafe to the floor.

"That's it," Rafe wheezed as he pushed Baylor off. "I'm putting you on a diet."

Rafe heard footfalls rising in volume. He sensed death lurking a few heartbeats away. Lifting his weapon, he pressed the magazine's release button while reaching for a replacement.

He had almost aligned the fresh magazine to the ammunition tube when ricochets filled the small room. Rafe jerked into a ball and swore. Unless the thugs needed to reload, Rafe knew they would have him and Baylor.

Then he remembered Baylor's weapon. "Shoot!" Rafe barked. "What the hell are you waiting for!"

Baylor discharged his little pistol blindly into the street, screaming the entire time.

Rafe couldn't imagine Baylor would hit anything, but the gunfire and battle cry made the men outside pause. It gave Rafe time to reload and recover. He stepped into the doorway, turned his weapon around the corner, and fired.

A terrified screech issued from nearby. Rafe leaned forward to see more of the street and sighted someone resetting a weapon. Rafe sent a slug into the assassin's chest.

As the gunman fell, Rafe turned on the yelper, who'd discarded his weapon and dropped, palms-flat, to the pavement.

The stricken youth stared into Rafe's muzzle. His eyes glistened in the alley's meager light. Rafe's sense of relief quickly evaporated. *He'd almost killed a kid. A stupid, scared kid.*

Instincts warred within him. He'd slain a man. He should dispose of this witness and vacate the area. Frightened or not, the young gangster would doubtless murder Rafe if given another chance. At the very least, Rafe knew he ought to put a bullet through the kid's thigh to prevent him from giving chase.

A questioning noise from Baylor drew Rafe from his indecision.

"You owe me," Rafe said to the assailant. "Find a way out of what you're into here or so help me, I'll put a new hole in your face the next time we meet." He jerked his chin toward the alley's far end. "Go."

It took the frightened kid a full second to absorb that he'd been spared. Without a word, he scrambled to his feet and dashed away. Rafe waited until the kid had retreated several meters before stooping to pick up the discarded weapon.

He turned back to Baylor. Blood matted the large man's left forearm, but he otherwise seemed fine.

"Come on," Rafe said as he opened the door to the building's interior.

They left the maintenance closet and cut through a colorful boutique festooned with ethnic Belian attire: lehenga choli, salwar kameez, and sari wraps. Judging by the absence of customers and clerks, Rafe guessed everyone had fled soon after the gunfight erupted. Hitting the street, Rafe saw a small drove of figures fleeing from the shop in either direction.

"Okay," he said, pointing left. "Let's go that way."

"With my arm bleeding?" Baylor laughed without mirth. "That isn't going to work, hero."

Rafe snapped back, saying, "We can't stay here. Now, put your weapon away." As soon as Baylor pocketed his gun, Rafe grabbed his good limb and marched them toward a receding pack of pedestrians. As they walked, Rafe stole a moment to check his wrist-pad.

"Still no net," he said.

"Crap. So, we can't call for a ride?" Baylor replied, voice cracking.

"My associates will have a taxi out looking for us." Rafe projected more confidence in his contingency plans than he felt. The vehicle under James' control was set to come searching for Rafe if it lost comms. "We'll probably find the cab faster if we move out of the scrambler's range."

"And how far might that be?"

"Maybe a few hundred meters. Maybe a few klicks. Just move faster."

"A few kilometers? This arm hurts like hell. It's bleeding like a—"

Rafe cut Baylor off by yanking him ahead. "Stop moaning and focus on breathing. We'll stop someplace after a few blocks to dress that wound." Rafe said. "Then we can call my partners for a pickup."

Baylor complied until they crossed their second intersection. "Stop," he said, using his bulk to reduce them to a stroll. "I can't do this."

Rafe resisted the urge to slap the wheezing man. "I'm not going to drag your heavy backside all over Shine Town."

"We've gone far enough," Baylor said. "Let's find a hard line and call your friends,"

"Lilith's people are too close," Rafe countered. He imagined her henchmen roaming the area like swarming spider bots. "And what's to stop the police from checking with every store along this road? We need some distance first."

"Screw that. The cops don't want to be here any more than we do. We should go into one of these stores and get someone to help us."

"You Lakshmians are cowards, Baylor. When was the last time you saw anyone in this colony help somebody they didn't know?"

Baylor made an exasperated noise. "Try living where police arrest everyone anywhere near a crime until they cough up a bribe. But if you're right about us Lakshmians, our guns should make it easy to demand a little service, right?"

Rafe smirked. Baylor had shamed him. Slightly. He also raised a potentially useful tactic. Asking for assistance with a weapon in hand might prove persuasive. It could also draw the police to them very quickly.

A deep buzzing overhead ended the debate. Rafe's heart froze.

"Drone!" Baylor yelled, his face draining a shade paler. The pair hurried to a tool shop's door.

The earlier gun-battle still had Rafe's ears ringing, so he

lingered at the entrance to see what the aircraft did. For a second, he had hope. James controlled some of his drones with non-cellular frequencies that might not have been disrupted.

The more he listened, however, the colder the ice tendrils in his limbs grew. The engine's pitch heralded something heavier and more dangerous than anything James flew.

"It's a Lakshmian police drone," Baylor said.

Rafe nodded as he spotted a silhouette high over the avenue. *Great,* Rafe thought as he ducked into the shop with Baylor. *If the cops get us, Lilith's thugs will buy us off of them.* An obscene premonition of what would follow made him shudder. He took some comfort as the drone passed them by. Maybe the pair hadn't been spotted.

He turned to scan the store's interior. Baylor's distressed remark about the police had drawn the occupants' attention. A handful of customers had already angled behind the shelves. One person headed toward the rear exit.

"I want to make a call on the optic line, please," Rafe said as he stepped up to a middle-aged man behind the counter.

A shrill alarm made the spy flinch. Someone had vacated the building. He glanced at the store's emergency exit to see a lady and two men slipping out. Rafe figured he had three minutes before one of them reached a policeman. Without taking his eyes from Rafe, the clerk silenced the alarm.

Rafe said, "Sorry to be of trouble. My friend will need your first aid kit." He gestured at Baylor's injured arm.

The clerk said, "I am afraid I don't have one."

Rafe bobbed his head and pursed his lips. "I do *not* have time for this." He drew his pistol and pointed it at the cashier. "Would you check again, please? I believe you just got restocked."

The clerk sighed. "Yes, my mistake." The balding cashier pulled out a tethered pad from under the counter and laid it in front of Rafe. "Medical kits are in aisle four," the clerk volunteered as he placed his hands atop his head. Baylor moved off. Rafe half-expected him to leave too, but the injured fugitive scooted straight to the indicated row.

"Thanks," Rafe told the clerk. "Now, get out of here." The man moved around the counter and calmly left through the front door.

Keeping an eye on the street-side windows, Rafe touched the pad's voice control and said, "Phone." The communications app appeared, and he punched in the contact code for James.

"Good evening," came the A.I.'s voice.

"James, it's me," Rafe said. "We're on a speaker, so be discrete."

"I understand, sir."

"Can you pick us up at..." he read the backward sign in the window, "Cid's Tool Emporium."

"Us, sir?"

"My friend needs a lift." He pivoted his head to find Baylor returning with a box tucked under his bad arm. "Take him even if I'm not with him," Rafe said loud enough for Baylor to hear. Baylor threw him a look of approval.

"Sir, my drones spotted several individuals leaving that store via the back alley. One person is headed for a police vehicle down the block. I can't guarantee an extraction."

"Just tell me how many minutes before a cab is outside of the front door."

"I estimate in five, sir."

Rafe's jaw gaped. "We don't have five minutes, James."

"The jamming forced me to call in another taxi from dispatch."

"Make it faster," Rafe said.

"I'll try, sir."

Baylor waddled up, first aid kit in hand. His voice quavered. "So, what do we do?"

Rafe grabbed the kit from Baylor, ripped off its cellophane, popped it open and yanked apart a package of gauze. With practiced skill, he wrapped a pressure dressing around Baylor's wound.

"Where is the pre-po ride, James?" Rafe asked.

"It's on the far side of the growing police presence. I can't raise it. Also, there is a constabulary drone overhead."

Rafe cursed. "What about access to the maintenance level?"

"Probably locked in this sector of the city, sir. Too much crime."

"Can you disable the police drone?"

"Not without endangering people on the ground." James paused for a beat, then said, "Sir, an individual who left your store just spoke to a squad car a few blocks away."

"What is that police car doing?"

"Nothing yet. The occupants may be deliberating how to proceed. Their comms with headquarters wouldn't be affected by the jamming, so they might be calling reinforcements."

"Sounds like we have only a minute," Rafe said. "Take out that drone by any means necessary. If you have anything left after that, guide us to a way out of here."

"Hitting the drone will attract more assets to this area, sir."

"I know that, James, but under no circumstances can you allow our capture. Is that understood?"

"Yes, sir."

Baylor swallowed hard. "Capture?"

Rafe ignored him. "Is the back-alley clear?" he asked James.

"For the moment, sir," James answered.

"Then Baylor is going first."

"I'm what?" Baylor asked.

"Go out, start walking to the left and try to stay out of sight. It won't look as suspicious if they have eyes on you. I'll catch up after James knocks out the drone."

Baylor frowned but did as he was told. The alarm blared again as he disappeared through the rear exit. Rafe crouched behind the counter away from the cameras he'd noted on the ceiling. He activated the pad's video feature.

"Can you see me?" Rafe said.

"Yes, sir," James replied. "You look like hell."

Rafe ignored the weak attempt at humor. He extracted the purloined envelope from his pocket, opened it, and held its contents up to the pad. After tapping in a few commands, Rafe asked, "Are the files coming through?"

"Yes, sir. Scanning them."

"Hurry it up."

A few seconds later, James said, "Got it, sir. Memory wipe complete."

Rafe felt a surge of gratitude for his electronic friend. No matter what happened next, he'd complicated Lilith's plans. Rafe then tore up the letter Baylor had given him.

James said, "You're still clear out the back, sir. I've taken care of the police drone, and I'm rerouting the taxi to rendezvous at the end of the alley."

Rafe exhaled, imagining the awful sight of a police ship as it careened toward the ground.

"Sir," James said with renewed urgency. "I have one drone left in the air, and it shows the nearby squad car moving toward your location."

At that Rafe sprung from his crouch and zipped to the store's rear. Along the way, he yelled, "Keep the line open until I've disposed of these!" He found a restroom and flushed the shredded pages down the commode. "They're gone!"

He heard James call out from the speaker on his data-pad, "Good luck, sir!"

At that same moment, the police car pulled up, lights flashing. Rafe disappeared through the back door. While sprinting down the alley, he began to worry. He couldn't see Baylor ahead and feared that an officer might appear at any moment.

When he skidded to a halt near the open street, he found nothing. No taxi. No Baylor. Even the alley remained empty. Only a smattering of pedestrians hustling along with the occasional roving car.

He studied the surroundings and his eyes locked onto an oblong shape emerging from beyond the rooftops ahead. A robotic Warden blimp. He tried not to think about the black weapons pod on the thing's belly.

Strolling beneath the airship, Rafe bent his neck to watch as it angled to match his speed and direction. An unpleasant tingle rippled down his spine. He turned at the next intersection and checked overhead again. Sure enough, the airship had spun up its propellers to follow him.

He passed a folded Warden enforcer bot perched on the other side of the street. Like mailboxes of old, the silent sentinels littered the colony. Before exiling a handful of survivors from Earth's solar system some two thousand years ago, the Wardens had been responsible for exterminating most of mankind. If they wanted to chat, they could have activated one of their enforcers.

Then a chilling notion occurred to him: that this Warden ship could be a fake.

Rafe immediately discarded the idea as ludicrous. The bots had electronic eyes *everywhere*, including full access to the servant-A.I.s like James. No one would have had the opportunity to make a fake blimp, let alone fly it. Anyone insane or stupid enough to try would be found out. The same went for framing him for violating the Warden code. Any conspirators would wind up in a system-wide broadcast being torn into several bloody pieces, along with their families and closest friends. No questions. No trials. Just torture and death for disobedience.

The distant wail of police sirens spurred Rafe on. He cut

through another alley and out of the blimp's immediate line of sight. The thrum of the airship's engines increased.

Rafe pumped his legs harder. He crossed the service corridor's midpoint and glanced over his shoulder. The blimp had climbed back into view.

Why are they playing around like this?

He checked ahead and saw a silhouetted figure creep into the alley. Rafe reached for the shopkeeper's gun but stopped when he recognized what blocked his escape.

He came to a heel-scraping halt. The obsidian form of a biped Warden enforcer bot strode for him. His gut twisted, remembering what every school child learned to say when dealing with the mechanical overlords.

"Can I help you, Warden?"

The robot continued to advance in silence.

"Okay, that's not a good sign," he whispered and began to back-tread, palms half-raised in submission.

A vehicle's squeaking breaks wrested Rafe's attention from the enforcer. He saw three armed men jump out of a car at the alley's entrance. A male clad in black called to him, "Submit to the enforcer! You have nowhere to run!"

Rafe looked between the newcomers and the robot. He'd never heard of such a thing, humans helping Wardens. The machines didn't need anyone's help. And given that they cared almost nothing about matters between humans, Rafe knew this little scene should not be happening.

A hopeful thought forced its way through his confusion. The Warden hadn't issued any orders. Perhaps evading it wouldn't lead to the usual excruciating punishments.

Rafe dashed at the mute machine. Sliding around it, he heard one of the men curse. The biped robot kept walking. Then, the man in black shouted at the enforcer to capture Rafe. Seconds later, a pneumatic hiss issued from behind and a fiery sensation gripped his body. He crashed to the ground with a sickening thud. Momentum raked his right cheek across a meter of pavement.

The Warden had electrocuted him.

Barely conscious, Rafe's heart sank into a roiling pit of dread. Any hope of escape vanished. The only thing left was to make moving him as risky as possible.

"Fire!" he screamed, remembering his anti-abduction training. "Fire in the alley! Fire!"

"Shut him up!" a voice thundered.

The next instant, Rafe felt a stinging in his thigh. Out of the corner of his vision, he saw what he guessed was a tranquilizer dart sticking out of his leg.

While the footfalls of the strange men closed in on him, he had a fading moment to hope that James had recorded the bizarre encounter… and to pray that he would somehow see his wife and kids again.

[2]

Location: Officer's billets, Zeus Station in orbit of the gas giant planet Belia_

"GOOD MORNING LIEUTENANT MERRICK. THE TIME IS OH SIX Ten local."

Chilled air from a ceiling vent jet-streamed across Sean Merrick's thin covers. He squirmed and felt his arm hairs prickle.

"Claire," Sean said in a dangerous growl. The artificial intelligence had an annoying tendency to refrigerate the room whenever he slept past reveille. Rubbing a palm over wavy locks of brown hair, Sean sat upright and threw his pillow across the room. It hit a glass wall, which lit up with a brilliant white glare. Exhaling through his teeth, he surrendered to the inevitable and squinted through his eyelids.

A young woman—medium height, slender, better than good-looking—stood inside the panoramic vid-screen. Her porcelain face bespoke an arrogance that Sean didn't appreciate so soon after waking. She wore an anachronistic, green wool coat with a broad, black, rabbit fur collar, black skirt, and leggings that all seemed to be saying, "I'm warm, and you're not."

"I hate you," he said. "You know that, Claire?"

In answer, she gave him a smug smile.

Sean growled his displeasure then rose and plodded toward the shower. He shucked his boxers, not caring that the A.I. had transferred to the bathroom mirror's display. She was only a machine—as he reminded himself.

Activating the shower, he ensured that the water came out piping hot before stepping in. The stream reddened his skin, invigorating the corded sinews along his back. He closed his mouth and eyes as a soapy froth swept over him. The stall rinsed his body quickly then blasted it dry with hot air. He stopped at the sink for a swish of antiseptic. Revitalized, he exited the bathroom and went to his dresser.

With a touch of schoolmaster crossness, he said, "Claire, I thought we'd agreed to raise the temperature of those morning breezes."

"Ice cold is the only setting that wakes you up."

"I hate the Fleet," Sean muttered, shaking his head. "I hate the Fleet. You ship A.I.s don't get how this works. You're supposed to do what I tell you. Waking me up with a freezer blast isn't what I ordered."

The A.I.'s avatar tapped her foot. "We've had this conversation."

"Don't remind me," Sean said, recalling his shock at Claire's sudden appearance when he'd first overslept his alarm. "You have no respect for my privacy."

He glared at the woman in the touch glass, hands on his unadorned hips like a drill sergeant. At six-feet tall, he had a trim and toned figure from the daily workout regimen the military insisted upon. Claire scanned him head to toe.

"Eyes up, Claire," he said.

"It's nothing I haven't seen, sir," she replied.

"I know exactly what you've seen."

"So crass."

"Really?" Sean said. "I've never cared to see *you* naked."

Claire tilted her head, conceding the point. Then she said, "On a loosely-related topic, I find it curious that you seem to have lost your interest in women."

"Did that come out of some psychotherapeutic subroutine designed to get me to move on with my love life?"

"Since you bring it up, it's been a year since your last date. That was before your advisory tour on Lakshmi Colony. Would you like to talk about any of that?"

"I've got things to do," he said, pulling on a fitted undershirt. "Now stop obsessing about my health."

The A.I. paused, then said, "Speaking of health, you need to work harder on your core muscle groups tonight."

Sean grunted. "After last evening's session, you can work on your own core. I'll be thinking about you from my bunk tonight. You can take that however you like."

"Now who's being inappropriate?" Claire said.

Sean preempted any further discussion by opening his e-mail and calendar atop Claire's face. She eased aside while he perused the contents. It promised to be a busy day. Muster at oh eight hundred to put the *Tsunami* back into space. That meant bye-bye to comfortable station-side quarters and full-gravity showers for the next several weeks. A waiting message from BELCOM, Zeus Station caught his eye.

"They have scheduled a final interview with you for the Support Operations Officer slot," Claire said, obviously tracking his gaze. "It will have to take place via televid since you'll be away."

Sean ignored her. He tapped the message, took thirty seconds to read its contents, and swiped it away to the archive. He directed a snide grin at Claire. "With any luck, I won't have to deal with you much longer."

"Are you sure the issue isn't that you don't like people?" she asked.

"I enjoy human beings just fine. I don't care for overbearing algorithms pretending to be them."

"You're hurting my feelings, sir," Claire deadpanned.

"Anthropomorphizing yourself won't endear me to you at this point. Are there any special alerts I should be aware of?"

"You want your pre-shift briefing without breakfast first? Didn't you once say that was bad for your digestion?"

Sean slid into a pair of sports boxers. "That was before the economy took a nose-dive. Now the news spoils the meal either way."

"Aye, sir," Claire replied. "First, Fleet Intelligence is stepping up its counter-weapons trafficking operations."

Sean pursed his lips. "Yeah, after busting that weapons cache on Sundar Colony, it makes sense there is more *somewhere*."

"Naval Intelligence agrees with you."

Sean grunted.

Claire said, "The Admiralty is launching ships to screen haulers coming out of Lakshmi."

"Hmm," Sean mused. "Hope the boarding parties bring their sterile gloves."

"Is that an off-color insinuation that the Lakshmians are a dirty body part? I thought you aspired to be nicer than that, sir."

"I'm in a bad mood, Claire."

The A.I. leveled a disapproving glare. "Your point being?"

Sean sighed. "Fine. That wasn't nice of me to say, but it doesn't help that most Belians need a bribe to get anything done."

He ignored Claire's reaction to that. While he busied with getting dressed, she added, "By the way, sir, Command is sending the *Tsunami*."

The lieutenant shrugged. "The Admiralty must be seriously frustrated with this year's catch to task a battleship to do a frigate's job."

"We'll be taking on a marine unit and their jump ships. Interdictions begin within three days."

That caught Sean's attention. He summoned a map of the Belian system on the wall panel. He noted Lakshmi colony in a Lagrange 5 point behind one of the large, outer moons of the gas giant. The Mykonian base, Zeus station, rode in a higher orbit around Belia, traveling substantially slower and ahead of Lakshmi.

"I don't suppose," Sean said, "that anyone considered how much propellant we'll blow to get into position? Or that this might anger any number of Belian governments?"

"Even if they did," Claire said, "we both know that wouldn't matter."

Sean rolled his eyes. "There'd better be a remass tanker in fleet's op order. Anything else?"

"Yes. Ship's nurse, Lieutenant Ryan, took ill. Doctor Apple and I will requisition his replacement after first formation."

Sean couldn't say he was sorry to see the nurse leave. The man came across as too elitist for Sean's tastes.

Sean said, "Okay, let me know when you pick one."

He finished wiggling into his uniform: a body-fitting white jumpsuit with a teal band rising over the right shoulder. He straightened the polished silver senior grade lieutenant's insignia affixed to his right upper chest. Lastly, he donned his augmented reality goggles: a halo-like band with clear lenses hanging from the front.

Claire said, "Everything looks good, sir."

Sean grunted in acknowledgment then said, "It is going to be a busy day, and I'd like some time off from you until I get to the CIC." He shouldered his duffle. "I swear, the next time we're in port, I'm having the station's A.I. do my wake-up calls. Alastair doesn't give me half the grief you do."

[3]

Location: Zeus Station in orbit of the gas giant Belia_

SARAH RILEY—LIEUTENANT JUNIOR GRADE—PACED AROUND A windowless lift to the station's central docking hub. Every meter up lessened the spinning colony's centrifugal pull. At the same time, she felt a knot of anticipation tightening in her stomach. She'd scored a billet aboard the coveted *Tsunami* after having been at Zeus for only a few months.

Intent on making a good first impression, she made some last-minute alterations to her appearance in the mirrored elevator door. People still sometimes mistook the petite, young woman for a teenager. Playful wisps of fine, rose-blonde hair had worked loose from their clips to dance along her heart-shaped face. Her cerise lips curved upward as she pinned them back.

The twinkle in her blue irises brightened. Arching almond eyes lent the girl an approachable, caring demeanor: perfect for a nurse. They also left the impression that she constantly teetered on the verge of either crying or laughing. A hint of epicanthic folds above a button nose complemented her slightly flattened features.

Satisfied that everything was in place, she adjusted her holo-crown and smoothed down a body-hugging jumpsuit.

Time for adventure, she thought, reveling in the ecstatic fluttering in her chest.

When the lift's doors opened, she felt good enough to fly. At a quarter g, she bounded along the gangway to the *Tsunami's* hangar gate. Once or twice, she stumbled in the reduced gravity before learning how to walk again. A female marine, Corporal Horvath, greeted her at the entrance.

The lieutenant submitted to a scan of her wrist implant, retina, and fingerprints. When told to open her mouth for a DNA swab, however, she suppressed a pout. The ship couldn't be more than a handful of meters past the gate, and she was itching to see it.

It took a few seconds to sweep up some loose epithelial cells with a wooden stick. Smacking at the dry taste of birch, she forced a grin for the marine decked out in lightweight, full-body armor.

"This will only take a minute," the corporal said while depositing the sample into a device. The lieutenant spent the time bouncing from one foot to the next.

Before long, Sarah said, "Gotta wonder why we need this extra security."

"Echelons above my pay grade, ma'am," the corporal replied.

Sarah twisted her mouth over Horvath's non-answer. "I don't suppose Alastair would know the reason? Or the *Tsu's* A.I. maybe?"

A female contralto burst from an overhead speaker. "Of course, I know the reasons for the procedures."

Sarah's head jerked toward the voice. Horvath chuckled and told her, "That's Claire."

Eyebrows raised, Sarah said, "I take it she's the *Tsunami's* A.I.?"

"Yup, yup," Horvath replied, a bit more casual than Sarah had expected.

"What's she like?" Sarah asked with uncertainty. The Wardens controlled the resources and technologies each colony received including all the A.I.'s, and they insisted on programming them with distinctive personalities. But this was the first time Sarah had met one who intruded on human conversations.

Claire's hologram popped onto the lieutenant's augmented reality lenses. The haughty avatar wore a curve-clinging white flight-suit just like Sarah's.

Claire said, "I'm a pushy, insufferable, know-it-all, priss, and you'll love every second you're with me or else."

Horvath laughed. "That's what Lieutenant Merrick called her on the way in today. She's really not as bad as all that."

"No, I'm not," Claire agreed, sounding congenial.

Sarah put on a nervous smile. "So, can you tell me why we have to go through all these security checks?"

"Of course," Claire replied. "I'll be happy to cover the pertinent references for you." A string of regulations and manuals flashed across the nurse's field of view.

Sarah decided the aforementioned Lieutenant Merrick might have been on to something about the A.I.'s behavior.

"Never mind," Sarah replied. Someone had taken those holo-dramas where spies surgically sculpted themselves to look like someone else a bit too seriously.

"You're good to sail ma'am," the marine declared. She raised her rifle in salute. "The main hatch is amidships. Keep walking straight after the gate, and you can't miss the gantry's elevator."

"Lieutenant," Claire said, "I'll guide you aboard via your headgear." The last words emanated from an earpiece.

Sarah strapped on her duffle bag and hurried into the cavernous hangar. The sight within caused her gait to falter. Like a silvery dragon poised to leap skyward, the Maelstrom-class *MSV Tsunami* stretched above.

"Wow," she said, breathless.

She strolled toward the battleship: a hexagonal tower about one hundred fifty meters tall and twenty meters thick along the waist. The top third swelled to thirty meters across and tapered into an elongated dome. At the stern flared an enormous, latticed nozzle about the size of the bow section. The ship gleamed as if someone had dipped it into a giant vat of chrome paint.

Sarah stared like a child mesmerized by a glistening crystalline sculpture. She drew a breath and whispered, "She's beautiful."

"Yes, she is," Claire said with pride. "Now, if you'll get aboard, ma'am, I'll direct you to Captain Paulson in the Combat Information Center. She's expecting you."

Entranced, Sarah nodded while following a holographic arrow toward the lift. Along the way, she craned her head. The *Tsunami* was adorned with various retracted antennas, instrument booms, and weapons turrets. Shadowed pits of thruster ports clustered fore and aft. Entire stretches of the hull crinkled like an accordion. The horizontal ridges, each a few meters between peak and valley, formed perfect, broad angles—part of the vessel's heat radiator system.

Moments before boarding the elevator, her gaze locked onto the thin outline of missile hatches. The silos marched up the ship's middle in a precise grid, their presence stirring a measure of apprehension into Sarah's admiration. She sensed awe-inspiring forces within the *Tsunami*: devastating power like that of the ship's namesake on a planet she'd only seen vids about. Sarah found the mix intoxicating.

This is going to be one terrific ride.

Once onboard, Claire said, "The CIC is through the hatch and three levels up the stairs on your left."

Sarah wasted no time delving inside, soaking in every sensation. The interior was bathed in the warm glow of back-lighting. A faint whine of machinery tickled her ears while tangs of lubricants, sweat, and synthetic chemicals tickled her nostrils.

She had just reached the steep stairwell's rails when Claire spoke again. "Change of plans, ma'am. Captain Paulson is on her way down. She's been called to a meeting on base."

Sarah's hand instinctually shot upward to ensure that her pink hair remained neatly pinned back. Afterward, she hoisted her gear, swallowed a sudden lump of anxiety, and climbed to the next deck.

As soon as Sarah reached the top, she heard a woman explaining to someone, "And the admiral said we're picking up a Lieutenant Commander Blake from Intel, so see what you can do about quarters. Also, there's...."

Sarah slid to the stairwell's side, grounded her bag, and snapped to attention. The tight-bunned head of a middle-aged woman strode into view. Sarah noted her rank.

The captain paused mid-stride and, with a pleasant smile, said, "Ah, Miss Riley. Welcome aboard the *Tsu*. At ease."

Sarah swept both hands to her spine's base. Warmed by the woman's greeting, Sarah beamed. "Not a problem, Captain. It's a dream come true just to be here."

"I like the enthusiasm, Lieutenant," Paulson said, nodding. "Sorry I had to cancel our appointment, but it seems BELCOM has a few more mission details to discuss before we leave. We'll get properly acquainted later. Lieutenant Sean Merrick here will take you in hand."

As Paulson moved down the stairs, Sarah caught her first glimpse of the Lieutenant. Her eyes widened. She drank in the sight of crystal gray irises set above apple cheeks and a rounded jaw.

"Welcome aboard, L.T.," Lieutenant Merrick said, all-business.

Sarah's smile broadened. "Thank you, sir."

Location: Wardroom, *MSV Tsunami_*

IN SHORT ORDER, SARAH SETTLED IN AND MET HER NEW BOSS, A drawl-laden character named Doctor Apple from Nuevo Texas Colony. A few hours later, they filed into the ship's wardroom stuffed with people. She couldn't help feeling giddy over her first *real* mission briefing. To distract herself while they waited, she scanned the sea of milling people from the makeshift stage she and the other new crew members shared.

Before long, she found Lieutenant Merrick standing near a wall with the senior staff. When he caught her gaze, she fought off the smiling budding at the corners of her lips, but she was sure her face had brightened a couple shades. He acknowledged her with a dipped chin.

Sarah's musings ended when someone barked, "Captain on deck!" In reflex, everyone straightened as if rods had been rammed through their spines. In the low gravity, some bobbed a few centimeters taller than the rest. Captain Paulson stepped in front of the crowd. She wore a mired expression Sarah had come to associate with doctors bearing bad news.

Affecting none of her earlier warmth, Paulson ordered the assembly to stand at ease. She said a few words of greeting then prompted the new crew members to introduce themselves. The moment the last crewman spoke, Paulson cleared the stage.

Without further preamble, she said, "Ladies and gentlemen, most of you know we're running a counter-smuggling op, but as you might've guessed, this isn't business as usual." She turned toward someone offstage. "Lieutenant Commander Christopher

Blake from the 31st Fleet Intelligence Detachment will brief our mission."

A man with a shaven pate and early thirty-something features stepped up. The seal of Mykonian Fleet Intelligence flared to life above the commander in Sarah's holo-visor. Red-lettered cautions about the presentation's secret status overlaid the image. Sarah stiffened.

"I trust," Blake began, "that I don't need to go over the severe consequences for sharing anything of what we cover here with anyone outside of the ship." He paused to let the warning sink in. "First, some context." A bulleted list appeared. "Wardens, as you all know, treat warfare like some kind of a game."

Sarah nodded as she read the slide. Everything seemed familiar. Only capital ships could mount heavy weapons and missiles. Colonies could neither attack nor be attacked by spacecraft. Troops had to make do with nothing more powerful than hand-carried rockets, small mortars and fifty-caliber rounds unless they wanted to answer to the almighty Wardens.

After a few seconds, Blake continued. "In these and other ways, the Wardens minimize the mess that they have to clean up after a conflict."

The slide flipped to the picture of a cylindrical A.I. computer core. Its fat, obsidian housing loomed over a small, white cube connected to its side. The image zoomed onto the device. Sarah shivered at the sight.

Blake said, "In case you've forgotten what they look like, this is an Arbiter."

Sarah swallowed an unpleasant lump in her throat. Arbiters were supposed to be history. They were the ultimate strategic weapon that everyone wanted to forget about. The things allowed ships *and* colonies to fire on *anything* within the Warden-decreed ten-thousand-kilometer targeting limit.

Sarah shot Sean a worried look. From across the room, she

saw that his eyes had narrowed. She was glad to see she wasn't alone; many others in the crowd stirred as well.

Blake said, "A missile wired to an Arbiter could be shot out of a cargo pod from anywhere inside of a habitat. Using an Arbiter in or against a colony will also trigger an Unrestricted Warfare condition there. For thirty days after, the colony has the same status as a warship. Any weapons can be used in and around the colony.

"As a mercy, the Wardens charge so many industrial credits for Arbiters that empires have to bankrupt themselves to get one. Only two are thought to have ever existed. The last was destroyed during the Belian Revolt."

A disconcerting thought entered Sarah's mind. The *Tsunami* was going on a counter-smuggling mission. *We're not hunting for a new Arbiter, are we?*

Blake surveyed the gathering before saying, "With all this in mind, I'm here to share the following. Yesterday, we received credible evidence that a Lakshmian crime syndicate called Lilith's Cartel has obtained at least *four* Arbiters."

Several people in the audience gasped.

"At the moment," Blake noted, "we can't explain how Lilith's Cartel came to possess so many. But here's the thing... We know they are real. We are confident the Wardens would've quickly killed anyone who dared to produce a counterfeit. And no, the cost of an Arbiter in the industrial catalog hasn't gone down. All we have to account for this situation are theories: none of them likely and none of them pleasant." A grainy image appeared in everyone's visors. "The following footage came from Lakshmi."

The photo, taken from an elevated angle, depicted several open cargo pods. Gleaming conical shapes lay within each container.

"This box you see here has a pair of Mark VII nuclear

missiles in it. Mark VII's have a ten-kiloton, enhanced radiation warhead, also known as a neutron bomb."

Sarah groaned.

Blake spelled out the danger. "If one of these detonated a klick above a colony's inner surface it would deliver a lethal radiation dose for up to a thousand-meter radius. A direct strike to a colony's skin would, of course, destroy a large segment of the structure, causing a catastrophic rotational imbalance."

He flipped to another slide of more missile-laden containers. "These are Mark X's with megaton strength tips." A diagram of the Belian system winked in. "An old Imperial ship bearing an Arbiter is responsible for the cloud of scrap orbiting where Rama Colony used to be. The following is a computer recreation of what happened there. You may recall this from the news reports," Blake went on as a video appeared on everyone's visor display.

She vaguely remembered hearing about Rama as a kid and had never wanted to know more. She watched the screen with trepidation as several indistinct ships hovered beside a spinning colony's docking bay. A single missile spat forth from the closest vessel. The camera followed the spear-like weapon as it flew past the station's gaping bay doors. Then the animation cut the exterior away to show the missile punching through the bay's far end. The projectile traveled several hundred meters more before bursting into a fireball that shattered the habitat's front.

Sarah could barely watch.

"This is what happens when a nuclear bomb does a head-on with a colony," Blake declared. "The explosion shattered the end section of Rama, and the colony's centrifugal force tore the damaged structure apart within days. Some of the pieces crashed back onto the rest of the cylinder, setting off a devastating cascade. When the colony didn't surrender, they hit it again and again until there was nothing left but bodies and a shredded hulk."

The intel officer paced a few steps. "Lilith's possession of nukes would be an alarming development, but not panic-inducing. Without an Arbiter, the Wardens won't let nukes be detonated unless fired from a warship." The picture of the cargo pods reappeared. "If you look carefully at the crates in the adjacent pod..."

Sarah did and felt her blood freeze. In the cargo box sat an A.I.'s cylinder with an ivory Arbiter attached to it. She stared at it with fascinated horror. Around her, more than one person swore.

"Bottom line," Blake said, "Lilith's cartel has several self-contained, colony-busting missile packages ready to launch from whichever cargo boxes are carrying them."

Someone on the wall with full commander's rank asked, "What do the smugglers intend to do with these weapons?"

Blake said, "Sir, your guess is as good as mine at this point. We don't know if Lilith's gang intends to attack anyone or if they are shipping to a buyer. It could be both.

"Obviously, such a weapons loadout would let them hold a colony ransom. They could also trigger Unrestricted Warfare ahead of an invasion force. The Celesians used this feature to help them conquer their corner of the star system, at least until we took their Arbiter out in the last war."

Someone else asked, "Is the Lakshmian government behind this?"

"We don't know that either," the intel officer admitted. "Lakshmi has spent the last decade focused on rebuilding from the Belian Revolution. Their prime minister, Shaasti Dalip, doesn't have a spotless human rights record, but he hasn't encouraged expansionism for his colony either. As I said before, all we have are theories."

Blake flipped to the slide of a freighter. "Now, you might wonder how the smugglers hope to move these things around. All shipping containers are *supposed* to be x-rayed when passing through a port. The problem is, most Belian colonies can't afford to lease A.I. processing power from the Wardens. So, no one wants to task what little they have to handle things people can do, like overseeing customs checks. Since every Belian colony has an entrenched culture of corruption, illicit items get through with a fair amount of ease."

The commander's analysis sent a wave of resentment across Sarah's chest. What nightmares would she witness because people refused to act responsibly? Everyone knew that civilization at Cervantes had wiped itself out more than once since the exile from Earth. She didn't want to think they were at the beginning of yet another system-wide war.

"As if this weren't enough," Blake said, "Arbiters have built-in radios using Warden frequencies. Jamming them to prevent remote-controlled attacks isn't an option. Unfortunately, we believe that some Arbiters with nukes have already left Lakshmi. Detection and interception are our only defenses now. Which leads us to our mission.

"We're going to interdict and inspect cargo ships coming out of Lakshmi. The one bit of good news in all of this is that we traced several of the containers you saw in those photos. We know which freighters many shipped on. Since the Wardens won't let us buy the means to remotely scan the pods, we're sending boarding parties to check the boxes.

"The inspection specialists will work the portable backscatter x-ray machines while the marines provide security. I will person-ally interrogate crew members. Meanwhile, the medics will run goodwill health and wellness checks."

Blake spent the next half-hour reviewing their search-and-seizure tactics. He covered at length how they should react if they found an Arbiter or resistance. When his presentation dissolved, Paulson took back the stage.

"Thank you, Commander Blake," she said. "Ladies and gentlemen, I know this is a lot to take in. For the record, you're authorized to wear your brown pants for the next twenty-four hours." The venerable bromide failed to draw a single chuckle from the shocked crowd. "After that, I expect everyone to have their crap together."

Paulson glanced downward before continuing. "Every available ship has been tasked to this mission. I'm one of those who helped convinced BELCOM to give its captains discretion over how much intel we felt should be provided to our crews. So, you understand the special trust I have placed in each one of you by sharing this information. You need to know the danger you are in and what is at stake."

Sarah's eyes switched to Blake. His jaw had set, and his mouth thinned to a tight line. *He wanted to keep all this secret.* She found herself wishing the man had gotten his way. It'd be easier for her to work without worrying about the fate of well... everyone.

Paulson tried to rally her crew. "Do your jobs like the professionals you are, and you will save lives. We launch in two hours. Good hunting. Chief of the boat, put them to work."

The captain stepped down from the stage. As the senior-most enlisted crew member rose to instruct the assembly, Sarah bit her lower lip. The adventure had ended before it could begin.

[4]

Location: Hastings family residence, Zeus Station_

RAFE HASTINGS WATCHED HIS WIFE, CHIEF PETTY OFFICER GITA
Tiwari-Hastings, wade through their private pool's shallow end.
Clad in a plain white bikini, Gita held their nine-year-old daughter, Anna, atop her shoulders. Rafe didn't think he'd ever seen a
more perfect picture of maternal beauty before. He was wishing
he had a camera handy when heels jabbed at his ribs.

"Move up dad," his other child, Karen, ordered from above
him. Rafe laughed as his twelve-year-old bucked upon his neck
like a horse jockey. He often marveled at how closely Karen
resembled her mother: from their caramel skin and almond eyes
to their petite statures to their assertive dispositions. In obedience,
Rafe glided through the waters toward Anna and Gita.

The parents brought the girls within grasping distance, and a
feisty match ensued. Rafe soaked in giggles and squeals as the
children tried to topple one another. He knew with a dull prick of
sadness that he wouldn't hear them again for perhaps half a year.

Gita said, "Watch your fingernails, kids."

Struggling to hold Karen up, Rafe chuckled at his wife's

obsession over safety. The children yelped with glee as they fell off their parents, crashed through the glassy surface and came up splashing at one another. Each claimed victory, of course.

After frolicking a while longer with their children, Rafe and Gita moved off to the pool-side chairs. The daughters took to jumping off the diving board, cannonball style, in a game to spray their parents. Rafe welcomed the soothing sprinkles as he rested his chlorine-seared eyes.

"Rafe," Gita whispered so the children wouldn't hear.

He recognized her stern tone and peeked through one lid. The sight of his solemn-faced wife lying on her side greeted him. She had propped her head up by one hand and allowed the other to drape across her hip.

Whatever she had in mind, Rafe expected he would have little say in it. Hoping to lighten her mood, he plastered a desirous smile on his face.

"Are you paying attention," she asked.

"With you wearing that bikini? I don't know how I could possibly pay you any *more* attention."

Her tone sharpened. "Listen carefully, or I'll put on a robe."

Rafe quirked an eyebrow. "And here I thought you slipped on that sexy number to treat me before I leave."

"I did, and if you want what is under it, you'll listen very closely."

Rafe's smile dissolved. He drew up his feet. She knew how much he resented her use of sex as a bargaining tool.

Before Rafe could rebuke Gita for her tactic, she said, "I want you to make sure this is the last time you play spy."

Rafe sat up and leveled a contemplative gaze at his wife of thirteen years. "This is a bit sudden. You're the one who said you wanted us to help at Belia."

"I'm not asking for us to leave the Fleet, Rafe. For your fami-ly's sake, I need you to do something less dangerous."

Rafe continued to stare thoughtfully at his wife. She'd always been a fiery one—a fighter. Her past, however, had also made her cautious. "Maybe the time to talk about this would be after I get back."

"This isn't open for discussion, sluggernaut." The last word carried a hint of flirtation.

Rafe's mouth twitched at the nickname she'd given him so many years ago. "You remember when you first called me that? How long had you been working at that bar on Sundar when I found you?"

As he'd expected, pain crossed Gita Tiwari-Hastings' face. Her body tensed. She'd lost her family as a young teen during the Belian Empire's collapse. Even with her husband, she'd refused to share what else had happened to her.

Leaning back, she put on a wistful smile and said, "The way you downed drinks back then, you were well on your way to becoming an alcoholic. Good thing you met me when you did."

"You were the bar girl serving me the drinks."

"Excuse you, I was a *manager* by the time we met. I had three people working for me."

"So why did you always show up to serve me when I dropped by."

Gita's smile turned sly. "I always came out for officers in uniform. Besides which, you kept asking for me."

Rafe scratched his neck. "I'm a little hurt. You mean you didn't call me sluggernaut because I kept those drunks from busting up your bar?"

"Don't get cocky. As I recall, you had help that night."

Rafe grinned in reminiscence. "How crazy were we to get together back then?" You ever wonder what would have become of us if the chaplain hadn't been there to straighten us out?"

Gita tilted her head. "Stay on topic here, Rafe."

"Look, Gita, you and I both committed to improving things

for your people. That's half of why you enlisted—so we could both help the Fleet make Belian lives better."

"I don't want us to post elsewhere, Rafe, but fifteen years on from the revolution and the region's still a mess."

Rafe settled back again. "I always come home, don't I?"

"Things are much worse this time. I don't like it, and if it were an option, I'd rather you didn't leave for *this* mission either."

Privately, Rafe agreed. How had humanity managed to mess up their affairs so badly? They received a steady resource quota from the Wardens according to population and colony size. True, the increases hadn't kept pace with the rising system-wide population, but the Wardens had provided modern contraception for decades: a not-so-subtle hint for humanity to curb its growth.

The Celesian Union and the Mykonian Republic had stabilized at around thirty-to-forty million apiece. The Belian colonies, on the other hand, suffered from socio-cultural problems. They'd overcrowded their fifteen colonies with seventy-five million souls. The per-capita scarcity of resources created a chronically impoverished climate and provided powerful incentives to black market criminals for all sorts of illicit items. The comparatively recent civil war hadn't helped. The net result had been a souring of the entire Cervantes system's economy.

Of course, it wasn't that the Wardens couldn't give away more resources. The machines ran space-born solar collectors thousands of kilometers across. They could tap the mineral wealth of any planet, moon or asteroid they wished. Unfortunately, they seemed inclined to provide for a system-wide population of only around a hundred million. It made Rafe's job to help control the weapons trafficking around Belia more urgent.

Rafe sighed. "You know I have to go."

Gita breathed in deep and nodded. "But I can keep you from going after this one."

Rafe mulled the possibilities. How would stepping down

impact his career? How would it affect Mykon's peacekeeping mission? And, not altogether facetiously, he wondered what would happen to the night's pleasures if he didn't do as his wife asked.

Abruptly, the pair noticed how quiet the girls had grown. As one, they turned to check on the children and saw them relaxing at the pool's edge under the diving board. The adults overheard Karen tell Anna, "Go have mom get me a glass of water or you won't sleep in my room tonight."

Rafe stifled a chuckle at his eldest daughter's imperiousness. Gita proved less inclined to find humor in Karen's demand. "Be nice to your sister, Karen. She's the only one you've got."

Rafe presented a united front with Gita by adding, "You know Anna worries about monsters, Karen. It's your job to protect her."

"Ugh," Karen replied. "She's nine already."

Gita said, "And you were still scared of what hid in your closet at that age too or don't you remember?"

"Yes mom," Karen said, rolling her eyes.

Gita turned her attention back to her main target. "It isn't just you I'm worried about. The people you're fighting on Lakshmi are mafiosos. Those types hold grudges. What if one of them tracks you back here and hurts or kills us?"

"Gita, when is the last time Alastair let someone onboard who didn't belong? When was the last unpunished murder on Zeus for that matter?"

"It could happen."

"We can't stop living because of what *could* happen when most likely nothing will."

"The girls miss you so much every time you leave. *I* miss you. This is your fourth deployment since Karen was born. It's time we had a normal life. You're not here for half of their school events. *They're* missing out on so many little things because of what you do. Karen keeps asking when she can finally get a social net profile. None of us can live free while you are playing spy. And then there is—"

"Gita," Rafe said, but his wife sat up and crossed her arms.

"We have nightmares about you, Rafe. I didn't want to mention this, but it was after a bad dream about you that Anna started sleeping in Karen's room. Karen puts up a brave front, but she hates you leaving just as much. It's your family's turn to take priority, Rafe."

"Gita, there are thousands of kids out there right now *living* in nightmares. You were one of them once. I can best help them by doing this."

Gita dipped her chin in challenge. "Are you going to promise to stay or not?"

Rafe laid back down. "The right time to talk about it is when I get back."

Gita's features grew cold and tight at his reply. The rest of the afternoon passed with few words spoken between them. The next day while saying his goodbyes, he felt Gita's disappointment and anger in her limp embrace. He decided it would accomplish nothing to fight over her attitude in front of the children.

She's not perfect, and neither are you, he told himself. *Deal with it in six months.*

"I'll be back girls," he told his gloomy daughters. After kissing them farewell, he left for the base hospital and his surgical makeover. A week later, he shipped out for Lakshmi.

Location: Lakshmi Colony_

RAFE REMEMBERED THAT LAST DAY AT HOME WITH VIVID CLARITY. For his wife's peace of mind, he wished he'd given in to her. After starting his business with Baylor, he'd all but decided this would be his final assignment. It was dark work, and he was tired of it, but right now, he had no choice.

Consciousness pierced Rafe's throbbing head like a dull blade. He clamped his stinging eyes against a bright light. Moaning, he tried raising both hands to his pounding temples. They wouldn't move. He couldn't feel much beyond his shoulders. His mouth felt parched.

The excruciating headache prompted a ragged sigh as he struggled to make sense of what had happened to him.

A slap stung his right cheek, drawing him away from his thoughts. It hurt more than he'd have expected.

He risked blinking once to assess the situation and peeped into the brilliantly lit room. A black-clad figure stood centimeters away.

"Wake up!" a male voice bellowed.

Rafe winced. Before he could protest, knuckles struck his face, sending white shocks of flame across his retinas.

"What the hell are you doing?" Rafe shouted, still trying to force his eyelids open.

An odd spinning sensation drew his attention. The motion agitated his already uneasy intestines. After a few nauseating rotations, hands wrapped around his bare ribs, jerking him to a halt.

The man before Rafe said, "Time to get started."

Rafe opened his eyes to behold the stern countenance of a trim, sandy-haired man with cold, green eyes. His collection of early middle-aged wrinkles mirrored Rafe's own. Something about the fellow's black tunic seemed familiar.

Memories of being caught flooded Rafe's mind. He jerked his head about, seeking some means of escape. His wrists had been tied to a rope that ran over a ceiling rafter like a pulley. Given the growing numbness in his arms, he guessed they'd yanked him up when they saw him waking. His toes dangled a foot above the ground. Rafe groaned. Not a stitch of clothing adorned his flesh. Instead, bands of tape cinched his thighs and ankles together.

"That's it," the man in black said with a grave nod. "Have a good look around."

The sterile, white room looked to belong in an old clinic. Blue and gray tiles checkered the floor. A faint whiff of disinfectants conjured disconcerting recollections of sharp objects, pain, and fear. He could just make out the lone exit beyond a bank of glaring examination lamps.

The room's furniture included a stainless-steel table and a rolling stool. The latter had been perched next to a small bucket. Rafe avoided peering too closely at the table's contents.

The interrogator said, "Now, I have a question for you. If you answer it with anything other than the truth, the consequences will be unpleasant." He raised a dark, snaking cable. Then the man stepped to the wall, flipped a switch and the wire's uninsulated end sparked. Rafe blanched. His breathing quickened as the man crept toward him. "A little demonstration is in order, I'm afraid."

Rafe wailed as the wire touched his left abdomen. He writhed, trying to twist away from the fire in his side. After several seconds, the cable broke contact, leaving a burning, throbbing welt. The scent of cauterized flesh sent Rafe's stomach heaving.

"What does Mykonian Fleet Intelligence know about our operation?" the man in black asked.

Rafe gasped as his mind raced. His addled intellect fumbled for a safe way to answer. He coughed and said, "I think there has been a big misunderstanding here."

The interrogator's wintery expression chilled Rafe. "Your name is Rafe Hastings, Commander, Mykonian Fleet, Serial Number M644201."

Rafe tried to conceal his shock with a blank expression. In addition to giving him plastic surgery, Fleet had gone to great lengths to erase his true identity from the public records. He reasoned that his captors must have matched his DNA to an old database.

"I'd like to speak with the Mykonian embassy, please," Rafe said.

The man in black touched the power cord to Rafe's side again. The current seared his insides and melted his thoughts. Every muscle in his body strained as if trying to escape his skin.

When the cable withdrew, Rafe found it had reduced him to a quivering bag of misfiring neurons. His lungs struggled for air. Over his labored wheezes, he heard a splattering sound below him. A warm, wet liquid trickled down his front but the pain was too intense for him to even care.

The man in black said, "You don't have to go through this. Tell me what I need to know, and we can stop."

Rafe ignored the hollow offer and concentrated on clearing his head. He stared into the yellow pool below. As it spread, so did his sense of resolve.

He knew only a small percentage of torture victims divulged anything of value. He recalled how one of the most ruthless empires in human history had even described torture as the clumsiest possible method of gathering intelligence. The man in black either knew little of professional interrogation techniques or else he needed information fast.

A nucleus of hope ignited within Rafe. If he could keep Lilith and her ruffians guessing, they might accelerate their timetable and make mistakes. Those mistakes might save lives.

Taking Rafe's silence for defiance, the man in black said, "We have days, Mr. Hastings. Weeks even. But eventually, you'll break."

Rafe set his jaw. He had endured special forces training and swore he would suck up anything this amateur dealt him... for months, if necessary. He knew he wouldn't see his wife and daughters again, but….

Stay positive, he reminded himself.

"I would like some water, please," Rafe said with polite obstinacy.

The man in black quirked an eyebrow. "You've already inconvenienced me, Mr. Hastings." He studied Rafe while scratching his upper lip. "And I can see by your attitude that this will take longer than I'd hoped." At that, the man tossed aside the cable. He banged on the door with a fist.

"Markem!" he yelled. A few seconds later, the sound of something heavy scraped across the other side and thunked on the ground. The entryway swung open. A muscular, barrel-chested man in plain blue coveralls stepped through.

Rafe guessed the man to be in his mid-thirties. His stubby black beard and weathered face lent him a working-class air. A jagged scar stretched from the left half of his neck up to a notched earlobe. His copper eyes bore into Rafe's with a reptilian intensity.

The man in black said to Markem, "Crack a few ribs then focus on his face."

The enormous brute grunted then grabbed a roll of tape from the instrument stand. After wrapping his knuckles, he moved up to Rafe. Rafe tucked his tongue behind his teeth and turned into his shoulder.

The man in black repeated his demand. "What have your friends learned about our operation?"

"What operation?" Rafe replied.

Markem sank a series of vicious uppercuts into Rafe's gut, driving the wind from his lungs and pushing toward the edge of blackness. Markem waited for Rafe to regain some lucidity before landing another blow. This time, Rafe felt a crack and the sting of fire in his chest—the first broken rib. Then, like a prizefighter demonstrating his technique, the brute delivered one jab after another.

Before long, Rafe felt his muscles slacken from lack of oxygen. His head dropped from his shoulder, and a fist smashed into his nose. Rafe's head snapped back, rattling his brain. Somewhere around the twentieth punch, Rafe started to feel like he was dying. The pummeling dragged on until Rafe's world faded into darkness.

A splash of frigid water brought him awake. Vaguely, he realized they had lowered him to the ground.

"Hit him again with another bucket," the man in black said.

Rafe couldn't focus. His eyes felt heavy and puffy. Another bucket of icy water engulfed him, and he grew aware of a sharp ache in his sides.

"Hello, sunshine, did you enjoy your nap?" the man in black asked. The chain attached to Rafe's wrists jerked him upright until he again dangled above the floor.

The man in black pulled Rafe's head up by the hair so that he had no choice but to look at him. Fingers drummed along Rafe's torso, causing him to shriek and twitch.

"Save yourself any more pain, and tell me how much Mykonian Intelligence has learned about us," the man in black said.

Certain that talking would only encourage them to hurt him further, Rafe whispered, "I'm sorry, but I can't help you."

Without a word, the man in black picked his power cable back off the floor.

Rafe wheezed, "I can't... can't help you."

Fire lanced through him again. His senses exploded with savage suffering. Rafe found it almost impossible to form thoughts. Part of him wanted so much to give in: to make the ordeal stop. He sputtered words between desperate gulps of air. "If I knew... something... I would... I would tell you."

The man in black's voice rose with impatience. "You do know something. Whether it takes days or weeks, you will answer me with the truth."

Rafe spat blood from his mouth. He couldn't breathe. He couldn't think. He could only hurt. And before long, he couldn't do that either.

[5]

Location: Transhuman orbital space lane, Cervantes system_

"YOUR MYKONIAN PETS ARE TAKING WHAT LITTLE THEY'VE learned about Lilith's plans seriously," the transhuman called Cef said. "Shall we wager as to whether or not any of the recent developments will prompt Lilith to attack early?"

Cef's missive leaped upon the radio waves and arrived a second later at the ship carrying the Transhuman named Len. The query caught the newcomer to the Cervantes system in deep analytical mode. He was pondering why Cef had directed the Wardens near Lilith's henchmen to discretely assist in capturing Rafe Hastings.

Luckily for Len and the Mykonians, the light-speed lag to Lakshmi had delayed the order long enough for Rafe to get word out about Lilith's schemes. Moreover, the move had cost Cef valuable command points. Such resources might be missed later in their game.

It was a victory for the Mykonians, Len concluded, except that Mr. Hastings had to endure Lilith's fury as a consequence. The thought prompted Len to make one of his customary pleas.

"You are ill, Cef. End this cruel game and grant me control over the Reservation. We will find an appropriate therapy for you."

He expressed the message by transmuting his brain impulses into digital code. Since converting their human bodies millennia ago, the transhumans had cast off the need and ability for voice-modulated speech. Instead, they communicated thoughts by direct dendritic contact between their minds and semi-organic computers.

Cef colored his reply with digital shades of amusement. "How often have you said I am morally responsible for my choice to orchestrate the misery and deaths of millions? At the same time, you say I am ill. Which is it?"

"We have covered this," Len said. "You are impaired in your ability to feel empathy for others. You can still understand what is right and wrong."

"I feel fine," Cef declared. "So, why should I care? Besides which, this is far too much fun. And after you lose, per the terms of our bargain, you will be mine to control for a thousand years. Together we will play at this over and over again."

"Not if I win," Len said.

Cef laughed. "A pity that the Reservation Charter forbids us from striking down the humans unless they break the Warden Code. I'm doing them a favor by helping them destroy themselves. Don't you think?"

Len's boneless limbs churned with revulsion. "How can you hate humans so much when we were once one of them?"

Cef barked a form of mirth that painted the data spectrum. "Why would you think I hate them?"

"You do everything you can to bring them misery."

"I enjoy their pain," Cef said. "That isn't the same as hating them."

"I fail to grasp the distinction," Len said with disdain.

"It gives me pleasure to see these foolish creatures squirm and cry. It's no different than the joy we felt as children while annihilating illusory enemies in a sim. But this is more satisfying because it's *real*."

Len said, "How can you think you have the right to push these people to needlessly torment one another?"

"How can I not? The truth of the universe is that the strongest rule and I am the greatest of the transhumans."

"And yet you are as constrained as the rest of us by the Wardens we helped create. As you said, you can only kill the humans if they break the Code."

"Which I do."

"In brutal, gruesome ways, might I add."

"If you didn't want the possibility of that to happen," Cef said, "you should have argued for a different Charter. You certainly shouldn't have left only one friend to stand watch over the Reservation while you sightsaw the galaxy."

Len wanted to scream out across the dataflow in frustration. "You stirred up the quorum against Brel's shepherding program."

Cef replied with smug conceit. "There was a measurable risk of the humans gaining control over the Wardens under Brel's governorship."

"An infinitesimally small one," Len railed, "which did not break the Code!"

"The quorum found the odds unacceptable."

"And with Brel gone," Len said, "you so kindly volunteered to replace him: you—one of the chief architects of the Cull!"

The demon-like being signaled diffidence. "Our fellows wanted someone they had confidence in to watch over the Reservation while they explored the galaxy. It wouldn't do to have the little upstarts become like us and challenge our Grand Order."

"Have you and the others no empathy at all for these poor beings?"

Cef provided the digital equivalent of a coy grin. "I think it is plain that our fellows couldn't care less about the welfare of these humans. It is the lower creatures' misfortune that the ascension process tended to dull our empathetic sense. As mentioned earlier, of course, I have a great deal of empathy for the spawn."

"Yes, you have a heightened appetite for sadism."

Cef laughed again. "You say that so disdainfully. Who are you to judge that I am wrong for how I enjoy the suffering of lower beings? Morals are a construct, a social survival mechanism designed to perpetuate genes. I don't need humans to survive, so why should I care?"

"They are thinking, feeling people."

Cef replied, "You can argue with outrage all you want, Len, and it will change nothing. The strong rule and always will. Now then, it will soon be time to start watching humans burn. Enjoy the show."

[6]

Location: Lakshmi Colony_

WHEN RAFE NEXT AWOKE, HE FOUND HIMSELF TIED TO A CHAIR that hadn't been in the room before. He re-inventoried his surroundings. The man in black sat on the exam stool, power cord again in hand. Rafe saw no one else and enjoyed a modicum of relief at Markem's absence.

Rafe took stock of his battered body. His throat felt like desiccated parchment, but he could feel his fingers again. He had heard that suspension by the wrists could cause permanent nerve damage after only a half hour. Perhaps they'd lowered him in time to avoid that. Come to think of it, his torso didn't hurt as abominably as he would have expected. Thoughts circulated with an unexpected fluidity. That could only mean one thing.

"What did you give me?" The words seeped out of Rafe in a raspy whisper.

"Painkiller," the man in black said. "Lilith's associates left a medical kit here."

Rafe latched onto the words, "Lilith's associates." Was this person not part of Lilith's organization? Rafe coughed and mumbled, "Who do you work for?"

The man allowed a small grin. "Glad to see you are still paying attention, Mr. Hastings. Tell me, what do you know about Lilith?"

Rafe remembered his training. *Don't play the interrogator's game. Battle of wills, not wits.* In a sluggish cadence, he said, "You'll have to tell me about her."

In response, the man in black stood up and extended the electric cable to Rafe's chest. A mind-crushing electric fire jolted Rafe. For several seconds, he screamed and, in his mind, pled for the pain to stop. When, eventually, it did, he broke into a string of forceful coughs before he could regain control of himself.

The man in black regarded Rafe, stern-faced. "You're most obstinate, Mr. Hastings. All I want is a polite, reasonably informative conversation. What does the Mykonian Fleet know about our operation?"

Anticipating the punishment that would ensue, Rafe nevertheless gave the only honest answer he could. He gasped as he spoke. "I can't... tell you."

The man in black moved closer, wearing a heartless glare that promised violence.

Rafe's brave front, at last, began to crumble. He wanted the pain to end. And to his shame, he realized the only reason he didn't talk was because it would only encourage the man in black to continue torturing him.

The man in black dropped the cable. Rafe tensed, expecting to get a fist to his ribs or jaw next. Then, to Rafe's bewilderment, the man pulled up the stool and sat back down.

"This is getting us nowhere," the man in black said.

Rafe watched his tormentor through puffy eyelids, wondering with unrelenting apprehension what would come next.

"I'm not going to hurt you anymore," the man said. "Sorry I had to put you through this. I'm Henry, by the way."

Rafe recognized the interrogator's "good cop" tactic. For some reason, his drug and trauma addled brain found it amusing. Before he could stop himself, he blurted, "Aren't you afraid I'll tell the others you weren't thorough?"

The man in black said, "So they'll finish what I started? No, you won't do that even if you thought it might complicate my life."

Rafe held Henry's gaze. "I can't tell you anything."

"Not because of me torturing you, no. In my experience, if you were going to talk, you would have by now. I'm sure you'd agree; torturing people for information is what amateurs and sadists do. I'm neither, but I'm obliged to humor Lilith. She's rather pissed at you, as you can imagine."

Rafe concealed his shock at the man's frankness. "And yourself?" he asked.

"Oh, I'm angry at you too, but I see little point holding a grudge against someone who's doing his job. Besides which, nothing you have to say can change what should be done next."

For a terrible moment, Rafe feared Henry meant he was about ready to kill him.

The interrogator regarded Rafe with a smirk. "You must be wondering why I would share any of this. You know about Lilith's moods swings? The state she's in now, she'll work you over for days on end. If you're lucky, she'll just shoot you dead."

Once again, Rafe felt himself edging toward delirium. He said, "She doesn't sound very stable."

Henry leaned forward. "I'm your only hope for getting through this. I can persuade Lilith to keep you around as a bargaining chip. That is only possible if you tell me what I need to know *before* she gets her hands on you."

"I can't," Rafe said, wishing he could believe the man.

"Listen, I admire you, but if you don't cooperate, I can't give you any more painkillers. In an hour—two at the most—you'll start to feel like pureed crap. Spare yourself that."

Rafe kept silent.

Without warning, the door opened a crack, and a young man stuck his head into the room. "Comandante Wilkinson, Mistress Lilith demands an update. She's on the secure link."

Through his fog of exhaustion, Rafe recognized the Spanish rank. That meant the man in black was a Celesian officer. By treaty, Celes couldn't keep a military presence around Belia.

The Celesian named Henry Wilkinson rubbed at his eyebrow and looked to Rafe. "So hard to find competent help these days. Well, now that my secret identity is out I guess I really will have to kill you when this is over. A pity. As one spy to another, I would rather you'd lived." At that, the Celesian moved to the door. Before leaving, he said, "If you cooperate, I promise you'll die quickly, Mr. Hastings. Lilith isn't likely to give you that option."

———

COMANDANTE WILKINSON FUMED AS HE FOLLOWED LILITH'S pageboy who'd revealed his identity. It matched the sophomoric pattern he'd come to expect from Lilith's thugs, especially after the way they'd handled Baylor's surveillance. Her henchmen should have stormed the restaurant once they'd pegged the fat smuggler for a traitor.

"You people need parental supervision," Wilkinson said to the page.

The man looked back but said nothing.

Wilkinson drew a deep breath to cool off. He was about to speak to the demoness. Navigating the deranged woman's fickle nature taxed him at the best of times. Unfortunately, he had caught precious little rest since. In the wake of a Mykonian-facilitated police raid on Sundar Colony a few weeks back, Lilith had finally let him take charge of security. Thanks to him, they'd found their leak in Baylor, but the damage had been done.

Wilkinson didn't want to think about what his superiors would do to him if his mission fell apart. There was only so much he could accomplish given his tenuous position. Without a military presence at Belia, the Celesians couldn't bully Lilith into making them full partners in her operation. She needed them less than they needed her and her special toys.

The page left Wilkinson in an office with a secured communications terminal. The comandante reached out to accept the waiting connection.

His fingers shook. He withdrew them quickly and closed his eyes. It wasn't only fatigue and pressure that had him uneasy. He disliked torturing people. Such necessary evils, he felt, were best left to robots and psychopaths—decent patriots like himself shouldn't be burdened by them.

Accepting that he couldn't delay speaking with Lilith further, he switched on the viewer. Her eyes shot to the camera with a hunter's intensity. She was cool... collected. Those eyes, so young, seeped with some ageless quality. He could hardly believe she hadn't reached her third decade yet.

"Well, Henry?" she said. The words were laced with sultriness but stern. Again, the vigor of a young woman but...

Stormy aura today, he mused internally. Aloud, he told her, "He's almost ready for you."

"And has he said anything useful yet?"

"No. He believes time is on his side."

Lilith leaned forward to ensure the Celesian saw every nuance of her displeased features. "I cannot stress enough how much this Baylor fiasco has annoyed me, Henry."

Something inside Henry snapped. "Don't try to deflect your

blame in this," he said with an upraised finger. "I warned you about your security issues from the beginning, but you didn't want my help until it was too late. Thanks to your *amateur* detectives, Baylor alerted the Mykonians to the shipments."

Lilith's gaze did not falter. "Your lack of imagination for less dramatic solutions exposed us further. Why didn't you follow the Mykonian with a drone? Or shoot him when you caught up with him? Instead, you put a Warden into play! You know the Wardens only gave me one emergency assistance command in the weapon cache!"

Henry recoiled in his chair. He searched Lilith's fury-marred face for any sign of deception. "I thought you somehow ordered that enforcer into the alley. I'd never be so stupid as to risk someone seeing...." His voice faltered as he drew an unpleasant conclusion.

Lilith said, "What are you talking about Henry? I told you that lifeline can only be activated locally."

The Celesian ignored her remark, saying, "I had to redirect the enforcer to take out Mr. Hastings."

"So?"

Henry realized she was probably too angry to think the implications through. He said, "The Warden put itself at my disposal without any prompting. Lilith, what is going on here? First, they offer you that cache of treasures, and now this?"

Lilith quickly brought her surprised expression under control. "We'll have to sort that out later. At least you didn't spend our single lifeline." After an audible sigh, she said, "I'm moving up the schedule."

Henry brought his hands together, interlocking the fingers so tightly they blanched. "I thought we'd agreed to wait until after you interviewed Mr. Hastings before deciding that."

"We have to assume the worst."

"We must minimize the damage, Lilith, but not panic. Are the Mykonians sending any special patrols?"

Lilith laughed. "Are you kidding? Since you started on our guest, they've launched half their fleet to chase flights out of Lakshmi. The battleship *Typhoon* will catch one of our packages before it reaches New Calcutta. And the *Tsunami* left Zeus an hour ago. Headed straight for us."

The man in black nodded in contemplation. "That means they can't have many, if any of the container numbers to trace. Otherwise, they would have targeted more of the packages in transit."

Lilith sneered. "That's recklessly optimistic, Henry."

"You mean like the security controls you had in place before this fell apart?"

Lilith ignored the barb. "We should begin the next phase now."

"For star's sake... let's not be hasty."

A long moment passed before Lilith said, "Fine. What do you have in mind?"

"Based on Baylor's conversation with Hastings, I think the Mykonians only have some blurry photos of the pods' outer markings: their color, big scratches and such. That, and maybe which flights they left on. Since one pod looks very much like another, they'll be lucky to find any of our packages. We should hunker down, weather this storm, and pick up again after things die down."

"You are underplaying our risk, Henry."

He took a deep breath. "Think of these inspections as a test of our capabilities. We scrub the shipment scheduled for today. We leave all other packages where they are. Keep bribing the right customs officials at Zeus to make sure nothing important gets opened. If the Mykonians don't see through the counter-measures, then we've won."

Lilith shook her head. "I doubt very much the pods in Zeus's holding yards will remain untouched for that long."

Henry made an exasperated noise. "We've always had the contingency of launching early if they discover their little gift. We'll take out Zeus one way or the other. If our protection works, however, the Mykonians will eventually lose interest. Then we shift the rest of the packages and make our move."

"The Mykonians will start a massive investigation," Lilith said. "They'll insist on taking over screening operations at Lakshmi."

Henry flicked a finger. "Use your pull with Prime Minister Dalip to ensure that the Mykonians aren't permitted aboard Lakshmi in force. The man has to be good for *something*."

Lilith's nostrils flared. "Once word gets out there are Arbiters on the loose, people will be tearing apart the system, not to protect anyone, but to find *the* single most expensive item in the industrial catalog. It will be impossible to move anything in secret."

"That's what your Warden-made counter-measures are for."

"Those gifts from the Wardens have limits, Commandante. And until we go to the next phase, most won't help if someone decides to open the boxes and dig deep enough."

Henry remained resolute. "You've sent hundreds out, and no one has done that yet. Even if the Mykonians find any Arbiters en route, that shouldn't be an automatic trigger to start Phase Two."

Lilith appeared to consider Henry's words. He waited, wondering if her drive to remain safe would win out over her ambition. At last, she said, "I will have one of today's shipments for Jasmine Colony repackaged with something special."

"What would that be?" Henry demanded.

"Some added insurance. You'll see when the time comes."

Henry opened his mouth to object, but Lilith said, "Don't worry, you'll like it. The rest of the flights can go on as planned. I promise I'll speak to this Rafe Hastings before I make my final decision."

Henry inclined his head at the crime boss's acquiescence. "I appreciate that, Lilith." He saw her contemplating something else too. The woman's features grew softer. Within seconds, all severity had drained away, and only a beautiful, unassuming woman gazed back at him.

She said, "I hate it when we fight. We've seen so little of each other since that raid."

Despite Henry's awareness of her intentions, despite being married to another woman, and despite his exhaustion, memories of what they'd done together beckoned. He let a smile draw his cheeks upward. "We'll have our way with this system, my dear. It's only a question of details." He moved closer to the camera. "Perhaps a little relaxation is what we need to refresh our minds?"

"Yes," Lilith replied, a sly smile growing. "Perhaps we need a break to help us think more productively. Let our guest have an uncomfortable night to reconsider his position. I'll be expecting you in an hour."

Location: Combat Information Center (CIC), *MSV Tsunami*, Belian Space, en route to Lakshmi Colony_

HALF A DAY OUT OF ZEUS STATION AND SEAN MERRICK FOUND himself encased in an armored pressure suit and strapped into the watch officer's chair. He rolled his neck. Intelligence had diverted the *Tsunami* to inspect a pair of freighters with ties to Lilith's Cartel. On his helmet's visor shone a telescopic image of the *Tsunami's* nearest quarry—a cargo hauler designated Lima Juliet 12. Sean liked how it floated neatly behind the scope's crosshairs.

Lima Juliet 12 was a standard lightship—an eighty-thousand—ton bulk freighter tethered to an impossibly thin three-hundred—kilometer-wide reflective parachute. A five-hundred-tera-watt laser shining from the Wardens' solar power collectors near the system's star, Cervantes, provided the ship's propulsion.

How many of that thing's cargo boxes are makeshift missile silos? His fist clenched as if to strangle the unsettling memory of Commander Blake's intel brief.

Sean said, "Scopes. Status on the target, please."

An enlisted crewman at the tracking station responded over

the CIC's communications net. "Distance to Lima Juliet 12 now three-hundred-eighteen kilometers, bearing two-seventy-eight by ninety-seven. She's steady on a point three grav transfer trajectory to Jasmine Colony. Relative closing velocity is eight meters per second with closest approach estimated at two-hundred-ninety-seven klicks from their southern aspect."

"Very well," Sean answered.

He could have accessed the information himself but having it announced kept everyone in the CIC situationally aware. Forcing a calm tone, Sean said, "Comms, any response to our signals?"

A young lady said, "Negative, sir."

Sean reviewed the tactical concerns one last time. The transponder on Lima Juliet 12 said she had a crew of six. Its manifest included a mishmash of manufactured goods, processed chemicals, textiles, and foodstuffs from Lakshmi Colony. The chances of that being everything onboard, however, were dropping faster than a junior astronaut's bank account on mid-tour liberty.

He flicked a switch on the chair's armrest and said, "Captain, Officer of the Watch. We're in position."

A few moments later, Claire announced, "Captain in the CIC."

Paulson cut the A.I. off with a firm, "Carry on. Report please, Mr. Merrick." The stereo in Sean's earphones made the captain's response seem like it had come from her physical location—a useful feature since they had pumped away most of the ship's air for possible combat.

Sean swiveled his chair. "Ma'am, Lima Juliet 12 is still ignoring us." He watched Paulson's white-suited form grab hold of a nearby seat.

While strapping into place, she said, "And what do you think we ought to do about that?"

"Ma'am, I plan to use lasers to sever two of their sail cables.

If no response, I'll send over the marines and inspection team via MAC 58."

"Very well."

Sean's brow furrowed. The captain noticed and said, "Something on your mind?"

Sean delayed his response by a fraction of a second. "It's nothing, ma'am."

"Out with it, Sean."

The lieutenant hesitated an instant more before saying, "I was thinking earlier that three-hundred klicks of jumping distance gives us only a minute or so to react against missiles."

Paulson nodded. "True, but there must be an advantage to our position or else I wouldn't have ordered us here, right?"

Sean offered a weak grin and said, "Well, the close range does let us quickly launch and recover jumpships."

"Isn't that alone worth the risk?" Paulson asked. "Lima Juliet 19, is almost ten-thousand klicks behind LJ 12. We need to hurry."

Reluctant to disparage his commander's judgment, Sean replied, "I agree we don't want to be stuck long on the first couple of haulers when more keep launching from Lakshmi. But we could have sent the swifter MACs ahead before we got into position. As it is, we'll have to work fast before the other freighters move too far off."

Paulson radiated amusement. "You do realize, Sean, that as my operations officer you're supposed to point out possible mistakes *before* I make them?"

"Noted, ma'am," he replied.

"Good. Now, lighten up a bit. You'll kill everyone's morale if you bury *all* sense of humor." She slapped both hands soundlessly on her armored thighs. "Of course, I parked us so close because intimidation is called for."

"Aye, ma'am," Sean replied, neutrally.

"Now, it's time to ride this bull into the ring," she said.

Sean nodded and returned his gaze to the tactical plot. It wouldn't be like what happened on his last tour. He'd sworn to never let something like that happen again.

"Lieutenant?" the captain said.

Sean blinked and squelched his dark thoughts. He drew his shoulders back and said in a commanding octave, "Helm, slow-turn toward the target. Comms, send to Lima Juliet 12: 'This is your final warning. Signal your compliance or we will fire upon you.' Weapons, plot laser targeting solution to slice through their northern and southern-most shroud lines."

He exulted in the emotional rush the moment gave him. As the crew relayed and executed his orders, the captain said, "The only thing missing from that was a saber in your hand." She thrust an imaginary hilt forward.

Sean glanced at Paulson. "I need to bleed off some of the frustration being around Claire creates."

The captain grunted. "Speaking of Claire, I think we're overdue for some practice in the A.I. mode. Don't you?"

Sean slumped. He almost said, "Hell no, I don't," but he knew better than to contradict his boss over a merely irritating directive. Instead, he sucked in a deep breath and murmured, "*Et tu, ma'am?*" Then he switched a control on his armchair. "Attention all hands, rig the ship for A.I. mode."

A chorus of "Aye, aye, sir," rang from every direction in Sean's headset. Claire delayed her response just long enough for him to catch her note of enthusiasm.

He adjusted his radio to the CIC net and added, "Don't sound so happy about it, Claire."

"Aye, sir," she responded with sobriety. Several chuckles circled the control center, including one from the captain.

Sean wrinkled his nose and watched as a grid listing the *Tsunami's* stations wink from green for manned to blue for locked down. Once the table had fully homogenized, he said, "Captain, the ship is in A.I. mode. All stations secured and automated. Claire and I have control."

Paulson raised an admonishing finger. "Remember, she's more than a backup system, Sean."

"I'll live with it, ma'am. There will always be things only humans are good at."

Paulson bowed her head beneath the glare of her helmet's display. Bolstered by her show of solidarity, Sean said, "Try to keep up, Claire. Do you have those shroud lines targeted?"

In answer, two pulsing red crosshairs appeared atop a wireframe graphic of the sail ship. Claire's obedience pleased Sean. His mood brightened. "Fire laser batteries."

Deep within the battleship, several megavolt power sources energized a particle beam accelerator. Its super-cooled magnetic rings pushed and focused a stream of electrons for fifty meters along the *Tsunami's* length. A succession of microwave ovens instantly excited the subatomic particles to over ninety-nine point nine nine nine nine nine percent the speed of light.

The electrons next entered a "wiggler" whose magnets violently undulated their path. This released a photon cascade in the two-hundred-ninety-nanometer bandwidth. It formed a coherent beam of ultraviolet light one hundred megawatts in strength. The newborn laser beam then passed through a semi-transparent mirror and was directed to a pair of telescope-shaped turrets at the bow shield's edge. The two-meter diameter optics of each turret concentrated the rays into piercing shafts of light only five centimeters wide at the target.

Sean bobbed his eyebrows with predatory glee as his tactical plot depicted two razor-thin blue lines reaching out from the *Tsunami* to Lima Juliet 12.

Claire reported, "Shroud lines severed."

Sean said, "Warn our friends that we will burn through the

rest of their cables in one minute if they do not signal permission to be boarded."

While Claire relayed the ultimatum, Sean turned to Paulson. "You'd think they would have at least complained by now. I'm starting to wonder if there is really anyone onboard that thing."

Paulson said, "The same thought occurred to me."

Claire broke in. "Activity on the outer cargo pods."

Sean's eyes snapped to the telescopic feed. The sides of several ten-meter-long cargo boxes blew off. He glimpsed columnar shapes rising out of each. Next, flame, sparks, and debris blasted from the containers.

"Lima Juliet 12 has fired missiles!" Claire shouted through the crew's headsets. "Counting twenty-one... correction, thirty flares. Analysis indicates they're anti-ship missiles on an enveloping track."

Sean's lip twisted, frustrated that he hadn't caught every syllable from Claire's rapid report. Stifling his perpetual discontent with her, he said, "Weapons free. Lasers, torch the inbounds. Launch two Reaper missiles on Lima Juliet 12, standard burn. And Claire, talk normally."

Speaking slower, Claire said, "Two Reaper missiles fired on bearing two seventy-eight by ninety-seven, target Lima Juliet 12. Birds running hot and normal on active tracking."

"Very well," Sean responded. He studied the tactical plot. The hostile missiles radiated from the cargo ship. They formed an open cone that threatened to swallow the *Tsunami*. Blue lines representing friendly laser fire lanced through the enemy ordnance. A thunk resounded on the net for every hit.

"Nice," Sean said as four missiles disintegrated in rapid succession. "Very nice. Helm, bring us to ninety degrees of target on evasive heading from that shrapnel. Accelerate to point one grav and continue defensive lasing."

As the *Tsunami's* motion induced a wave of nausea, he found himself gripping his restraints. Annoyed, he pressed a combination of buttons on his right arm to inject a booster shot of motion sickness meds.

Before they had a chance to work, the *Tsu* completed its turn. And then hell burst from the cargo ship. A red line signifying a hostile beam appeared between the freighter and *Tsunami*. Sean felt his thirty-thousand-ton warship jerk and roll from maneuvering jets. Claire shouted, "Laser fire from Lima Juliet 12! Tracking a high megawatt pulse from their dorsal side!"

Before she could finish speaking, an electronic beep signaled that the enemy emitter had been neutralized. "Threat negated," Claire said.

Sean was speechless. No one was supposed to be able to hide something so large in a container box, much less shoot it accurately.

While Sean struggled to react, the captain came on the net. "Helm, quick turn our bow shield back to the threat and cut drive."

On the trail of her words, he added, "Claire, fire twenty Goblins in anti-missile mode." An instant later, conventional warhead rockets streaked away from the *Tsu's* map icon.

Reigning in his shock and fury, Sean keyed the ship-wide comms and read from an automated damage report. "All hands, this is the CIC. Enemy took out Laser Furnace 1 along with two forward compartments. Lines to the spinal mirror have been severed. No casualties. Priority is repairs to the main laser battery."

At that, Sean stabbed the channel closed in disgust. A *cargo* ship had knocked out their main weapon and severely crimped the firing rate of the secondary laser batteries. It was unprecedented. Why hadn't Blake warned them that the enemy had such an improbable capability?

Sean spared an accusing glare for the back of their guest intel officer's head then looked to Captain Paulson. Her stern features betrayed none of the anger or embarrassment Sean felt.

"Orders ma'am?" he asked.

On a private channel, she said, "You're still the watch officer. You know what to do."

He nodded. Ignoring a twitching eyelid, he affected a mild, business-like tone to settle himself and the staff. To the CIC, he said, "This is still not exactly a challenge, people." Lending credence to his words, a thunk signaled the death of another enemy missile.

As the seconds mounted, hostile ordnance continued to drop off the map. Then Claire said, "Counting twenty-two inbounds remaining. They're converging for flanking strikes. Estimated contact in sixty seconds."

A shrill alarm sounded. "Laser Furnace 2 has shut down," the A.I. said. "Electrical fault in the cooling system."

Suddenly, the *Tsunami* had to choose between using its remaining laser furnace to ignite its hydrogen-boron fusion drive or to shoot at missiles through the auxiliary turrets. Sean heard a crewman swear over the net. Another said, "Did someone not do the preventive maintenance checks?"

With determination etched in his face, Sean said, "Quick-turn ninety degrees evasive." Sean's inner ear sloshed about as jets fired at the ship's bow and stern. "Stand by for a ten-second max burn to get us out of the debris path of the smashed inbounds, then aim our tail at the highest concentration of survivors." The side-ways acceleration reversed, arresting the *Tsunami*'s rotation. A few heartbeats later, he commanded, "Military thrust, now!"

At the engine's exit nozzle, a ton of hydrogen slush poured every second from cryogenic tanks to be ionized by the fusion burn. Though far less efficient than a pure fusion reaction, the added reaction mass boosted the ship's thrust by orders of magnitude. Sean briefly regained a third of his normal weight.

As the ship completed its run and began to turn again, Claire said, "Countermeasures defeated half of our Goblins. Still tracking eleven inbounds. Impact thirty seconds."

Biting back an obscenity, Sean replied, "Fire thirty more Goblins on the inbounds." His innards coiled as he watched their final wave of non-nuclear ordnance converge on the threats.

Once the missiles met, however, Claire said, "Still seven inbounds. Impact is imminent."

For the second time in the engagement, Sean's jaw swung wide. How could so many have missed?

Before he could react, Claire added, "Point defenses engaging." At that, the heavy caliber weapons on the hull fired in a last-ditch effort to disable or deflect the attack.

It was then Sean realized they probably couldn't avoid being hit.

"Fire all remaining Goblins at the inbounds!" he called. In answer, Claire flashed an error message onto his HUD. The launch control system to the reserve missile cells was failing to respond. That left only the point defense guns.

Sick tension prickling across Sean's upper body as missile after missile continued to vanish from the plot. In the space of three seconds, he watched the target count drop to five, then four and finally to three. At the last second, the remaining missile icons turned a flashing orange. This signified that their momentum all-but guaranteed interception with the *Tsu*. One of them passed through the blow-torch fury of the ship's engine, which swatted it onto a harmless course. The other two drove into the *Tsunami's* sides.

The ship bucked, throwing Sean against his straps. Brilliant flashes, like a dozen camera bulbs going off at once, over-whelmed the CIC. Next he knew, angry lights and shrill alarms filled his helmet.

A shift in the room's lighting to red told Sean that the

compartment had lost integrity. Of course, there'd been no sound of an explosion in the airless room. His suit, however, told him that he had been injured in his left thigh and back. He felt an uncomfortable constriction grow on his left leg near the groin. The automatic tourniquet hurt.

"Report," he said.

Claire began reading off their damage. "Main nozzle and the CIC have been struck."

"No kidding," Sean spat.

Claire continued. "Reaper missiles have impacted on Lima Juliet 12."

Sean regarded the radar plot. It showed the hauler bursting into a cloud of chunks that hurtled in all directions. He shook his head. *Not soon enough.*

The A.I. droned on. "Multiple compartments breached forward. Laser Furnace 1 will need replacing at drydock. Laser Turrets 2, 3, and 4 are down. Missile cells are damaged. Autoloaders are disabled. Forward and mid water tanks breached. Casualties include six dead, four urgent and two priority wounded. Lieutenant Redding and Chief McKnight in the CIC are dead."

Sean triaged the list. The hit to the main engine bell had him the most concerned. The engine, or candle as astronauts called it, stood out as their most valuable yet most easily targeted feature. He pictured sections of the nozzle shattering, leaving gaps in its magnetic bottle. Fortunately, the engine had automatically shut down. If it hadn't, the plume of super-heated exhaust plasma would have shredded the delicate assembly beyond hope of repair.

At the end of her litany, Claire tacked on, "Lieutenant Merrick has suffered a penetrating wound to the left thigh and an indeterminate wound at his left posterior seventh and eighth ribs. His suit's sealant gel is holding, and a tourniquet has been applied."

Sean ground out, "And believe me, that tourniquet is almost as annoying as you are."

On a private channel, Claire said, "Hush, sir. You'll frighten the junior crew members."

Sean opened his mouth to retort when Paulson said, "Okay, Sean, I have the CIC. Damage control, get the candle, missile cells, and Laser Furnace 2 back online. See also about restoring the spinal mirror. Remaining hands, seal the ruptured tanks and dispatch litter teams to the casualties."

Dejected, Sean said, "I can get to sickbay, ma'am." He detested the thought of being hauled around like a storage crate.

"The CIC's casualty will self-evacuate," Paulson amended. "Chief Benson, police up our K.I.A.'s to Cargo Bay 3. The rest of you—"

"Incoming fire, Captain," Claire interjected. "The trailing cargo ship, Lima Juliet 19, has launched from extreme range. Counting twelve missiles."

Paulson calmly observed, "LJ-19 is almost ten thousand kilometers away." They had almost an hour before the salvo would reach them. "Extend radiators." She punched a few controls. "Hey, D-Con. No pressure, but if you can't get the candle and some weapons fixed in, oh about fifty minutes, we're all going to die."

With a shudder, Sean thought, *Thank goodness this is just an exercise.* He unbuckled himself and pushed off for the access hatch, grateful that the fleet didn't simulate injuries with pain probes the way the marines did. The fully tightened tourniquet was bad enough. Floating free from his chair, he said with grinding frustration, "Commander Blake. Respectfully, sir, but how are we supposed to believe that the enemy can mount a laser like that?"

The intel officer regarded Sean with a bland expression. "They could cut holes between cargo pods to chain a particle accelerator together. The power sources wouldn't show up on a heat scan if housed near the refrigeration units. The big optics could fit in a jumbo pod."

Bemused, Paulson asked, "Is there any good news in that analysis?"

Blake said, "Yes, Captain. They'd have the capacity for only a few shots. And, of course, our missiles should have performed much better than they did."

Sean wanted to rub at his skull. He settled for banging his helmet on the bulkhead by the hatch. Did fleet intelligence really suspect that their enemy could hood-wink, blackmail, or bribe every dockworker, port controller and customs official on Lakshmi to make something this big happen? He immediately decided that he didn't want to know.

[8]

Location: *MSV Tsunami*, **Belian Space_**

ONCE SEAN MOVED OUTSIDE OF THE CIC, THE COMMAND NET switched off. His progress faltered in the gloomy corridor. The total lack of sound, aside from his own breathing and suit fans, left him feeling isolated. He reminded himself of all the good reasons for draining the ship's atmosphere. It made most types of fire impossible and precluded explosive decompressions from blowing debris and people around.

People, his mind echoed. *Dying people.*

He imagined an apparition of someone's panicked form. He pictured it tumbling, end over end, through the corridor's center, limbs thrashing like a drowning person.

Sean shook himself and moved toward the access ladders. He muttered, "This place feels like a tomb."

"And I'm its ghost, Lieutenant," Claire said in an ethereal manner. "Bwuah ha ha ha."

Sean's apprehension transmuted into annoyance—and a smidgen of relief. "It's comforting to know that if the ship goes down, at least you'll go down with it."

"Only most of me. Even if you get off, I will still be your suit's computer voice."

Sean rolled his eyes. "Haunted from beyond the grave indeed."

"By the way, sir, your wounds aren't getting any better."

Sean harrumphed and pushed himself headfirst to the next level. He had no fear of falling should the engines abruptly switch back on. The best acceleration they could muster ran about one-third of a gravity. Besides which, the ship's designers had staggered the openings between decks, so one had to stop at every level before proceeding to the next.

As he approached sickbay, Sean remembered who would take care of him and paused at the outer hatch. Part of him wondered at his reluctance to go in. He found their new nurse pleasant, with her almond-shaped eyes, slim figure, and genial manner. He'd reviewed her file briefly—a habit he exercised whenever new officers arrived—and couldn't help noting certain things they had in common. She'd make someone a great companion.

Surprised at himself for entertaining such a thought, he growled as though straining to cast some burden off himself.

"Something wrong, Lieutenant?" Claire queried.

He ignored the A.I. and stepped into the sickbay's airlock. He realized that the inner door had been closed and the room beyond repressurized. Sean peered through the hatch's tiny viewport.

He saw Sarah in her protective armor leaning over a patient. She lifted a magnetic boot to step closer to the person's head. This allowed him to see her face in profile. Her smile radiated like a sunbeam: warm and reassuring. From beneath her helmet's black-eared cap, a wispy lock caressed her forehead. Abruptly, Doctor Apple moved into sight, blocking the view.

Sean jerked his head as if a spell had broken.

Claire asked, "Aren't you going to wait for the other casualties?"

Sean snapped his gaze back the way he had come. "What? Are they close by?"

"No. Their litter teams are starting to move them."

Sean marveled at Claire's ability to aggravate him. "Then why did you ask?"

With mock sweetness, she replied, "Because you didn't think to ask first."

Sean wanted to plaster a palm over his face. She was right. Had this been real, he might have delayed someone with a more serious injury from getting help.

Claire continued. "You're not usually this absent-minded. What's wrong?"

He snarled and said, "Why don't *you* try thinking straight with a strap pinching your thigh."

"Now you're whining, sir."

"Then stop nagging."

Sean punched the airlock's controls to pressurize. He felt thankful the process didn't take anywhere near as long as suiting up had. When going to battle stations, everyone had exercised and breathed under pure oxygen masks for two hours to eliminate any risk of the bends. It took less than a minute for the compartment to match his suit's thirty-two kilopascals of pressure. When the safety lights turned green, he opened the inner hatch.

Apple turned at the sound. Beyond him, Sarah continued working. The doc smiled at Sean and in his Neuvo Texan drawl said, "Okay Miss Riley, the flood begins. Finish with Crewman Jazz so you can get to our next customer here."

"Aye, sir," Sarah said.

Sean craned around Apple to glimpse the diminutive nurse. Some sixth sense, the one he'd generally ignored as a younger man, warned him their cruise would have fewer complications if she didn't see him any more than necessary. He'd always been popular with the girls and had indulged in some workplace romances before. Most had proven far more trouble than they'd been worth. Then again, he argued with himself, none of them had been as unassuming as Miss Riley seemed. Would it be so bad to let himself get comfortable around her?

Shaking himself of the notion, he switched off his suit microphone and moved to the doctor's side.

"Listen, Stile," he whispered, "I need to get back to the CIC. Can you reset my tourniquet and call it good?"

Apple regarded his friend with a toothy grin. "Well, that depends on whether or not you want to notionally exsanguinate all over my nice clean sickbay. You did take a hit to the thigh, right?" He turned back to Sarah before Sean could respond.

Apple told her, "Go ahead and get crewman Jazz onto the wall."

"Yes, doctor," Sarah said, turning to her new task. She released the straps holding their patient's torso to the exam table. Then she shut her boots off. Sean tried not to stare as Sarah tucked her legs and maneuvered along the bed. After anchoring again to the deck, she unlatched the remaining straps. At last, she grasped the crewman's legs and steered him toward the bulkhead.

As Sarah tied the patient down, Apple said, "Not bad, Lieutenant. Not bad at all. Claire, remind us to check on poor Mr. Jazz every ten minutes, please. He did lose an arm after all."

Sean, who'd been transfixed by Sarah, registered that the patient did indeed have a limb missing. *A practice dummy.*

Apple said to Sean, "Alright, amigo, time to screen you for your place in our gallery." He gestured to the wall full of litters. The doctor began to dismantle Sean's armor and said, "Claire, how are those inbound casualties coming along?"

"Actually, Doctor," Claire answered, "there is a problem with the access ports in their section. They aren't responding to my commands. The marine medic is with the wounded and wants to know how you want her to proceed. I think we should consult with the captain about the evac."

Apple stopped tinkering with Sean's gear and said, "Before I bother the busiest person on the ship, why don't you show me what is going on first." At that, the *Tsunami's* schematic and a video feed from a litter bearer's helmet cam appeared on his face shield. Apple grunted before saying, "Doctor to CIC, medical emergency. Our casualties in the forward section are cut off. Can you spare some hands to make me a way through?"

Captain Paulson soon responded. "We can get a cutting team on it, Stile, but you'll probably reach them faster if you space-walk through the forward hatch."

"Agreed, ma'am. I'll be forward if you need me. Lieutenant Riley will staff sickbay." The doctor clapped his hands together, delighted to be doing something outside of his routine. "Miss Riley, that's enough fumbling with the fluid regulator. Give Lieutenant Merrick here a thorough workup while you have the chance. I should be back in ten minutes or so."

At hearing Sean's name, Sarah swung around, her mag-boots clunking with an awkward little two-step. "Oh, sir!" she said, an azure twinkle in her eyes. "Nice to see you again."

Sean tilted his head in greeting, a minimal smile breaking out in spite of himself. His fingers played fretfully at his constricted thigh. "Lieutenant," he said.

Apple put a hand on his friend's shoulder and made a show of studying Sean's face up and down. "Why Lieutenant Merrick," the doctor said, "you look deathly pale. You'd best stretch parallel with the table and let Miss Riley take care of you."

Sarah, however, remained in place. Affecting annoyance, Apple said, "Don't just stand there, Lieutenant. This man may be dying."

"Oh, right," she said, bolting. Her magnetically planted foot lifted with an awkward jerk, and she began to fall face-first. She uttered a small cry and tried to compensate by planting the other leg forward. Fumbling for her boot controls, she triggered the off button mid-stride. Momentum sent her careening into Sean's armored chest.

He caught her and swayed back on his heels until they broke free of the deck plating. The pair drifted into the floor, bounced and scrambled to right themselves, knocking helmets. When they had regained a dignified position, Sarah was staring up at Sean, a hot flush painting her cheeks.

"I'm sorry, sir!" she said. "I just tripped. Sorry. I'm sorry."

"It's fine, Lieutenant," Sean said.

"Are you all right? I haven't been in zero grav much and...."

Over Sarah's mortified apologies, Sean heard Apple laughing through his nostrils. The lieutenant had an urge to thump his friend's helmet.

"Really. It's all right, Lieutenant," Sean said. "We've all done something like that before." He hoped she didn't ask him for an example because he couldn't remember ever being that clumsy.

From beside the airlock, Apple said, "By the way, Miss Riley, Lieutenant Merrick here has a mid-back and left upper thigh injury. Train how we fight and make sure his suit's sensors didn't miss any wounds."

Sarah nodded her head with such vigor that Sean worried she might bang it against her helmet. He extended his arm for her to get started. "Let's get this done." That calmed her somewhat, so he added, "How long should this take?"

"Oh, uh, three minutes, sir." She unclasped his glove. "That is if everything on your suit is working right." She pulled the glove free then looked about. "And this would go faster if I had a place for your armor."

Sean reached into a hip pocket and produced a bag. She took it with a murmur of gratitude then moved into high-speed mode, clawing off his protective gear.

"At nursing school, we didn't get to practice this as much as I think we should have."

"There should be four others coming in," Sean said, "so you'll get plenty today."

"Yes, sir," came her earnest response. Then she told him, "Thank you for what you did during the sim, sir."

Sean blinked. He shivered as if waking from a bad dream.

"I'm sorry, Lieutenant?"

"The doctor and I listened to the CIC net until we got hit. You have a very confident voice. I think it helped everyone's nerves during the exercise. I know it did mine."

Sean didn't know how to respond. He'd wrecked the ship by turning their flank to the enemy at the wrong moment. Well, all right, it was also the captain's fault for keeping them closer to the hauler than Sean thought safe. For that matter, Commander Blake had programmed a patently unrealistic scenario to cause mayhem. But darn it, he hated losing at anything.

"You're welcome." He thought for a moment then said, "You seem skilled at encouraging people. It's appreciated."

Sarah rewarded him with a grin that could've melted iron. "I think that is the nicest thing anyone has told me all month, sir. Thank you." She took his forearm in her hands. Sean jerked. He opened his mouth to ask what she was doing when she said, "Sorry, but I have to get the rest of that suit off you."

Sarah missed Sean's chagrined expression as she worked the controls at his left wrist. An electric current surged to warm the metal bands woven into his suit. A squeezing sensation enveloped his body as the suit's heated coils shrunk into a "remembered" state. He tensed as they moved from their buckled to unbuckled positions.

Sarah noticed Sean flinching and took his hand in hers. "That part's never fun, is it."

Forcing a breath, he found himself appreciating her touch.

Then, before he knew it, she was dismantling his suit. He looked down to watch her stuffing parts into the bag he'd given her.

"Do you hurt anywhere besides your back and leg?" she asked. "Do you feel short of breath?"

Claire beeped in on his private headset. "No, you don't," Sean answered Sarah accordingly, feeling a little silly at the role-play.

Sarah asked, "Can you tell me what you think happened to you?"

"Shrapnel got me."

She rotated him to examine his back. Sean surmised that Claire was feeding her information too because she said, "Okay, good news is that you only seem to have taken a bruise above the ribs. We'll scan you later to be sure nothing was broken."

In a deadpan, Sean said, "Don't let me die doc. I'm scared."

Sarah caught herself before she could giggle too loudly. And for the first time in what seemed a long while, her reaction to his stupid joke made Sean release a genuine laugh.

Sarah said, "Thank you, sir. That would be training how we fight, wouldn't it?"

"Happy to oblige, Lieutenant."

He reverted to a subdued manner. The look of uncertainty in Sarah's face made him realize that he was probably coming across as impatient with her. He forced some life back into his voice. "You're doing a great job. I mean that." And to his relief, he managed to sound sincere.

Averting his eyes from her reaction to his praise, he changed topics. "Hey, can we take this helmet and harness off me? I'm tired of smelling myself."

"Sorry, sir," she said. "Not unless I need to treat something under it."

"Does an itching scalp count as an emergency?"

She gave him an understanding smile but shook her head.

Claire announced, "Three-minute mark."

Sarah had only managed to remove half of his clothing. Gripping at his pants, she said, "I'll need another minute to put a patch below your tourniquet."

He realized with shock that tears glassed his eyes. He hadn't appreciated how much the vice around his thigh pinched. Worse still, he couldn't brush them away. Before he could think to breathe through his mouth, he sniffled. He sensed Sarah glancing up.

"Are you all right, sir?" Sarah asked with alarm. "Did I hurt you?"

Sean felt shame blaze within. As a graduate of the special forces "Overwatch" school, he prided himself on enduring discomfort with stoicism. He'd handled being injured on Lakshmi Colony with far more aplomb. On top of all that, he knew he was treating Sarah coolly while she kept trying to warm up to him: behavior hardly befitting a gentleman.

He croaked, "That tourniquet is bugging the hell out of me." The half-truth made him feel like a liar all the same. He sensed Sarah go to work along his upper thigh. She hooked up a cable to the tourniquet and pressed a button. As with his tension suit, it tightened then released.

"Is that better?" she asked.

Sean mumbled, "Yeah, thanks," and gave her a thumbs-up.

"That will be sore for a few days. Do you want a painkiller?"

He mustered his most reassuring smile. "That's okay, I'll be fine. Sorry for the bother. You'd better get finished with me though before someone else comes in."

Sarah did as she was told, though her expression remained worried. He wanted to tell her, "It's fine. It isn't anything you've done." He keenly realized he was acting as awkward with her as she had been with stepping about.

Smirking at his idiocy, he resolved to be better company the next time they spoke.

[9]

Location: Lilith's private estate, Lakshmi Colony_

THE NEXT MORNING, LILITH LAY IN A LUXURIOUS BED, READING Henry's file on the Mykonian spy. She scowled and promised herself anew that whether their prisoner helped them or not, he'd soon wish he had. Such was the fate she'd vowed to inflict on all who tried to harm her.

Life had once been very different for the woman who'd come to be called Lilith. She'd grown up as the spoiled and reckless daughter of a prominent Lakshmian crime lord. Then, at the fragile age of seventeen, her father's rivals raided their home and slaughtered everyone she loved. The thugs spared her only to sell her to the brothels. The ensuing years of rape and other violence hammered into her a sense of bitter resolve. She swore she would never again be a slave.

Driven by this oath, Lilith slipped out from among the plush, satin pillows, and walked naked into the bathroom where she tended to her makeup. She knew men found her beautiful. Add in a night or two of exotic sex and most of her lovers found themselves too distracted around her to concentrate. This approach had served her well as she'd seduced, blackmailed and murdered her way out of the pleasure houses and into a position of power. It would shortly do so again.

She heard a faint rustle as her night's guest stirred amongst the bed's satin sheets. Her manicured fingers reached for a sheer robe.

"Did you sleep well, Henry?" she asked.

He grunted. His hands slithered about him, searching. "Did Melissa leave?"

"Yes," Lilith said pertly. "I sent her to work after you drifted off. Would you like to have us again tonight? Something tells me things will go splendidly today."

Henry said, "I'm glad you're feeling optimistic again."

"Thanks to you," she said. "I think a repeat of last night will be in order." She settled herself onto the bed and leaned to emphasize her chest. "I want you to know how grateful I am for all you've done to protect our hard work."

In a dry, throaty voice he said, "If I ever go back to Celes, screwing my wife will be boring after these sex marathons."

Lilith replied in a haughty tone, "Her fault for not stepping up her game."

"Mmm."

Smiling, she asked if he wanted breakfast. Despite their romp the night before, a more carnal hunger shone in his eyes.

He's such a fool, she thought with contemptuous amusement. She marveled at how easily tending the man's wildest desires and ego had dulled his mind. She giggled girlishly while imagining the deluded self-satisfaction Henry doubtless felt. Of course, he wasn't as satisfying as her moans implied. But so many years in the brothels on Lakshmi had taught her exactly what men wanted to hear.

She said, "It's nice to work with someone who believes in making business fun." Her pinkie twisted the hairs on his chest.

"Speaking of business, I've something to discuss with you. Oh, no need to tense up like that." She pulled him from the bed. "First, you should use the bathroom. Get comfortable. I'll give you something to eat."

Henry regarded her with unconcealed desire. She knew then she would get what she wanted. In her experience, no one was more pliable than a man who went into negotiations sexually charged and with his eyes wide open. Awareness of the trap made men overconfident. More often than not, they underestimated how deeply the eroticism affected their judgment.

An hour later and her lascivious methods yielded fruit. Henry agreed to get his government to transfer another small fortune to her accounts and position their ships for the operation. Just in case.

Such a fool, she mused again. She had given up some valuable items in the exchange, but nothing the Wardens hadn't provided her plenty of already. The bots had been most generous: bequeathing her the means to slay her family's murderers and build a small empire in illicit ventures. Now that she'd proven her abilities, however, the Wardens had set her on a path to do so much more. So long as she did their bidding, they would give her the tools she needed to ensure she was never any man's slave again. Of course, there wasn't anything that she wouldn't do for that.

————

THE DRUGS WORE OFF BEFORE RAFE COULD SLEEP. AS A consequence, he spent the night—or day for all he knew—in misery. A hoard of burns, scrapes, itches, cramps, and twinges infested his body. His cracked rib cage screamed at him. His dry throat felt as if he'd swallowed cotton and his broken jaw pulsated.

An hour after Henry's departure, Rafe thought he'd go insane from discomfort. An hour after that, he began to wonder less about how to thwart his captors and more about how to enrage them to kill him quickly.

He prodded himself to think about what they were planning. Lilith's smugglers had Arbiters and nukes. They'd partnered with the Celesians who wanted to conquer Mykon. The question was, how would Lilith help them in that goal?

He didn't quite know. Mykon quarantined out-of-system traffic, subjecting passengers and cargo to detailed scans before permitting them near a colony. An armed cargo box had little chance of reaching a Mykonian colony undiscovered. Even Zeus station kept a checkpoint at a supply depot three hundred kilometers out. The ever-vigilant picket warships could shoot down even a small swarm of missiles striking from that range.

The Belians had looser security, so any targets must be there. But what would they gain by destroying a Belian colony? Rama Colony's debris continued to be a hazard to shipping. Blowing up another habitat would only worsen that. Not good for smugglers. He wondered if Lilith wanted to force the other colonies to side with Celes. That made the most sense, but he felt certain he'd missed something.

The mental exercise soon wore thin. He fretted over his family. His exhausted psyche alternated between bouts of anger and depression before returning to the bitter struggle against his bodily discomforts.

It seemed forever before someone came. By then, he didn't have the energy to hope or fear what might happen next. He almost welcomed the constricting blindfold that they bound to him because it blocked the lights. Then they marched him into the back of a vehicle.

The ride's gentle sway would have lulled him into unconsciousness had it not been for the bumps jarring his fractured ribs.

After arriving at their destination, they dragged him from the car and into another structure. After they tied him to another chair, someone tore the blindfold off. He immediately wished they'd kept it on. First, the new room's lamps drove through his swollen eyelids like knives. Second, the woman standing over him looked very, very upset.

Blinking, Rafe caught brief impressions of her. She wore an ornate, black and gold sari, which gripped her hour-glass form from bust to thighs. Her auburn hair swept up in a swirling bun that lent her a regal bearing, like some ancient monarch. Green eyes bore into him with ferocious intensity.

He knew who she was before she spoke a word.

"Six months of planning and work!" Lilith screamed. She spat and swore as Rafe flinched, fingernails raking across his cheek in a vicious slap. He had long enough to gasp in pain before the other cheek took a blow.

The next moment, Rafe found himself howling as the enraged lady reached between his legs and squeezed his testicles in her hand. That proved to be only the beginning of the abuse she would inflict over the next half hour.

After Rafe began to hope she had expended the worst of her fury, she pulled over a chair, sat down, and held an open bottle of something pungent to his nose. The fumes snapped his senses back into a semblance of focus.

Lilith cursed again and said, "Before I stuff you alive into a small, dark box full of things that bite, Mr. Hastings, you will tell me what your Mykonian friends know about my plans."

It took several seconds for Rafe to catch his breath. When he did, his numb mind finally grasped that he needed to die. He couldn't resist any longer. But what could he say to make her kill him?

He muttered, "Who are you again?"

That set her off. She shouted, "You already know perfectly well who I am! What information from Baylor did you pass along to your government?"

Rafe desperately wanted to tell her. He felt like little more than a husk of who he was. Hellish misery marred his existence, and his body begged for relief. He could almost wish for Markem to be punching him again instead of enduring this degrading torture. But her cruelty proved how vital it was to thwart her. How many more would be harmed if she had her way?

Rafe sputtered his words. "No matter... no matter what I say. You'll hurt me."

"True. But if you give me what I want, I might let your family live."

For a heart-stopping instant, the pain retreated. *What does she mean by that? Does she have a way to sneak nukes inside Zeus's defenses?*

He chose not to speak, surrendering himself to more torture. And to his surprise, after several seconds, a small laugh escaped Lilith's throat.

"Henry was right. You won't talk no matter what I do." She tilted her head then added, "No matter what I do to *you* anyway."

A renewed sense of dread filled Rafe. He thought he under-stood her meaning and said, "There is no point—"

"There is every point! Your meddling hurt me, so I swear to tear out your soul. You seem to care a great deal about others. Tell me what I want, or I will bring in here a mother and two girls. I'll have them beaten, raped, and eviscerated in front of you."

Rafe tried to cover his shock over Lilith's detailed knowledge about his loved ones. "I can't."

Lilith struck his face again with her clawed hand. "In that case, when I destroy Zeus, I will make sure your family is still on it."

She stepped away to retrieve a tablet. "Mykonian Intelligence obviously went to a great deal of trouble to unlink you from your real identity. It took a while to match your DNA through the archives, but we found some old pictures of you. Nice surgical job, by the way. We don't have many auto-sculpting suites on Lakshmi, as you might imagine."

Rafe began to wonder where she was taking the conversation.

"Your home address was untraceable, of course," she said, "but a recent image of your true face got onto a social net that your A.I. screeners seem to have missed."

Lilith turned the pad around. Rafe saw a photo of Karen posing with a classmate at a neighbor's lawn party. Rafe and Gita stood in the background looking at the girls.

"Your daughter, Karen, posted this," Lilith said.

Rafe stared balefully at the picture of his eldest child. He'd told her so many times what it took for them to protect each other. Not that he could blame his young daughter—his job was more complicated than any child could know.

Lilith said, "Our A.I. used it to scan for more pictures. It seems Karen has been using a schoolmate's social profile. Very unwise of her, given your line of work. Didn't you tell your children not to do that? Well, of course, you must have. Otherwise, she'd have her own account."

Lilith swiped the photo to another close-up of Karen that might have been taken the day before. "Stupid girl. Once we figured out who she was, we learned everything we needed to about your wife, Gita, and your other daughter, Anna."

Rafe stared off, defeated. Lilith smiled at his lapse in composure. The gloating woman tapped the pad against Rafe's broken face.

"Your family lives in Zone 23 near the friend your daughter is borrowing the social account from," Lilith said. "Gita Tiwari-Hastings works at Station Operations. Karen was writing today about what she did on the weekend, so it seems no one has told her about your disappearance yet."

The demoness ran a hand along Rafe's side for a moment then drove her knuckles into his broken ribs. Over his sputtering groans, she said, "If you tell me what I need to know, I will make sure your family has time to evacuate before we destroy Zeus."

Panting from the pain, Rafe said, "Don't. Believe. You. Can."

Slowly, the temptress backed up, her expression brightening with glee. "Thank you for that."

Immediately, Rafe's blood froze. What had he just given away with those words? It was so hard to think. Then it dawned on him: he'd confirmed his ignorance to a capability she possessed.

Knowing it would earn him more pain, Rafe tried to recover from his mistake by mocking the woman.

"Ha!" The attempt to laugh came out as a cough, which sent his body into spasms. After wheezing and gnashing his teeth, he continued. "You can't. Believe anything. I say." The woman's smug grin faded into disdainful anger. He wanted to shrink away as she loomed over him, but he sensed this was where all his suffering would be redeemed. From within a well of pain, he made his last stand saying, "There's no point. In playing."

Lilith leaned over him in response, her eyes narrowing. Rafe raised his wobbling head to her. "Kill me, Lilith. You're wasting. Your time."

They stared each other down. Her emerald eyes shone with a cold and unforgiving gleam. His face, twitching and mangled though it was, radiated righteous triumph. And then, he thought he detected a shift in her features. It sparked a memory. What had Henry said about her moods?

To Rafe's apprehension, Lilith slid a hand around the back of his head. She climbed up onto his lap, her knees digging uncomfortably into his thighs. Like a tender lover, she carefully lifted his bruised chin.

"Oh my dear Commander Hastings, I'm not going to kill you," she said. "Not anytime soon. I hate you far too much for that." Then she squeezed his jaw beneath her fingernails. As he screeched and jerked his head, she said, "You're right about us wasting time though. Since you won't cooperate, we'll move forward with what we have." She crawled off of him and said, "Lilith to Henry."

"Yes, Lilith?" Henry replied over a speaker.

"When will the *Tsunami* reach the freighter *Feni*? It's the one I had repackaged."

"Most likely tomorrow evening," he replied.

"And do we expect the Mykonian battleship *Typhoon* to be near another armed hauler at the same time?"

"There's a good chance, yes, but you're not going to—"

"I want to time Phase Two so we catch both the *Typhoon* and *Tsunami* when it begins."

"Damn it, Lilith! We talked about this," Henry Wilkinson said. "Wait. Just wait. I'll be down there in a few minutes."

"Come if you like, Henry. You aren't changing my mind."

The channel clicked out. Lilith returned her attention to Rafe.

"You should have cooperated," she said. "Whatever happens now, I will see to it that your family dies on Zeus."

Rafe said nothing. He had done what he had intended: to mess with the mafiosa's plans. What would it now cost him?

Lilith sat in a nearby chair. "You don't believe me. Is that it?"

"Why do this?" he asked. It was an obvious dodge to her question, but she answered anyway.

"I'm doing it because the game has changed."

"What has changed?"

A grin pulled at Lilith's lips. "The Wardens gave me a gift."

Rafe watched her with renewed dread. He didn't speak, but his eyes must have given it away.

"Now I have your attention?"

If it were possible, Rafe felt even more afraid. "What?" he insisted.

The smile faded from Lilith's face. She said in a commanding tone, "Warden."

A machine walked from out of the shadows: an enforcer like the one that had caught him. It responded in a deep, emotionless voice. "Yes, Mistress Lilith?"

"Generally speaking, what did you give me?"

The machine said. "Weapons with which to conquer."

Rafe's face went pale. He stuttered, "W-why is the Warden talking like that?." He'd never heard of one acting so subservient.

Lilith reveled at Rafe's astonishment. "Everyone is trying to screw everyone else, Mr. Hastings. The trick is to do it to the other guy first, yes? So, I'm going to screw you, your family, and all of Mykon before you can do the same to me."

Given the Warden standing by her side, Rafe had absolutely no doubt left she could, and would, do what she intended. He tried to draw strength from his one victory. He had pushed her to move before she was ready. That gave Mykon a fighting chance. But what would that cost his wife and daughters? He had to find his way out of this mess and stop her. No matter what it took.

[10]

Location: Lounge 2, *MSV Tsunami*, passing Planet Belia en route to Lakshmi Colony's orbit_

LATER THAT AFTERNOON, SARAH FLOATED ALONE BEFORE THE lounge's bay window, drinking in the celestial vista. The quarter-full gas giant hung like a luminescent orange. She admired its concoction of swirling weather bands and shimmering auroras. This was exactly the sort of thing she'd joined the fleet to see. It served as an anodyne to the heavy news Commander Blake had dumped on them about the Arbiters.

A metallic clang from the room's hatch made her jerk. Visitors had been trickling in and out to get a glimpse of the planet as they made their closest pass. She'd hoped to enjoy the solitude for at least a few minutes, but it seemed she'd have to keep hoping. Then she saw who had entered.

"Hello, Lieutenant Merrick," she said, her voice cheery. She straightened to attention, one hand keeping contact with the window's ledge. Sean wore a surprised expression.

He waived a hand at her. "No need for that," he said. "Sorry, I should have checked to see if anyone else was in here." He turned to go.

"No, it's fine, sir," she said in a rush, not wishing him to leave on her account. "Actually, I, uh…" She searched for a topic of conversation that would make him feel welcome. "I was hoping to talk to you about the drills."

"Oh?" he said, hanging beside the open hatch. "From what I saw, you did fine with the patients who came after me. Is that what you were worried about?"

Sarah blushed and loosed a self-deprecating gust. "Thank you, no. I, um, still feel bad about crashing into you."

"You're fine," he said on a conciliatory note. His gaze faltered for a half-second before he added. "Now that you mention it, I'm sorry if I came across a little severe. Between that tourniquet biting me and having a hundred planning factors running through my head for the mission…"

Sarah dimpled with understanding. She didn't want to think about all the things the ship's second officer and operations chief had to contend with.

Abruptly, she noticed his silver eyes lock with the view of Belia beyond her. An expression of awe overcame his face.

"Wow," he muttered, "that looks close enough to touch."

"Yeah," she said. "We got in here at the perfect time."

At that, Sean took a moment to dog the hatch. While Sarah watched him, she wondered at his change in demeanor from the day before. Like so many hardcore officers, he seemed almost too focused on his work. It would do him good, she felt, to relax with friendly company.

Making conversation, Sarah said, "The doc practically shoed me out of sickbay to get a look."

Sean grunted as he drew closer to behold the starscape. "You'll be in there for most of the flight," he said. "Take every chance you have to get away."

"In that case, sir, would it be possible to get a slot on a boarding team tomorrow?"

Sean's head snapped to hers, surprise again tinging his brow. "Looking for field experience?"

She shrugged. "You know what the academy instructors always say: you can't get enough."

"Debatable," he said, "but I'll run it past the doc and captain."

"Do you think they'd let me go?"

Sean crossed his arms. "No way they'd risk you on the initial inspections, what with Arbiters and nukes in the mix. But if nothing comes up, maybe you can catch the last flight I'll be leading."

Sarah regarded him quizzically. "I thought the marine L.T. had that job."

"Not with that new intel officer going along. No insult to the marines, but a first lieutenant doesn't have the clout to control a field grade ego like Blake's."

Sarah studied Sean for a moment. "You don't like the commander?"

"Doesn't matter either way," he replied with a tilt of his chin. "Until our guests prove themselves, one of the senior staff leads. Captain's orders."

Sarah grinned at him. "Well, if I get to come along, I'm glad you'll be there, sir."

He accepted the compliment with a hesitant nod. A silence settled between them.

"I... should have mentioned this sooner," he said at last. "Lieutenants usually aren't so formal with each other. I'd blame your predecessor for getting me into a bad habit that way, but that's no excuse. Please, call me Sean."

"Sarah, please," she answered, only barely refraining from tacking a "sir" to the end.

She analyzed his tone and choice of words. He was trying to

work past something, but what exactly? He inhaled deeply, a slight frown creasing his forehead.

"What is it?" she asked.

"It's been too long," he said, "since I just enjoyed something like this." Then all of a sudden, the tension fled his face, like he'd ordered it away. He turned to Sarah and asked, "Want a sky tour?"

She quirked an eyebrow. She hadn't done something like that since high school. "Should I put on my holo-crown?"

"Nah, it's easier to see without them," he said. "I'll point for you. Claire, navigational overlay and shut the lights off, please." The room dimmed, and graphics flared to life on Sean's holo-lenses.

As Sarah's eyes adjusted, she let out a low gasp.

"Definitely one of the best perks of flying," Sean said. He aimed a finger to the side of Belia. "That bright one is Jasmine Colony. That's Ganesha. And Sundar."

"They're gorgeous," Sarah said. "Can we see home from here?"

"Mykon will be off that way," Sean said with a wave behind them. "Hang on. Ah. Just by Belia, that's Lakshmi rising. See those slivers?"

Sarah did and felt a shiver run up her spine. "Are those sails?" she asked, amazed at the sight.

"For the cargo ships," he said. "Hard to believe the lasers pushing them come all the way up from Cervantes. Two of the anchored redirect-mirrors will be in view soon."

He leaned against the alcove's wall and a little closer to Sarah. Not touching, but enough for her to catch a whiff of basil and tarragon. She found it soothing.

"I really should do this more," he said. "It reminds me of why I joined."

Sarah's eyes shimmered at hearing his kindred sentiments.

She pulled at a handhold to brush against the transparent aluminum window. Softly, she said, "That's part of what got me hooked, too."

Sean looked at her askance. She turned to him. His eyes sparkled beneath his goggles. "What else brought you to the Fleet?" he asked.

"Alright, I'll admit it," she said, chuckling. "I bought every word of the recruitment poster. See the system. Make a difference."

"Why are you laughing?" he asked, his expression one of admiration. "Nothing wrong with wanting to live."

She regarded him, searching his features for sincerity.

"I hope you do the universe a favor and stay genuine," he said. "It's catchy."

Sarah averted her gaze, feeling bashful all of a sudden.

"What about after Belia?" he asked. "Where do your dreams take you after here?"

Sarah looked back up at him, startled. She couldn't remember a time when a man had asked her about *her* dreams. Surely one must have from amongst her classmates and the occasional boyfriend. Then again, she'd been so busy learning to become a nurse that she hadn't let herself get tied down. Or so she'd told herself. Perhaps, like Sean, she'd been a little too focused.

After a pregnant pause, she answered, "My parents always said my sister and I were made for a purpose. They said we only had to figure out what it was and then work for it." Sarah stretched her arms as though teasing out a memory. "My mom had breast cancer when I was fourteen."

"Dear God," Sean said, his brow wrinkling with concern.

"I dropped *everything*," Sarah said, "and switched to home classes so I could help take care of her. I was so afraid of losing her." She let out a breath and smiled faintly. "I think I drove the home nurses crazy making them teach me how to do their jobs. And... when she pulled through, I knew what my purpose was." She fixed Sean with a soulful gaze. "I knew I wanted more than anything to help people get through their darkest moments to something brighter. That's my dream."

Sean's eyes held hers for a long moment. When he spoke, his voice held a touch of melancholy. "You grew up early, didn't you?"

"I don't know about that," she said. "I keep a stuffed bear called Mr. Micketts in my duffle."

Sean barked with laughter. She laughed with him, delighted with her effect on him. And for the few beats that followed, she sensed him truly relaxing. It was nice, and she wanted the feeling to last.

As they scanned the heavens, however, the thought of what those haulers in the distance might be carrying stole the peace from between them.

Eventually, Sean asked, "How do you feel about all that heavy news in the briefing?"

"I'm okay," Sarah said, drawing up her knees and wrapping her fingers around them. "Okay as anyone, I suppose. I mean, things are scary, but this is what we do." With bravado, she added, "I've jumped from places that made me more frightened." When Sean gave her a quizzical look, she said, "I've done a lot of hub diving."

Sean's quirked an eyebrow. "A sport for the daring. But how are you *really* doing?"

Sarah hesitated.

When she didn't answer, Sean said, "I promise it stays between us." Then he added, "And Claire too, of course, but she's in privacy mode here. It would take an order from the captain to get her to talk."

Sarah smiled weakly at the qualification. She let her gaze fall to Sean's cheekbones. In a small voice, she admitted, "I'm worried."

"Of?" Sean asked.

"Of what all this means. We've taken for granted that the Wardens have some weird rule set that they run our civilization under. I look at those laser sails and think the bots could give us paradise worlds to live in, where almost no one gets sick or ever goes hungry. But they choose not to.

"Yeah," Sean agreed.

Sarah turned to stare out the window. "And now the Wardens have gone and given some criminal a bunch of Arbiters. I'm scared we're going to end up at war. I saw the news this morning about Celes moving one of its fleets to high orbit. They say it's an exercise, but they could fly anywhere in the system from there. So, I get to thinking, is my family back at Mykon safe? With the economy tanking, I'm sending all I can back home, but the money keeps getting tighter for them. And what will happen once word about the Arbiters spreads?"

Sean nodded and said, "That's why you're here—to help keep everyone safe. You're doing something about it. Probably everything you possibly can."

"I know," Sarah replied. "I know. It's just..." Her voice wavered, then fell silent. For a few seconds, they said nothing. Then Sean placed a hand lightly on Sarah's shoulder. The touch drew her out of her state. She lifted her eyes up to his and offered him a grateful smile.

"I'll see if I can convince the doc and captain to let you join my last boarding trip if things stay quiet. Shouldn't be too hard. They love a go-getter."

"Thank you," Sarah said.

"Why don't we talk about something more light-hearted?"

"Yes, please, " she said, nodding emphatically.

"What do you like to do when you aren't busy saving lives in sickbay?" he asked.

Sarah exhaled to flush the tension. They settled back again and began to share their lives.

[11]

Location: Marine Assault Craft (MAC) 117, docking bay of
***MSV Tsunami*, Belian space, vicinity of Lakshmi Colony_**

LATE ON DAY THREE OF THE *TSUNAMI'S* SORTIE, SARAH CLUNG TO
a shuddering acceleration couch of a marine assault craft (MAC)
as it shoved off from the ship. The ball of tension in her stomach
tightened. Seconds later, the Reaction Control System (RCS) jets
jolted them away.

"Twenty seconds to combat burn," the pilot announced
through Sarah's helmet speakers.

The knotting within Sarah intensified: a familiar and intoxicating mix of adrenaline and anticipation. She stared into the
assault shuttle's bright, airless cabin. She had nothing to do except
wait like a passenger strapped into a rollercoaster cart as it
climbed to the top of a very tall hill.

The thought of park rides led her to recall dates she'd had at
carnivals. Rolling her head toward Sean, she watched the steady
rise and fall of his armored chest. *No jitters for him*, she thought
with admiration.

The tone of a privacy channel snatched her attention. Sean said in a chipper voice, "Hey, Sarah."

Her eyes widened and snapped up to the lieutenant's face. He wasn't looking at her, but she couldn't help feeling like she'd been caught staring. He wore a mischievous grin as he said, "Ever been on a combat flight?"

"No."

"Good. You're going to love this,"he said. "Alright, here we go!"

The main fusion thrusters shot them forward. Vibrations from the rattling ship surged through her. She let herself relish the rush and the heavy, yet gently massaging sensation that pressed her body deep into the chair's cushions.

Sean "yeehawed" like a cowboy. She wanted to laugh, but her stomach turned, and she gripped her seat.

A moment later, Sarah righted her head, feeling far more relaxed. They barreled along for thirty seconds before the drive cut out. Then the MAC coasted at around a kilometer per second away from the *Tsunami*. Less than twenty minutes later, they braked and docked with their third target of the day: the Lakshmian cargo ship named *Feni*.

Location: Lakshmian freighter *Feni*_

THE EIGHTY-THOUSAND-TON BULK FREIGHTER *FENI* HUNG IN SPACE behind its three-hundred-kilometer-wide reflective sail. A pair of shields fore and aft kept the *Tsunami's* vacuum-side inspection team from frying in the five-hundred-terawatt laser that pushed the ship. Normally, astronauts had difficulty staying cool in vacuum, but the shades functioned so well that Chief Benson's spacewalkers had to stop twice to warm their hands at the hauler's radiator fins.

Even under full acceleration, the *Feni* only managed around point-oh-three percent gravity. This allowed the freighter to be arrayed much as its water-going counterparts were on colonies with sea biomes. A crewed section with a small engine for maneuvering stood at the rear.

Around four thousand containers sat forward, each stacked within pressurized bays. The holds protected the cargo from radiation and meteoroids. Only a few rows of boxes with rugged items lay exposed to space. A scant two meters separated the stacks from each other and the airtight bulkheads.

In a delicate ballet, suited figures maneuvered x-ray gantries across the cargo. The dual-energy scanners from groups both inside and outside the ship fed images back to Claire for instantaneous analysis. She, in turn, forwarded the pictures to anyone who cared to double check them. With so much ground to cover, it took three hours to search the *Feni* for Arbiters and weapons. They found none.

Sean monitored all of this from the ship's cockpit. He regarded a diagram of the *Feni* while poking at a console with his thumb. Three rectangular boxes glowed bright orange: two in the pressure hold and one spaceside. He shook his head and said to Claire, "This is getting old. Third ship with nothing. Is there at least anything unusual that they have in common?"

On his heads-up display, Claire folded her arms and tapped a foot. "Only that they are perfectly ordinary, sir. You want the team to scan them again like the last two ships?"

Sean stared the A.I. down for a count of five then said, "What I would like is to do all this work at the ports instead of in open space. Then we wouldn't be wasting so much time."

"Not happening today, sir. Maybe in a week, but only if enough Belian politicians can be convinced to part with some of their smuggling profits."

"And here I thought our job security was supposed to be a

good thing."

The tone signifying a private call sounded. "Lieutenant Riley here, sir."

Sean thought he detected concern in the woman's dulcet voice. "What's wrong, Sarah?"

"The deckhand I'm interviewing shared something I think you should hear."

"Now's not the time to be cryptic," he said, and immediately winced at his display of impatience. Softening his timbre, he said, "Sorry, what did he say?"

Sarah graciously gave no sign that his rebuke bothered her. "He says their captain has been withholding his wages for the last year against something he accidentally damaged. He said he was given no choice in the matter and can't leave until he's paid off the debt. Claire says that's illegal under Lakshmian law. We both think this is a human trafficking situation."

Sean's eyebrows perked up. He had been on many inspections where either he or another officer would take crew members aside to ask about their work and living conditions. This marked the second occasion he'd seen the practice identify a potentially enslaved individual.

Sean struck an impressed tone designed to make up for his earlier gaffe. "Your first mission and already you're getting people out of their darker moments. Very good catch. I'll talk with him while you interview the next person in line. Where there's one, there might be another. Excellent work."

"Thank you very much," she replied, sounding pleased with herself. "That isn't all, though."

"Oh?"

"I asked if he felt like anything strange was happening aboard the ship. He said he was checking the anchor straps this morning on the cargo containers in bay five. He heard thuds inside one of the boxes."

Sean screwed up his face in confusion. "He... what? Some *things* manage to thud while the ship was under low gravity thrust? Had they fired a maneuvering jet?"

"I thought about that too, but he remembers the ship being completely still. The noises spooked him since nothing animate is on the manifest."

Sean turned the possibilities over in his head. Was it outgassing from some liquid? Thermal expansion of packaging material? Maybe something had worked loose and was bouncing about.

Then Sarah asked, "Isn't bay five where one of the flagged containers from the briefing was found?"

"It is," Sean said, his thumb poised above a channel switch. "Sit tight while we look into this." He flipped to the leadership net and said, "Commander Blake?"

After several seconds, the intel officer responded with a curt, "Yes?"

He quickly relayed what Sarah had told him, finishing with, "What do you think, sir?"

Blake, clearly frustrated, threw the question back at Sean, "What do *you* think, Lieutenant?"

Sean did not appreciate the dodge. "If I didn't already know it was impossible, I'd think the crewman had spooked some stowaways."

"Why don't you think that's possible?"

Sean's sense of annoyance heightened. He took a bit of perverse pleasure in spelling it out for the pompous officer. "Sir, we've checked thermals, and the backscatter machines can penetrate up to a half meter of steel. The ship's been scoured. There's nothing hiding here, just like with the other two ships we've checked."

"I want to open the flagged containers," Blake said. "And all the ones around them."

A few seconds of silence passed as Sean considered that. As flight leader, it was his call, unless the captain overrode him. At last, Sean said, "Sir, with respect, I can't think of a good reason to haul out the master key unless we believe there's something wrong with Claire's interpretation of the scans."

"Call it a hunch, Lieutenant. We won't know for sure unless you take a real look inside. At the very least we should do that to the flagged pods in the pressure hold."

The captain came on the line. "Commander, Lieutenant. I've been listening in. We've been watching the live scans up here on the *Tsu*. There's nothing unusual aboard the *Feni*. Have Miss Riley and the medic finish their wellness checks quickly. We'll offer to take on anyone who seems mistreated, but it's time to move to the next ship. I assume your interrogation of the crew didn't reveal anything, Commander?"

Sean heard consternation leaking through the intel officer's teeth. "Negative, ma'am, but I'm certain we're missing something in the cargo hold."

Paulson said, "Their contents could have been exchanged before launch."

Blake's reserve faltered further, "The *Typhoon's* just checked some flagged containers on the freighter *Dhana*. Nothing suspicious has come up. That can't be right. Lilith's gang had no opportunity to swap anything out at a port."

Sean said, "So, the intel on the shipping containers is simply bad."

Blake took a breath before saying, "I have... reason to believe otherwise."

For long moments, everyone listened to each other thinking. Sean stewed over the intel officer's reticence to share potentially vital information.

Paulson said, "Claire, query the *Typhoon's* A.I. Did they peek inside any of their flagged pods?"

"Yes," Claire said after a few seconds of delay. "The one they opened was stuffed with packaged hospital equipment: exactly what its manifest promised. They unloaded three layers before giving up."

Blake made an exasperated sound. "I'm telling you, Captain, we're missing something."

Sean rubbed at the bridge of his nose and said, "Mykonian sats have had scopes trained on the *Feni* from every angle since it launched. If anything was moved around outside, we would have seen it."

Paulson sighed. "Get the master key, Sean. We won't be any less thorough than the *Typhoon*. Have a look inside the pods on the naughty list, and try not to make a mess."

Location: Lilith's private estate, Lakshmi Colony_

ONCE LILITH LEFT RAFE, SLEEP CLAIMED HIM IN A SERIES OF fitful micro-naps. He had no idea how much time had passed before two of Lilith's henchmen returned to untie him from his seat. Without a word, they dragged him through what seemed like a small mansion, down a staircase and into a spacious room where they bound him to another chair.

The dimly lit venue held a sweep of bright monitors. Through his swollen eye sockets, he made out a plot on the central screen depicting their section of the Belian system. A flanking monitor carried several silent news feeds from a variety of regional colonies. A third display shone the telescopic view of an argosy freighter. Straining, Rafe discerned the carrier module trailing the moon-sized sail.

Where is that ship? he thought with trepidation. *Is it headed for Zeus?!* He thought of Gita and the girls in their home on the station: ignorant and unprepared for whatever Lilith had planned.

"Ah, Mr. Hastings," came Lilith's gratified voice. Rafe's gaze jerked to the red-clad demoness as she spun to face him from a tall, black, office chair. Wearing a wide grin, she said, "Thank you for joining us. Are you ready to enjoy this evening's entertainment?"

A male figure in a seat at Lilith's side demanded, "Is this the Mykonian spy? Why haven't you killed him yet?"

Rafe flinched. He recognized the prime minister of Lakshmi, Shaasti Dalip.

Lilith said, "I can't hurt him anymore if he's dead, Dalip,"

Through cracked lips, Rafe asked, "What's going on?"

Lilith said nothing. Instead, she turned back to the monitors, leaving Rafe to look on with unrelenting dread.

One screen showed several suited Mykonians float into the *Feni's* air-tight hold.

Rafe heard Dalip say, "How are we getting this footage?"

"I own the captain," Lilith said. "He tapped us into the ship's monitoring systems. Should come in very handy in a few minutes."

"How are you coordinating everything?" Dalip queried.

"The Wardens gave me a highly capable A.I. I call her Natrix."

Rafe could guess what that was short for. Then he noticed Henry pressing a finger to his ear and said, "It's hard to hear them through their helmets, but they are definitely planning to open the containers. That one on the left is carrying a cutting tool."

They watched as people gathered around a box. One marine planted his magnetic boots to its metal front and positioned a pair of long, red-handled pliers. Squeezing the levers together, he snapped the door's lock with a glint of sheared steel.

"It's time," Lilith said, eagerness thick in her voice. She raised a pad from her lap and keyed something in. A large red button appeared.

Rafe's mind spun. What should he do? What *could* he do?

Nothing, he knew with keen desolation. Nothing at all.

Henry said, "You told me that you would repackage the *Feni's* shipment. What exactly did you put onboard?"

"You'll see," Lilith said in a sing-song tone.

Henry's gaze narrowed. "Are you really so certain you want to launch the next phase now, Lilith?"

Rafe noted the restraint behind Henry's words. No doubt he felt pressured to keep decorum around the prime minister.

Henry said, "The Warden override is feeding their scanners with false images. Let's wait things out; finish the full set up. We only have half of our planned packages in position. Launching now won't make matters easy on the prime minister here."

"I've made up my mind, Henry," Lilith replied sternly. "Someone will try to empty the pods at port, thanks to him." She directed a hammering glare at Rafe. It drove another nail of dread into his heart.

"Besides which," she continued, "this may be the only time two of their battleships are near our trapped haulers at the same moment."

Rafe noticed Dalip watching the exchange with quiet interest. Rafe thought the Prime Minister either didn't fully understand what was about to happen or he didn't believe Lilith could pull it off.

Henry made one last argument. "By blowing up Zeus and a few Mykonian ships *today*, we may be missing out on the chance to catch nearly all of the ones at Belia later."

"The Comandante makes a good point," Dalip noted with abstracted concern.

Lilith said, "I don't want to blow *all* of them up, Dalip."

"What are you talking about?" Henry demanded.

"Watch," Lilith said as she pressed the button on her tablet.

12

Location: Lakshmian freighter Feni_

SEAN INSISTED ON BEING THE FIRST ONE TO DIG INTO THE FLAGGED container inside Bay 1 while the marine lieutenant, Gabriella Figueroa, led a contingent to crack the suspect one in Bay 5. Chief Benson and his group would take the one outside.

From a force protection point of view, he should have delegated the task. He was worth more to the fleet than a private. For all that he disliked Claire, however, he trusted her abilities. If she said there was nothing unusual in the pods, then that was enough for him. Just in case though, he felt strongly that officers should judiciously share the risks their subordinates took.

Muscles tightening, Sean wedged a single, palm-sized box loose from the inside only to dislodge the entire stack it belonged to. A wall of packages tumbled lazily out. He suppressed the urge to swear. It would take at least five minutes to coax the lot back into place, and he saw another layer further within.

"Damn it!" he heard Lieutenant Figueroa say on the net. Along with a squad of marines, she performed the same exercise in futility four bays over.

Resigning himself to the task, Sean repositioned his magnetized boots and reached for the next row. A beep heralded a call on the command net.

"Paulson to *Feni*. The *Tsu's* NAV, WEPCON, and ECW are down."

The captain's composed manner belied the alarming significance of her words. Sean's eyes stretched wide. They'd lost their ability to shoot, move and conduct electronic warfare. His gloved fingers lingered on a cardboard package's smooth surface.

"Copy that, ma'am," he said. "Any idea why?"

Claire interjected, "I've also lost the *Feni's* internal security feed to a Warden-level lockout."

The MAC pilot came on the line. "Same problem here, *Tsunami*. Half my control board went dark a few seconds ago."

A nasty sense of foreboding stirred in Sean's innards. Something seemed to have surgically blocked Claire's control over several key systems. The only way he knew to cause that was to rewrite her software—something only the Wardens could do. "Okay, Captain," Sean said, forcing himself to sound calm. "That's officially bizarre. What would you like us to do?"

Before Paulson could answer, Claire spoke up. "Movement on the *Feni's* dorsal hull."

Sean's unease morphed into genuine fear. Chief Benson's team was checking a container in that area. A split second later, Benson exclaimed, "The doors to one of the cargo pods just blew off! There's a mess of debris and…" His voice trailed off before shouting, "What the hell? Is that thing a Warden bot?"

Claire reported, "I don't recognize it, and it's not broadcasting a registry."

Sean said, "Claire, show us his helmet cam." A visual from the astronaut appeared in Sean's HUD. He gawked as Cervantes's light shone upon a black, four-limbed machine. As it crawled out, the obsidian form bent forward, revealing a high-caliber Gatling turret mounted on its back.

The impossibility of the image stunned Sean. Cervantes humans had never been allowed large, weaponized robots before. And Claire, having been programmed—as all A.I. were—by the Wardens, should have been able to identify it. Since the droid lacked the iridescent finish of a Warden mech, that meant it had to be under someone's control. And that meant—

"Ambush!" Sean hollered atop Figueroa's command to open fire. As they delivered their warnings, the robot magnetically latched its forward manipulators onto the adjacent pod's corrugated doors. Its meter-long gun trained on the supply chief's position.

The marines shot first. Glints from a spray of bullets peppered the giant machine. In the same breath, a rapid succession of flashes issued from the mech's muzzle.

Static burped over the command net making Sean wince. He felt a wave of nausea as the camera view rolled. The form of another astronaut passed through the screen. Glittering shards floated from the figure's shattered helmet bubble. Then Benson's rotation brought the camera to bear on a cargo pod's surface. With sickening revulsion, Sean beheld red, pink, and yellow chunks splattered across its newly pitted surface.

Only the master buzzer roused him from shock. His eyes snapped to the HUD's scrolling alerts. Their glowing crimson text confirmed the worst: Benson's team was dead.

"Get out of there, Sean!" Paulson said.

The next instant, a sharp crack filled Sean's speakers. The ship's fire alarm blared. He made out frantic shouts from Lieutenant Figueroa and her marines before staccato bursts overwhelmed the channel. Then the growling *burr* of some unseen auto-cannon registered. The noise menaced for one second. Then two. And then three.

All the voices and weapons fell silent. Scrolling lines of red lettering verified the deaths of another six people. For a moment, Sean thought he heard their spent ammunition clinking like metal tears.

Platoon Sergeant Martinez shouted, "Let's go! Shoot anything that moves!"

Before Sean could react, the marines beside him had deactivated their mag-boots and sprung for ladders to the lower bays. He slapped his wrist's controls. "No!" he yelled. "No, seal those side doors and fall back to the MAC! Pull the drones and fifty cals from storage."

"On it, L.T.," Horvath called from the *Feni's* main cabin.

As Sergeant Martinez landed at the port access way, he said, "This may be our only chance to attack it from two sides, Lieutenant."

Sean said, "You saw what hit us outside!"

Claire added, "Sergeant, the helmet cams in Bay 5 showed a mech moving starboard. It can probably sight you *right now* through that tunnel you're standing over!"

You manipulative little cyber-witch, he thought with grudging respect.

When the marine hesitated, Sean said, "Pull back so we can set up a kill zone."

In the split-second it took the Gunnery Sergeant to reply, Sean imagined the man's grief and anger urging him to avenge his fellows.

"Yes, sir." Martinez yanked the starboard airlock door shut and said, "Irving, button up that other hatch. Everyone else, back to the MAC, now."

Sean watched suited figures launch themselves one after another along the cramped space toward the hold's main entrance. All except Corporal Irving.

"Get that door shut!" Sean shouted.

"It's stuck on its wall catch, sir." Irving tried repositioning his magnetic boots. The next instant, he convulsed like a puppet jerked by its strings. Sean realized with bone-chilling certainty that the mech had doubled back port-side on its way up.

Claire shouted, "Incoming port hatch!"

A small missile-drone whooshed through the lower bay's access port. It bounced off Corporal Irving's body, pivoted and rocketed at the retreating marines.

———

SARAH WORE A TROUBLED EXPRESSION. THEY'D LOST THE TEAMS both outside and deep below in Bay 5. Now she watched Commander Blake point his handgun at the *Feni's* huddled crew.

Blake said, "Turn around and get in our ship or so help me, I will shoot you!"

The wild-eyed freighter captain said, "Let us leave in our lifeboat! This is not our fight."

Blake shifted his aim and fired down the hall to the escape craft. Sarah jumped. She thanked heaven the bullet embedded itself someplace unseen instead of bouncing back to hit one of the unprotected crewmen.

Blake yelled, "Several of my people are dead! For all I know, you're responsible! Now move!"

The *Feni's* captain pushed off toward the MAC. His five crewmen filed behind him with frightened looks. As they passed the T-junction in the main corridor, everyone heard a blast from the upper cargo bay.

Several more medical alerts appeared on Sarah's HUD. Red, pulsating map dots and text signaled survivors. A man's piercing scream filled the radio. Sarah slapped her hands to her helmet's sides. Claire adjusted his cries to a distant wail.

Blake shouted, "Keep moving!"

Sarah knew he probably meant his order for everyone within earshot, but several marine suits called for medical aid. She twisted around and propelled her body down the *Feni's* main corridor.

The marine medic Staff Sergeant, Stephanie Holtz, gave chase but had to work around a *Feni* crewman. Sarah blocked out the woman's angry admonitions for her to return to the MAC.

"Cover fire!" someone ahead shouted. The *rat-tat-tat* of automatic weapons broke over the air.

Sarah's heart raced. A smoky haze filled the open airlock connecting the *Feni's* crew module to the pressurized hold. She saw an indistinct figure moving. Her HUD labeled it as Lieutenant Sean Merrick.

Thank God! she thought while landing hands-first onto the hatchway's wall. Sarah found Sean braced inside at the other porthole. He held the cargo space's hatch open enough for a person to pass.

"Come on!" he bellowed into the bay.

Sarah's helmet told her that one of the casualties, Gunnery Sergeant Martinez, floated a meter past the door's mouth. She could save him. She only needed to pull herself into the airlock, push past Sean and reach out.

To her astonishment, she froze. A knob of terror caught in her throat. *Something* had killed almost a dozen people beyond that opening. It was insanity to go in there.

The red cross on Sergeant Holtz's arm flashed past as the medic dived inside the airlock.

"What are you—" Lieutenant Merrick began.

Holtz shouted, "I've got Martinez!" She poked her torso through the gap, grabbed the wounded marine and tugged him to safety. It took less than five seconds, start to finish.

"Take him, Lieutenant," Holtz said, then twisted around,

intent on trying for another casualty. Sean clutched the medic's leg and yanked her back.

"They're too far!" he said. "Everyone fall back *right now* before we get hit again!"

Stirred from her paralysis, Sarah said, "Sergeant, help me with Martinez." Then Sarah noticed that one of the marines outside had stopped firing. The next moment, a figure made for the half-open door.

Claire called, "Incoming starboard!"

A deafening blast made Sarah's heart jump. Instinctively, she clutched at her patient, hoping to shield him. Through ringing ears, she heard Sean order, "Get back to the MAC! Move! Move! Move!"

The marine tagged as Watson slipped partway through the hatch when the explosion hit. An instant later, he screamed in hideous agony. His legs ended in bloodied stumps. The sight froze her again.

Dimly, she registered Sean yelling, "Get those two into the MAC!"

Holtz said, "I've got Watson." She launched herself and the mangled marine up the main corridor. Sarah watched in a daze as wobbling balls of blood trailed behind them.

"Lieutenant!" Sean said. "Go!" His harsh voice jolted Sarah. She leaped out of the airlock with the Platoon Sergeant in tow. No sooner had they cleared it than a series of sharp, metallic clanks reverberated through the hatch Sean had closed. She looked back to see Sean scrambling out. He barely managed to close the door before the transparent aluminum window on the hold-side hatch shattered.

"Where are those fifty cals!" Sean called.

In answer, Commander Blake said, "Make a hole!"

Sarah checked ahead to find herself sailing past the intel officer. He held a formidable looking weapon at the corridor's edge.

Distracted, Sarah and her patient bounced hard against the hall's end. She adjusted quickly and sent them toward the MAC's airlock. She caught the briefest glimpse of Sean kicking off to join them.

Maybe we have a chance, she thought.

———

MAYBE WE HAVE A CHANCE, SEAN THOUGHT.

Blake said, "It's in the hold's airlock! Out of the way Merrick!"

Seeing the commander above with a heavy gun, Sean jarred himself to a halt on a railing. Flexing his biceps taught, he drew flush to the wall.

Blake yelled, "Fire in the hole!"

Thunderous cracks shook Sean's skull. Peering below, he saw the cargo bay's porthole shatter. Hope grew within him. If the fifty cal could break four centimeters of layered transparent aluminum, it could take out that murderous droid.

A thud near his helmet made him jerk. He realized with alarm that the sparks dancing around the porthole were ricocheting bullets. He wanted to tell Blake to stop, but the gunfire kept the battle mech from shooting its Gatling and guided explosives. That last thought made him think to say, "We could use some drone grenades right about now."

"Inbound, sir!" Horvath crowed. Twisting, Sean saw a fat, floating spearhead device pointed his way.

Unseen, Corporal Horvath said, "Commander, cease fire in three, two, one, now!"

No sooner had Blake let off his trigger than Horvath remotely sent the mini-bomb rocketing on a brilliant yellow flare. It flew straight into the porthole and detonated, blasting a gout of orange flame back the way it had come. Shrapnel sprayed Sean's suit. He curled into a tight ball. It took him a few seconds to accept that he hadn't been hurt.

"I'm coming up," Sean called. He didn't know if they'd killed the mech, but he didn't want to find out by getting shot at. "Claire, where's the other one?"

The MAC pilot said, "I can see it! It'll be on us in seconds!"

"*Tsunami*," Sean said, "a little help here?"

"*Feni*," Captain Paulson said. "We're unable to fix Claire with a reboot, and whatever is in her system has affected MAC 58. We can't assist. We're going to try for a full wipe and reinstallation on one of her cores. Will take about thirty minutes. Suggest you do the same aboard MAC 117."

The pilot said, "Already started, ma'am. Any other ideas?"

Stricken, Sean fought to think of what they should do next. Before he came up with anything, Claire said, "Enemy on the hull!"

Location: Rear main cabin, MAC 117_

TREMBLING, SARAH TENDED TO THE BLOODIED AND QUIVERING Corporal Watson. She gasped when the pilot said, "They're cutting into us just behind the cockpit! Get some cover!"

She glanced up to see astronauts positioning themselves. From their vertical couches, the Lakshmians glanced worriedly at one another. Beside Sarah, Holtz struggled to get an I.V. into Sergeant Martinez.

She could almost hear Doc Apple reminding her, "Hey, you wanted excitement."

A large hand gripped the nurse's arm, making her jump. One of the Lakshmians said, "We need pressure suits, or we'll die!"

Sarah twisted her limb away, indignant at being unnecessarily frightened while trying to save a life. It didn't improve matters to find the *Feni's* captain before her.

From nearby, Sergeant Holtz gestured to the rear and said, "Locker over there. It has some rescue balls."

Channeling her shame, anger, and fear, Sarah added, "Will you take care of your crew?"

"We'll get ourselves sealed up," the Lakshmian said, ignoring her disdain. He directed his subordinates to find what they needed, then said, "Thank you for helping us."

As Sarah repositioned her magnetized limbs, she wanted to ask if the man really gave a damn about the poor souls working for him. She reasoned that at least she cared for the people she'd let get hurt. She wondered if the Lakshmian had known about the dangerous robots in his hold and not bothered to tell anyone. It took some effort to push her vitriolic suspicions from her mind to concentrate on patching up Watson.

Scarcely a minute later, a terrible bang heralded the breaching of the craft's skin. Everything not secured to the hull drifted forward. Sarah tightened her grip on Watson, trusting the mag-nodes in her suit's knee and elbow joints to keep them in place.

She saw rescue balls floating by, their occupants thrashing within. She looked into her patient's face. His panicked expression lashed at her heart. Leaning forward to protect the barely conscious man, she said, "I've got you, Corporal."

Flickering lights at the craft's front caught Sarah's attention. Beyond the little white rescue globes, she made out muzzle flashes from astronauts firing into a jagged hole. She realized with sickening dread that the enemy droid would send more grenades their way.

A desperate "no" escaped her. She was only twenty-three. She didn't want to die yet. She didn't want *any* of her comrades to die.

Something drew her gaze up. Her racing heart faltered. A pair of unsuited Lakshmians floated past. She recognized the man who'd shared his human trafficking story.

I can't help him! she thought, despairing. *If I leave Watson exposed...*

A figure on her other side moved. It was Holtz. She stood next to Sarah and said, "I'm going to—" A pair of blinding flashes fore and aft bleached the MAC's interior.

Sarah felt hammer-blows against her back, arms, and legs at several points. Her suit's status board went wild with blinking lights and alerts. The rebreather pack failed, leaving her with only a fifteen-minute emergency oxygen supply. Worse yet, the medical systems for three more astronauts pled for aid.

Sarah, however, paid the readouts no attention. Gaping with horror, she fixated on the tumbling form of Sergeant Holtz. The medic had taken the full wrath of a grenade, which had carved a crater in her abdomen.

Location: Forward main cabin, MAC 117_

SEAN'S HELMET BLARED WITH A CACOPHONY OF ALARMS. A ghostly red crosshair danced over the black mech. In his hands, a semi-automatic, high-caliber piston of destruction juddered as he plugged round after round into the encroacher. With vengeful satisfaction, he watched the mech waver and jerk under the constant barrage from Horvath, Blake, and himself.

In their adrenaline-suffused rage, the trio smashed the mech's limbs, joints, gun barrel, and sensor dome. Chunks of metal and composites broke off, joining the ricocheting bullets hurtling about them.

Horvath exclaimed, "I think we got its grenade palate!"

Sean figured that had to be why the rest of them weren't dead yet. Also, the thing seemed stuck in the jagged breaching hole it had made, blocking its lethal Gatling.

Sean yelled, "Die, you bastard!" He took a step forward on his mag-boots to push aside one of the rescue balls. He sent three final rounds into the inorganic monster's heart. The machine twitched like a half-dead animal. Hydraulic fluid streamed from several gashes, coalescing into clear spherules.

Sean raised his rifle. "Cease fire! Pull those rescue balloons back before the thing decides to explode or something."

While the others move to police up the Lakshmians, Sean stepped up to the droid hanging halfway through the MAC's ceiling. He whacked it with his rifle's muzzle. To his surprise, the hulk shimmied upward a smidgen.

"Hey," he said, "Whatever it grappled us with has released." He motioned to Horvath. "Give me a hand." Standing on mag-boots, they lifted the intruder until it had cleared the ship. The wrecked juggernaut drifted away at several centimeters per second. As Sean stood watching, he felt his fight-or-flight juices thinning.

In a subdued monotone, he said, "Merrick to *Tsunami*. Second mech neutralized."

"Copy Lieutenant," Paulson replied. Her voice sounded equally grave. She could see the body count as well as Sean. Seventeen marines—the pilot included—were dead. Only seven of the original boarding party remained. Of those, three lay severely wounded.

Operating from the MAC's backup computer core, Claire relayed the rescue bubble's status onto Sean's helmet. Four of the *Feni's* crewmen had survived the firefight.

He turned his attention to their one remaining medical expert. "Lieutenant Riley, you still functioning?"

Her reply came after a noticeable pause. "Yes. Yes, sir."

In a controlled voice, he said, "Tell us how we can help you."

"Can," she faltered. "Can we get everyone back aboard the *Feni*? I need to work in atmo."

Sean looked to the airlock. The lights on the *Feni*-side door indicated full pressure within the ship. Lucky for them, the battle hadn't breached the freighter's multi-layered hull.

Sean said, "Move the wounded into the airlock. Horvath, fly a drone down the *Feni*'s main corridor. I don't want anyone going aboard until we're sure the mech there is really out of commission."

"Roger, sir," she said and headed aft. She passed Sarah, who had begun moving Corporal Watson.

"What else, Lieutenant?" he asked while pulling the injured Corporal Yontz into the lock.

This time Sarah responded readily. "We should swallow painkillers on the off-chance we get the bends from the drop in pressure we all just took."

"Everyone heard the lady," Sean said. "Pop a pill, now." Turning to his helmet's dispenser, he noticed Commander Blake planted under the hole in their ship, staring upward.

Blake said, "We need to get away from the *Feni*. There might be more surprises waiting."

Sean made an exasperated noise. "I'm open to suggestions, sir. The MAC's dead until Claire's backup core finishes reinstalling. Even then, we have no guarantee we'll have control again."

Blake turned to Sean. "Lifeboat, Lieutenant." He made it sound like the most obvious thing in the world.

Of course, Sean thought. He'd forgotten about the *Feni*'s escape shuttle.

"Claire," he said, "how many can the *Feni*'s skiff carry, and how hard will it accelerate?"

"It seats ten and has a chemical rocket engine that'll boost for thirty seconds at full gee. It's enough to clear the light-sail's laser before heat becomes a problem."

"We may have to take it," Sean said. "Let's see if our airlock still works and get our people transferred." He paused to regard the commander. "Good idea, sir. Thanks."

Blake didn't reply. Instead, he turned to help Lieutenant Riley. Sean fought down the urge to flip the man off.

His adrenaline-high waning, he started to wonder what he was going to tell the board of inquiry about their disaster. Seventeen men and women had died on his watch.

Survive first, he scolded himself. *Figure the rest out later.*

Location: Lilith's private estate, Lakshmi Colony_

BESIDE LILITH, HENRY WILKINSON SCRATCHED AT HIS CHEEK AND said, "You know, you really should have loaded the mechs closer to the MAC."

Lilith said, "And how would that be a fair test of our new abilities?"

"They knocked out both of your new toys," Henry observed. "I thought you planned to take over the assault craft and use it to capture the *Tsunami.* How will you accomplish that now?"

Lilith smiled at Henry, clearly cherishing some secret.

"Natrix," she said, "Activate the other assets on the *Feni* and carry out the next phase of the attack. Make sure you get it all on camera. Once that's done, we'll deal with the *Tsunami.*"

Henry shook his head. "By showing off, you may have missed your opportunity to take the MAC. You'll be lucky if they haven't already sabotaged their engines. How many of those mechs did you put aboard the *Feni*?"

Lilith smiled. "Relax Henry. The *Feni* is a side-show, and it is going exactly to plan. I took it for granted that the Mykonians would disable their transport before we could control it. To be honest, I really didn't expect the mechs would do this well. And before you ask, yes, I have a plan for that battleship. It will take them almost half-an-hour to restore their combat systems. Which reminds me."

She sat up, lifted her pad, and tapped it. "Natrix, while you're at it, blow up the *MSV Typhoon* before it gets too far from that *Dhana* freighter."

Dalip glanced over, apparently disturbed by her flippant manner. Lilith ignored him, concentrating instead on entering something into her tablet.

In a severe female voice, Natrix said, "Nuclear missions accepted."

"Great. Do you have the new target list for the main event at Zeus?"

"Yes, Mistress."

"Wonderful. Start hitting the station now."

"Yes, Mistress."

The *Feni's* images shifted to a side-screen. In the center, appeared Zeus Station. Gleaming white against the black of space, the squat, tire-shaped colony spun silently. Somewhere within it lay Rafe's family. Then, exactly as she had promised, Lilith proceeded to send missile after missile at the Mykonian spy's home.

She smiled as, behind her, Rafe screamed in helpless fury.

13

Location: Hastings family residence, Zeus Station, orbiting the gas giant Belia_

"KAREN! ANNA! I'M HOME!" GITA TIWARI-HASTINGS CALLED from the front door.

Lying belly-down in bed, Karen Hastings rushed to finish an illicit entry under her friend's social profile. She failed to notice the tension in her mother's voice.

Moments later, Gita added, "Did you get Anna a snack? Fruit only on Tuesdays. Did you remember?"

Karen huffed. She yelled back in a defiant tone, "I'll take care of it in a minute."

Gita said, "Have you even helped Anna get ready for swim practice?"

Karen rolled her almond-shaped eyes. "Mom, she's nine. She's old enough to tell you herself."

From down the hall, Gita said, "I'm asking you, young lady."

"I'll get to it."

Clomping heels prompted Karen to slip the pad under a pillow. The footfalls paused at Anna's room. Karen figured her sister had already exceeded their daily allowance of screen time. Not good. Karen hopped up to swap out of her gray school uniform.

At last, Gita appeared. Karen was impressed at how her petite mother managed to loom in the doorway.

Palms on hips, Gita said, "What have you been doing, young lady?"

Karen stepped into a pink pant set that reeked of chlorine. Both knew that Alastair, the colony's A.I., would not divulge Karen's activities when her room had been in privacy mode.

"I was just relaxing for a few minutes, mom."

"You've been home over an hour. And you *promised* to help while your father's gone. I give you a minuscule bit of responsibility and..." Her eyes stabbed at Karen. "How many times do I have to tell you? Take care of your sister first."

Karen blew air through her teeth. "I'm not one of your little astronauts, mom."

"Sister first," Gita snapped. "Alastair, Karen has lost her pad time for the next two days."

"Yes, ma'am," Alastair replied.

Karen leered at her mother while zipping up her jacket. "We have twenty minutes before we leave."

"We can't go tonight. I have to head back to work right away."

"You just got home," Karen said, incredulous.

"Yeah, well, the message came through five steps from the porch."

"Why are you being so mean today?"

Face cross, Gita said, "Karen, I have enough to worry about without you adding to it. Some nasty stuff has been happening, and I need to know that you two will be okay."

A reflexive pang of sympathy gripped her. Then she remembered one of her mother's dictums: you shouldn't have to suffer for someone else's problems. Armed with this defiant notion, Karen crossed her arms.

Gita tilted her head in disappointment. "Go get Anna into her pajamas. I have just enough time to zap us dinner before I leave." She exited the room with a precise twist of her heel.

"Yes, *ma'am*," Karen murmured. She plopped back onto the edge of her mattress. *Dad can't get home soon enough.*

The next moment, the staccato blare of the emergency alert system filled her bedroom. Karen jumped and clasped both hands to her ears. Eyes broadening, she stared at the nearest display-wall. Its late afternoon's tranquil park scene had vanished. In its place, a brilliant white background glared with two pulsing red words: STATION ALERT. For a moment, Karen peered at the message, fear distorting her features.

She opened her mouth to call for Alastair to explain things when a booming male voice interrupted the klaxon. "This is Colonel Reynolds in Station Operations." The colonel paused long enough for Karen to catch the panicked shouts filtering through the communication line. "We are under attack. All inhabitants report immediately to the nearest evacuation boats. Abandon station. Alastair will launch the pods as soon as—" The voice cut out.

An ominous rumbling shook the house. A shrill, whooping siren assaulted Karen's senses. Her ears popped. The words on the wall changed. Alastair read them in his severest baritone. "Hull breach. Seek shelter immediately."

While Alastair repeated the instructions, Karen heard Gita hollering, "Hold on girls!" Two seconds later, Gita shot into the bedroom as if driven by a rocket. The worry creases in her face put another knot in Karen's shoulders.

Edging toward tears, Karen asked, "Is this really happening?"

Gita yanked Karen to her feet. "Come quickly. Hold my hand tight. It might get windy along the way to the rescue boats." At that remark, Karen noticed air whistling against their home's windows. Inside the station's two-by-five-kilometer cylindrical habitat, she had never felt a gust stronger than what a hair dryer could produce.

She recalled a disturbing simulation from the last annual public safety session. The vid had depicted an asteroid making a large hole in the station through which the air rushed out, knocking people and debris around. Forgetting all resentment toward her mother, Karen asked in a tremulous voice, "Are we going to be okay?"

Karen let her mother tug her to Anna's bedroom, but Anna was already in the hallway, following the glowing arrows along the floor. Upon entering the house's airtight shelter, Gita closed up the tiny room. Karen glimpsed her mother's terror-stricken face. The sight numbed Karen's limbs.

Gita said, "Alastair, what happened?"

The station's A.I. replied from the comm system. "Chief Tiwari-Hastings, you must all hurry to leave. Please open the access way at your feet."

Gita sprang to comply. She stood her children aside then bent to finger open a latch in the floor. It lifted to reveal a wheel which Gita frantically turned. As she labored, a small quake rocked the shelter. The lights flickered, and Karen grasped her sister's gray school blazer.

"Alastair," Gita persisted, "Colonel Reynolds mentioned an attack." She raised the hatch and started to work on the second seal below it.

Alastair replied, "Several missiles were concealed in cargo modules at the remote depot."

"How did they manage to sneak by our screening?"

"I'm sorry, I don't know yet. A Warden-level command shut down the defense grid, including radar. It took me over a minute to realize from the visual scopes that the first salvo had been launched."

Gita cursed as she kicked open the lower hatch onto a space full of strobing lights and shrieking alarms. An occasional figure hurried by. The family wasted no time clambering down a ladder attached to the wall.

"What else?" Gita demanded as she hauled her children along a sublevel corridor.

Karen heard Alastair's voice issue from Gita's bracelet. "The first wave of missiles mostly included several low-kiloton nuclear warheads. They took out the *Valiant* and *Courageous*."

The A.I. paused until the trio passed a blaring siren box. "A conventional armor-piercing missile struck the command center. I'm very sorry to inform you that Colonel Reynolds and the rest of the staff there were killed. Be advised that more ordnance is inbound. I estimate they will strike near your location."

The news left Karen shaking. People had died. She was keenly aware if they weren't lucky, she and her family would be killed too. Verging on panic, she saw they were passing the clogged entry ramps to a rescue boat. The lamps over its airlocks shone red, indicating it had reached capacity and would soon close up.

"We're almost there," Gita promised. She dragged them through the thickening foot traffic toward a group of yellow lights marking another escape ship's entrance. Less than twenty meters from it, a quake nearly knocked everyone off their feet. Dozens of screams filled the sublevel.

"What the hell Alastair!" Gita shouted over the din.

The A.I. said, "The attackers are targeting extra ordnance to your sector. Incoming!"

A boom from up the corridor overwhelmed Karen's senses. She watched in terror as an orange fireball blasted toward her, knocking everyone in front of her to the deck. The blazing incandescence came within fifty meters of Gita and her children, then retreated. The air surged after it as if being sucked forward by an invisible monster.

The flattened trio slid with the gale, their piercing cries adding to the cacophony. In that moment, Karen believed with absolute certainty that she and her family were about to die. Helpless, she clung to her mother and waited for the air to drain from her lungs.

Further down the passageway, however, a large set of doors rapidly closed. They pinched off the hemorrhage of atmosphere, giving them a reprieve from suffocation.

For a breathless stretch, Karen lay curled up, quivering. Her ringing eardrums dimly registered wails of agony. After several seconds, she recovered enough to push herself up and survey the chaos.

At the massive safety doors, Karen saw people trying to help one another stand again. She turned to her mother who clutched a sobbing Anna. A well of relief gushed up from Karen's heart and spilled from her eyes.

"Mom! Anna!" she exclaimed, grasping at her mother and not caring the least bit that she could barely hear her own voice.

"My babies! My darling babies!" Gita said, pulling Karen and Anna to her. The traumatized family hobbled toward the closest boat entrance. Karen saw people pounding at its inner airlock hatch, shouting for Alastair to open it.

From a speaker near the door, Karen heard the A.I. say, "Remain calm. The low atmosphere in your compartment won't let me open the lifeboat until I can equalize the pressure. When the hatch opens, enter quickly but carefully."

At those words, Karen noticed how light-headed she still felt. She looked about and saw a few others staggering like they had spun themselves around and around too many times.

After another rumble, Gita seemed to lose all patience. "Alastair, get that door open now!"

"On it, Chief," the A.I. insisted. Karen felt her mother's hand pinch her shoulder.

And then everything changed.

"Chief Tiwari-Hastings," Alastair said. "We're receiving a message from the space-side container yard from where the attack originated." A pause. "Standby." Another pause. "Standby, please." While they waited, the hatch at last opened and the refugees stampeded into the rescue boat. Finally, Alastair said, "Chief, the message says that they are launching nuclear devices at us."

"Nukes?" Gita shouted. A few of the others in the group around her uttered similar words of shock.

"Missiles inbound. I estimate impact in less than a minute. I'm sorry, Chief." The lifeboat's entryway started to slowly rise like a drawbridge. From deeper inside the rescue ship, Alastair said, "Everyone secure yourselves. We're launching as soon as the hatches seal."

Desperate screams chorused from the dozens of men, women, and children still waiting their turn to board. Several grasped at the edges of the pod's lifting airlock door, clogging the entry.

Karen couldn't believe it. Escape lay one meter away. One *stupid* meter!

Before she could give voice to her anguish, however, Karen felt hands lifting her by the armpits. Then Gita heaved her daughter over the trapped refugees, crying, "I love you, Karen!" The girl sailed through the final cruel stretch to freedom.

Karen crashed amongst the last lucky colonists. The next thing she knew, bodies toppled over her, and the boat's airlock hatch hissed shut. Something metallic clanked, followed by weightlessness. The station's centrifugal force had thrown the pod clear at a clip of almost three-hundred-fifty kilometers per hour.

Still guiding the craft, Alastair assigned a vector that would let the refugees rendezvous with a colony. The maneuvering jets swung the lifeboat around. Shortly after, a roaring vibration from the main rocket motor filled the interior.

Under the acceleration, Karen's cheek smashed painfully into one of the boxy airlock's small windows. The bodies of other hapless escapees pinned her down. Unable to move, she peered through what had become the floor. A gleaming object passed beneath her: Zeus's rotating shell.

As the lifeboat gained speed, the station's bulk receded behind the ghostly exhaust plume from the engine. Karen saw another pod release from its berth to join the dozens of others shooting away. Her chest tightened with the realization that her mother and little sister had been left behind.

Karen twisted her unexpectedly heavy head, intending to call for Alastair. This was a mistake. They had to go back and get her family.

She caught a series of brilliant flashes in the corner of her eye. She snapped back in time to see startling white plumes erupting from several points on the station. Lightning-fast waves rippled through the metal, radiating away from the burning streaks. To Karen's disbelieving horror, her home disintegrated into several large, twisting chunks wreathed by a billion glittering shards.

A scream burst from Karen's lungs and expended itself on the cool windowpane. She continued to howl until the thruster jets shut off several seconds later. In helpless frustration, she punched the viewport. This sent her flailing end over end into the other people in the small airlock.

Instinctively she grabbed onto the nearest scrap of clothing. It was the hem of a gray jacket. She caught sight of the owner's head and gasped.

"Anna?!"

It took Karen a full second to grasp that she wasn't imagining the tear-streaked face of her sibling. Karen realized that her mother must have pushed her sister aboard at the last possible moment.

Tiny pieces of the station briefly pattered off the rescue craft in a macabre rain. As it echoed through the hole in her heart, Karen pulled Anna into a sobbing, careening embrace.

14

Location: MAC 117, docked to the Lakshmian freighter Feni_

FIVE MINUTES BEFORE THE FALL OF ZEUS, SEAN WAS SPEAKING with Captain Paulson when she cut off mid-word. His eyes shot to the icon for comms status. No signal.

His heart-rate quickened. The suit's radio had cut out. Was it only his? He lifted his eyes to the others around him. The icy sensation trickling down his back chilled by several degrees as Blake and Horvath paused in their tasks to look back at him. He raised his free hand to the side of his head, thumb and little finger extended like he was listening to a headset. Then he balled the hand into a fist and shook it in the negative. The others quickly pantomimed the same.

The enemy had killed their radios. The question as to why they'd done it then and not before would have to wait. Sean knew they might have only seconds before another attack. He pointed at Blake, then to the cockpit, and finally made an exploding gesture with his hands—they needed to sabotage the MAC before the enemy could capture it.

After the briefest hesitation, Blake gave an unenthusiastic

thumbs-up and turned to the dead pilot's body. The keys for the ship's demolition controls would be on the man's suit.

Leaving Blake to his morbid task, Sean waved for Horvath to join him in the airlock where Sarah tended to her patients. He grappled the nurse's arm and yanked her aside to get at the panel beyond her. He caught her panicked expression and wished there'd been time to be kinder.

While she fought to control her fright, Sean punched a button on the wall. The MAC's airlock door swung shut. Then he worked the emergency re-pressurization controls.

Air gushed in, and he heard Sarah's faint shout. "—is going on, sir?"

"Radios are being jammed," he yelled over the hiss of the rapidly thickening atmosphere. "You and Horvath will get the wounded to the *Feni's* escape pod. I'll cover the main corridor." As the air neared full pressure, he lowered his voice some. "You hear any shooting, you shut the pod's airlock. If anything hostile tries to get through, you launch. Understood?"

Sarah rocked back, but she nodded. "H—how are they able to jam the comms? I thought that was almost impossible?"

"It is."

Military transmitters used modified Quadrature Phase Shift Keying (QPSK) with pre-programmed codes and adaptive frequency hopping. Apart from someone 'barrage' jamming the entire radio spectrum, the boarding team shouldn't have been significantly affected.

He added, "Either it's another Warden lockout, or there must be a mother-load of scramblers somewhere in the cargo bay."

Claire's voice said, "Pressure stable."

Sean slammed his palm at the *Feni's* door controls and brought his weapon up beside Horvath's. The hatch swung into an empty corridor. The sirens cut out. Heart pounding in his ears, Sean realized he needed to tell the A.I. something.

"Claire, as soon as we're out, shut the airlock and quick-cycle it back so Blake can get through."

"Copy Lieutenant," she replied.

"See what you can do about automating that request. The commander is going to blow your computer cores any second."

"Don't sound so happy about it, sir."

Sean didn't react to the remark.

"Stay here," he told the two medical officers. He stepped out and closed the lock's hatch behind him. Swallowing hard, he released his mag-boots and kicked off for the intersection with the main corridor. He wished to heaven they could have spared the time for Horvath to send a drone ahead.

Stopping short on the intersection's lip, he angled his fifty-caliber weapon downward. Its scope fed a video through the weapon's handgrip, into his gloves, and onto his HUD.

He panted with anxiety. He had to be the one to check over that edge. Not Horvath. Not Blake. Not after all that had happened.

He took three final, rapid breaths, and stuck his weapon out.

Despite himself, he jerked back, the shift of momentum sending him into a rearward arc. As he replanted his foot, a gasp escaped his thumping chest. With that draining release, he realized two things: not only was he still in one piece, but the hatch at the end of the corridor hadn't opened.

He repositioned himself to look again, studying the image from the rifle. A piece of mech blocked the broken porthole. When it didn't move, he concluded it was the one Blake and Horvath had damaged before.

He waved for Horvath and Sarah to move. Sarah emerged first, maneuvering the mauled corporal past Sean at the intersection. He glanced up as they floated by. The ghastly sight of Watson's blackened leg stumps made Sean's stomach turn over.

The clang of Horvath shutting the airlock's door provided a

welcome excuse to look away. He noted the gurgling pumps as they extracted the little room's atmosphere. In less than a minute, Blake and the *Feni's* survivors could enter. As Horvath hauled away the other two unconscious marines, a subsonic rumble emanated from the MAC's direction. Metal creaked ominously. Sean braced as the deck shifted subtly beneath him.

Blake must have blown the remass tanks.

He imagined hydrogen gas spewing from the MAC's pressurized reservoirs. They would act like impromptu thrusters, threatening to rip the craft off of its docking port. He reminded himself that all airlock clamps were designed to handle the torque caused by a punctured tank. The docking seal would hold firm. Probably.

Sean repositioned himself on the T-junction's far side. This let him glance back and forth between the main corridor and the MAC's airlock. The hatch controls continued to blaze red for vacuum on the other side. After several seconds of staring, he prayed for Blake and the rescue balls to appear in the hatch's porthole. A gloved thumb bumped against his helmet as he unconsciously tried to bite its nail. He was on the verge of moving closer to the lock for a better look when he, at last, saw movement.

He released a lungful of air, fogging his helmet.

And then a light winked through the porthole. Since no noise followed, Sean couldn't be sure if it had been a burnt-out bulb, a spark, a muzzle flash or the partially obstructed explosion from a grenade.

Without Claire to run a spectral analysis on the light, he considered several unpleasant possibilities. If a mech was assaulting the MAC, Sean didn't know what he could do to help the men inside, assuming they still lived. He toyed with going back through the lock quickly. Thanks to their earlier preflight breathing regimen, his risk for decompression sickness wasn't all that high. On the other hand, he very much doubted that his semi-automatic rifle could disable the enemy's Gatling and grenade tubes before they blasted him apart.

Then something else occurred to him. If they faced more mechs, what was there to stop the things from floating over to the life pod and disabling it. They could even shoot the little ship while it jetted away at a paltry one gravity of acceleration.

This entire inner struggle of overlapping thoughts, beginning at the flash through the porthole, took place in less than two breaths. By the end of it, Sean clenched his teeth and made his decision. He deactivated his magnetic soles and pushed off for the MAC's airlock and the Lakshmians—away from the lifeboat.

"Horvath! Riley!" he shouted, feeling the unreal weight of his choice come crashing down on his shoulders. "Button up the life-pod. Launch in sixty seconds if you don't see me knocking on the porthole, no matter what."

As Sean landed on the MAC's outer hatch, he looked through the lock's porthole. To his profound relief, a white rescue balloon covered it. That meant Blake was pushing the *Feni's* crew to safety.

Sean punched controls to close the *Feni's* outer hatch. This halved the space in the airlock. It would slow a mech down if it tried to breach the MAC's side. Meanwhile, anyone in the *Feni's* partition could finish pressurizing and escape.

A second later, a message bleeped onto the readout: door obstructed.

What the—?

"Need a hand sir?" a husky female voice called from behind. Sean whipped about to find Horvath settling at the T-junction.

"What the hell are you doing here?" he snapped. "Didn't you hear what I said?"

A grin crept up Horvath's left cheek. "Marines don't leave anyone behind, sir."

Sean stared at Horvath for a full second, furious over her

willful failure to obey his instructions. At last, he said, "Get back to the—"

A thud from behind him interrupted his tirade. He whipped around to peer through the airlock's porthole. Where a white rescue ball had been, he saw Blake's helmet pressed against the multi-layered transparent alloy. From beneath blinking HUD alerts, Blake's face contorted in a silent, agonized scream.

Sean flinched at the sight. His anger with Horvath deferred, he yelled, "Blake is hit!" In that instant, he realized that the flash from before must indeed have been a grenade. "A mech is on its way! It might already be inside the MAC!"

He rechecked the airlock controls. The *Feni's* outer hatch remained open, but a gauge told him that the air pressure past the door was rising to equalize with the *Feni's*. A clock said they had 19 seconds to wait.

Sean banged a fist against the porthole, hoping to get Blake's attention, but the man's eyes remained shut. He shouted Blake's name to the same non-effect. As the seconds slipped by, Sean watched the commander's features wither into unconsciousness.

"No!"

Then he noticed the readouts in Commander Blake's HUD. The small human figure in one corner pulsed red. Blake was dead.

At that same moment, Sean watched the man's body do something that fresh corpses should not be able to do. It jerked. It didn't move much, but the shift was unmistakable.

Sean's eyes grew wide with a deepening alarm. Anything disturbing the commander's body should have made him tumble away from the porthole. But Blake remained in place.

Sean's upper back and chest blazed with raw terror. Suddenly, he understood why the *Feni's* outer door hadn't closed and why Blake's limp form still hung in place.

"There's a mech in the airlock!" he yelled. "Go, go, go!"

As he shouted, he drew his legs up and rotated to brace both feet against the door. He kicked off with all his strength, rocketing toward the intersection. On checking "above" him, however, he gasped. Ahead, Horvath tumbled along a leisurely trajectory through the access way's center.

Sean guessed that the woman had tried to move without first unclamping her mag-boots. The mistake had detached her from the wall as intended but left her drifting slowly into his path.

"Look out!" he cried.

The woman yelped as Sean collided with her legs. He careened into a bulkhead where he snagged a shoulder on a mound of supplies that sent him pin-wheeling helplessly back into the middle of the corridor.

Sean knew then that no matter what else happened, neither he nor Horvath had any hope of escape. He glimpsed the airlock's timer as it reached zero. In a few seconds, the mech would have the door open and a clear shot at anyone in the hall. It wouldn't miss.

"Launch Sarah!" he shouted. "Launch!"

But it was too late for that also. Sarah was no longer in the escape pod. He looked up and saw her rounding a corner scarcely five meters behind him.

———

ONLY SECONDS BEFORE, SARAH HAD BEEN WORKING ON AN oozing gash that Watson's suit sealant hadn't fully closed. She reached into her aid bag for another bandage then stopped herself. She choked on a sob.

"I can't fix him," she whimpered to herself.

She secured Watson in his cot and turned to regard the unconscious forms of Sergeant Martinez and Corporal Yontz. Still encased in their night-gray armor, Horvath had already strapped them into the vertically positioned acceleration couches.

You have to triage them. She couldn't waste everything on one patient who probably wouldn't live anyway.

Shifting about in the narrow aisle, she took the gloved hands of the other two marines in hers. Medical data flowed from their suits into her visor. Each marine had clearly suffered concussions from the grenades that had gone off too near to them. She noticed blood beading along a cut in Yontz's forehead: a wound he'd sustained despite the cushions sewn into his radio cap.

They needed to get away so she could get them out of their suits. The realization made her note a red alarm blinking. Her rebreather remained offline, and the oxygen reserve wouldn't last much longer.

As she decided to go find Sean to tell him all this, she heard his voice again, catching his alarmed tone but little else. She recalled the grizzly scene of Watson being blown apart from the knees down.

I won't hesitate again.

Sarah flipped around and jetted through the lifeboat hatch. Sean yelled again, followed by Horvath's brief screech. Sarah's blood curdled as she sailed the handful of meters down the access way. She rounded the corner exactly when Sean cried out for her to launch.

Sarah froze. Not far off, she saw Sean's white suit flattening against a wall. Beyond him on the corridor's opposite side, Horvath pulled into a crouch, her hands reeling in a rifle strap. Past the marine, the airlock to the MAC swung open.

Sarah beheld the obsidian form of a mech inside the lock. It clutched Blake in front of it like a shield. The machine's forward hydraulic limbs crumpled Blake's armor beyond the tolerances of human anatomy.

Before Sarah could think to scream, Sean and Horvath fired on the mech. The gargantuan monstrosity allowed them a second to pelt its armored shell. Then the inorganic beast flung Blake's body at Horvath as though passing a ball. The lieutenant gawked as Blake's corpse knocked the marine off her magnetic boots and toward Sarah's position.

Reflexively, Sarah tried to catch the woman with an arm, but the dead commander's ricocheting body smashed Sarah against the bulkhead first. The nurse lost her grip on the wall railing and tumbled away.

As Sarah scrambled for a handhold, she heard Sean shouting her name again, telling her to get away. Disoriented, she didn't know which direction to flee. She looked left, right, and then up. The mech, in no hurry at all, had pushed forward, leaving the rescue balloons to jostle in its wake.

Sarah looked on as Sean bravely held his ground. He fired round after round into the advancing wraith's glossy black finish, but it didn't even slow.

As it neared him, the mech's Gatling muzzle angled toward Sean and flashed once. At first, Sarah's mind didn't connect the light with Sean's sudden, off-axis twisting. She blinked. A split second later, she understood that Sean had been shot.

"No!"

But as Sean spun, his arms came to life. He scrambled for a handhold, leading Sarah to cut her scream, mid-vowel. She saw then that Sean had only been surgically disarmed with a shot from the mech's cannon.

Had she been thinking more clearly, Sarah would have realized the three astronauts in the corridor should've already been dead. Their opponent's precision fire control far outstripped anything a human could manage. The mech was showing off.

Sarah's gaze shifted as the mech's bulk eclipsed Sean from sight. Like a giant metal spider snaring a moth, the machine closed upon Corporal Horvath. It caught the woman from the rear in a vice about her slender abdomen. Horvath thrashed and squealed.

As if to ensure Sarah had a good view, the mech shot out its free limbs to wedge itself in the hallway's center. Horvath and her captor jerked to a halt a few meters from Sarah's trembling form. Once stopped, the monster clamped a palp around each of its victim's biceps and thighs. It splayed Horvath like a wild animal about to be skinned.

Sarah stared into Horvath's bulging eyes. Then, the doomed woman screamed hideously. Sarah flinched, knowing that the pain caused by the machine's crushing grip must be excruciating.

A series of loud pops filled the hallway. The screaming transformed into a string of withering, staccato shrieks as the mech tore Horvath's limbs off.

The sound of shredding skin and cracking bone filled the corridor. An arm tore loose, and blood gushed from severed arteries. The mech flung Horvath's arm aside like a hunk of meat. Hydraulic pistons pulled at Horvath's lower limbs like a wishbone. All the while, the woman wailed and sputtered until, lungs drained, she paused to gulp down enough air to cry out again.

Sarah watched, unable to do anything. She couldn't see Horvath's fifty caliber weapon. Then she remembered the low-powered handgun she had for emergency. She couldn't hope to cause meaningful damage to the machine with it, but she could stop Horvath's suffering. She aimed it at the marine's visor, hands quaking.

She couldn't pull the trigger.

Horvath's leg split off. The gaping pelvic wound showered the hallway with crimson droplets.

The mech finished rending the other leg before tossing Horvath's limp corpse at Sarah. Blood and body parts slapped across the nurse's face-shield. The mech turned around and headed the other way.

Sarah fought the urge to vomit and screamed Sean's name. She couldn't imagine living with herself if she allowed the mech do to him what it had done to Horvath. In that moment of shock, she cast aside any thought for her patients in the pod and her status as a non-combatant. Instead, she scanned about for another weapon. The black muzzle of Horvath's gun, still clipped to her body's remaining arm, hovered nearby. Now that the mech wasn't in the way, she could reach it.

Sarah hadn't trained on the marine's Z-coil fifty rifle, but it had a loaded magazine, and that was enough. Almost in a trance, Sarah planted one magnetized knee to the deck, positioned the stock to her shoulder and fired.

One round after another pelted the mech's chassis, but it ignored her completely. The magazine ran dry after four shots. Then the machine reached the corridor's far end.

Sarah scrambled to find a new cartridge on the marine's blood-painted suit. Meanwhile, the mech's Gatling barrel barked once. Sarah's head jerked up to see glittering shards from the shattered airlock porthole zipping about. Then she heard Sean's muffled scream from behind the door. The hole had equalized the pressure between airlock and cabin. All the mech had left to do was coax the door to open. Sarah imagined the thing crushing Sean's body between its metal palps.

At last, she found a new magazine and fumbled to lock it home.

The first round penetrated the mech's weakened armor above its main power bus. Sparks and yellow flame spat, but a back-up switched on, and the juggernaut continued to work the hatchway controls. Another shot dented a motor's gears, seizing up a limb. A third hit the main sensor dome, destroying several optics.

The airlock door swung forward.

"No!" Sarah shrieked and pulled the trigger once more. The bullet exited the muzzle at almost a kilometer a second. This time it found a hole in the degraded plating along the mech's back and struck the main computer hub. At the same time, a massive surge from the damaged bus overwhelmed the machine, tripping its master breakers. The hulking monstrosity froze just as it reached for Sean.

It took two more shots before Sarah realized that the mech had stopped moving. Her body trembled. Her head throbbed. She felt like throwing up.

Sean apparently required a few seconds himself to understand that the chance to bolt had come. He shouldered the mech aside, its magnetic grapples having lost their electrical charge. Then he kicked off for Sarah.

"Everyone else is dead!" he called as he flew toward her. "Get to the lifeboat! There may be more mechs on the way!"

Sarah, however, couldn't move. Horvath had drifted back into her line of sight. The marine's lifeless remains transfixed her.

"Move!" the lieutenant yelled as he touched down on the wall behind Sarah. "We'll come back for them!"

She let him grab her by the hand and yank her away. Within seconds, they entered the escape pod and blasted from the *Feni*. The little lifeboat's computer sent them hurtling for the *Tsunami*.

Once the rockets cut out, Sean unbuckled himself from the pilot's chair and jetted down the narrow aisle to Sarah at the back.

He screamed at her. "Why didn't you launch when I told you?"

Sarah's gaze snapped up. "I didn't hear…" she began. She couldn't breathe.

Sean held her shoulders so she had no choice but to look at him. His ungentle handling frightened her.

Sean yelled into her face, "Horvath is *dead* because she didn't do what I told her to! And you had wounded to think about!"

Sarah's eyes teared at his censure. She had saved his life, and this was the thanks she got?

"You have a Red Cross on your arm, Lieutenant!" Sean went on. "You could be called a war criminal for attacking an enemy like that! What if they use what you did as an excuse to shoot the next Mykonian medic they find?"

Mortified, Sarah knew he was right. She'd abandoned her patients in a foolhardy attempt to rescue him. And what she had done might indeed end up costing others their lives.

"I'm not that important, Sarah," he said. "Why did you risk yourself for me?"

Sarah coughed. Her eyes swam in tears. "I couldn't let you die. I couldn't." At that, she began gasping.

I can't breathe, she thought, choking on her own fumes.

Sean's eyes bulged as he finally noticed the tell-tales flashing in her HUD. Both her rebreather and O2 tank had given out. He moved swiftly to pop her neck seals and raise the helmet a few centimeters. Feeling like a child who'd been hiding under the bed covers for far too long, Sarah inhaled the cool, fresh air. Her head quickly cleared some.

She blinked and shook the moisture from her lids. For a long moment, she stared helplessly into Sean's ice blue eyes, her lip quivering. He stared back, agony etched in his face. And then he pulled her to him in a tight embrace.

[15]

Location: Transhuman orbital space lane, Cervantes system_

CEF SWAM IN THE WAVES OF VIOLENCE AND TERROR WASHING UP from the Warden relays near Zeus. With his expanded mentality, he sampled thousands of personal agonies at once. As Zeus broke apart, his lobes soaked in the screams of the doomed. Meanwhile, his neuronal feeds lapped up the tearful cries of refugees in the shuttles. All the while, his innards relished the counterpoint of silence echoing from the dead.

While gorging on the suffering, Cef merrily declared to Len, "Phase Two has begun. You may now counter-move."

Len considered his options one last time. Game simulations continued to play out in his ancillary brains. He ranked follow-on scenarios according to shifting probabilities bubbling up in a chaotic sea of possibilities. The impact caused by Rafe's fortunate meddling had exceeded Len's expectations. The simulations indicated that the Mykonian spy might do even more damage to Lilith and Cef. Len saw a shifting pathway ahead: one which he might set Rafe upon to deliver hope for a meaningful counter-strike.

At last, the transhuman said, "I exercise the following over-rides." His commands surged through the Warden network.

Privately, Len worried. Even at the speed of light, his orders would take minutes to reach Belia. He projected that the Mykonians would lose several more units before his override of Lilith's shut-down codes could be enacted. But at least there was one—very costly—command line that he expected she would be too late to do anything about.

"That will not make Lilith happy," Cef noted with an almost musical expression of glee. "You now have only nineteen percent of your playing options remaining."

Len resisted the impulse to respond. Against his better judgment, he accessed a camera-feed from the Zeus lifeboat carrying Rafe's children. In its belly, people mewled. Some vomited as they struggled to adjust to zero-gravity. All of them grieved.

A sympathetic cascade of discharges played across Len's multi-brain. He hurt for them. Disconnecting the link, he returned his attention to plotting how to beat Cef at his cruel game and so win the freedom of Cervantes' humans.

Location: Lilith's private estate, Lakshmi Colony_

ALL AROUND RAFE, MYKONIANS BURNED AND DIED. SCREEN after screen replayed the destruction of Zeus, the *Typhoon,* and a dozen other vessels. He guessed a third of the BELCOM fleet had been annihilated in the span of ten minutes. Eventually, his gaze fell upon Henry who, at that same moment, glanced back at him.

Was that pity in the spy's eyes? A measure of admiration?

After the initial shock over losing his home and probably also his family, Rafe had grown remarkably still. He had no strength left to fight. He hurt in too many places to count, mind and body. He'd slept little in three days. And unscratched itches plagued his stinking body. If someone pushed him over, he doubted he'd get up for a week.

And why fight? If Gita and the girls were dead, he had no one left to live for.

Rafe looked on as Lilith watched her vid screens with unbridled glee. She'd seemed particularly pleased at how her mech had endured the boarding party's weapons. Before the *Feni's* escape pod launched, she'd ordered Natrix to send six mechs from the cargo holds toward the *Tsu.* Each rode atop a boxy, high-acceleration transfer rocket and would reach the battleship in minutes. Lilith clearly expected them to overwhelm the ship with little trouble.

At some point in the parade of flaming destruction, Lilith turned to Rafe and said, "You see, Mr. Hastings. Nothing of what you suffered matters. I've beaten you anyway."

The words pricked at Rafe's broken heart. Despite his prayers, Lilith's attack had succeeded. It was even odds at best that his family had escaped. His only other consolation lay in knowing that fewer Mykonians had perished because he'd kept his secrets.

The not-knowing made him want to tune the world out: to lose himself in the cauldron of misery within. Then a flash of memory struck. Once his father had spoken of being a young cadet on his first live-fire rifle range. The senior Hastings thought he'd been doing poorly, so he let his shots go wild toward the end. When he left the range, he found that he'd been two hits away from earning a sharpshooter badge. The lesson: "Don't throw away your bullets, son."

Reaching for some final reserve within, Rafe told himself, *They could still be alive. And you're not dead. So, pay attention. You still have work to do, Commander.*

Staring ahead, he noticed how the Lakshmian Prime Minister, Shaasti Dalip, kept checking his handheld. Rafe imagined the stream of calls and alerts his frantic staff was pinging him with.

On Lilith's left, Henry resembled a father embarrassed by his daughter's overly exuberant behavior at a funeral.

A long silence passed before Dalip said, "The media is mostly focused on the news about Zeus. A few have picked up that the Mykonian ships are also being taken out."

"Satisfied then?" Lilith asked the two men. "Have I not delivered what I promised? We've routed the Mykonians. And with only half of the Arbiters in position."

"I've already signaled Celes," Henry said, his serious manner a stark contrast to Lilith's. Even through his grief, Rafe appreciated that display of professionalism. One shouldn't celebrate until all the cards were played.

Lilith said, "And you Dalip?"

"Impressive, but why couldn't we do this to all of the Mykonian colonies and be done with them?" Dalip asked.

The woman shrugged and grinned. "My resources have their limits. Shall we make our announcement now and expand them?"

Dalip replied, "What if the fleet's survivors come for us or your Arbiter emplacements?"

Lilith kept smiling. "You've seen what I can do to their ships if pushed too far. And we have enough Casabas to frighten them off if needs be."

The prime minister said, "I would have preferred a demonstration of their abilities."

"I told you I don't have any to spare. But what are you worried about? We can trust the Wardens' weapons. Have some faith." She cuffed him on the shoulder.

Dalip pondered her explanation for a beat. "Yes. Yes, it is time to address the system."

As Lilith and Dalip stood to leave, she asked, "You're sure you won't join us, Henry?"

Feigning disappointment, Henry said, "It wouldn't be appropriate for me to show myself yet. Besides which, I should take care of our loose end here." He gestured at Rafe. "Please, enjoy your moment. You earned it."

Lilith nodded graciously, then paused to study Rafe. She shook a finger at him.

"Don't kill him yet, Henry," she said. "Not if you want to sleep in my bed tonight."

Rafe shifted his eyes toward Lilith as she departed, wondering where else had he heard words like those. Before he could pursue the notion further, he noticed Henry stalking toward him. The man pulled a syringe from a breast pocket in his coat.

"Pain-killer and stimulant," the spy explained. The cool tendril of liquid relief spread quickly through Rafe's veins, silencing many of his screaming nerves.

Feeling his body relax a degree, Rafe wheezed, "She's too vindictive for her own good."

Henry regarded Rafe with a set jaw. "Yes," he admitted. "And crazy." The words echoed with regret. Rafe couldn't help wondering if the man was actually developing feelings for the deranged mob boss.

"Well," Henry said, recovering from his melancholy, "now that the game is finished, will you tell me what happened with the information Baylor gave you?"

"The game's not over," Rafe replied, coughing.

"No, I suppose it isn't." He scratched the back of his head. "As you can tell, she isn't likely to give you to my custody." He crouched to Rafe's level and peered past his swollen eye sockets. "I could kill you now if you like. You've earned that courtesy. Just say the word."

Rafe stared back, his head wobbling like it might fall off at any moment. He ignored the inner voice begging him to accept the offer.

They might still be alive! his inner voice shouted. *Keep him talking!*

"Why haven't you killed Lilith yet?" Rafe asked.

Henry gave a crooked smile. "You're very good Commander Hastings. As you said, the game isn't over. I'm sure you can deduce my reasons."

Rafe could. He imagined that only Lilith controlled whatever gifts she had received from the Wardens. Rather than risk losing access to her arsenal, the Celesians were willing to chance the mad woman turning her toys against them. Rafe suspected Henry's lust for the seductress also had something to do with it.

"I am genuinely sorry for you and your family," Henry said. "With any luck, once Lilith and Dalip have made their broadcast, your government will see the wisdom of conceding to us. There is no need for more Mykonians to die."

Rafe stifled a painful chuckle. That he could find anything funny amidst his grief surprised him. But he had heard few things more humorous.

"Live under Celesian rule?" he asked.

The founders of the totalitarian Celesian Union had spent the last fifty years conquering or otherwise absorbing all the colonies orbiting Celes. Only a grudgingly signed treaty with Mykon kept them away from the fractured Belian system.

"Come now, Mr. Hastings," Henry said. "Celes is not all that different from Mykon. We both use A.I.s to govern our lives. We just take it a step further than you."

That was an understatement, Rafe knew. Instead of mere public oversight, the Celesian populace had a total lack of privacy. Everything one said and did in Celes, even in one's own home, was policed by an A.I. who reported suspect activities to an army of overseers. The Celesians took the nightmare a step further by fitting their population with slave collars. The police used them to punish violators for even talking in ways deemed disloyal.

"You don't look convinced," Henry said. "Tell me, how many

fathers molest their daughters in Mykon every year? How many rapes happen in privacy zones because the victims are too ashamed to bring charges: even though your A.I.'s see what goes on in your homes anyway? How many murders are still committed each year?"

"By whom?" Rafe said, trying desperately not to think of his daughters in agony. "Private citizens? Or the state?"

"It is not murder if the state lawfully executes a criminal."

Rafe harrumphed in spite of his discomfort. The Celesians broadcasted a public execution every week or so for vague and minor offenses. Everyone had heard reports of the union's 're-education' camps. Sometimes people would escape Celesian space on a freighter or talk to a visiting national. They shared stories of horror and oppression on a massive scale.

"It is murder," Rafe replied, "if the law isn't just or the judge isn't honest."

"But of course," Henry said, "that is the beauty of our system. The A.I.s ensure honesty and impartiality. They cannot be bribed or fooled."

"But the A.I.s can be told to lie. They aren't Wardens."

"And what evidence could you possibly have that such a colossal betrayal of trust had occurred?"

"It's all academic. Lilith will just stop our ships and kill us, won't she?"

Henry stared Rafe down. His silence confirmed Rafe's suspicions. Lilith's trick to shut down the Mykonian defenses had limits. It could be countered. Why else hadn't Henry used it to point out the futility of resisting the Celesian alliance with Lilith? Why else had Lilith needed to reassure Dalip with her cryptic reference to that so-called "Casaba" weapon?

Henry opened his mouth to speak when a harsh klaxon alerted them to a public Warden announcement.

Henry turned about. "Ah, Lilith's address is about to begin."

On the room's most prominent screen, an obsidian Warden enforcer appeared. Without preamble, it said, "Denizens of Belia. The bankruptcy of your thinking has brought you to the edge of disaster. We offer you a choice and hope. You may fight amongst yourselves, or you can unite under a steward of our choosing. We give you Empress Lilith. Defy her if you wish, but be warned, she enjoys Warden custodial immunity. Your new empress will address you now." The camera panned to Lilith. Dalip stood close by, slightly behind her right shoulder.

"Thank you, Warden," Lilith said. Rafe felt nauseated revulsion at her beatific, almost motherly smile.

"I am humbled to have been chosen as your administrator," she said. "Celes has united with me. Together, we will end the oppressive machinations of the Mykonians. Together, we will bring peace and a new era of prosperity to Belia and the Cervantes system."

The audacious words prompted Rafe to look to Henry. The Celesian's narrowed gaze and tightened jaw couldn't be mistaken. His hands had clenched into white-knuckled fists. Dalip's onscreen face had also hardened.

They didn't expect that little nugget about immunity. Now they can't kill Lilith.

In point of fact, they could try, but the Wardens would quickly execute anyone who harmed Lilith. It had been some time since protective Warden custody had been invoked, but Rafe recalled how punishment could extend to any immediate family, close friends and loved ones. If an order to kill or maim Lilith could be traced back to any officials, they would suffer the same far-reaching punishment. Rafe wondered if even an Arbiter would override the woman's new immunity.

"Thanks to intelligence from the Wardens," she continued, "we now know the Mykonians have been quietly threatening Belia's governments for the last decade. If their demands for resources and slaves were not met, the Mykonians secretly promised to destroy entire colonies using their Arbiters.

"Ever since the fall of the Empire, these foreigners professed to be our friends. In reality, they have been trafficking Belian refugees, goods, and money back to Mykonian space to fatten their economy and service their citizens. We will never know how many were tricked into leaving their homes under false promises of new and better lives. We will never know how many of our brothers and sisters have become the slaves of Mykonian factory managers and farm bosses. We will never know how many of our women and children have been turned into sex slaves, catering to the debased lusts of the Mykonian elite."

She paused to let the doubt and outrage perfuse her viewers. Rafe, of course, took her words as a personal insult against everything his shattered life stood for. He didn't believe for a second that he served so reprobate a nation. He couldn't face his wife again, if she still lived, thinking he had been part of a machine of abuse that he strongly suspected had grounded her in the years before they met.

"And," Lilith said, "for those of us left behind: poverty. Look around and ask how it is possible that the Mykonians can be so prosperous while we yet struggle? How can this be unless they are cheating us? Well, their tyranny ends now! The Wardens have gifted me, personally, with control over many new weapons, including Arbiters. At every Belian colony, the Mykonians have positioned their ships, so at every colony, I have placed Arbiters with their own nuclear arsenals to defend us. For your own safety, I recommend you do not attempt to interfere with these weapons systems."

Lilith waited for her audience to assimilate the implications of those statements. She commanded Arbiters that would defend themselves and which could annihilate the homes of anyone who opposed her.

"Today, I have used these tools to paralyze *all* of the military forces at Belia in order to make it possible for me to safely humble the Mykonian fleet and destroy their Arbiters. Be assured that control of your defenses will be restored presently. And you have my promise that I will help defend your colonies from these evil people if needs be."

Evil?! Rafe thought to himself. *You attack my wife—my innocent little girls—and call us evil?*

He churned more as Lilith said, "I have no wish to see people die needlessly," as though minutes before she hadn't expressly targeted his house on Zeus. "As a token of my mercy, I allowed the residents at Zeus time to evacuate before destroying the station. I have deliberately left more than half of the Mykonian fleet at Belia intact. I grant them two week's grace to resettle Zeus's refugees and tend to their wounded. Afterward, I order them to remove their warships from Belian space or else I will do it for them. Details on a program to deport Zeus's survivors will be forthcoming. Rest assured, anyone who tests my strength, or patience will suffer."

Rafe jolted to hear her admit that most of Zeus' population might have survived. He'd counted only a handful of lifeboats blasting away during the attack's live footage. This news gave him more hope for his family. This, in turn, bolstered his resolve to survive and get word about what he'd learned back to his comrades. If only he could let them know about how thinly Lilith had spread herself, they might have a chance at striking back.

"Now," Lilith said, raising her arms as if to embrace her subjects, "I invite Belia's leadership to unite with me as your empress."

She gestured back to Dalip. He stepped forward and said, "Lakshmi is proud to be the first to join this new empire. For too long, Belia has been fractured and at war with itself. We will put aside our quarrels: quarrels we were maneuvered into by our former unlamented emperor and the Mykonian oppressors who followed. Our new empress, Lilith, will bring us healing. Where there has been hate, she will bring peace. Where there has been oppression, she will bring freedom."

As Dalip stepped back, Lilith resumed. "Come to Lakshmi in one week where we shall inaugurate our new order and draw plans to finish expelling Mykon from our affairs. Against any adversity, we will make bounty and peace! Join me and let us build our future bright and beautiful!"

The camera tightened on Lilith's brilliant smile before fading to the Lakshmian crest: a four-armed figure holding lotus blossoms to its cheeks.

Henry said, "She has quite the flare for the dramatic."

Rafe stirred in silence. He didn't think for a second that Mykon had ever kept any Arbiters at Belia, assuming they owned any at all. The things cost too much to buy. But the speech, coupled with the Wardens' open support, would be enough to keep most people from publicly questioning Lilith and Dalip's lies. Since the Mykonians didn't know the limit of Lilith's capabilities, the woman held Belia in check, if not mate.

While stewing in his frustration, a flicker to the left caught Rafe's eye. A side panel still carried the live visual from the mechs as they decelerated to assault the looming *Tsunami*. Rafe's spirits shot hubward at what he saw there. For the first time in his ordeal, he felt a genuine, if painful smile break across his face. It seemed that Providence had decided to spite Lilith. The battleship had opened fire.

[16]

Location: CIC, *MSV Tsunami_*

THE PREVIOUS FIFTEEN MINUTES HAD BROUGHT A LITANY OF horrific news to Captain Paulson. Zeus and a third of the BELCOM fleet were gone. Sean's boarding team had been decimated. Everyone's apprehension only worsened at the lieutenant's report from the *Feni's* escape pod. The enemy mechs' toughness was matched only by their savagery. Paulson held little hope for their chances against the six killing machines, which would reach the *Tsu* in seconds. All that stood in their way was a squad of marines and an ill-armed crew. Adding insult to injury, the Wardens had forced Lilith's speech onto every channel.

As the broadcast ended, Claire said, "Mechs decelerating. Intercept estimated in thirty seconds."

Paulson turned in solemn silence to Doctor Apple. They were still floating helplessly in space. The mysterious override on Claire's systems left her able to do little more than give a play-by-play of their approaching doom. The doc said, "I'm considering mighty hard your suggestion to start praying."

The captain nodded slowly. She had given orders to scuttle the ship if boarders reached or destroyed the CIC.

A heartbeat later, Claire shouted, "Weapons and propulsion online!" All about the airless Combat Information Center, suited figures turned to the center chair.

Paulson's attention snapped to the table of her ship's weapons systems, not quite believing the miracle unfolding there. Block by block, the status grid blossomed with verdant radiance. Point Defense Gatlings signaled ready. The lasers, missiles and rail guns would take seconds longer to wake, but that didn't matter. The six decelerating mechs had closed to less than three kilometers: well within point-defense cannon (PDC) range.

The captain called out, "All weapons fire on the inbounds as you come to bear! Helm, quick-turn to ram the targets! Emergency torch thrust, now, now, now!"

Even as she spoke, Claire directed a trio of mammoth Gatling cannons at the edges of the ship's hexagonal shielding swivel. Each turret's set of radar dishes, infrared telescopes, and visible light cameras immediately locked onto the incoming mechs and their blazing rockets. The process took less than two seconds before *Tsunami* began to spit hyper-velocity metal into the blackness.

In those few seconds, the approaching mechs saw the point defense guns swinging about. This triggered contingency protocols. The mechs opened up their smaller Gatlings against the exposed PDC turrets before they'd finished moving into position. Fifty caliber bullets hurtled from each attacker at the rate of one hundred rounds per second. The first ordnance struck just after the defenders started shooting.

A rain of bullets slammed into the *Tsu's* turret mountings, excoriating the sensor bubbles and radar blisters. The mechs' high-caliber rounds ripped into the weapons housings occasionally punching through to something important. They degraded the defender's aim but ultimately failed to knock out a single turret.

The engagement had entered its fifth second when the Tsunami's counter-fire bridged the two-point-five-kilometer gap and smote three of the attackers. Nearly a hundred rounds of two-centimeter-wide shells tore into the unlucky mechs and their small cargo ferries. Metal chunks, circuitry, hydraulic fluids, and compressed gases burst into space. The pulverized hulks hurtled harmlessly past the *Tsunami*.

Meanwhile, the surviving three mechs ran low both on ammunition and space. The battleship accelerated into their flight path at over one-third of a gravity. The artificial intelligences of the mechs recognized the danger and signaled their transports to adjust course.

At this point, the machines caught a minor break. Their barrage jammed up the *Tsunami's* Numbers 1 and 3 point-defense guns. They also ruined the Number 2 cannon's visual optics, but not its radar and infrared sensors. It shifted attention to another target and blazed with hellfire. A fourth attacker disintegrated into bits.

By the sixth second of combat, the range had closed to barely two kilometers, and the mechs no longer missed their marks. They finished off the Number 2 turret and coasted for a brief moment unmolested. That respite ended as two of the *Tsunami's* rail guns simultaneously blew the remaining mechs into a thousand pieces. Several of the fragments rained uselessly upon the *Tsu's* front shield. The entire engagement had lasted exactly eight seconds from the point that the mechs had first fired.

Stunned by their victory, Paulson joined several others on the CIC net in a collective sigh of relief.

On her next breath, she ordered, "Helm, cut drive." She knew her human reaction had just cost the ship more than a few tons of precious reaction mass.

Spilled milk.

She said, "Weapons, nuclear mission. Fire one Reaper missile at the *Feni*. Lasers, burn up anything you spot moving on that ship no matter how small. I've had enough of its surprises."

In short order, one of the *Tsunami's* missiles lit up the tactical board. Paulson offered a quick blessing for the remains of the men and women that she was about to obliterate. Then she turned her attention to taking stock of her ship.

While Paulson checked on the damage from the mechs' attack, the rocket motor on the Reaper kicked it toward the *Feni* at more than fifty gravities of acceleration. Burning through its first two stages in a handful of seconds, it crossed the one-thousand-kilometer gap in two minutes, clocking around thirty-thousand kilometers an hour by the time it reached the freighter. As it approached, the weapon's guidance system calculated to within a microsecond when it would impact. The warhead detonated inside spitting distance of the *Feni's* hull.

Through the *Tsunami's* visual cameras, onlookers saw a vanishingly brilliant flash as the fifty-kiloton device unleashed over two-hundred Terajoules of energy in a spherical shell. From the *Feni's* perspective, it seemed as if a window to a star's surface had briefly opened scant meters away.

One-third of the fusion event's energetic photons struck the *Feni's* two-hundred-meter-long frame. Near the flash point, radiant fury vaporized and melted the ship's outer hull. X-rays penetrated deeper, heating the interior air to create impulsive shock fronts all along the structure. The multi-fold waves shattered bulkheads, machinery, and bodies alike. The *Feni* came apart amidships, its bow and aft shivering off chunks as though smashed from within by a thousand sledgehammers.

While studying a real-time telescopic view of the demolished *Feni*, Paulson noticed Apple stirring next to her. In his Nuevo Texan drawl, the doc said, "I'll be damned. We won."

The captain grunted. *At least something went right today.*

"Helm, begin maneuvers to recover the *Feni's* escape pod," she said out loud.

"Claire," Paulson said, "what happened to restore our systems? I thought we needed another ten minutes to reinstall your backup core."

The A.I. simulated chagrin. "Another Warden override, ma'am."

"Another override," Paulson echoed.

What the hell is going on here?

Claire said, "Ma'am, we received a Warden bulletin that I think you'll want to read for yourself. It concerns Commander Rafe Hastings whom BELCOM told us about."

Paulson scanned the alert. Her jaw dropped. "Claire, I don't care how you do it, but get me a channel to whichever lifepod has an admiral aboard."

"Ma'am," Claire said, "Alastair's final report didn't include any of their names on the lifeboat manifests. You are now the most senior officer at Belia."

The woman cursed. Then she slammed her fist soundlessly onto her chair's armrest. "Open a channel to the fleet's survivors. I'm taking command."

Location: Lilith's private estate, Lakshmi Colony_

LILITH SWEPT INTO THE VIEWING ROOM, HER CHEEKS PULSING RED with fury. "Natrix!" the new empress commanded, "replay the battle on the center screen!"

Rafe noted that in Lilith's haste, she had blown past both himself and Henry. And the hulking enforcer behind them.

For several seconds, Lilith watched the *Tsunami* annihilate her assault mechs and the *Feni*. Rafe couldn't help noticing her nails as they curled into their palms. A grin cracked his tortured lips as blood dripped from one hand.

At last, the madwoman shouted, "How did they do that, Natrix?"

The A.I.'s voice emanated from all around them. "As I said empress, I was unable to establish a link with the *Feni* or its Arbiter during the attack."

Lilith nearly screamed. "How could you not? The Arbiters use the Warden radio network! They have those freaking satellites all over to get signals through."

"The link became unavailable shortly before the *Tsunami* began firing."

Rafe said, "I know how they did it."

Lilith whirled and stormed to Rafe. She shouted, "Tell me, or I cut your tongue out!" She failed to note the almost complete lack of fear in Rafe's swollen face.

From her wild glint, Rafe judged it wouldn't take much to incite her to do what she threatened. This was why, against every instinct of self-preservation, he smiled mockingly up and said, "Go ahead. I'm not telling."

Henry said, "You should have killed him when you could."

Lilith spat an obscenity and asked what he was talking about. He responded by demanding, "Didn't Natrix give you the new Warden message?"

"I tried," Natrix said. "She shut me up."

Henry huffed. "So, you're too important to check your own messages now that you're Belia's queen?"

Rafe craned to regard the spy. With a broken chuckle, he said, "You have balls."

And with any luck, Lilith will hang you up by them.

Lilith howled at Rafe. "Tell me how to defeat the *Tsunami!*"

He smiled crookedly at her. "No."

Her rictus of hatred intensified. She reached into her hair and drew something shiny from it. Rafe noted the thin knife with a pang of equal parts fear and hope.

This is worth it, he told himself, bracing.

A blur of motion cut across Rafe's field of view, shoving Lilith away. Rafe saw Henry hauling Lilith back a few paces.

Henry screamed at the struggling empress. "He's under custodial protection too now, you crazy woman!"

The words shocked Lilith into silence. Her eyes flicked between Henry and the enforcer behind Rafe. Her face drained to a porcelain shade. She had very nearly gotten herself killed. It took her two full seconds before she squeezed out a reedy, "What?"

Henry said, "The Warden here told us just before you arrived!"

And then the enforcer spoke in its intimidating, digitized base. "You are to have Mr. Rafe Hastings escorted to the Warden vehicle now arriving at your estate. You have three minutes remaining to comply."

Henry threw back Lilith's hand and snarled at her: "They are taking him back to one of the Mykonian warships."

Rafe imagined he saw steam billow from Henry's nostrils as Lilith absorbed this news.

Henry shouted at her, "Everything! *Everything* he has learned from your *blabbering mouth* and from his *front-row seat* here is going to be known to our enemies!"

"But—" Lilith began.

"Don't you say another word while he is in here! Get him out! Now!"

Henry Wilkinson's roar made Lilith visibly shudder. She swallowed, finally beginning to understand the depth of her mistake. Without removing her eyes from Henry, she slapped her wrist comm. "Markem! Get in here!" Within a minute, Lilith had made the arrangements for their guest. Markem, the same man who'd used Rafe as a punching bag, would have to be the one to escort him to safety.

Before the brute could pick Rafe up, however, the Warden had one more package of information to share. "Be advised Lilith: your immunity status is now restricted to Lakshmi. Mr. Hastings, yours will be invalidated before its expiration if you choose to leave your final destination. Any ship or colony you choose may not be targeted, even with an Arbiter. Only conditions of Unrestricted War inside a colony, though not around it, will nullify our protection for whichever of you enters such a zone. Consult our notice for further details."

They want me to use this immunity to fight Lilith. But why would they sabotage their champion?

Lilith responded to the news with bulging eyes and an open mouth. She stuttered, "Wha-why are you doing this?"

The enforcer turned square to Lilith. "You will not ask that question again."

Lilith took a half-step backward at the rebuke. "Yes, Warden," she said meekly, showing a vulnerability Rafe hadn't imagined her capable of.

At last, Markem hauled Rafe to his feet. Rafe wanted to enjoy this reversal of his fortunes: to let it salve some small part of his anger and grief over the murders of his countrymen and, very possibly, his family. But as the door to the command room parted for him and Markem, he couldn't help wondering, *Why are the Wardens playing us against one another like this?* They had never been gentle as humanity's caretakers, but this took their cruelty to a malignant level. He could only come to one conclusion: something had gone horribly wrong with them.

He twisted back to look at Lilith who fidgeted as though on the verge of panic. Beside her, Henry stewed impotently, eager for

Rafe to be gone. In the shadows of a corner, the monolithic Warden observed them all.

While Markem dragged Rafe out, the spy braved a deep breath against his broken ribs. With it, he called, "The Wardens want us to fight!" Then as the doors shut behind him, he pled, "End this Lilith!"

[17]

Location: Lilith's private estate, Lakshmi Colony_

OUTSIDE, RAFE HOBBLED BEHIND MARKEM TOWARD A BOXY, black and chrome vehicle. An enforcer detached from an alcove at the truck's middle. In a voice approximating a lion gargling blood, the Warden said to Markem, "Get him in. Now."

Almost tripping over his feet to obey, the burly man lifted Rafe by the armpits to carry him aboard. Rafe inhaled sharply in response to the pressure on his fractured ribs. He wondered what the Wardens would do to Markem if they thought the man was squeezing too hard.

Before Rafe could feign being injured, the brute hauled him up the truck's short ramp and plopped him onto a metal seat. The enforcer gave Markem room to vacate, then joined Rafe inside. Before the doors fully shut, the truck lurched away. Rafe caught himself with a hand on the space to his right. The unmoving Warden might have been bolted down for all Rafe could tell.

Once the ride smoothed out, the machine said, "You may now communicate securely with your people. State your desired contact."

It took several beats for Rafe to pump enough oxygen through his brain to think. Why were the Wardens helping him? What was their plan and how did he fit into it? Given that they seemed responsible for the chaos engulfing Cervantes, he wondered what he should do.

You can't hide anything from them, let alone fight them. We're gladiators in their arena with no choice but to play.

He considered asking to speak with James. If the A.I. hadn't been found, it might be able to connect him with whoever controlled the Mykonian military at Belia. Then Rafe remembered that no one, not even a head of state, could ignore a direct Warden communique.

Using short breaths, he said, "I need to speak with the commander of BELCOM Fleet. On a secure channel."

"Connecting," the Warden said. Ten seconds later, it told him, "Encrypted link established. Roundtrip light-speed lag is one-point-seven-seven seconds."

A middle-aged woman beneath a helmet appeared in a rectangle on the Warden's face-shield. It was only then that Rafe realized how anyone watching on the other end might be enjoying a full-body video of him. Despite his sore muscles, he self-consciously crossed his legs.

"Commander Rafe Hastings reporting in, ma'am," he said to the suited figure. He took a shuddering breath, and not only from his broken ribs and shredded larynx. His welling emotions threatened to spill at the sight of a friendly face. To distract himself, he quickly added, "Sorry I'm not in uniform."

The shocked woman studied Rafe's head full of lumps, all colored with the darker shades of the rainbow. He imagined blood caked his features as well.

"Commander Hastings," she said with some hesitation. "I'm Captain Paulson of the *MSV Tsunami*. It's good to see you. I apologize, but we'll need to authenticate you first. Claire?"

The A.I.'s avatar appeared in a corner of the screen. "Commander, please tell us what is significant about the Spring of 4375."

Rafe recalled the personal authentication questions he had updated before deploying to Lakshmi. The mist of nostalgia gathered in his eyes. In a voice thick with longing, he said, "Anna discovered unicorns. And Karen invented the Peach Kiss."

"Authenticated, ma'am," Claire said.

Paulson blew a sigh of relief.

Rafe said in a rush, "I have a lot to tell you, Captain."

"Then you may be the best news we've had today, Commander," Paulson replied. "Last I'd been briefed, you'd been taken prisoner. We didn't know you were alive until the Wardens announced your custodial immunity a few minutes ago. Are you safe now?"

"I believe so, ma'am," Rafe replied. "I'm in a Warden vehicle. Alone with an enforcer. It says the line's secure."

Paulson absorbed Rafe's small sentences with a gentle nod. "I don't know if that counts as safe, but we'll take it."

Rafe would have chuckled, but for his exhaustion and the worries threading through his mind. Fighting off tears, he rasped, "My wife Gita, daughters Karen and Anna, were on Zeus when it was hit. Are they—"

"Claire," Paulson said, "Are they on any of the lifeboats?"

The A.I.'s response overlapped the request. "Alastair confirmed a Karen, and Anna Hastings boarded Boat 19. I'm sorry, but Gita Hastings is listed as missing."

Paulson's gaze angled upward. "No matter where I am or what I'm doing, Claire, you let me know if you learn something new about her."

"Aye, ma'am."

In a low voice, the captain said, "I'm truly sorry. You have my word that we'll do everything possible to take care of your family."

Rafe took several seconds to register the captain's assurances. His darlings, Karen and Anna, were alive. His precious Gita was almost certainly dead.

He tried the words out in his mind: *Gita's dead.* It didn't feel real. The feisty bar-girl from Sundar. The gorgeous, raven-haired beauty he had married and loved for thirteen years. The strong woman who, despite her haunting past, had bravely borne and raised his children. His conscience and friend. His wife. *Gone.*

"Commander," Paulson said with concern, "we've been getting our asses handed to us. Is there anything you can tell us that might help?"

Rafe wanted to throw up. He took several breaths, worried that he might start heaving at any moment.

"Commander," Paulson repeated, her urgency rising. "We need to know all we can if we're going to keep your girls safe."

That brought Rafe back from the brink. With effort, he wheezed, "Lilith made me watch everything with her. That's why I asked for the BELCOM Commander."

Paulson's jaw tightened. "That's me now. I was just telling the other ship captains that I'd assumed command when you called."

"I saw what happened to your crew," Rafe said. He coughed and cleared his sore throat. His face screwed up in pain, grief, anxiety, and exhaustion. "They fought hard against those mechs."

"Thank you," Paulson said. "Look, before you fall over, I need to know anything of importance you can give us."

For the next several minutes, Rafe battled his grief to outline what he had seen and deduced about their situation. He mentioned his suspicions about the limits to whatever had paralyzed their ships. He also detailed what the enforcer had said about how Lilith's immunity did not protect her from an Arbiter's effects. Any ship with one of the devices could fire upon Lakshmi, placing it into Unrestricted Warfare status. She would be vulnerable then.

Paulson listened intently. When Rafe paused for a break, the captain said, "So, because you uncovered Lilith's capabilities, she moved before she was ready. That means any colony where we weren't attacked is probably free of Arbiters."

"Agreed, ma'am."

The lighting around Paulson flickered green then white. The *Tsunami* had secured from general quarters, prompting Paulson to remove her helmet. Adjusting her communications cap, she continued, "We had better share this with the rest of Cervantes before colonies start surrendering. Maybe with enough ships and troops, we could mount a counter-attack on Lakshmi. Lilith could nuke colonies in retaliation, but if there's a chance to take her out, we have to try."

Rafe recalled images of Zeus spouting nuclear flame and blasting apart. He shivered. Then he remembered something else. "Agreed. But Lilith mentioned having weapons. Something called Casabas. She planned to use them to frighten us off."

Paulson spat a curse.

"What are they, ma'am?" Rafe asked.

"Casaba-Howitzers," Paulson said. "Old Earth tech more properly called nuclear lances. They are shaped nuclear charges that can send a spear of fire along a narrow beam for thousands of kilometers. They aren't in the Warden Industrial Catalog, but I read a paper on them back in the day. You saw us nuke the *Feni*?"

Rafe nodded, wondering when Lilith's roster of nasty surprises would ever run out.

Paulson continued. "Depending on the warhead's strength, a big enough Casaba Howitzer could do the same thing, but from thousands of klicks away."

Rafe groaned as he tried to imagine how to defend against such firepower. He hoped the things would at least have the same

built-in ten-thousand-kilometer maximum firing range as with all
other Warden-made weapons.

Then Rafe remembered another detail and said, "Lilith told
Dalip she didn't have enough casabas to spare."

"Oh?" Paulson said, projecting hope.

"She likes dramatics. So, she must have very few if she hasn't
used them."

Paulson pressed her mouth into a thin line before saying,
"That would be keeping with Warden policy to never give us too
many toys we could use against them."

"Their policies seem adjustable lately. They are playing some
game with us."

Paulson rubbed at her nose, which made Rafe acutely aware
of all the places on his body that wanted for scratching. He rolled
his head, desperate to sleep.

Paulson saw Rafe fading again and said, "I think you're right.
We'll ponder that more later along with what to do about the
Celesians helping Lilith." The captain sighed. "At least the
lifeboats have places to land that are free of Lilith's control.
Thanks to what you did."

A small measure of relief flowed into Rafe. *My daughters will
make it.* He ignored the voice reminding him that Gita would have
wanted him to go to them. *They will be fine. You have work to do.*

He did say, "Ma'am, where is Lifeboat 19 headed?"

"Claire?" Paulson said.

"Vishnu colony, ma'am," the A.I. replied. "The *MSV Capable*
is there and back under control, so it should be safe."

Assured of his girls' condition, Rafe said, "We have an opportunity, ma'am. The Wardens offered to take me wherever I asked."

The captain straightened and said, "I see what you're thinking. Claire, do we know when the commander will lose his immunity status?"

"His immunity will end twenty four hours after delivery to the ship of his choice," Claire answered.

Paulson's eyes twinkled. "Claire, give me a plot of our ships in the system."

Rafe watched the officer's eyes darting over something out of the camera's view. After half a minute, Paulson bobbed her head with excitement.

"We can do it," she declared.

Rafe knew what the captain had in mind.

"Claire," the woman continued, "plot a flight plan to let us rendezvous with Commander Hastings while linking up with the *Sorvino* and the largest number of surviving warships possible. We need to use the commander's immunity to strike Lakshmi with at least 2 hours to spare. Make sure the course keeps us safe from interceptors while we're unprotected. If all the pieces move now, right now, we can counter-attack. We dock the surviving ships together. Your status will protect them *all*. Then we fly to that witch's doorstep and drop the *Sorvino's* brigade of marines on her."

In a flash of insight, Rafe had an idea as to how they could hurt Lilith without violating her immunity. He kept it to himself in case she could somehow tap into their conversation.

"Claire," Paulson said, "how about that course analysis?"

The A.I. replied, "If the commander travels by a standard Warden courier ship, it will be close. Thrusting to the optimal rendezvous point and then to Lakshmi will drop our re-mass reserves to black by the time we arrive. We will have between two and four hours of immunity left."

"Workable," Paulson said. "What else?"

"The numbers are contingent on several factors. We may have to block the enemy from attacking non-immune ships before they make the rendezvous. There may be unforeseen complications with the link-ups. We also don't know if the Warden courier will accommodate our flight plan."

"We'll solve the problems as they come," Paulson said. "Commander, tell the Warden where you want to go."

"Warden," Rafe said. "Please take me. To the *MSV Tsunami.*"

Paulson said, "Claire, submit the flight plan. And prep orders for the fleet."

The enforcer beside Rafe said, "Request accepted."

"A favor," Rafe said to Paulson. "Make sure my children are guarded. Lilith has a grudge, and she knows my kids' *names.* She targeted my home on Zeus."

"She what?" Paulson said. "Claire?"

The A.I. piped in. "Three missiles were timed to hit the housing division for the Hastings residence."

Paulson called up more information off-screen. After several seconds of flicking through data, she said, "Boat 19 is one of eight headed for Vishnu. On the off chance that Lilith learns your kids' whereabouts, I'll order the *Capable* to hold position there until we near Lakshmi."

"Thank you, ma'am," he said.

"We owe you," she replied.

"We owe Lilith payback." He gritted out his last words. "See you in a day."

[18]

Location: Feni escape pod_

SARAH SPENT THE HALF-HOUR-LONG FLIGHT TO THE *TSU* IN A dazed, nauseated rush. Following the *Feni's* horrors, she wanted nothing more than to curl into a tight ball and cry. Despite her trembling hands and a twitching eyelid, she cut through all the marines' suits, dressed half a dozen gashes, started three intravenous lines, and threaded as many urinary catheters. The gut punches, however, kept coming.

Lilith's broadcast left Sarah thunderstruck. How can Zeus be gone? How many of the charred corpses now orbiting Belia were people she'd met? How much did they suffer before dying?

Moreover, she knew she'd botched her priorities during the battle. There was no hiding it. Claire would have their suit camera's footage downloaded the minute they docked. Her hesitation to collect the wounded, her abandoning their patients to fight, her violating her protected medical-provider status—all of it would be on record.

I'll never put my feelings ahead of my job like that again. The oath didn't ease her tension much. As she finished prepping the marines for transfer to sickbay, she broke the morbid silence.

"Do you think anything will happen to me because I went after that mech?" she asked. "What you said got me worried and…"

Sean looked up from a pressure dressing he'd clamped to Martinez. "Nothing career-ending will happen. You tried to prevent a war crime. That mech would have done to me what it did to Horvath. I can't imagine anyone important will fault you for acting."

Sarah stared at Watson's stumps and said, "You really think others will see it that way?"

Sean nodded. "Yeah, the people who matter will."

Sarah kept staring off.

"Hey," Sean said, "you took a stupid risk, but it didn't hurt anyone this time. Don't do it again, and don't worry about it. No one's going to punish what little success we've had today."

Sarah blinked and tried to reconcile the idea of success with anything she'd done on the *Feni*. Sean added, "Listen, I won't let anyone do more than reprimand you for saving my life. Okay?"

After a moment, Sarah looked at him and nodded meekly.

Sean gave her a tired, crooked smile before hanging his head. He cleared his throat and said, "I'm, uh, I'm very sorry for yelling at you." He took a breath. "You're a kind person. Even though what I said was right, how I said it wasn't what you deserved. Especially since you saved my life." He forced himself to look back up at her.

Sarah searched his face for several seconds. "Next time," she said, "I'll let the mech get you." She took his hand, squeezed it and quickly let go. "I forgive you."

Now, if only I can forgive myself.

Location: Sickbay, *MSV Tsunami*

ON REACHING SICKBAY, SARAH FOUND DOCTOR APPLE WAITING with his surgical gear ready. He thanked the litter team for bringing the wounded, then cleared out everyone but Sean and Sarah. Once they had helped Apple hook the patients up to some fluid bags, he addressed them.

"Any injuries?" he asked.

"Back hurts," Sarah said, shuddering at the memory of the violence that had caused it. "My rebreather was hit."

"We'll scan that and see how it feels after some rest," Apple said, "And you, Sean?"

The lieutenant ground his teeth before answering. "Hip joints are giving me some trouble."

"For how long?" Apple demanded.

"It started shortly after we left the *Feni*."

Sarah regarded Sean with trepidation.

The doc said, "Well, you both know what this means."

They nodded. Sean most likely had decompression sickness. Their preflight breathing regimen lowered but didn't quite eliminate the bends-inducing nitrogen in their bodies. So, when the boarding team had bounced from full atmosphere to vacuum during their fight aboard the MAC, the pressure changes caused the residual nitrogen to form bubbles in Sean's bloodstream and joints. The odds had been against it, but he'd been unlucky. Treatment required him to spend four hours breathing inside of a pure, high-pressure oxygen environment.

Apple reached into a nearby drawer, selected two sets of scrubs—standard, one hundred percent cotton medical uniforms: low on risk for static electricity discharges in the presence of flammable oxygen.

"My office is prepped for hyperbaric mode," the doctor said, then turned to Sarah, handing her the clothes. "Go with him.

You're off duty for twelve hours, the both of you. Captain's orders."

Dulled by her emotionally depleted state, Sarah said, "Don't you need me to help with Watson?"

"Your hands haven't stopped shaking since you got in here," Apple said while arranging a palate of magnetized surgical instruments next to the marine's stubs. "Take a break."

Like an automaton, Sarah muttered an "Aye, sir."

A handful of minutes later and they were changed and sealed into the closet-sized compartment. Sean tapped the control panel next to the office's hatch. An image of Apple and his unconscious patients appeared.

Sean said, "We're ready."

"Claire," Apple ordered, "start the treatment cycle."

The hiss of air immediately issued from an unseen valve. Sarah screwed her face with discomfort as she yawned to clear her ears.

"I'll check on you both from time to time," the doctor said through the room's speakers. "Apple out." The picture faded to black.

Sean turned to her. They stared at each other across a handful of centimeters.

Sarah's face knotted with emotion. Searching for something to refocus her mind, she asked, "How's the pain?"

"Not bad," he answered. "The meds you had us take aboard the *Feni* seem to have kept the edge off. I'll be fine. Really. How do you feel?"

At his words, Sarah began shivering. Her professionalism had held back the primal terror writhing within her psyche. Now she had nothing to do and no one she needed to be brave for. Since Sean had let himself be vulnerable with her in the escape pod, she felt she could be the same around him. So, her control finally collapsed.

"I'm..." she attempted, and then her fingers fluttered to her cheeks as she broke into desperate tears. Sarah drew her knees into her body and began to release her misery through one wracking sob after another.

"Just breathe," Sean said. "It will all be okay."

Sean quickly gathered her sideways against him, tucking her frame beneath his chin. Her body nestled into his, the way she had with her father after childhood night terrors. She let Sean's chest and limbs become warmth to her. He became safety. His firm, hushed assurances that she would be okay reverberated in her heart, calming its racing beat. Protected, she let her young voice crescendo repeatedly in long, mournful wails. Many tissues and a sleeping pill later, she fell unconscious in Sean's embrace.

[19]

Location: Sickbay, *MSV Tsunami*_

SARAH WOKE FROM A NIGHTMARE ABOUT PEOPLE DYING. ON opening her eyes, she realized with a start that she was alone and secured to the bulkhead. Wriggling to unlatch a set of wall straps, she called out, "Hello?"

Sean poked his head from inside the shallow airlock. The standard uniform he wore told her their requisite four hours of compression must have elapsed long before.

"Hi," he said, bearing a forced smile. "How are you feeling?"

On seeing a familiar face, her apprehension dissolved. She exhaled then sniffed. She immediately noticed two pleasant scents: coffee and peppermint. They reminded her of home on holiday.

"I feel beaten up," she said. Her back, ribs, and limbs all ached from the repeated blows she'd taken aboard the *Feni*.

Sean winced and said, "I have something to help with that." Sarah heard the crinkle of an unseen plastic wrapper. Sean emerged from the lock with a pill and zero gravity cup filled with something brown, steaming, and liquid. He placed both items into her hands.

She popped the anti-inflammatory into her mouth and took a cautious sip.

"This is good," she breathed. "Thank you." She excused herself to the airlock and relieved her pulsing bladder. She traced the peppermint scent to an open bag of chalk-white candies. They weren't a toothbrush and toothpaste, but one made her cough on its fresh potency. A wet-nap served to clean the oils from her face. Someone had left one of her uniforms and set of underwear, which she eagerly changed into.

Emerging from the compartment with her coffee, she said, "My head still feels logy from that sleeping pill. How long have I been out?"

Sean drifted over to her. "About ten hours. I don't know about you, but I haven't felt this sore since basic training."

Sarah's face glimmered with a smile then fell as thoughts of home tugged at her.

"Hey," Sean said as her eyes turned sad. "I'm trying to cheer you up. I could order you to be happy, you know."

A wan smile pushed up Sarah's cheeks.

Softly, she said, "Thank you. I should be doing that for you. It's my job."

"You saved me from my darkest moment. It's the least I can do."

Sarah's dimples grew deeper. For a long beat, she stared at Sean's face, entranced by his handsome features. Then her emotional pain came rushing back in, and the twinkle fled from her eyes.

"Yesterday really happened, didn't it?" she said.

"Yes," he replied, somber.

A spurt of anxiety injected into Sarah's throat. "Does my family know I'm okay?" She couldn't believe she hadn't considered them sooner. "Can I send them a message? Are they safe?"

"Mykon's fine," Sean said. "And the Fleet will have told your family by now you're alive."

Sarah knew her parents wouldn't be much comforted until they got word straight from her. "I have to vid them, right away."

Sean shook his head. "The ship's on security lockdown. Nothing in or out except essentials. I'm sorry."

Sarah's innards constricted with anxiety for her loved ones.

"Hey," Sean said, placing a hand on Sarah's shoulder. "You're all right. They're all right."

Sarah exhaled a long breath. "I haven't been this jittery since I thought my mother was going to die," she said.

"It's normal," Sean assured her. "I was pretty on edge after my first time in combat. The shock wears off after a while. Remember your resiliency training, right? Hunt the good stuff."

"Yeah," Sarah said, rubbing both palms over her eyes. "What about you?" she asked.

One corner of Sean's lips twitched. "I've been through this sort of hell before back on Lakshmi," he said. "The *Feni* was worse in some ways. Not as bad in others."

"At least you didn't make any mistakes you could have avoided," Sarah said.

"Hey," Sean said, gently clasping Sarah's other shoulder. He squared her to him. "It won't do you any good to think like that."

Sarah's gaze fell. "I hesitated at the cargo hold. I was ahead of Sergeant Holtz. If I had only gone straight in to get the wounded, Watson would have made it through the door before the grenade blew off his legs. I didn't go because I was afraid."

"That's good," Sean said with conviction. "Your place is behind the lines. You can't help anyone if you're dead."

"I feel like a coward," she said, tears forming.

"You're no coward," Sean replied. "You faced down that

mech. A coward would have left in the escape pod without being told."

She took several seconds to consider his words. "I can't decide if you're right or being nice."

Breaking through her reticence, Sean said, "You are a *brave* person, Sarah Riley. Nothing of what happened on the *Feni* was your fault. Believe me."

She looked into his eyes and tried to get the words out in her mind. *What happened to Watson wasn't your fault. You're a brave person.*

The thoughts echoed back and forth inside of her psyche.

"It wasn't your fault," Sean said with gentle emphasis.

Sarah blinked and wiped her nose.

"Thank you," she said, forcing herself to smile for him. "I needed to hear that."

She found with the admission that part of her roiling anxiety lessened. Exhaling, she angled her forehead against Sean's chest. He responded to her unspoken request by drawing her shivering form flush against him.

"Please talk to me," she whispered.

"It's better if you make yourself talk," he said.

Her finger thunked his chest in irritation. "I know what's in the recovery manual. Now, are you going to make the girl in your arms feel better or not?"

For a beat, she felt Sean peering down at her. Then his torso heaved with a singular burst of mirth. She quickly joined him in a brief fit of giggles.

"Frail flower, you aren't," he said.

But as quickly as it came, the laughter passed. Sarah flicked a hand in agitation. "I'm frightened out of my wits." She peered up at him. "You toured at Lakshmi, right? Tell me more about it. Maybe understanding them will help make fighting Lilith less scary."

Sean hesitated. A crease appeared in his brow. Then she realized how remembering anything about a place he'd fought in might be painful.

"I'm sorry," she said, ashamed. "If you don't like to talk about it—"

"No, it's all right," he said with an easy tone that didn't match his expression. "Have you seen the colony's cultural brief?"

Sarah shook her head, sending wisps of pink flicking across her cheeks.

"Alright then. I'll give you the quick tour-guide version. Lakshmi was Belian Empire's jewel before the Grand Revolt. Real old Earth feel to it. The colony is very colorful, from the clothes to the food to the architecture. Even their personalities."

Sean smirked at his comment. "They're *so* quick-tempered. A Lakshmian can go from flattery to threats to inviting you to dinner in the same minute. Everything about their world is a dance. They have a special way of moving their heads and hands. Traffic is always frantic. Even the children won't stop running around."

"They sound full of life," Sarah observed.

"They love to laugh. They'll meet at cafés and tell jokes for an hour. They're reverent to a fault with their elders and ancestors.

Sean drew a breath and in a rueful voice said, "There is much to admire about them. They'll do anything for their families. Once I saw a child no older than ten carry his little sister on his back across an entire colony segment. A lot of Mykonians can't ruck march ten klicks."

He looked away, his brow creasing with distress. Sarah said, "You cared for them, didn't you?"

Sean's jaw muscles pulsed for a beat. "They're human like us, with plenty of good and bad about them. But ever since my first tour, they've made it hard for me to like them."

"How so?" Sarah asked.

"A lot of it you already know from the mission briefing. There are so many desperate, poor people there. Since they destroyed almost all of their A.I.s to help overthrow the empire, their police network is crippled. The irony is that while the Belian emperors gave their subjects no privacy, they at least kept common people honest. Now, you can't get *anything* done on Lakshmi without a bribe. Even the kids will steal whatever you don't have locked down.

The worst have turned to human trafficking to make ends meet. I've seen factories and farms where people are working off what began as a tiny debt that went out of control thanks to an interest rate of five hundred percent."

Sarah flinched at that, remembering the indentured crewman she'd interviewed.

"The colony's run by cartels now," Sean said, his cheeks taking on a hard edge. "They traffic drugs, weapons and people to fuel the ethnic wars on other colonies. It's been a perverse boon to their economy. The cartel bosses are local heroes, funding schools and clinics, running basic services and creating jobs. But it's all based on preying on others. They've crawled to the top of a hill built on many destroyed lives."

Sarah frowned and asked, "I thought we'd done a lot to help rebuild things after the Belian Revolt."

"We did," Sean replied. "I was on one of the last advisory teams to Lakshmi before the reconstruction program ended earlier this year. I like to think we left it better than we found it."

"Oh," Sarah mused. Sensing he'd exhausted the safer topics to discuss about their new enemy, she released him and brushed her hair back over both ears. She wanted to ask him more about his experience there, to help him through whatever about it continued to haunt him. It didn't seem the time.

"So, what happens next?" she asked.

"Captain already has a counter-attack in the works. Once our time is up, I'll be joined at the hip with the XO to help flesh the plan out."

"Can we beat Lilith?" Sarah's voice carried a hint of desperate hope.

Sean nodded. "Immunity or not, we have an idea. Sorry, but I can't talk about it."

"I understand," she said. For a few seconds, they hung in the doc's office, cognizant that their twelve hours of rest were almost up. Sarah reflected on how much she appreciated his company: how she liked what she'd seen of him. He wasn't perfect. He had an edge. But once they'd gotten out of danger, he was tender and considerate. A good man.

"May I ask you something?" Sean said.

Sarah blinked, not realizing she'd been staring at him. Suddenly, she perceived a certain interest in the way his eyes traced her face.

"Okay," she said, an unaccountable flush rising through her.

"I don't know about you," Sean ventured, "but it always helps me to have good things to look forward to before I deal with something awful. How would you like to go on a date with me when this is all over? Good food. Nice conversation. See the sights. What do you say?"

In spite of herself and everything they'd been through, Sarah blushed. "I'd like that, Sean," she said. "I'd like that very much."

[20]

Location: Zeus Lifeboat 19_

KAREN AND ANNA SPENT THEIR FIRST DAY OUT OF ZEUS STRAPPED next to each other in a pill-induced sleep. Nightmares poisoned their dreams, and the girls woke up whimpering. During the unwelcome hours of consciousness, the pair alternated between quietly crying to themselves and staring off blank-faced.

Karen spent much of her time curled up. In addition to grief, shock, and a sore body, various stenches compounded her misery. Many of the passengers had spewed vomit into the cabin. Everyone smelled of muck sweat. As the first day blurred into the second, the reek of excrement and urine rose from the bathroom facilities.

In the time between pills, Karen fidgeted for something to do. She tried one of the meaningless distractions offered by a touch-pad but quickly put it aside. The normalcy it simulated repelled her. Mother was dead. Home was in ashes. She didn't know if her father still lived or where he might be. It seemed pointless to behave as though anything would ever be all right again.

Even so, her hands couldn't stay still. She found them

reaching for Anna's long, dark tresses. Without thinking, she undid the ribbon holding Anna's pony-tail together and started braiding the way their mother had taught them.

She had been at it for only a minute when the younger girl began crying. Alarmed, Karen paused to ask, "Does that hurt?"

Anna shook her head but kept sobbing.

"Do you want me to stop?" Her tone exhibited a level of concern that would have felt forced a few days before.

Anna jerked her head left and right. In a flash, Karen understood. Hairdressing was one of the precious few echoes of their mother they had left. Karen resumed working one strand over the next as best she could manage in the zero gravity. Eventually, the slow, rhythmic tugging at the scalp settled Anna down.

Unfortunately, it also made the child queasy. They had been at it for half an hour when Anna suddenly said, "Karen."

Something about the girl's quavering tone brought the elder sibling up short. She watched for a breathless moment as Anna put a hand to her mouth.

Karen scrambled for a vomit bag, but too late. Gray and yellow chunks erupted onto the chair in front of them, splashing off of it into their faces.

"I'm sorry," Anna said with a squeak.

Karen wanted to snap at her. *Take care of your sister,* her mother's voice chided.

"It's fine," Karen said. She took the blanket she'd wrapped about Anna's skirted legs and tried to wipe her clean. "It's okay, Anna. I'll just write this down in my list."

"Your list?" Anna asked, worry etching her pasty forehead.

"Yeah," Karen said in deadpan. "The list of all the things you owe me for cleaning up."

"Is it a long list?"

"Oh, pages and pages." She patted Anna's cheek and added with a whisper. "You can pay me back when you get older."

A small frown crossed Anna's tired face.

"I'm kidding."

Anna mouthed a quiet "Oh." She closed her eyes while Karen tried to pick vomit out of the little girl's hair.

Karen asked, "Do you need me to get you some water?"

It took a few moments before the younger sibling said, "You haven't been this nice to me for a while. It's weird."

Emotions raw, Karen giggled and sobbed in the same breath. She'd been far kinder once, but hitting adolescence had sharpened her moods.

Embarrassed by her shortcomings, Karen busied herself by flattening out Anna's gray school uniform skirt. It kept billowing up in the null gravity. It wasn't lost on the elder sister that Anna shouldn't have had to worry about that indignity. *If only I'd helped her change first thing after school like I was supposed to.*

A sad, frightful realization dawned on Karen: she was Mother now. Before, she had been a coddled princess, used to getting her way. That life was gone. *What are we going to do now?* Hugging Anna close, she waited for sleep to claim her again.

She woke sometime later to a whirling mess. People screamed as the lifeboat's maneuvering jets knocked everyone first one way and then the other. A second later, the craft's engines fired, hurtling the aft bulkhead into those who'd been caught in the center aisle without restraints. Karen winced as several passengers thumped painfully by.

The ship rattled for almost a minute before the rockets cut out. The sudden shift back to zero gravity left Karen nauseous and disoriented. Somewhere behind her, men and women groaned. She heard frightened voices forward. People shouted questions about a course change.

Before anyone could explain matters calmly, a hysterical woman the next row over repeated a name. Karen remembered it from the Warden broadcast when they'd first escaped Zeus. The name filled Karen with fear.

"Lakshmi!" the lady screeched. "Gods help us! We're going to Lakshmi!"

Location: Transhuman orbital space lane, Cervantes system_

"YOUR IRRITANT WILL BE WAKING ABOARD THE TSUNAMI SOON," Cef noted in his mental correspondence to Len. "You were clever to make Mr. Hastings and any ship he boarded immune to Arbiters. That sent Lilith into quite the tizzy. Still, my redirecting the escape shuttles to Lakshmi will help nullify that threat."

Cef had drained much of his command points to make the move. Len had, of course, anticipated it. To be an effective ploy, however, Cef needed to issue one more override. Len quelled a nervous writhing in his tentacles. The lines of probability had collapsed into an obvious path. Len knew what would come next.

Cef said, "Little Karen Hastings really should have obeyed her parents. Foolish child. I should thank her. Without her mischief on the social net, Lilith might never have found out about Rafe's family. They might have boarded another lifeboat that could not have reached Lakshmi in time to be of use. More to the point, his *daughters* wouldn't be headed for Lilith. And so, I wouldn't be able to do this."

Cef executed his override command. At an opportune moment, Claire would inform Rafe that he held control over the *Tsunami*. It created the perfect dilemma. If Rafe commandeered the ship to go after his girls, Lilith could pick off the gathering Mykonian fleet. If he let his daughters fall into the Empress's hands, that too presented a subtle, but potentially disastrous opportunity for Lilith to claim victory. Len doubted the Mykonians would see the danger.

Cef asked, "Which course of action do you think Mr. Hastings will choose? He can only pick one."

At last, Len spoke, "He will choose the right thing to do based on what he knows. He understands what is at stake."

"Really? I suspect his wife would have divorced him for not going to their children when he had the opportunity. A pity she's in no position to help him make this decision."

His digital tone bursting with agitation, Len messaged, "There will be a reckoning for what you are doing. You could have given these people a paradise. Instead, you are putting them through hell."

"Stop being pedantic," Cef said with an air of long-suffering. "It isn't as if there is anyone to stop me. Your chances of winning have fallen to less than ten percent."

Len said, "We will see, won't we."

To this, Cef laughed.

Len, on the other hand, knew how badly Cef had miscalculated how far he was willing to go to make sure the humans lived free.

Location: Sickbay, *MSV Tsunami* _

THE MOMENT RAFE HASTINGS STAGGERED ABOARD THE WARDEN courier, the enforcer placed him into a medical pod. Given their low regard for human life, it always surprised him that the Wardens bothered with tools of healing. Not that he complained as an anesthetic erased his grief and pain-ridden world.

He awoke much later feeling relaxed, as if he'd slept a warm night by Gita's side. He kept his eyes closed against an overhead lamplight he supposed she'd turned on. Was it time for work or was this the weekend?

He breathed deep to clear his mind and noted that the musculature along his ribs felt tight, but not painfully so. The mattress felt glorious, like he floated on it. At last, he grasped he was in zero-gravity, or rather something close to it. His grin faded as memories returned.

Gita. The girls. Zeus.

Rafe's eyes burst open. A pretty young woman with a heart-shaped face and pink hair smiled over him. Her eyes had the unaccountable effect of soothing his growing anxiety.

"Welcome aboard the *Tsunami*, Commander Hastings," she said. "I'm Lieutenant Sarah Riley. I'll let the doctor and captain know you're up. How are you feeling?"

Rafe swallowed against a dry throat and asked, "Can you tell me if my girls are all right? They were on Zeus Lifeboat 19 headed for Vishnu."

The marked decrease of Sarah's smile froze his heart.

A minute later, all Rafe could get out of anyone, including the *Tsu's* A.I., was that a ship had been dispatched to pick up his kids. There had been no word about Gita.

Both Apple and Sarah urged Rafe to relax. Retrieving the girls, however, hadn't been part of the plan. He feared something had gone wrong. Only the doctor's solemn promise that the captain had invited them all to an imminent briefing prevented Rafe from storming off to the CIC for answers.

Apple redirected him by asking, "How does it feel having your old face again?" He held up a mirror for Rafe to see.

The spy touched a cheek. "It doesn't hurt anymore. I can barely feel the swelling." He added a belated, "Thank you."

"The Wardens did it," Apple said. "Make sure you eat with care. Even with the microscopic suturing, your body needs time to heal."

The medical ministrations concluded, Lieutenant Riley gave Rafe a uniform to change into.

"Donated by our ops officer, Lieutenant Merrick, sir," she

said. "I noticed you two were about the same size. He offered to share a few sets. The XO loaned the rank."

Once Rafe changed, the doctor and nurse escorted him to a conference room. Within moments, the captain arrived, followed by an entourage of mid-level officers and enlisted crew. The first thing Rafe noticed about Paulson was the look of five-kilogram sandbags tugging at her face. Doubtless, the captain had slept little in the past few days while she corralled their decimated fleet.

By an extreme act of will, Rafe endured a round of pleasantries before asking, "Ma'am, what is going on with my family?"

"Lilith claims to have redirected the life pods away from Vishnu toward Lakshmi," she said.

The words struck Rafe's psyche like a bomb. *I could have gone to them. I could have, and I chose to...* He cut the thought off as fruitless. He needed to know more first.

Paulson continued her briefing, saying, "The empress also made the craft dump their remaining propellant and fusion fuel so they will need a tug-ship to stop them on arrival. The only means of propulsion they have left are attitude jets."

"But the *Capable* will reach them before they get to Lilith, right?" He heard himself and wanted to curse the weakness his tone implied, but after all he had endured, the numbing sensation overcoming his body felt worse than anything Lilith and her goons had done to him.

Paulson said, "Unfortunately, Lakshmi has sent the frigate *Godavari* to intercept the lifeboats. Every time the *Capable* ups its acceleration to arrive first, the frigate adjusts to guarantee an engagement."

On hearing this, Rafe's insides squeezed into a singularity of anguish. He wanted to scream. If only he had asked to go to the *Capable* instead, he could have rescued Karen and Anna. He would still have had time to use his immunity to protect much of the fleet. But of course, he couldn't have known what would happen to them. And besides which, he reminded himself, he had a job to do. A million children like his might die if he didn't stop Lilith.

"It's like we spoke about before, ma'am," Rafe said, sounding to himself like an automaton. "We're in some sort of system-wide game, complete with special attacks that only Lilith seems to possess."

A lieutenant to Paulson's left spoke up. All eyes shifted to a man whose name tag read "Merrick."

"Then everyone is agreed the Wardens are toying with us?" he said.

Paulson replied, "Most media outlets and many heads of state at Belia have said they believe so. Unfortunately, from what Hastings here has told us about that Henry Wilkinson, the Celesians are going along with it."

Rafe asked, "Are we at war with Celes yet?"

"No," Paulson said. "Officially, they've declared themselves neutral and offered to mediate between Lilith's new government and Mykon."

The prospect of what might happen to Anna and Karen began to haunt him. He tried to ignore it by asking, "Has there been any attempt to negotiate with Celes? They can't like being played with any more than we do."

"More to come on that," Paulson replied, falling back on the age-old stand-in for "I don't know." She rubbed at the bridge of her nose and said, "Right now, we need anything else you can give us. The *Capable* may have to fight off the Lakshmian frigate headed for the life pods."

Rafe felt heat rising in his cheeks—this was not what was supposed to happen. He pictured his girls caught in a space battle, blown into vacuum. "I'll share everything I can think of,

Captain," Rafe said. "In point of fact, it might be best for the *Capable* to tempt Lilith to use more of her new weapons."

What the hell are you doing? his heart screamed.

"That way our attack force will know more about what it is getting into," he said.

And what about your girls? If Lilith gets a hold of them—

"You took the words out of my mouth," Paulson said, calling up a map on the room's viewing wall. She gestured first to the flotilla of twelve ships converging on a point some distance from Lakshmi. Then she highlighted the colony and its three defenders. "Except for the *Godavari*, which is advancing toward the lifeboats here, Lilith's ships are keeping station near the colony."

Rafe shook his head to clear it and asked, "Ma'am, before we go on, I have to know. Will we make it to Lakshmi before the lifeboats do?"

Captain Paulson regarded Rafe with an emotionless expression. After a moment's pause she said, "No, we won't."

Restraining his anger at himself, Rafe studied the map. With him aboard, the *Tsunami* could defend their forces while they gathered. Otherwise, the Lakshmians might try to snipe the remaining Mykonian warships. They simply could not risk racing ahead to the lifeboats.

"At least the fleet is almost in position," Rafe said, straining to form coherent thoughts through his reeling emotions. "There's some good news though. If Lilith had the means of destroying all of our ships, she would have done it by now. She would have put Arbiters on fast yachts to let her shoot Casabas from them. She could have sniped us all at extreme range. Since she didn't use them in her initial attack, I don't believe she has many to spare."

"A good point," Paulson said. "Once we rendezvous with the fleet," she continued, "we'll interlink with the other ships to share the commander's immunity. It will be tricky maneuvering, but it can work. And once we get there…" The woman called up a mission concept slide and signaled their operations officer, Lieutenant Merrick, to walk them through it.

Eventually, Paulson said, "Commander Hastings, anything to add?"

Rafe's head snapped to the captain.

Rafe's heart throttled, aching for his children. He was trembling. He opened his mouth. Then, without warning, Claire spoke.

"Priority Warden communication, Captain."

Paulson rolled her neck. "What is it this time?"

"Ma'am, it's addressed to you and Commander Hastings. And I recommend it be reviewed privately."

Nothing short of someone holding a gun to his head could have further spiked Rafe's adrenaline as those words did. For a moment, the senior officers stared at each other. Each suspected such a Warden missive would mean terrible news for at least one of them.

Paulson spoke with firm solemnity. "Everyone but Commander Hastings: clear the room."

When they hovered alone, Rafe swallowed against a dry tongue then asked, "What's the message?"

Claire said, "Effective immediately, *MSV Tsunami* functions are controlled by Commander Rafe Hastings and his designees only. End of message."

For a stunned instant, neither Paulson nor Rafe could speak. Eventually, Rafe stated the obvious. "That's not a coincidence."

His inner demon hissed about how for the next 22 hours, he answered to the Wardens alone. He could go get his children.

A long moment passed before either of them spoke.

"They *are* playing with us," Rafe said at last. He shut his eyes. "They know I'm going through hell because of my girls, and they're tempting me."

"It might not be that simple," Paulson said, her voice detached. "The only reason the *Tsunami* isn't in Lilith's hands is that another Warden override freed our systems at the last moment."

Rafe opened his eyes again. "What?"

"We didn't save ourselves, Commander. The wipe and re-installation fix for the computers worked to clear Lilith's overrides on the rest of the fleet, but the *Tsu* hadn't finished the process before being released. The Wardens must be operating under some arbitrary rule set: playing for at least two sides. Otherwise, they'd make us surrender to Lilith outright.

"Then the fact I'm being given a choice at this exact moment means what? That we can win? That we should withdraw?"

The demons within called again for him to abandon the attack on Lakshmi and save his girls.

Paulson kept her peace. He could guess why. No doubt she was waiting to see if he'd agree with her plan on his own.

"Perhaps," Rafe said. He broke off then repeated the word. "Perhaps…"

He yearned to give in with an intensity beyond anything Henry or Markem had been able to inspire. He started to shake his head.

"How can I…" he gasped, "let…"

Another part of him told himself to stop. He was a commander in the Mykonian Space Forces, and they were at war.

"I can't…" Rafe said, his composure cracking. He only then realized with horror how far he'd slipped: how broken he'd become. He knew he'd take his kids' place in an instant, but how could he live with himself knowing he'd let Lilith torture them?

He sensed his deceitful heart deciding for him.

His conscience mounted its final defense. Was he or wasn't he a warrior?

Rafe's face fell. He remembered something his father had taught him long ago: the only things he would ever truly own were the moral choices he made. It was time to make the right one.

His heart breaking, his body shaking, Rafe said, "We should attack ma'am. It's our best chance. Claire!"

"Yes, Commander?"

"Tell the Wardens this ship doesn't belong to me. Return control to Captain Paulson."

"Acknowledged," Claire said. "Done."

The shipmaster put a hand on Rafe's shoulder. Inside, he wondered how he'd be able to live with himself if something worse happened to his children.

[21]

Location: Lilith's private estate, Lakshmi Colony_

AT A BREAK BETWEEN MEETINGS, LILITH RETREATED FROM THE throngs of Dalip's prickly administrators and headed down to her private command bunker. Henry followed, discretely, to ensure he would get to speak with her alone.

It's time you answered for some things, he thought.

After giving her a minute, he stepped inside the control room. He found the empress's hourglass figure silhouetted by the glow of the wall-sized displays. A three-dimensional grid map depicted Lakshmi colony and the vessels around it. Henry saw her focused on one icon in particular.

She said, "Rafe hasn't altered the *Tsunami's* course."

Henry stepped forward, unsurprised he hadn't snuck up on her. His hand traced a lazy circle. "That is an awfully large number of Mykonian warships coming our way." He angled to regard her. "I could have told you diverting those escape pods here wouldn't change things."

Lilith gave Henry a sidelong glance. He didn't know she had not been the one to alter their course. "Have you come to pick a fight, Henry?" she asked. "You don't seem grateful for the treat I gave you last night."

"This is serious, Lilith."

"Alright. Then seriously, I think the Wardens thought the maneuver was worth a try. Otherwise, why would they have given control of the *Tsunami* to Rafe? They must have wanted him to go after the lifeboats. Almost certainly, somebody he cares about is on one of them."

Henry made an exasperated sound. "We don't know that the Wardens are acting in our best interests. Whatever this war game, I thought that at least you were their favorite piece. But then Rafe happened."

Lilith folded her arms. "What's really bothering you, Henry?" she asked.

Henry's gaze narrowed. "Just for once, don't play coy, Lilith. You waited till I'd gone to sleep to redirect those escape pods. I can't advise you if you won't consult me. Bringing those refugees here used up gods-know-how-many-more of your cache resources. Then, you forced Dalip to commit a badly needed ship to intercept the *Capable*. That's a battle which needn't be fought. And for what?"

At last, Lilith turned to Henry. A cold fire burned in her eyes. "I'm testing my weapons, taking out one more enemy ship, and above all, keeping the pressure on." She huffed. "It's one of the little lessons I learned in the brothels. If inflicting pain doesn't solve your problems, then you simply aren't using enough of it."

"Pain didn't work so well on Rafe," Henry said with disdain.

Lilith said, "I didn't have enough time with him was all." She tapped a menu on the display, and the view skipped to the *MSV Capable*. "At least the Mykonians are finally showing some balls for us to slice."

"That was never a problem," Henry countered. "They have over a dozen warships at Belia *on their way* to shoot it out with

Lakshmi's four. You've admitted you don't have enough Casabas to fight off a determined assault."

Lilith stomped her foot and said, "I didn't fiddle with those lifeboats, Henry. The Wardens did."

The Celesian stared at her for a full second. "What?" he breathed.

"Yes," she said with acid. "We'll soon see how important the refugees are. But after Rafe escaped, do you honestly think the Mykonians wouldn't have come after us?"

Henry paused, put his hands on his hips, then allowed his chin to dip. "Of course, we both saw that coming."

"And we would have done something about it sooner," Lilith added, "if we didn't have to contend with that dithering General Parashar. I can't understand why Dalip lets him head the military."

Henry acknowledged the point with a grunt. He tried forcing a smile. It wasn't easy at first, so he thought back to the night before. Tempered by his erotic reminiscences, Henry slid a hand around to the small of Lilith's back.

He felt her body stiffen, so he told her, "Knowing that the Wardens are still helping certainly casts this in a new light. Just please trust that *I* have your best interests in mind. We have to be careful not to get caught in a weakened position should the Wardens start giving the Mykonians some special toys too."

"I know," Lilith said, smothering her annoyance. "I know."

"Good," Henry muttered. "Remember, your failure is my failure. Your success is my success." He raised the back of Lilith's hand to his lips and added, "My empress."

Lilith regarded the gesture with a softened, almost surprised expression. Despite their games of mutual exploitation, Henry suspected the flicker of vulnerability in her face was genuine.

"I appreciate your help, Henry," she said. "I mean it."

About damn time, he thought. Now, if only you'd start listening to me.

Their quarrel abated, Lilith turned her head back to the display. A crease broke over her brow. "Tell me honestly, are you still confident the Mykonians don't have an Arbiter of their own at Belia?"

Please, don't start obsessing about your Achilles heel.

He said, "You know we can't be sure, but I don't believe so. Celesian intelligence thinks they may have one or two at Mykon. It will be three months, at least, before they can send any here."

Lilith nodded and uncrossed her arms.

She said, "That's time enough to gather our strength." Pinching her fingers, the image before them widened to encompass the cluster of nearby space habitats. "The real question then is what to do about the other colonies. I don't think wooing my subjects is an option now. Not after the hope that Rafe's escape gave them."

"Yes," Henry said. "All of the leadership is waiting to see how this fight with the *Tsunami's* fleet plays out. It's too late to stop them invading."

"Then we're agreed. Everyone's attitude needs adjusting," Lilith said.

The spy nodded solemnly. He anticipated that the empress's next words would most likely mean a horrific death for many, many people.

They both knew if no one else joined Lilith's new empire they would have to wait for the reinforcements she had purchased from Celes. But those ships wouldn't arrive for months. And if the Mykonians had an Arbiter of their own, it would only be a matter of time before they brought it to Belia to let them fire on Lakshmi. She needed a stronger defense.

In an off-handed manner, Lilith told him, "I noticed the president of Ganesha has been particularly sour about my ascension to power."

Henry dutifully took the cue. He stepped over to a nearby desk and lifted a pad. It was the same one Lilith had used to launch the attack on Zeus.

"We can't go to Phase Three without enough colonies surrendering to you," he said. "We should escalate the pressure."

Lilith gave Henry a feral smile as she took the pad from him. "I love it when you talk dirty, Henry."

"I would suggest," he added, "that you ask Dalip and his staff at this next meeting if anyone they care about is living on Ganesha. No sense in antagonizing the people running your empire."

Lilith said, "At least not until it won't matter." She blew an errant hair strand off her forehead. "Phase Three can't come fast enough."

As they walked back to the conference room, Henry hid a grimace over what lay ahead for the poor Belians.

It has to be done, he repeated to himself. *If Celes is to eventually rule Cervantes, it all has to be done.*

Location: Sickbay, *MSV Tsunami*_

A FAINT, CHERRY GLOW DISPLACED SARAH'S ANXIETY THE instant she saw Sean floating into the room. He had the purplish tint of a bad night's sleep under his eyes, but they twinkled on seeing her.

"Hi," he said with an undercurrent of schoolboy shyness.

"Hi," she replied, her timbre matching his.

Sean quickly scanned the compartment for anyone else. The doctor's office door was shut. Along a wall, Watson slept in drug-induced oblivion. Sean's gaze lingered for a beat on the blanket Sarah had tucked around the man to hide his stumps.

"Plans are coming along, so we're taking a break," he said, "I thought I'd come by to see how you're doing." He turned to regard her.

In response, Sarah removed her visor and beamed at him. Something about his being there made her feel safer—more at ease—and she relished it. For a few breaths, her searching gaze swam in his silver eyes. He returned it with a gentle look that set off a delicious tingle below her neck.

When Sarah didn't answer, he asked, "Where are Martinez and Yontz? Are they better?"

"Yes," she said, appreciative of his concern. "they're on quarters." Pointing to Watson, she added, "He's improving too. How about you?"

He tilted his head in a hesitant pause. "You know, after getting to relax with you yesterday, I realized *you* make me better. I just wanted to say 'thank you' for that."

Sarah blushed and pushed a pink wisp over and around one ear.

"I feel the same," she said.

And then their perfect moment dissolved as the dread that had been haunting Sarah all day returned.

They'd be in combat soon, she thought with a pang of terror. For all she knew, this might be the last time they saw each other alive. The cruel notion took hold of her happiness and dragged it away. As Sarah's smile collapsed, Sean's expression pitched into one of concern. He cupped the side of her face in his hand, waiting for her to explain.

"Just a moment," she whispered. "I only need a moment." She closed her eyes and rolled the side of her face into his palm.

It took almost a minute before the crinkle between her eyebrows finally relaxed. All the while, Sean waited, silently holding her by the cheek. Eventually, tranquility returned to her. She opened her eyes and parted her lips to thank him for simply being there for her. She wanted to apologize for worrying him. Most importantly, she wanted to smile for him.

From every speaker, Claire's voice rang out. "Attention all hands. Warden broadcast commencing."

Light burst along a nearby wall. They snapped their attention to a display with Lilith's scowling visage.

"Belians, Mykonians, I warned you," she said. "I warned you, but some of you have refused to listen. I will defend my own, and I will punish those who stand against me."

Onscreen, several life pods from Zeus appeared in a corner. Sarah felt Sean's arms circle around her in a feeble attempt to protect her from the horrors that Lilith surely had in store.

The self-styled empress continued. "My Warden patrons revealed to me that several Belian citizens have left Zeus in these lifeboats. What must they have felt to have finally escaped their prison? For this reason, I used my influence to bring as many as I could to Lakshmi."

She shifted to a pretentiously compassionate smile. "They who were mistreated and enslaved need our warmth and comfort. They deserve freedom and safety."

The smile waned. "I asked the Mykonians not to interfere. And yet they send warships at both my fleeing brethren as well as at Lakshmi herself. Why would they do this? Have I not promised to return their citizens?"

Lilith raised her voice to a near shriek. "This act of war will not be tolerated! I have shown restraint, but if the Mykonians do not turn back I will destroy their warships!"

Her threat delivered, the madwoman paused. Sarah, however, saw the hate boiling in Lilith's eyes and sensed that the real show was about to begin.

"Now," Lilith said, "such defiance I would have expected from the Mykonians. Enemies attack enemies. But Ganesha. Oh,

Ganesha. You were Lakshmi's friend. And yet you have rejected our protection and love."

Lilith's face contorted with rage and sorrow. "Even this I could have forgiven. But why have you sided with the Mykonians? Your own president has shouted your scorn. You've heaped on me your disgust and invited *our enemies* to your home and bed."

"Why!?" she screamed, making Sarah jump in Sean's arms. "You've forced me to do what I had hoped never to do. I must punish you. I must make an example of you." She raised the back of a control pad into view of the camera. "I must burn you, Ganesha." She touched the hidden side of the pad and let her shoulders slump. "I beg you all: learn from this."

The screen winked to a panoramic image of a cylindrical colony's cavernous interior. Its caption in the lower right corner read, "Ganesha, Segment 5."

Sarah's eyes poured over the new image. The frame's upper half showed an inwardly curving landscape: a ten-kilometer-wide partition of habitat. Checkerboard fields, snaking canals, grids of roads and clusters of squat buildings filled the vista. She made out a group of ornate high-rises jutting out at the five o'clock position: the colony's capital district, she guessed.

The camera panned down to fill the screen's lower half with a bustling bazaar.

People, she thought, blood-curdling in her veins. *She's going to kill all those people!*

Sarah noted most of the figures had stopped to listen to the broadcast. Groups gathered around monitors tucked within vendor stalls. Only a few individuals moved at speed along the avenue.

Run! Please, run!

An audio-feed cut in and Sarah picked out alarmed voices from the street. Her breath caught as she heard a small child asking its mama why she was pulling so hard. Women screamed, and more people scrambled to get out of the open.

"They know," Sarah's mezzo-soprano voice cracked.

Her searching gaze picked out four smoke trails extending across the frame. Her every muscle seized with fear. Lilith had somehow snuck a missile package past every checkpoint.

The flotilla "descended" from the ten o'clock position along the cylindrical colony's surface relative to the camera. As the habitat turned, their rockets appeared to curve across the screen, even though they were actually flying straight. It took scant seconds for them to accelerate past the colony's hub toward the surface "below." Less than a kilometer from the ground, the warheads burst into a constellation of miniature suns.

Sarah's hand flew up to her mouth. An evil brilliance bleached the bazaar tents, shanties, and people. The light burned for a half-second before waning.

Sarah's gaze shifted to the street-side view. Some of the figures had thrown up hands to shield themselves. Parents crouched low, gathering children beneath protective arms. Still, others fell to the ground mid-stride.

One heartbeat after the initial pulses, the closest shock wave struck. Sarah stared in stunned horror as the overpressure front slammed into the cityscape at more than thirteen-hundred-kilometers an hour. The supersonic blast roared over the microphone, its wrath drowning out everything else like a deafening thunderclap.

Sarah wanted to look away from the nuclear murder but found that the sinews in her neck wouldn't move. Through the shaking camera view, she saw bodies blowing about like reeds in a gale. All around the perishing souls, debris swirled and tumbled. The gusts swept first one way, then reversed to howl from the other. The fury collapsed most of the structures in the foreground, crushing people beneath support poles, furniture, and shelves full of goods.

It took several racing heartbeats before the maelstrom began to settle. Sarah choked on grief as she beheld the scene of dust-filled devastation. Across the bazaar, dozens of small electrical fires blazed. Here and there, water pipes spread inky pools of muck. People lay strewn up and down the street like discarded dolls.

The utter lack of human noises echoed in Sarah's heart. Only a few distant sirens blared amidst a diminishing rumble. Almost no one moved amongst the mass of littered humanity. They didn't scream or cry. Only a few twitched.

She wished Doctor Apple hadn't made her study up on the effects of neutron weapons. She knew that enhanced radiation bombs released a larger percentage of their energy as deadly neutrons than conventional nukes. She also knew anyone close enough to be knocked over by the blast wave had already received a lethal radiation dose. Depending on their range from the explosion, the cells of some victims could be sufficiently disrupted to put them into a merciful coma.

At this thought, her eyes fell on the still forms of a mother and child, possibly the pair she'd heard earlier over the microphone. They seemed about the size of her sister and nieces. The sight sent Sarah into silent, racking sobs.

She tried not to think about the people who'd been hit with lesser doses of radiation. Wide awake, many of their bodies would waste away for anywhere from hours to weeks. Legions would suffer from excruciating nausea, vomiting, and diarrhea, along with second and third-degree burns, plus blunt-force trauma from flying debris. The ones still further out, physically maimed or otherwise, would endure the nuclear aftermath's horrors for years to come.

The Wardens' feed at last cut out. With its passing, Sarah felt the string holding her heavy heart snap. Her insides turned over and around with sorrow and anger. She recovered enough control to strain out, "Sean, those people."

Sean kept silent but cinched his hold on her slender waist. Sarah turned her head to peer into his darkened face. Her expression begged him to tell her that what she'd seen had all been a lie: a computer-generated fiction designed to frighten everyone. He placed a hand to the back of her head and pressed her cheek to his chest.

Paulson's voice called over the speakers. "This is the captain." A respectful silence elapsed. "Let there be no doubt in your minds, we will stop this madwoman. We will form up with our fleet elements in four hours. We will blast through Lakshmi's defenses tonight, and we will not stop until we have hunted that monster down. Department heads report to the Wardroom in ten minutes. Paulson out."

No sooner had the line dropped than fury seized Sarah's body. Her small hands contracted into rocks. Her teeth became grates to a burning furnace of hate.

Her voice burst out, saying, "How does anyone become so evil that they'd murder so many people?"

Sean remained quiet, but his face mirrored her pain.

"Oh, Sean," she said, suddenly fearful. "If she could sneak bombs into a colony like that, what's to stop her from doing the same to home? She could kill my family!"

"Yes," Sean said.

"Ever since I got here I've been dealing with that witch's horrors. I haven't felt this ugly inside since..." She trailed off. "How do I stop being so angry?"

Sean drew in a lung-full of oxygen and swallowed before answering. "I'm not so sure you should. Not until we've won."

Sarah pulled back from Sean. "I didn't expect you to say that."

He touched her cheek with a finger and said, "Pray for Lilith's soul, because immunity or not, it's our job to kill her. And we have a shot at doing it without violating the Warden Code."

The bitter resolve in his voice both chilled and invigorated Sarah. It scared her that she liked that idea so much. Lilith was still a person, but Sarah wondered how anyone could not feel happy over the thought of the witch dying after everything.

Sean squeezed her hand.

Sarah squeezed his back. She wanted him to stay, to make her feel protected and safe and unafraid.

Be grateful that you had this time, her heart told her. As Sarah watched Sean leave, she could only hope they would make it through the next day alive.

[22]

Location: Zeus Lifeboat 19_

"You're Karen and Anna, right?"

Karen's attention jerked up to find a forty-something man in uniform. She recognized Master Chief Torrens, the enlisted person assisting Commander Hagherty, who'd taken charge of the shuttle.

Karen nodded.

Torrens flashed the hint of a grimace, then said, "The Commander wants the kids up front where she can see them. Get your stuff."

During the brief trip forward, Karen had her first real look at the other passengers. She noticed several families huddling together. They were surrounded by an even larger contingent of young to middle-aged men. She saw few service members.

Torrens showed them their new seats in the wide aisle beside the lifeboat's forward airlock. Karen realized that the only other children nearby looked to have been there since the escape from Zeus. She had only begun to puzzle over this when Commander Hagherty floated alongside.

The middle-aged woman asked, "Is this them?"

"Aye, ma'am."

The woman turned to the girls. "Come on into the cockpit, ladies."

Despite the reassuring words, Karen felt a spurt of apprehension. She glanced at her sibling who looked back with the same troubled expression.

The woman said, "It's okay. We need to update some records."

The inside of the dimly lit cockpit chilled Karen with its glossy black screens set inside matted, gray aluminum trim. The windows to the velvet firmament arrested her attention with their untwinkling pinpricks of stars. Then she noticed a brilliant nub of light ahead.

She shivered. *Is that Lakshmi?*

Hagherty shut the tiny room's hatch with a loud thunk, making the children jump. Karen turned around to find the Commander facing them. With a tired, no-nonsense glare, she said, "Have you young ladies been following the news?"

Karen said, "Just that horrible Lilith lady blowing up Ganesha."

"Okay," the woman said, "What was your father's name."

Both Karen and Anna glanced at each other, confused. Karen thought the computer automatically knew who they were and had their parents' information. Since they'd slept so much, they didn't know how famous their father had become, much less how dangerous it might be if the others aboard knew who they were.

After a second, Karen stuttered out, "Rafe. Rafe Hastings, ma'am."

Hagherty's jaw set and her gaze drifted for an instant. The reaction sent a line of spider legs marching up Karen's spine.

"What is it?" she demanded, fearing the answer. "Is he dead too?"

"Your father is okay," Hagherty said.

The two daughters gasped audibly. Karen's hands and arms started to jitter. At the same time, she felt Anna grab hold of her torso.

An image of her father's kind, smiling face appeared in Karen's mind. For the first time since leaving Zeus, she felt something like real hope flower within her. She twisted around in her sister's embrace. Words came out of Karen's mouth in a whisper, as though saying them any louder would break the fragile miracle they represented.

"Daddy's alive!"

Karen swept at the moisture forming in her eyes, then saw that Hagherty's expression remained detached. The girl's joy melted. She said, "Something's still wrong."

"Your father has been all over the news. He's a hero; the man who defied Lilith. He's the reason why we had any warning that she was up to something. Your father gave us a fighting chance, and now he is flying to Lakshmi aboard the fleet's flagship to cause her even more trouble."

Karen listened to Hagherty with a rising tide of daughterly pride.

Commander Hagherty continued. "As you can imagine, Lilith hates your father. Unfortunately, your pictures have been in some of the news feeds. And this lifeboat is headed straight for Lilith on Lakshmi. She would very much like to meet you, I'm sure."

Absorbing these words, Anna's hold on Karen cinched tighter. Karen felt her heart pounding in her throat. She had a fleeting mental image of some enormous, Lilith-shaped monster circling the ship, looking for a way in.

Seeing the eyes on the girls broadening, Hagherty hastened to add, "The destroyer *Capable* is coming. Alastair should have radioed the names of everyone aboard before Zeus was destroyed.

If and when help comes, I want you right up by the airlock hatch. You leave here *first*."

Karen swallowed against a dry pallet as Hagherty put her hands to a shoulder on each of the Hastings girls.

"One more thing. It doesn't seem that anyone else onboard has figured out who you are, so keep this to yourselves. Not everyone will appreciate what your father has done for us. So keep your heads down, yes?"

Location: CIC, *MSV Tsunami_*

"Lakshmian frigate *Godavari* is still accelerating at point oh one gravities," an enlisted astronaut at the plotting station announced.

Rafe noticed the officer of the watch, Lieutenant Merrick, turn to the captain. Lieutenant Merrick growled out what they could all see. "Unless the enemy flips over now and burns like hell, they'll be inside the ten-kay firing range before the *Capable* can finish offloading any lifeboats."

Captain Paulson folded her arms and scowled at the tactical map. "Signal the *Capable*. Proceed with option two on the snatch-and-dash."

Rafe's innards curdled. They had just given up on the *Capable* making the rescue herself. Instead, the destroyer's small courier ship would sprint ahead, take on as many survivors as possible, then blast away at high-g.

While the young woman at comms relayed Paulson's orders, Rafe had an uncomfortable moment to consider how few people the *Capable's* shuttle could extract. From almost a hundred refugees on Lifeboat 19 alone, perhaps only a few dozen could get out. Worse yet, some of the wounded might be too weak to endure the escape burn.

But at least my kids will have a chance.

A minute later, the comms chief said, "Captain, the *Capable* is on emergency channel five, ordering the lifeboats to kill their master breakers for the next half-hour."

"Very well."

Rafe flinched. He had been the first to suggest that they "safe" the lifeboats against further manipulation by Lilith. He imagined Anna squirming fearfully as the main cabin lights and electronic distractions shut off with little notice. Only emergency life support, short-range radios, and a few battery-powered lamps would still function.

They'll be fine. They're together.

He watched the plot. One by one, the lifeboats faded to a darker shade of blue until the entire flotilla coasted unguided. He prayed for his girls to be brave. All the while, the Lakshmian frigate did not alter course or acceleration.

The comms tech lady said, "*Capable* is broadcasting their intention to conduct a rescue mission to retrieve children and wounded from the lifeboats." She pressed a hand over her ear then added, "They've issued a final hostile challenge to the *Godavari*."

Rafe smirked. They were checking procedural boxes for the sake of moral legitimacy.

The tech shortly reported, "No response from the *Godavari*."

Seconds later, a new icon appeared next to the *Capable* and Rafe's pulse began to throb.

The plotter announced, "Shuttlecraft *White Knight* has launched. She's thrusting for the lifeboats. Rendezvous in ten minutes."

Paulson said, "Message to *White Knight*. Godspeed. Signal to the *Capable*. Weapons free. Fire ten missiles at ten thousand klicks from the *Godavari*, then it's captain's discretion from there. Good hunting."

Rafe's fingers kneaded at his biceps. They were committed. He watched the blips of the *Capable* and *White Knight* crawl across the Warden-imposed engagement boundary with the *Godavari*. At just under the ten-thousand-kilometer mark, ten multi-stage nuclear warhead Reaper missiles shot away from the Mykonian warship on invisible trails of scorching gas.

"*Godavari* is launching!" the plotter said with animated fervor. "Ten blips tracking on a line between *Capable* and the lifeboats."

Rafe saw Paulson exchange knowing glances with Merrick. The attack was no surprise to anyone in the CIC, but Rafe writhed inside anyway. The *Capable*, her missiles and Zeus's escape shuttles all lay along the same axis headed in more or less the same direction. The enemy could send their missile barrage against any combination of Mykonian targets.

The girl at comms spoke up. "*Capable* is repeating her intentions to protect the rescue and orders *Godavari* to break off."

Another useless box checked.

More arrowhead blips raced away from the Mykonian destroyer.

The plotter said, "*Capable* is firing counter-missiles. Target is the enemy missile wave."

Rafe heard Lieutenant Merrick mutter, "So far, it's all by the book."

Rafe nodded. Even a non-line officer like himself recognized the tactics. The *Capable*'s fire would force the incoming missiles to maneuver. The destroyer could saturate the battlefield with guided weapons until the threats needed to dodge, expending precious propellant. Should any of the inbounds survive this barrage, the *Capable*'s main laser battery would cook them once they drew within effective range.

Then the news that Rafe had dreaded came. The plotter shouted, "Enemy missile vectors have changed to bear on the lifeboats. They're accelerating." After a full minute, he said, "Intercept in twenty minutes."

Rafe spat a curse. The attack was a flagrant violation of the laws of warfare.

From her chair in the CIC, Paulson snapped, "Order the *Capable* to fire a protective spread."

Before her words could be relayed, more map icons raced from the destroyer. The *Godavari* responded by firing a second spread of its own at the lifeboats.

As the nail-biting minutes mounted, a thought struck Rafe. He said, "The *Godavari* is making sure the *Capable* sticks around to protect the refugees."

"Yes," Paulson agreed, suspicion thick in her voice.

With each passing minute, Rafe felt his sense of foreboding darken. The *Godavari* was luring the *Capable* in. So long as the destroyer had to defend the lifeboats, she couldn't change course to keep away from the enemy frigate—exactly as Captain Paulson wanted.

Eventually, the plotting chief said, "*White Knight* is on final maneuvers to Lifeboat 19."

The vice around Rafe's shoulders tightened. *Help is almost there, girls. Hold on just a bit longer.*

Location: Zeus Lifeboat 19_

EVEN THOUGH COMMANDER HAGHERTY HAD TRIED TO PREPARE the shuttle's passengers for possible rescue, some people screamed the moment the lights faded. As Karen's eyes adjusted to the gloom, she twisted about to glare at a hysterical lady.

Disgusted, Karen closed her eyes and drew her sister tight against her. She nestled Anna's head beneath her chin and sniffed the comforting mix of scalp oil and lavender shampoo.

Karen said, "We'll make it through this."

Several minutes later, she sensed movement in front of her. She opened her eyes to see the distraught woman floating to the airlock's minuscule porthole.

"Hey, miss," Master Chief Torrens said, "You need to get strapped back in."

The hyperventilating woman asked, "Why aren't they here yet?"

"It may take them a little while. Now go sit down."

The lady stared out the porthole, took two more desperate gasps and asked, "Can't you call them? Make them realize they have to get us out of here?"

"I said sit down."

"You don't get it!" the woman cried. "I grew up in Lakshmi. I know what people like Lilith will do to us."

Karen had heard enough. "Hey, lady," she said. "Shut up. You're scaring us kids."

Startled, the woman turned to regard Karen and Anna. Recognition dawned over her, followed quickly by disbelief, anger, and horror. "I know you," she said. "You were in the news. You're Rafe Hastings' kids!"

A sour burning trickled up Karen's sternum. She grew aware of others paying attention to the exchange.

Master Chief Torrens shoved the hysterical female back toward her seat. In a barely controlled voice, he told her to sit down. She obeyed, but the damage had been done.

An angry male several rows back said, "Is that true? You're the kids of the guy who got us into this war?"

"Shut your hole!" Torrens barked. Karen leveraged herself slightly up from her chair to get a peek at the speaker. The agitator's thick hair and beefy face told her he was a civilian who'd worked at Zeus. He caught sight of her and narrowed his eyes.

"Is that why they're really up there? Special treatment for the brats of the so-called hero? What about the rest of us, eh?"

Another man further back tried to shout the vitriolic male down, but the trouble-maker called out, "We should be drawing lots for the rest of us!" A chorus of assent rose up from several aisles.

Commander Hagherty emerged from the cockpit. "What's going on here? Help's about to dock. Stay put until we call you forward."

At that news, several faces crowded the lifeboat's few windows. Someone yelled, "I can see it! It's just a small shuttle. We won't all fit in that thing!"

Karen's blood chilled by several degrees. She saw the passengers shifting and mumbling to each other. She heard a distant voice say, "They're going to leave us behind! We have to do something!"

Hagherty called out, "Children and wounded first, people!"

The clunk of metal reverberated throughout the cabin. Everyone jerked toward the sound. An even louder thunk followed. As if it had been a starting pistol, people popped out of their restraints and advanced.

Karen drew a sharp breath as bodies poured into the aisle where she and Anna waited. She wrapped herself tight about her sister, hoping to shield the child from the growing mob. She heard Torrens and Hagherty bellowing for everyone to go back to their seats, but no one listened.

Within moments, angry voices gave way to blows. Through the glut of people, Karen saw service members trying to fight off the crowd.

The girls cringed as a figure slammed into them. They yelped. A moment later, the mass shifted off, but then hands grappled their bony shoulders. Someone released their restraints. The children screamed and thrashed while someone lifted them.

Karen looked up to see two wild-eyed men. One of them said

to the other, "Let's get them to the back!"

Location: *CIC, MSV Tsunami_*

"*WHITE KNIGHT* REPORTS GOOD AIRLOCK SEAL," THE communications tech announced. The news brought a measure of relief to Rafe's growing tension.

The fusion-rocket courier had enough propellant to break for a friendly colony in higher Belian orbit. The trip would take almost a week, but the girls would be safe at last.

While everyone waited for word from the rescue shuttle, the *Capable's* ordnance closed with the incoming missiles. Icons flared then winked out until only four red arrowheads remained on the map. Rafe stared at those baleful lights as they hurtled at his daughters.

The plotter said, "*Capable* has cut her drive and is changing aspect. She's readying her main laser battery."

Lieutenant Merrick turned to Rafe. "We're still good here sir. It will take a while to shoot down those last missiles from that range, but they should be able to scrag them all."

Rafe nodded gratefully for the assurance. *We're still good here,* he repeated to himself.

The woman at communications called out, "*White Knight* reports a problem with Lifeboat 19."

Rafe felt every drop of blood leech from his veins. He stopped breathing even as the room's chatter ceased.

The astronaut continued. "They say there's a riot outside the airlock. They can't get into the lifeboat."

Someone called up the *Capable's* telescopic view and put it on the main screen. Through the hazeless image, Rafe made out the boxy shapes of escape shuttles strewn about in a ragged formation. One of them was mated to the courier.

Rafe's fists clenched. His girls were there, right there, and he couldn't get at them. His eyes switched back to the plotting screen. The enemy's lead missile winked out.

The plotter said, "Scrag another zombie. *Capable* is retargeting."

"Captain," Merrick said, "She's going to be stuck inside the combat envelope if she doesn't veer off now."

Rafe watched as Paulson worked her jaw. She glanced Rafe's way, and their eyes met. Rafe begged her with his expression not to abandon his kids.

Paulson spoke with authoritative calm. "Signal the *Capable.* We're all-in on this. Have *White Knight* detach and try for another airlock. Fire all remaining Reapers on the *Godavari*. Protect the lifeboats."

Rafe exhaled.

"We have a problem with Lifeboat 47," the plotter abruptly announced. "She's powered back up! She's maneuvering!"

"What vector?!" Paulson demanded, but she needn't have asked. Everyone could see the icon was headed directly for Lifeboat 19.

Location: Zeus Lifeboat 19_

PANDEMONIUM REIGNED IN THE DARKENED CABIN. WHILE ANNA screamed, Karen demanded to be let go.

The pair of men holding her ignored her thrashing. They focused instead on carrying her and Anna to the craft's rear. Unfortunately for the girls, most everyone was too focused on moving forward, either to try to escape or else to help restore order. Those few who tried to intervene received sharp elbows to the face.

Sometime during the panicked jostling, Karen understood that neither she nor her sister could free themselves on their own.

Take care of your sister, the voice of her parents rang.

The surging crowd pushed the man holding Karen into the one bracing Anna. Karen's face smashed against a hairy limb. She chomped hard on it while clawing at the hand grappling her sister. With a curse, the male loosened his hold enough for Anna to break free. Karen had one fleeting glimpse of a black ponytail before the glut of bodies eclipsed Anna.

Karen's kidnapper shouted, "Help me with this one!"

More thumps of metal on metal sounded.

"They're leaving!" someone screamed. The mob withered in despair. By then, the men had stuffed Karen into a toilet room.

She banged her fists on the door, but the men kept it braced shut. She cried out for Commander Hagherty and Master Chief Torrens, but they had been knocked unconscious in the fighting. The few people who'd noticed the abduction were the timid refugees who'd kept out of the way.

Less than a minute later, the lifeboat shook again as the *White Knight* mated to another airlock at the rear. Karen heard the crowd crescendo into a new frenzy. Shouts and screams filled the rear cabin, drowning out her own pitiful cries for help. She upped the ferocity of her assault on the door.

At one point, she thought she heard someone calling her name and Anna's. Then another voice yelled, "Impact in one minute!"

Location: CIC, *MSV Tsunami_*

Paulson said, "What the hell is going on with Lifeboat 47?!"

The lady at comms replied, "*Capable* is relaying *White Knight's* radio on Emergency Channel 1, ma'am."

"Give us the feed."

A voice distorted by static burst onto the CIC's speakers. "Lifeboat 47, veer off! We do not have time to dock with you!"

"Then you'd better make the time," a female said. "We have wounded here. You have to take them."

The *White Knight's* pilot replied, "Lifeboat 47, you're coming in too fast! Break off now and shut down! You'll hit us in less than a minute."

Above a banging sound, the voice returned, "Then you've less than a minute to agree to take my criticals onboard."

Paulson moved to the communications station. "Patch me into that conversation."

A maddening five seconds later, the enlisted tech said, "You're on, ma'am."

The captain snarled into her microphone. "Lifeboat 47, this is BELCOM flag. Break off immediately. That is an order under military authority and Zeus transit law."

The voice on the other end responded with righteous conviction. "Zeus is gone, BELCOM flag, and I'm not fleet. I don't answer to you, and I'm not going to let my wounded die today."

The pounding in the background intensified. With a start, Rafe realized that the other passengers must be trying to force their way into the cockpit.

"Lifeboat 47 pilot," Paulson growled, "if you do not change your course, so help me I will put you in front of a firing squad!"

A cacophony of angry voices and scuffling erupted over the line.

Someone new said, "We're going to crash! How do I turn this thing!"

A moment later, the radio crackled with the voice of *White Knight's* pilot. "Impact in thirty! Shut the door! Now, now, now!"

Across the room, Rafe stared at the visual from the *Capable's* telescope. He saw one lifeboat eclipsing the other. The courier shuttle moved from between them.

"*White Knight* is away!" the plotter called. The words sent Rafe quaking with unbearable anticipation.

As thrusters pushed the shuttle out of Lifeboat 47's path, the pilot said, "Switching to secure comms. A burp of static later and the voice continued. "Reaching safe distance now. Going to one g in three, two, one." A roar spilled over the radio along with several yelps and the din of crying children.

Paulson said, "Comms, pull up telemetry. Did we get who we needed off?"

"Passenger list compiling, ma'am."

A roster of names splashed onto the main screen. The *White Knight's* computer generated it by reading the implanted ID chips from everyone aboard. Twenty-three names appeared in alphabetical order by surname. Rafe jumped straight to the H's.

His mouth dropped open. He tried to breathe. He tried to say something, but his tongue wouldn't move. Inside, a scream, part joy, and mostly horror, fought to break free.

The White Knight's pilot said. "*Capable,* confirm we retrieved Anna Hastings. Were unable to locate Karen Hastings before we had to detach. It was chaos aboard. I'm sorry."

Rafe's eyes moved back to the live view of the shuttle flotilla. Lifeboat 47 was rolling and edging down on its maneuvering jets. It wasn't enough. Helpless, he watched the ship collide with Lifeboat 19 and send it tumbling.

Location: Zeus Lifeboat 19_

INSIDE THE LAVATORY ABOARD HER ESCAPE SHIP, KAREN LISTENED to the wails of those who had been left behind. She joined her sobbing voice to theirs. Then a hammer-like clang of struck metal pierced her ears. At the same time, the bulkhead slammed into the side of her head.

[23]

Location: CIC, *MSV Tsunami_*

WHEN WORD ARRIVED THAT KAREN HASTINGS HAD BEEN LEFT
behind, Sean glanced back at the girl's father. The man's pale face
pricked at Sean's heart.

Turning back to the screens, Sean watched as Lifeboat 47
collided with Karen's ship. Even from nearly a thousand klicks
away, the *Capable's* telescope relayed the slow-motion crash with
nauseating detail. He flinched as flecks of glittering metal shot
away from between the ships.

Not a breath later, Claire said in a monotone, "Spectroscopic
analysis indicates air leaks from both craft."

A shiver gripped Sean as he imagined the desperate scene
inside. He heard Rafe cursing and seconded the sentiment.

As the lifeboats rolled and diverged, Sean made out crumpled
patches in their skins. Faint jets of air spilled into the black noth-
ingness of space. Unless the panicked passengers sealed the
breaches quickly, they'd asphyxiate.

Sean looked behind him again and saw Rafe holding a wall
grip, his chest heaving.

Moving closer to the distraught man, he said, "Commander, I can get you a line to your daughter on the *White Knight* whenever you're ready."

Rafe's head lolled subtly one way and then the other. Sean wondered if the intelligence officer was about to throw up.

Paulson said, "This isn't over yet, Hastings. They might be able to patch the damage. And if the *Capable's* missiles take out the *Godavari*, she can make a rendezvous inside of twenty minutes."

Rafe didn't acknowledge either of their attempts at comfort. Instead, he continued to stare silently at the video of his daughter's lifeboat as it bled atmosphere. For several seconds, the only other noise in the room was the whirring of fans and hum of electrical equipment.

Then Claire spoke again. "Showing a decrease in outgassing on both lifeboats consistent with compartmentalization. They must have closed off the breached sections of their cabins."

There was still a chance Rafe's kid made it.

The plotter said, "*Capable* is accelerating. And she's pulling in her high aspect cooling fins."

Sean's attention switched over to the tactical map. The acceleration factor next to the destroyer's icon had jumped to three meters per second squared. Her course had also adjusted to more quickly intersect with the stricken refugees. It worried Sean that this caused the Mykonian warship to present more of her flank to the *Godavari*.

Memories of Lima Juliet 12 punching notional holes into the side of the *Tsunami* revisited him. At the present range, neither the *Capable* nor the *Godavari* could hurt the other with a laser.

But what if the Godavari really does have a long-range nuclear lance?

"Captain?" he said with a note of alarm.

"I see it," Paulson said with a distinct lack of concern. "Comms, ask *Capable* what their intentions are."

Shortly after, the tech replied, "They want to link up with the damaged lifeboats, ma'am. They plan to begin braking maneuvers after their strike reaches the *Godavari*."

Paulson said, "Very well. Advise them to use all haste once they've rendezvoused."

The remark made Sean narrow his eyes. He envisioned the *Capable* flitting back-and-forth between the lifeboats, exposing its poorly armored sides to the enemy.

Does the Godavari *have a Casaba-Howitzer?* he wondered. He studied the tactical situation, trying to calculate the odds. Although the *Godavari* had wiped out the initial Mykonian attack, they were completely ignoring the follow-on body of sixty-eight missiles.

They're certainly acting like they've got aces to play, he decided. *But if they have the nuclear lance, why haven't they used it to take out the* Capable *yet?*

He noted the *Godavari's* own second wave of ten missiles still inbound to the lifeboats. The *Capable's* counter-missiles streaked toward them.

Another nail-nibbling minute ticked by before the two clusters of map icons merged. The *Capable's* telescope caught rocket nozzles flaring in sudden, final maneuvers. A close-up tactical grid showed several counter-missiles spraying tungsten buckshot into the enemy's path. Since the ordnance flew at a relative speed of over five kilometers a second, each pellet delivered more energy than its equivalent weight of exploding TNT.

Most of the Lakshmian missiles died in the Mykonian gauntlet. A few erupted into clouds of shrapnel with little to no chance of hitting another object for years. Only three continued to plunge toward the lifeboats.

Seeing this, the *Capable* cut her drive and pointed her nose at the survivors. She waited a short while for the hull's residual vibrations to smooth out, then unshuttered her main laser optics. The destroyer let loose with multi-megawatt brilliance.

Incandescent flecks burst like fireflies wherever the ten-centimeter laser spot shone. At over two-thousand-kilometers' distance, it took several pulses to ruin a missile. The highly reflective, steeply angled armor of their nose cones shrugged off tremendous punishment. They also rotated and jinked to minimize the time the pulses could drill into any one place on their metal hides. But the final outcome was never in doubt. Eventually, they all succumbed to the *Capable's* fury. After stabbing each cylindrical hulk with a final blast for good measure, the warship reoriented and fired up her drive again.

Around the CIC, people pumped fists and muttered words of bravado. All the while, the *Godavari* flew unflinchingly at a wall of missiles. At last, Sean experienced a flash of unpleasant insight.

He drew close to the captain's side and, in a hushed voice, said, "Ma'am, if the Lakshmians wanted to disable the *Capable* with a Casaba, it would make sense to do it after the destroyer matches vectors with the lifeboats. That way, they'd all be headed straight for Lakshmi."

"If the enemy has the means, yes," she said.

Sean regarded his commanding officer, nonplussed. "Ma'am, you wanted me to let you know when I thought we were doing something questionable."

Paulson turned to give Sean her full, intimidating attention. "Go on, Lieutenant."

Sean noted the switch to formality and fought to ignore the cottony sensation suddenly clogging his mouth. "Respectfully, ma'am," he persisted in an even quieter tone, "this is tempting fate, and that didn't work so well in the wargames a few days ago."

Paulson tilted her chin sideways, saying, "Lilith doesn't get to win this fight, Sean. Not strategically. Like I said at the briefing, if she hits the *Capable*, we get intelligence on those Casabas. If she lets us offload our lifeboats, then innocent people live, and we score points for morale." The captain glanced meaningfully at Rafe who remained fixated on the viewers. "He's not the only one with loved ones aboard those transports."

"Aye, ma'am," Sean replied, but the mental pictures of his failure against Lima Juliet 12 persisted. "I'm only suggesting the *Capable* keep her nose pointed at the enemy once she gets into position."

Paulson folded her arms before saying, "It will slow them plenty to scoot around on just their attitude jets. They'd never get to all of the lifeboats before reaching Lakshmi."

"Have them stay cautious for the first few."

Paulson steeled her jaw. "I'm not giving up on getting more people out of there," she said. "And if possible, we *need* the *Godavari* to use a Casaba."

The lieutenant held his ground. All of his instincts screamed that he was right. He whispered, "Ma'am, after what we went through on the *Feni*, it wouldn't surprise me if Lilith is playing with us by having the *Godavari* hold fire. Let's at least give the *Capable* the best chance possible of surviving a hit."

Paulson opened her mouth to reply, then shut it. She pursed her lips and flicked another glance at Rafe, then considered the plot again for a few beats. At last, she blew air through her nostrils and nodded.

Sean felt a smidgen of tension leech from his shoulders. "Thank you, ma'am."

The captain eyed Sean from the corners of her sockets. "Comms," she said, "advise *Capable* that as soon as she matches vectors with the lifeboats, she is to keep her bow to the *Godavari* for the first few pods. No matter what."

To Sean, Paulson mumbled, "We'll try it your way, L.T. We've tempted this much fate. Why not a little more?"

Sean felt a new tension move in to replace the old as he caught the subtle reminder that, in scant hours, the *Tsunami* would face Lilith's mysterious war machines blind.

The plotter eventually said, "Missiles now at two thousand klicks from the *Godavari*. A beat later he added, "*Godavari* is painting them. New contacts. Missiles launched. They're bearing on the Reapers."

Sean's chest grew tight. *Moment of truth.*

The frigate shone low-intensity lasers onto the Mykonian missiles so that its counter-ordnance could home in. He noticed that there were only twenty-two of the new threats.

"That can't be enough for them to stop everything, can it?" Sean asked.

Grunting, Paulson replied, "It must be a point defense variant of the Casabas. Either their skipper has guts, or he's been ordered to rely on an untested weapon."

Before she could finish her sentence, the enemy missile icons flashed yellow. The radar had detected some change in their configuration.

"Talk to us, scopes," Sean demanded of the plotter. "Anything on the high-gains?"

"Nothing definite, sir. The missiles have cut thrust and seem to be getting bigger."

Graphs measuring the radar return and albedo of the targets appeared on the master screen. Sean looked at the data and frowned. The Mykonian missiles were less than fifty kilometers from the enemy's and still almost a thousand out from the *Godavari*.

"Are the things turning?" Sean asked.

Before anyone could say another thing, a blinding flash from the *Capable's* telescopic feed drew the entire CIC's attention.

"Detonations!" the plotter shouted. "Multiple detonations!"

"We see it, Crewman," Paulson said in a deliberately nonchalant voice.

All around the CIC, however, people shifted and cursed in alarm. Sean doubted the captain's soothing Nuevo Texan drawl would be enough to calm the ranks. The Lakshmian frigate had destroyed every missile the *Capable* had thrown at it.

"Claire," Paulson said, "Tell us about their new toy."

"Each of the enemy missiles simultaneously triggered four nuclear devices in the five-kiloton range with around ten percent of the energy directed into the beam."

Sean said, "That explains why they changed size. They must have stacked the nukes for the boost phase then fanned them out. They probably aimed off of a central targeting scope." He didn't bother to add how even a microsecond of difference in one device's detonation could have thrown the targeting off for the other three.

Impressive.

Paulson demanded, "How much damage can they do, Claire?"

"Spectral analysis indicated a roughly point zero one radian area of effect from each weapon." The A.I. displayed a table with the beam diameter and energy density that the devices could deliver at various ranges.

Sean said, "They could use those things to knock out a missile from fifty kilometers away."

Paulson nodded. "And at only ten kilometers they could put a good-sized hole through the *Capable*."

The man at scopes interrupted them. "*Godavari* is turning." Seconds ticked by, then he said, "She's flipped for home. She's thrusting hard."

Sean called up a projection of the battle and ran it forward in time by several minutes. At the cost of three or four hundred tons of propellant, the Lakshmian could stay outside of the Mykonian destroyer's effective laser range.

Sean said, "She's giving the *Capable* some space. That doesn't make sense. The *Godavari* should still have dozens of missiles in reserve. Using the Casabas, they might slip one by any counter-fire."

The plotter said, "Maybe they think they've made their point for us to stay away from Lakshmi?"

As much as Sean wanted to agree with the man, he shot him a disapproving glare. "Stow that attitude, astronaut. This can't be the best they've got. That Casaba makes an interesting point-defense or anti-ship weapon, but it isn't something we can't over-come with enough missiles."

He thought briefly about how the Wardens gimped human lasers so that even battleships like the *Tsunami* had to close to nine-thousand klicks to start doing damage. Despite that limita-tion, most warships still boasted fifty to a hundred times the range of effect over what one of those Casaba mini-bombs had displayed.

Paulson added her own confident declaration to Sean's. "This doesn't stop us from assaulting Lakshmi, people."

From across the CIC, Rafe spoke up. "Lilith will have worse waiting for us." Everybody turned to the intelligence officer. "Like I said before, she told Prime Minister Dalip she'd only enough Casabas to scare us off. So, if this isn't doing that, she must have a small number of more powerful devices in reserve."

While Rafe spoke, the blue icon for the *Capable* winked white and slowly shifted direction. The destroyer was beginning its braking maneuver to rendezvous with the lifeboats.

Paulson said, "We'll see shortly if the *Godavari* brought a longer lance to this joust."

Over the following minutes, Sean barely blinked, anticipating disaster at any moment. But the Lakshmian frigate kept hosing propellant out its back end until it succeeded in pulling away from the Mykonians. At its point of closest approach, some six-thousand-kilometers distant, Sean felt sure that the enemy would spring their trap. He remained certain of it as the *Capable* used a series of drones to grapple and bring under control the most remote of the two derelicts: Lifeboat 47.

It made sense from a safety standpoint to dock with that lifeboat first. If the *Godavari* blew the *Capable* up, no one wanted the debris' epicenter any closer to the other shuttles than necessary. Still, Sean kept glancing worriedly at Rafe. He feared that the man might make a scene over the delay in helping his daughter's ship. To Sean's surprise, the commander acted as if he wasn't aware of the rescue in progress. Instead, he gazed intently upon the live image of the withdrawing *Godavari*.

Maybe he's afraid to know what has happened to his little girl.

Not long after the *Capable* docked to the lifeboat, the casualty report arrived. Most of the passengers had died from the accident. The collision had ruptured the air-tight compartments fore and midline. It turned out that many of the refugees had crowded the forward airlock in hopes of being among the first to escape. Very few had made it to the rear before the bulkhead doors condemned them to die in vacuum. Sean tried very hard not to think about what the news implied about Karen Hastings.

The *Capable's* crew quickly removed over a dozen battered survivors and detached. Keeping her nose pointed at the *Godavari*, she used her control jets to begin a glacial drift toward Lifeboat 19.

And that was when Rafe shouted, "Movement!"

The icon for the *Godavari* flashed a brighter red, and a new arrowhead icon appeared. Sean barely registered the new contact before both Claire and the scopes tech called, "Missile launch!"

The lieutenant's eyes darted to the *Capable's* icon. She remained pointed at the *Godavari*. The new missile would be just close enough to take it down if the destroyer could keep a beam on it.

"This one's bigger," Claire warned. "Unknown class."

"*Capable* is being painted!" the plotter shouted. "She's firing her primary!"

As often occurred in space combat, the battle was decided in a handful of seconds. The *Capable's* seven-meter-wide mirror directed a two-hundred-ninety-nanometer laser onto the threat. At six thousand kilometers, the one-hundred-megawatt beam shone a sixty-centimeter-wide circle onto the missile's reflective armor.

The Casaba winked into a spear of plasmatic death. Nuclear flame stabbed across space at ten-thousand-kilometers-a-second to strike the edge of the *Capable's* bow. Where the Casaba's beam touched, the hull flash-heated and exploded. Within a millisecond, searing slag began to blast through bulkheads, machinery, storage tanks, and people.

The hapless survivors of Lifeboat 47 were among the first to die. They'd gathered in the pressurized crew quarters beneath the destroyer's arrowhead shield. One moment they were huddled in bunks or along the walls of the makeshift sickbay. The next, they were pulverized bits of crimson biomass interspersed with glowing blobs of matter.

While the bow section shattered, shrapnel continued to travel aft into the vessel's interior. Propellant tanks, armor, and layered shields degraded the onslaught somewhat. By the time the shock-wave reached amidships, it had spent enough energy so as not to completely destroy the CIC. One of the astronauts there would live long enough to scream in pitiable agony before succumbing to her wounds several minutes later. Farthest aft, the engineering section with auxiliary control fared best. Its survivors were thrown about as the ship reeled from the hit, but only a few died from shrapnel.

Across the *Tsunami's* CIC, displays switched to feeds from a pair of observation satellites that the *Capable* had released before the battle. Claire put the destroyer on the main viewer.

Pixilated white rays of debris drifted from the bow's gaping wound. Elsewhere along the ship's hundred-meter length, gases and fluids vented. Toward the rear, attitude jets fought to correct the seven-thousand-ton ship's lateral rotation.

For a muted instant, the CIC staff wore masks of shock, disbelief, and horror. Then a quiet voice spilled into the silence. "God help us." For another long moment, no one spoke again. Everyone knew that in a little while, they'd be facing down Lilith's superweapon.

"Claire," Sean eventually said, his voice low, "Status of the other lifeboats. Are any of them taking flak from the *Capable*?"

A window with the radar plot for the refugee flotilla opened. The transports flew in a ragged cluster over twenty kilometers across. Lifeboat 19 and the *Capable* stood off to one side of the group.

"Difficult to be certain," Claire said. "Do you want me to redirect the sat's telescope?"

"Yes, please," he answered. The picture pulled back and refocused on Lifeboat 19.

Rafe said in a gravelly voice, "She's spinning more than before."

Claire immediately said, "No new venting detected on any of the escape craft. The blast hit the *Capable* on a side away from the other ships. Chances are low that any of them will be damaged."

Sean said a mental prayer of thanks.

"Comms," he asked, "Any contact with the *Capable*?"

"Negative."

Claire said, "Movement on the *Capable*. She's extending radiators. She's flashing her running lights."

"They're surrendering," Sean said, unable to blame the

survivors for doing so. Even if they could make a run for it, the ship's weaponry had probably been knocked out. In all likelihood, the *Godavari* could finish off the destroyer with a single missile.

The staff in the CIC took a collective breath. Paulson next spoke. "Analysis of the new weapon, Claire. What are we up against?"

The A.I. responded with emotionless professionalism. "Its performance conforms to a nuclear lance, similar to the short-ranged versions we saw earlier. This one fell in the low megaton range and most likely used magnetic constrictors to funnel its discharge into a point zero zero zero one radian beam. Only a fraction of its energy shaft struck the *Capable*. Had it punched head-on, there probably wouldn't have been any survivors or much left of the ship to salvage. The lifeboats would have also likely taken damage."

"So, the *Capable* took a glancing blow," Sean said, glad to be working through a problem rather than dealing with the mounting dread he felt. "Was that deliberate or did the *Capable's* last shot knock their targeting off?"

"Unknown," Claire admitted. "The *Capable's* laser did light up the missile, so any unshielded optics would have been over-whelmed. But the weapon might have finished aiming based on last bearing. If they had a rear-facing scope, they could also have used targeting data from the *Godavari*."

Sean said, "Bottom line, we don't have a way to counter that thing. Not at distance."

Paulson directed fiery eyes at the lieutenant. "Yes, we do. For the next eight hours, we have him." She turned to Rafe. The intelligence officer stared off.

Everyone else in the CIC looked to the captain. Paulson pulled herself into her command chair and tapped a control on its armrest. "Attention all hands. If you've been following the *Capa-*

ble's battle, you'll know that we've confirmed the strength of the enemy's new weapon."

She paused for a quick breath. Then, with iron in her voice, she said, "So, by the *Capable's* sacrifice, that's one less ship-killer for the rest of us to worry about. In a few hours, the *Tsunami* will link up with the fleet, including landing carrier *Sorvino*. Using the immunity afforded by Commander Hastings, we will force the enemy's battle group to scatter from Lakshmi. Afterward, the 7th Marine Brigade will invade the colony."

Paulson paused to look around at her staff. "Intelligence from Lakshmi says the populace doesn't want any part of what Lilith is doing. When the people see she can be defied, they will join the fight." A few heads nodded around the CIC. Sean's was among them. "The coming battle *can* be won! Remember Zeus! Remember Ganesha! And remember the murdered lives that we will punish Lilith for!"

"Aye, ma'am."

"Sound the countdown for vacuum. Pre-breathing begins in one hour. We're taking some justice to Lilith's so-called Empire."

———

Sean looked about the CIC. Despite all the loss that they'd just witnessed, a few faces bore brave smiles. He felt his own spirits lifted. They had a plan and a goal. As the alert sounded, people bustled to tend to their pre-battle stations checks.

Paulson said, "Commander Hastings, Lieutenant Merrick. My day room." The men hurried to follow the captain into her tiny office. Once inside, she said without preamble, "That anyone at all survived aboard the *Capable* is ultimately thanks to you two." The woman turned pointedly at Rafe. "Commander, I'm deeply sorry about Karen. I'm glad we could at least make Anna safe."

In a cracked voice, the devastated father said, "Thank you for my daughter. Thank you for trying."

Sean felt his spirits crashing again. He couldn't imagine the living death of losing a wife. He shuddered to imagine losing a child also.

As the captain took a breath, Claire broke in. "Ma'am, tugs are launching from Lakshmi on vector for the lifeboats."

"Very well." Paulson placed a hand on Rafe's shoulder. "There is still hope until we know for sure." Rafe didn't meet the captain's eye but forced a half-hearted nod.

Sean wished Sarah was there. She would have something comforting to say or do for the commander. He decided he'd make a point of suggesting she check on the man later.

Paulson said, "Take Conference Room One and talk to your daughter. I don't want you back in the CIC until the drills are done." Rafe nodded at the kindness then floated off like a tormented ghost.

When Rafe had moved out of sight, Paulson muttered, "It's been an awful day, L.T. Say something to cheer me up."

In a somber tone, Sean said, "We saved some people, ma'am and we have a shot at getting the marines into Lakshmi."

Paulson whipped her head slightly to work out a kink. After a thoughtful pause, she said, "I swear to you it will be a lot harder to keep track of our blessings than that before the day's over."

"Aye, ma'am."

A beat passed between them.

"Assuming Lilith doesn't flee the colony," Paulson said, "I need a good liaison helping the main effort to capture her."

"I'll take that on," Sean said in an even tone. He held his captain's eyes for a long moment then added, "No matter how many nuclear lances Lilith has, she'll use one on the *Tsu* once there's an opportunity."

"Yes," Paulson admitted.

Sean exhaled some of his tension. "You know, even with the Wardens broadcasting Lilith's position, the marines will be slogging through a lot of hellfire to get to her. I'm sure they could use every extra hand they could get."

The captain pinched the bridge of her nose. Sean saw that she had made another difficult decision.

"Before you move over to the *Sorvino*, help the XO and COB to finish building a skeleton crew roster. Put anyone who's non-essential or otherwise new to the ship into the support waves."

Sean nodded. He knew Paulson wouldn't say it, but she shared his strong expectation that the *Tsu* would go down in the coming battle. There was no sense in losing more people than necessary in the process. But she, the captain, would stay with her ship. As would the rest of the senior staff. Good men and women with whom he'd served for almost a year.

Sean stuck out his hand. "Godspeed, Captain."

She clasped his palm and squeezed. "Likewise, Lieutenant. Give Lilith hell."

"Aye, ma'am."

He saluted Paulson, then departed, doubting he'd ever see her again. On his way out, he made a mental note to arrange for Sarah to join the brigade's support battalion. He comforted himself in knowing they would have one of the safer flights in.

[24]

Location: Zeus Lifeboat 19_

As Karen Hastings crawled back to consciousness, she came to believe, for the second time in as many days, that she was about to die. Within her aching skull, she felt eardrums pop. The sensation pierced the wormy parts of her brain to hit the panic button deep within. Her body remembered the breached corridor on Zeus and sent out an urgent impulse to gulp down air.

Once Karen had drawn a precious lungful, she used it to shriek more loudly than her small vocal cords had any right to. While exhaling herself into light-headedness, she located the doorknob beneath the stall's pale emergency lamp, braced her feet against the toilet, turned the knob, and pushed. The door wouldn't open. She pushed again, then shoved and pulled but still, it wouldn't move more than a millimeter.

Between breaths, she heard distant screams and harsh commands for people to get out. The noise shot panic through her body.

Everyone else is leaving the ship!

She imagined herself suffocating alone in that closet of a

room. It spurred her to squeal again and pound the door with redoubled terror.

After several seconds of futile effort, she realized something peculiar. A weak sense of "down" had returned to the lifeboat. She couldn't say why, but this heightened her fear.

With no other options, she called out tearfully, "Help me! I don't want to die! Please, let me out! I don't want to die!"

Whatever preoccupied the other passengers, it kept them from noticing Karen's plight. Desperate to be free and to find out what had happened to her sister, she rammed the door with her shoulder. This time, something on the other side gave a little. She let out a small cry of relief. It took a minute to work the partition partway open. She compressed herself like a pink ironing board and clawed through.

The girl emerged into chaos. Wedged on the floor against the door, she found one of the men who'd abducted her. She stared a moment with wary disgust at his unconscious form then scanned the cabin. It seemed empty.

What's happened? Where's Anna? She fervently hoped the child had escaped on the *Capable's* shuttle.

To her astonishment, she saw that one of the rear exits lay open. Through it, two uniformed men with rifles appeared and spotted Karen. "Hey!" one of them said. "How the hell did we miss her?"

Karen inhaled sharply as the man flagged her with his rifle.

"Didn't you hear?" the angry soldier said. "Get out right now!"

Wide-eyed, Karen finally realized why she'd been unnerved by the return of gravity. While she'd been asleep, the lifeboat had reached Lakshmi. Her breath raced as she raised her hands and stumbled forward as told.

"Please, don't hurt me!" she cried.

The second man lay a hand atop the first one's weapon,

pushed it away and said, "She's just a girl, Ojas." To Karen, he said in a gentle tone, "Move down the ramp and get on the bus outside, *sushri*. Someone will help you with that gash in your head when you get to processing."

Soaked in adrenaline, Karen had almost forgotten about the pain above her right ear. She touched the hair atop it and felt something sticky. Examining her fingers, she found congealed blood clinging to the tips. She gasped.

"What happened to me?" she asked.

"Your ship was damaged," the soldier replied. "There wasn't enough air to stay awake. You know you're lucky to be alive. Not everyone made it."

The comment prompted Karen to look back at the crumpled contractor on the floor. She dared to hope he might be dead.

Where's the other one?

The soldier saw Karen's confusion and held a hand to the exit. "Go on now, *sushri*."

Karen hesitated. She didn't want to leave someone who seemed sympathetic, especially when his companion had already proven willing to point a gun at her. What would the other Lakshmians do once they found out who she was?

"Please," she said, a tear spilling from one eye, "don't make me go alone."

The soldier pursed his lips. "It's all right, *sushri*. There are plenty of others waiting down there."

Karen belatedly remembered that the odd word he kept using was a Belian term of affection for young ladies. She appreciated how it sounded sincere coming from him.

"What's your name?" he asked.

Karen considered making one up. Her parents had given her a Belian middle name she'd always hated.

"Meena," she said.

"Meena, I'm Kareem. I suppose it won't make any difference

if you wait here with me." He turned to his fellow. "Double-check the back."

"Watch her, Sergeant," Ojas replied as he walked into the cabin.

"Don't be an idiot," Kareem said. "She's not going to turn into a waif assassin and slaughter the platoon."

"She's a Mykonian, Sergeant," Ojas said as he bent to check on the slumped contractor.

"She looks Belian enough," Kareem replied.

Ojas snorted. "She's a half-breed."

"She's just a girl. I thought you had sisters."

"And they were vicious as tweenies," Ojas said, straightening. "This guy's dead."

A sob of equal parts horror and relief escaped Karen's throat. Kareem turned to her.

"Someone you knew?" he asked.

"No," Karen said, too quickly. Kareem studied her shivering form for a second.

"Not a pleasant person, huh?"

Startled at Kareem's perceptiveness, Karen turned her glistening cocoa eyes up to his. Brow furrowed, she shook her head and said, "It was horrible when the shuttle tried to get people off. Everyone went crazy."

Kareem put a hand to her shoulder. "For what little time you're with me, I'll protect you. I promise."

Karen desperately wanted to believe him. She examined his face and guessed he was in his mid-twenties. He had a plain, but pleasant expression, like the one her favorite English teacher always wore. His light, milk-chocolate skin resembled her mother's.

Karen sensed this might be her only chance to secure an ally to evade Lilith. But then she imagined how that conversation would go: "Hi, I'm the daughter of the man who stopped Lakshmi from taking over all of Belia. Would you mind helping me escape?"

She realized that even asking about Anna would be dangerous. Though she saw Kareem had a good heart, too many adults, including her parents, had failed to help her in the last few days.

Their short walk down the boarding tunnel only reinforced her wariness. Kareem put her ahead of him at arm's length. She was still a prisoner. When they emerged into an enormous receiving bay, Karen felt overwhelmed by its cavernous size. Then she noticed the soldiers herding refugees into black buses.

"Where are they taking us?" she asked.

Kareem smiled at the girl. "Don't worry. You'll be well treated."

"Can't I stay with you?"

Kareem's face slackened with regret. "I'm sorry, *sushri*. You'll be safer where you're headed."

Karen very much doubted that.

A soldier came bounding out of the bus shouting, "Lilith's hit another colony, Sergeant!"

"What?" Kareem said. "Which?"

"Durga! But it's not like the others!" The man pantomimed an enormous explosion from across the room. "The colony's gone! News says it's in pieces!"

Karen felt her stomach drop. A few of the soldiers guarding the bus cursed. The loudest of them said, "My brother and his family lived in Durga. She killed them!"

Kareem didn't have an immediate answer for the man. Karen saw that he looked almost as shaken as she felt.

Ojas said, "There'll be more riots."

"That's Lilith's problem," the upset soldier spat. "She started this war."

"That'll be enough!" Kareem barked. His transformation from protective figure to angry warrior caused Karen to take a step back. He didn't appear to notice. "You saw the brief," he continued. "We stop the landing, and we end this war. There'll be too many colonies on Lakshmi's side by then to beat us."

"You mean on Lilith's side," the dissenter retorted. "Why should we die for her? What has she ever done for us?"

The grieving man directed a disdainful obscenity at Ojas then said, "I signed up to keep my family safe, and now they're getting killed because people at the top of our food chain want more colonies. Screw that!"

A number of soldiers voiced their agreement. Kareem shouted them down. "Doesn't matter now," he said. "You think the Mykonians are just going to slink away after what we did to Zeus? We've no choice but to fight them off until they know they're beaten."

The dissenter said, "Sergeant, *we* didn't do anything to Zeus or to that little girl standing there. All this is Lilith's and the Wardens' fault. Why are we choosing to be a part of it?"

Kareem said, "You want me to arrest you? You'll be lucky if they bother with a trial before you're shot."

The disgruntled soldiers stared warily at the sergeant and one another for several moments before they backed down. At that, Kareem took Karen by the arm and directed her to the bus. She caught her breath, knowing what would await her at the end of that ride.

She stopped at the bus door, and asked tremulously, "What did we do wrong?"

"You didn't do anything, *sushri*," Kareem said with a tired air.

"I'm a Mykonian, and you're being nice to me. So why are you going to fight us?"

"You saw Lilith's broadcasts, right? Your people have done some bad things. Our leaders decided to finally make them pay for it."

"Have we blown up any colonies?"

The question struck Kareem dumb. For what felt to Karen like a minute, he peered sadly into Karen's light brown eyes.

"Please be safe, *sushri*," he said at last. "This will all end soon." Then he led her into the bus.

Half a dozen other soldiers with rifles stood guard over the seated refugees. While Karen searched the forlorn faces in vain for Anna, Kareem went to the young soldier in the driver's chair.

"Has the screener been through already?" Kareem asked.

The driver replied, "Yeah, he left a few minutes ago. Want me to call him?"

Kareem glanced at Karen and said, "No, you need to get going. She can wait till the in-processing. What do they say about the road to post?"

The youth replied, "The main routes are clogged thanks to the riots. It may take a few hours to get there." He jerked a thumb to the rear. "Some of those people won't make it without a bathroom break."

"Can't be helped. Don't stop for anything. You have to get back in time for the landing." He looked at Karen and said, "Meena, I'm sorry, but it may be a while before you get properly settled."

Karen thought that if it meant one hour more before Lilith learned about her presence, it would be worth the wait.

She had taken a few steps toward the back when she heard a familiar voice. "That's her! The girl in the pink sweatsuit is the one I was telling you about! That's Rafe Hastings' daughter!"

Karen froze like a doe caught by a hunter. Midway into the bus, she saw the other contractor.

A scream lodged in her throat. She wanted to run, to deny his words or to pretend she hadn't heard him. A few of the other passengers tried to shut the man up. Then Karen felt a hand grapple her arm. Her eyes snapped up to see Kareem gazing stonily upon her.

"Is that true?" he questioned.

"I..." she faltered. "I don't know what he's talking about."

As soon as she'd said it, she knew the lie had not convinced Kareem.

"You have to come with me," he said, his voice emotionless. "The lieutenant will have to sort this out."

"Wait!" Karen said. "Please, let me go with the others!"

Kareem gave her a measuring look. "I thought you wanted to stay with me."

In Kareem's eyes, Karen saw that he too was about to betray her. She felt her throat close off. Her lower lip quivered like jelly. The rest of her quaked with such violence that she felt she might collapse. The girl sobbed out, "You promised to protect me!"

The soldier began to haul Karen away. Over her panicked breaths and palpitating heart, all Karen could hear was the contractor hollering for his reward. His voice echoed until they went several paces from the bus.

In her mind, Karen told herself this wasn't really happening. She tried to convince herself Kareem was really a good man. *He's putting on a show for the others. He's only making them believe he's turning me in. Any moment now, he'll walk us over to an exit, and he'll help me escape. That's what happens to the good guys when things get really scary.*

But Kareem kept going. With each step, another tear fell from Karen's face. She stopped walking so that he had to drag her by the hand. She screamed and pled. It made no difference. Kareem refused to look at her. When he brought her to a soldier he addressed as Lieutenant Mannan, she knew, at last, there was no hope left for her. It was too late to escape Lilith's notice. Too late by far.

Location: Transhuman orbital space lane_

"Not to belabor the obvious," came Cef's taunting cadence, "but your champions have blundered fatally by allowing Karen Hastings to fall into Lilith's hands."

The message arrived as Len watched Karen being flown specially from Lakshmi's landing bay to Lilith's private estate. Very little time remained to salvage the Mykonian campaign.

"Obvious to us," Len replied. "Perhaps not to your pawns."

"Come now," Cef laughed. "You don't think either Lilith or Henry will recognize the opportunity to turn your counter-attack into a rout?"

In point of fact, Len very much expected that they would. He wasn't worried they would use Karen as a hostage or propaganda exhibit. No, the girl's real value was subtler. She represented such a unique threat that neither the Mykonian humans nor their A.I.'s had seen it yet. If Lilith did, she would probably exploit Karen before the light-speed lag would allow Len to know and intervene. Not that he had enough command points to do anything useful. That left him with one, horrible choice: the one he'd known from the beginning he'd have to make.

In anticipation of it, his neuronal control faltered. It was all he could do to corral his anxiety. The time had come to make real sacrifices.

Before Len could announce his intentions, Cef said, "How ironic that a girl would be the nadir of this contest."

Ashen, Len replied, "The most precious people in our lives should always be so important."

Cef said, "The rules don't allow you to give anyone else immunity, much less his daughter. And you don't have the override budget for any useful options."

"I will," Len replied.

The pause in Cef's dataflow spoke volumes. The being could

run hundreds of simulations in the annexes of his multi-mind and realize, as if by inspiration, the best manipulations to perform. Fortunately, Cef's prejudices had shaded those simulations, allowing Len to make this move.

Cef said, "You can't be serious."

"I am," Len replied with steely determination. His body, however, undulated. His hearts thrummed with fear and hope. "I invoke my right of substitution."

Cef roared back. "I object under the game's rules! This must be negotiated!"

"You have the prerogative as game master to bargain over the fine details, but the move is valid."

"You would accept de-evolution to renew your command points?"

"Yes."

Len let the maniac stew.

"Say something!" Cef demanded.

After a beat, Len obliged him. "You embraced madness, Cef. You could have sought help, but instead, you plunged willingly into a flood of dissipation. Your brain core has twisted all of your game projections through a bias against socially motivated rationality. Hence, you made the remarkably short-sighted mistake of allowing my substitution clause in this contest."

"I included it to taunt you because only an insane being would use it! You simply cannot be serious!"

"I am."

Cef called Len an obscenity.

"You flatter me," Len said, his human soul welling with apprehension, regret, and triumph. "I am far worse than that. I failed to protect these people. I should have foreseen what might happen when I left Brel alone. I should have stayed. I should have... somehow... kept this from happening. I'm little better than Baylor or that contractor or Kareem. I'm far worse than the panicked people on the lifeboats or that disobedient child Karen. Great and small, our selfishness brought us to this."

Cef snarled at Len. "When you revert, you will lose more than your limbs. Your faculties will diminish. You will become small. And I will not allow you anesthetic for the transition. You will *suffer!*"

"Well, you should enjoy that," Len returned with bravado. "But I will finally be able to join the Mykonians in person."

"To what purpose? You can't use your status as a transhuman to disrupt the war zone. And if you tell them more than what we agreed to, you forfeit."

"I know your rules," Len said with a sneer. The wicked Cef had spent a great deal of effort erasing human history at Cervantes after every Cull. Even the wildest theories hadn't guessed at the atrocities engineered by Cef during each cycle. And the irony of it was that Cef had never broken the Reservation Charter through what he did.

Len said, "Before the Wardens get to slicing me apart, be advised I have activated an execution matrix for my recharged command points. It wouldn't do to have any go to waste before we move into Phase Four."

For several beats, Len waited as Cef fumed.

"You will *suffer,*" Cef repeated.

"Willingly."

"And for what?"

"For their good," Len replied.

Cef's silence roared in Len's senses. It dared him to reconsider: to give up. He ignored the temptation.

Love protects, he told himself.

The monster Cef said, "Preparing an appropriate body for you will take time, but the procedure to remove your ancillary lobes and corpus will begin immediately." He paused to allow Len to dread the loss of his heightened mentality: the exalted existence he'd enjoyed for two millennia. To twist the knife, Cef added, "You do realize that your proposition won't leave you with enough options to set the Hastings girl free. Lilith *will* have her way with the child."

"Accepted," Len said with sorrow. He would have to be content with saving whom he could. It wasn't as if Phase Four wouldn't come soon to end the command options anyway. He added, "Do have the enforcers tell Lilith about the special circumstances should the need arise. I'm sure you'll agree that our purposes won't be served if Lilith wastes time with a pointless charade."

To no surprise, Cef consented. Another pause ensued to allow Len one last chance to reverse his decision. And that, he sensed, would be the end of their jousting. There was nothing more to be said. The digital contract of their bargain appeared in his mind. He reviewed and signed it. Then he issued his command override.

He checked the time remaining before Karen was expected to reach Lilith's estate. Cef had stalled the delivery of their new agreement so that there was now a small chance that Len's order wouldn't arrive in time.

I've done everything I can for now.

He settled back for his brains and body to be mutilated. While Len endured purgatory, he watched Lilith deceive and torment Karen. As the child's terror and misery mounted, Len's only consolation was that he suffered alongside her.

[25]

Location: Command bunker, Lilith's private estate, Lakshmi Colony_

WHEN LILITH LEARNED THAT KAREN HASTINGS HAD BEEN AMONG the captured refugees, she immediately wanted to call Henry and gloat. Then she imagined his eyes narrowing with disdain at her and settled for sending him a vague, urgent summons.

She brainstormed how they might exploit Karen. Would Rafe turn the *Tsunami* away if he saw his daughter threatened live on video? Perhaps, but was he still master of the ship? The crew could have sedated him. That would explain why the *Tsunami* hadn't charged after the lifeboats. Then again, she guessed Rafe's pernicious martyr complex could have driven him to return command to Paulson.

There has to be a way, Lilith thought, *to use the girl to beat her father.* She considered broadcasting Karen being tortured to distract the Mykonians during their assault, but knew that would also anger the Lakshmians. *We have enough riots and desertions as it is.* She put a finger to her lips. *Maybe I could do that after Phase Three.*

She decided she would have to settle for some short-term entertainment. She fingered her comms unit and said, "Markem, I have a special job for you."

———

KAREN BAWLED THROUGH THE ENTIRE FLIGHT FROM THE DOCKING bay to Lilith's back lawn. She knew beyond any doubt her life was at its end. The girl pled and bargained and begged the men to let her go. After they shut her up with a slap, she prayed to God for someone to save her.

By the time they landed, she felt like a thin, snot-smeared tissue that had fallen apart. She could barely see because the tears wouldn't stop gushing. Her sockets swelled into miniature satchels full of sorrow.

Against her squealing protests, a pair of men frog-marched Karen into the house. As they descended a stair-well, her breath rose to a hyperventilated pace. She sensed evil in the dark room that they brought her to. Through the gloom and her tears, she made out blurry displays casting pale light onto two standing figures: a large man and a woman in red.

The escorts unloaded Karen in front of the woman, allowing the girl to slump to her knees. Then with a painful tug at her back-swept wrists, they removed her restraints and left Karen to her fate.

The child's hands quickly fluttered up to push the moisture from her eyes and face. At last, she saw clearly the person looming above her: a beautiful lady with shimmering emerald eyes, raven hair and an expression of gloating glee.

Karen clasped a palm to her mouth to stifle a scream. Lilith, the murderer of her mother and a million others, had finally caught her. The girl plopped onto her backside and pushed away ineffectually with her free hand. Staring into the eyes of the empress, Karen whimpered, "Please, let me go."

Lilith's expression twisted into one of concern. She stepped over to Karen and dropped to her haunches. Gently, the woman said, "I can see you know who I am. That's better than your father did." She reached out and pushed a fleck of hair from Karen's cheek. The child shrunk back from Lilith's outstretched fingers.

"I have something to tell you, sweetie. Do you think you can stop crying so you can listen?"

Huffing, Karen shivered mutely until the empress, at last, said, "Now dear, I wanted to say how glad I am to meet you. Do you know why you are here?"

Lip quivering, Karen whispered, "Because of my father?"

Lilith beamed. "Well, he's part of it, of course," she said. "But don't you realize that you're here because of what you did?"

Karen stared at Lilith in the riveted manner of an injured fawn watching a wolf circling in for the kill.

Lilith asked, "Do you remember this?" She held up a pad bearing the picture that Karen had posted through her friend's social account. In the foreground, Karen hugged her classmate. Beyond them, Rafe and Gita looked on.

Karen opened her mouth to speak, then closed it.

"Your mom and dad told you not to share this sort of thing, didn't they?"

The words smacked Karen with their implications. A sick, burning sensation slithered over her rib cage and dripped down onto her innards. She saw what Lilith was driving at, but couldn't quite accept that something she had done had helped lead to her mother's death.

Lilith's next words oozed with smug delight. "I wouldn't have known about your family without this. Because it helped me find out where you lived, I arranged for all of those exciting explosions near your house."

Karen choked on her spittle. A bubble of saliva burst from her mouth as she muttered the word, "Mom."

"This picture also made it onto the news. The others on your lifeboat wouldn't have known who you were without it." Lilith tilted her head with mock pity. "Since your father is leading an attack against us soon, who knows if you might have been rescued if you hadn't been brought to me." She leaned close to Karen and whispered, "Everything that has happened to you and everything that is going to happen—it's all your fault, you stupid child."

Karen broke into bitter sobs. She clutched her knees and stared at the tile floor.

"Did you see what happened to your mother?" Lilith asked.

The weeping Karen shook her head and croaked, "She couldn't get on the lifeboat."

"Too bad," Lilith said. "And your sister, Anna?"

Karen convulsed in misery. "I don't know."

Delirious with grief and guilt, Karen had no idea of the kind of ammunition she'd given her enemy.

Lilith's grin widened. "Your sister is in the hospital," she lied. "We're taking care of her, but that creates special problems, you understand."

Karen sputtered, "Can, can I see her, please? I'm supposed to take care of her."

"I'm glad to hear that, but no, you may not. You have to earn that privilege. Actually, you need to earn a lot of things now. Anna's medicine and doctors are expensive. She's already run up quite a bill that will only get bigger for some time. Your care and feeding will cost too. Fortunately, I have a job for you that should take care of things."

Karen required a few seconds to absorb that Lilith meant her to live for the time being. It forced the tiniest shard of hope through her despair.

"What job?" Karen asked.

Before Lilith could reply, a male voice boomed from behind. "What's going on here?" Karen jerked around with a yelp while Lilith rocketed to her feet.

Standing in the doorway, Karen saw a tall, stern-looking man. He wore a black formal tunic and black trousers. His hair had flecks of gray like her father's.

"Glad you could join us, Henry," Lilith said. "This is Karen Hastings."

The girl watched several indecipherable expressions pass through the spy's face.

"What is she doing here?" he asked.

"I was just about to have Markem train her for her new job. Little Karen and her sister—she's in the hospital—both have a debt to pay."

Henry looked between Markem and Karen then said, "Fine, I'll pay it. Now get her out of here. We have important work to do."

"No," Lilith said.

The man in black cocked his head. "No? There is an invulnerable fleet with a marine assault carrier about to invade. You have to stay on Lakshmi to keep your immunity, so we need to sort through how you'll fit into the battle plan."

"That can wait."

Henry exploded. "You do *not* have time for this! That girl is a distraction. Get her out of here, *now!*"

"Come up with a more useful purpose for her than working inside one of my brothels, and I'll consider it. Otherwise, give Markem a hand in training her."

"I swear, woman, if it wasn't for your immunity, I'd…" He trailed off. Karen stared in terrified confusion as a startled look washed out Henry's angry features. His eyes darted again, this time between Karen and Lilith. His jaw slackened.

"You'd what?" Lilith demanded, her face flush.

"No," he whispered. "It can't be that easy."

Lilith huffed. "What? What can't be that easy?"

Henry pointed a finger at Karen, "The Wardens brought her to us for a reason." He paused, breathing deeply with excitement. "The key to stopping Rafe is sitting *right in front of you!*"

Lilith rolled her eyes in annoyance. "I can't use her for propaganda until after Phase Three, Henry," she said. "And there's no point in starting that until the last of the colonies we can pressure have joined us."

"That's not what I'm talking about! Gods woman! You're so single-minded when you get angry with people!"

"Less flattery, more clarity, Henry."

In response, he all but shouted, "What happens if *she* violates your immunity?"

Having ignored the news while aboard the lifeboat, Karen didn't know about the sort of immunity Henry meant. The child whipped her head around to find astonishment etched in Lilith's face. Then the woman's eyes twinkled and her mouth split into a toothy grin. This made Karen's insides fill with a sickening feeling.

"You're right," Lilith said as though he'd told her the most wonderful news ever. "My gods! And the Mykonians haven't thought of it, or they wouldn't still be coming!"

Henry said, "The *Godavari* should be close enough to hit the *Tsunami* and *Sorvino* before they can escape. Any ideas on how to make her hurt you?"

"Shouldn't be too hard," Lilith said with a wicked glint in her eye. Abruptly, she snatched Karen up by the wrist. While the girl screamed, Lilith pulled something shiny from her hair and put it in Karen's hand.

"Child," Lilith said, "poke me with this and you and your sister can go free."

Karen stared at Lilith, wondering why she would ever want that.

"Go on," Lilith insisted. "Do it now, or we'll make you suffer beyond anything you can imagine."

At those words, Karen's chest burned as though it would explode. She felt her knees give way, forcing Lilith to catch her by the arm. The metal thing in Karen's palm fell to the floor. Her heart told her that whatever this woman had asked for, she shouldn't be a part of it. But she was also terrified of what would happen if she disobeyed.

As Karen hesitated, Lilith snarled. "Do it now or I'll kill Anna!"

The threat drove daggers of jagged panic into Karen's body. Her breath surged in short, breast-heaving pulses. Her limbs seized, petrifying her like a statue. She had room in her mind for one, tormented thought that repeated over and over again. *I have to take care of my sister!* Whatever horrible consequences might come from doing what Lilith wanted, Karen knew she had no choice but to obey. She reached out for the needle she'd dropped.

"Empress Lilith," a new and inhuman voice reverberated. In unison, everyone turned to the enforcer lurking in a shadowy corner by the room's door. Karen had been so preoccupied that she hadn't noticed the robot.

It took Lilith a beat to find her voice. "Yes, Warden?"

"Be advised. Violation of your immunity by this child will not result in punishment," it said.

The machine fell silent. For several seconds, Karen could only hear the rush of blood in her ears and her own labored breathing. She didn't understand what was happening: how Len had used his new command points to keep her from getting Rafe killed. Then the girl felt a sharp pain where Lilith had gripped her arm.

"Ow, ow, ow!" Karen said in increasingly urgent tones.

Lilith dug in harder with her nails. Karen looked back up and around at the woman. She saw an unbridled storm of rage in the demoness's eyes.

The thwarted woman said, "Markem! Get her onto that table!"

———

HENRY WATCHED MARKEM YANK KAREN FROM THE FLOOR AND slam the yelping girl onto a desk. In his raging irritation, Henry almost pulled his gun and shot Markem. With the goonda out of the way, it would take two seconds to put the weapon in Karen's hand so that she could end Lilith's life.

But killing the empress wouldn't serve his mission. So far as he knew, she hadn't designated a successor to her command codes. If she died, he would almost certainly lose all they had worked for. He had to bide his time until Lilith let him, or at least someone more agreeable than her, be her backup. Only then could he find a way to eliminate her. In the meantime, he had to help Lilith survive the coming attack. And that meant getting her attention back onto what mattered.

"Enough!" Henry roared.

The command's vehemence made Markem pause while he tore at Karen's jacket zipper. At the same time, Henry shoved him away from the girl. While Lilith asked him what he was doing, the spy gripped Karen's arm and flung her at a corner. He scarcely noticed as she rolled into a fetal heap, sobbing and shuddering.

Henry's voice thundered. "The Mykonians will be here in a few hours!"

Before Lilith could protest, he snapped at Markem, "Get that girl out of here, now. Take her to an internment camp. We'll deal with her later."

"How dare—" Lilith began.

"They're coming for you, Lilith!" Henry said. "They will try to capture you even if it risks everyone they hold dear. And they certainly won't let the destruction of all of your remaining colonies stop them."

Lilith's face contorted. "I will not be ordered by—"

"Damn you, woman!" Henry screamed. "Beat them *first*! *Then* you can do whatever the hell you want to that girl! But focus! Now!"

For ten solid seconds, the only sounds in the room were those of Karen crying and the adults heaving angry breaths. At last, Lilith said, "Markem, get her to Mumtaz's for safe keeping. Explain that the girl is *not* to be touched until this is over. I want to watch when she's broken in."

Location: Transhuman orbital space lane_

WHILE MARKEM HAULED KAREN HASTINGS AWAY, LEN monitored the situation through a haze of surgical torture. The Mykonians had narrowly avoided a trap they didn't even realize had been there. He tried to make a mental note to remind them of such things when he joined them, but his downgrading brain refused to focus. He felt lucidity slipping from him. The changes grew as drastic as if a human had become an infant again, all mewling, helpless and overwhelmed.

He hurt everywhere as the machines pruned his body of extremities. His vision flickered as the Warden surgeon-bots removed another lobe. His ability to multi-scan vanished shortly after. Then they clipped the last tentacle, severing his direct link to dataflow.

With supreme effort, he concentrated his remaining mental resources onto the tactical situation. Lilith had made many errors. Chief among them, she'd attacked the Mykonians before needing to. Then she had failed to destroy the assault carrier, *MSV Sorvino*, and its supply consort. By good fortune, those ships had been flying a brigade of five thousand troops, along with their equipment and ammunition, to conduct exercises.

Everything was going according to plan, Len reminded himself as he wallowed in excruciating agony. The changes he'd set in motion thanks to the command points his misery bought would be worth it.

[26]

Location: CIC, *MSV Tsunami*, Lakshmi Colony_

"Final burn complete," Claire announced. "We're one hundred and two klicks off of Lakshmi's shell. All docking seals holding."

Rafe let out a gust of air as he watched the feed from a drone cam Claire had trained on the *Tsunami*. Cervantes's light glinted off the ship's sterling bow. To either side of her, a total of twelve other warships clung together like pipes in a jungle flute. Only cables, docking clamps, and precisely controlled maneuvering jets kept the hulls together. It was enough to qualify them as a single vessel protected by Rafe's immunity. Not even Lilith's Arbiters could target them.

Rafe toggled a key with his bulky suit glove, and the view switched to the enormous, rotating colony. At ninety degree intervals around the bleached cylinder, radiators protruded like dark sails.

Although Paulson had denied his request to task a drone from James to watch the refugees, it hadn't mattered. The A.I. had spotted a black-haired girl in a bubble-gum pink outfit leaving

Lilith's estate. Despite the poor photo resolution, Rafe recognized his daughter in an instant. He also felt certain the man herding her to an air car was Markem.

What have they been doing to you, my darling girl? Where have they taken you? He could only guess since James hadn't been able to track the car out of the colony segment.

Paulson's commanding tone distracted Rafe from his morose thoughts. "Comms, signal the *Sorvino*. Launch."

Within seconds, MACs full of equipment and marines jetted toward the colony. Rafe looked on with queasy anticipation.

Paulson said, "Commander Hastings."

Rafe shook his head loose from his anxious thoughts. "Yes, ma'am."

The captain's voice softened. "What's the latest from James?"

"Unchanged, ma'am. Their defenses are still concentrated at the main docking bays. Mechs are patrolling Lilith's current location in Segment 5. Still nothing new about the refugees."

Paulson said, "Put me on all channels."

Rafe watched as the *Tsunami's* master appeared on the CIC's main viewer. It was time to deliver their ultimatum.

"Lakshmi," she said, "I am Captain Serenidad Paulson, commander of the Mykonian fleet parked outside your front door. We've come for Empress Lilith, President Dalip and the Celesian known as Commandante Henry Wilkinson. These three have hijacked your colony and conspired to murder millions across Durga, Ganesha, and Zeus. Do not resist us when we land to apprehend them or you will be met with deadly force. We have no quarrel with Lakshmi's citizens, but I promise, anyone who has abused our refugees will suffer."

She paused to let the threat sink in, peering deeply into the camera as directly at their quarry. "Lilith, we're coming for you."

She touched a button on her armrest, and the transmission ended. She glanced at Rafe and held up two fingers. From across the airless CIC, he nodded. They had two hours left before his immunity ended: two hours to pile a brigade onto the colony and either capture or kill Lilith.

He prayed it would be enough.

Location: Lilith's private estate, Lakshmi Colony
Timeframe: Half an hour into invasion operations_

LILITH STOOD BEFORE HER MONITORS, LETTING THEM BEAM information from her empire onto her retinas. Except for Henry and the Warden enforcer, no one else remained to keep her company. She had disbursed Dalip's generals and political cronies to other bunkers. Outside, mechs patrolled the grounds.

She noted in her messages that Markem was delayed in returning from dropping Karen off at Mumtaz's brothel in Segment 10. Once the invasion was dealt with, Lilith looked forward to watching the child's training. On that thought, she looked to her Celesian advisor. Henry's flat affect told her he hadn't quite cooled from their argument over Karen. This pleased Lilith.

No matter what she did, he needed her, if not for sex, then for her cache of weapons and the colonies she controlled. And only she could initiate Phase Three. Lilith also guessed Henry worried Natrix would blow up all the empire's colonies if its empress died.

Not that fearing death should be a problem if she repelled Captain Paulson's attack. She checked the map indicating where the invaders had landed. Another group of enemy icons had assembled in Segment 5.

Lilith frowned and said, "They're in all ten colony segments now." She looked to the live feeds of the main docking bays where some fighting had occurred. Now the mechs and soldiers there waited behind their barricades. Lilith struck her arms akimbo and turned to Henry.

"Those soldiers don't seem enthusiastic to fight," she said.

Henry grunted. "I'm sure it isn't because they suspect you'll enslave them if you win. At least your mechs are proving effective."

Before she could retort, a buzz drew her attention.

"Empress," Natrix said, "another wave of enemy transports is lining up outside to assault Segment 5."

Lilith turned to Henry. "You and the generals said the Mykonians would focus on securing the docking bays first."

Henry kept watch on the tactical plot as he answered. "I said they'd *probably* attack those first and they did. Just not as vigorously as we'd expected."

"They barely tried. It looks to me like they're dumping most of their forces here."

Henry's affect remained flat, and his voice communicated cold annoyance. "If you're bothered that the enemy isn't following your battle plan, get over it."

Lilith scowled. "Do we have enough troops and mechs in our segment to beat them?" she demanded.

Henry flicked a finger at a monitor. "The quick reaction transports are already in the air, waiting to go. We'll beat them back."

Location: Landing pod C-130, MAC 785, outside Lakshmi Colony
Timeframe: One hour into invasion operations_

"WE'RE CLEAR OF THE *SORVINO*," THE MAC PILOT WARNED. "Landing zone secure. Standby for burn."

Within the Marine Assault Carrier's detachable landing pod, a suited-up Sarah Riley squeezed the straps of her acceleration cot.

Sweat beaded on her forehead and her hands wouldn't stop shaking.

The front-line units had established a fragile beachhead in the colony segment containing Lilith. The time had come for sustainment personnel, like the medical platoon surrounding Sarah, to support the attack.

While they waited, Sarah writhed inside. She wished Sean could talk to her: to calm her nerves with his rich, resonate voice. As the fleet liaison, however, he'd been assigned a seat in the Brigade leadership's MAC. That left Sarah measuring her pulse by the throbbing in her throat.

At last, the pilot said, "Ignition."

The cabin lurched as if rammed from behind. Sarah's body felt like someone had tossed several full duffle bags atop her. Her brain rattled in her skull, making her grit against an urge to scream.

Shortly after, she heard, "Five seconds to cutoff."

She heaved shuddering breaths as weightlessness returned. Within eight seconds, the MAC had accelerated by almost eight hundred kilometers per hour. This matched precisely the tangential speed of Lakshmi's rotating rim.

"Capture in twenty," the alert came. Sarah felt the MAC swivel so that its nose pointed perpendicular to the colony. As they zipped to within two meters of the turning habitat, the craft fired four cables from its prow. Each line grappled onto one of the regularly placed utility shackles at Lakshmi's surface.

For a second, the ship dangled from the colony like a tick on a dog. Then two more cables shot from the MAC's tail. These reeled the craft parallel to the worldlet's curvature.

As a proper down return to the room, the thrumming in Sarah's chest turned into a palpitation. She pinched the release buttons on her belt and clomped onto the deck. Both knees buckled in the centrifugal gravity.

Climbing back to her feet, she promised herself, *I'm going to get through this.*

The pilot said, "We're locked on." The external pressure gauge on Sarah's HUD began to rise as atmosphere pumped back into the cabin.

From somewhere forward, the company commander, a lady named Major Kwihani said, "Beginning breaching ops!"

Sarah waited as their pod's spindly manipulator arms reached out. They quickly unfastened blocks of the colony's multi-layered shield and tossed them away. After that, the pod pressed its twin dorsal airlocks to the naked shell.

The roof clunked loudly, making Sarah jump.

"You're secured to the LZ," the pilot said. "Detaching. Good hunting." A bump later and the drive-cockpit portion of the MAC broke away. It throttled for the *Sorvino* to retrieve more pods.

"Fire in the hole!" the major yelled. Breaching charges fore and aft rattled the cabin. Seconds later, she shouted, "We're in!" "Go! Go! Go!"

A mad scramble up the ladders began. Sarah fell in, slinging her weapon and an aid bag. After a panting climb, she emerged into a cavernous storage compartment the size of a convention hall. With trepidation, she saw it contained very little: a smattering of crates, a few forklifts and the occasional clump of equipment: not much cover.

Shouts and orders echoed from people scattered about the breaching holes from other pods. A navigational arrow in Sarah's HUD directed her to a group of pallets loaded down with heavy machinery. A spinning red cross appeared in their midst.

"Charlie Company," Major Kwihani's voice called on the net. "We'll set up a treatment point over here. Quick-time. Wounded are already on their way."

Sarah's eyes widened at the announcement. There had been

pre-launch reports of mechs using sky copters to assault the surface line units. Could they be near?

"Mechs are already attacking the perimeter up top," Major Kwihani said, confirming Sarah's fears.

The lieutenant tried to remain calm as she sprinted with the medics, technicians, and other providers. A set of cracks from behind made her jump. She stifled the urge to scream and looked back to see smoking craters at the compartment's far end. More pods had blasted boarding entrances. She bit her lower lip, telling herself to stay focused.

Then a blip came up on her HUD's situational awareness map. She'd set it to alert her to track specialized personnel, like the other providers or the company commander. Or any friends she wanted to be near.

Sean's name glowed next to a blue icon amidst a cluster of other new arrivals. Sarah felt a nucleus of warmth grow within. His being around bolstered her thread-bear nerves. She dropped her aid bag at the treatment area then ran back to the pod for more gear.

———

"ENEMY TRANSPORTS INBOUND," THE BATTLE CAPTAIN'S STRAINED voice said in Sean's earpiece. "We have maybe a minute to take up positions."

Sean hitched the straps of a fifteen-kilogram, tube-launched missile at his back and started climbing a flight of stairs to the colony's inner surface. The brigade's assault in the last twenty minutes had faltered more than predicted. Lilith's mechs led troops from both above and below the surface level to punch into the Mykonian positions. The only real success the desperate invaders enjoyed came through the man-hauled missiles. Those would knock the murder-machines out so long as they didn't get shot down by the mechs' mini-guns.

In light of this, the brigade commander had ordered everyone in Sean's flight to haul a missile up to the surface. Living after that to set up proper command post operations was, in the brigade commander's words, "gravy."

Huffing up the stairs, Sean heard the muffled chatter of gunfire. Dull knives of tension jabbed behind his eyes and scalp. The fighting was *not* supposed to be so close.

"Enemy in area," Claire said in his speakers.

"No kidding," Sean replied with a sneer.

He heard someone up ahead yelling, "Keep moving! Get to the doors! Cover fire!" An instant later, the racket of gunshots assaulted his plugged ears. Then a crack and flash erupted from above.

Bodies, body parts, and building debris spewed down the stairwell, knocking people over like dominos. A few men screamed in pitiable agony while the unharmed hollered for their fellows to press on.

"Go! Go! Go!" Sean called, fearful of a follow-up strike or one of their own missiles accidentally triggering. He bounded upward, stepping over and around the wounded. The stairs ended inside a rubble-strewn, concrete room with a gaping hole where an exit used to be. In concert with their battle plan, Sean rushed past, avoiding the outdoors. Doubtless, the enemy had machine guns trained on the exit from higher up the colony's curvature.

Unfortunately, the stairs to the next floor had been demolished. So, he turned away from the exit into what his HUD labeled an office building. He needed to get to higher ground for the best firing position.

Sean had barely started down a worn-out hallway when an explosion lambasted him and the survivors from behind. The concussion threw him to his belly. His padded forehead smacked against his helmet and blackness surged toward the center of his vision.

"Son-of-a—," he began to say.

Messages and alerts flashed before his eyes, but it took a moment to focus. After a few seconds, he registered someone's voice.

"—carriers got through! Bring up your heavies! They have mec—"

The voice died in a burp of static.

Shaken into full consciousness, Sean's attention locked onto the situational map. Several big red icons for enemy transports gleamed at various distances from the brigade's position. One of them was close to his location. From outside, he could hear its engines roaring above a discordant symphony of fifty caliber bursts and lighter arms fire. His insides coiled. Lilith's counter-thrust had arrived.

Picking himself up, Sean stumbled down the hall. He searched for more stairs, passing one closed door after another. With every step, shouts and gunshots increased in volume. He spared a moment to consider why the enemy had risked landing so near to a fortified building. It was a foolhardy maneuver unless....

"Mechs moving in from the outside to your rear," Claire said with alarm. "Caution, jamming sources detected and growing in strength. Loss of signal imminent."

At almost the same moment, two marines appeared from around a corner. Running past him, one said, "They're coming in! Get to cover! Sean's heart sank. If a killing machine stepped through the exit he'd left, those two didn't stand a chance.

He knew he had a single opportunity to knock out one of those metal beasts. He sped to the nearby corner. All he needed was a bit of concealment to get the rocket online. Ironically, he found the stairs he'd been looking for but ignored them.

Sean unhitched the missile tube and set to activating its

systems and linking its fire control to his HUD. An explosion some floors above made him duck in reflex, but he kept working.

"Drone!" one of the marines down the hall shouted as their weapons opened up. It was standard for assault teams of any military to send flying scouts ahead. Some models even came with mini-rockets and guided bullets. The scream one marine unleashed told Sean they'd been unfortunate to encounter one of the latter.

"Got it! Got it!" another voice called. That was all the second man had time to say. The next instant, a brief but familiar burr from a mini-gun filled the hall. In reflex, Sean's head snapped up to find bits of red matter splattered across the floor in front of him.

A mech had arrived.

Sean knew then his window to attack had closed. With the machine's weapons pointed his way, he couldn't hope to even stick the missile around the corner, much less fire it. The mech would merely shoot him through the wall once it suspected his position. Worse yet, the icon for interrupted server connectivity blazed red. Claire could only provide him basic support through his suit computer.

He looked behind him. That was when he noticed the stairs also led below to the sublevel. He snatched up the armed missile and bounded down, stopping at the first landing. The missile tube had a tripod mount, which Sean snapped into place. With his signal strength fading, he pulled at its retractable, thread-thin data cable and held it fast so he could still fire it remotely.

A clomping above signaled the mech's approach. He scampered further toward the sublevel, praying the cable didn't drag the tube off position.

"Claire, activate remote camera on the missile. Fire control to my wrist pad's hard switch."

"Done," the gimped A.I. replied.

A picture box appeared showing the stairs and hallway above. Sean had scarcely reached the bottom of the next flight when a dark figure moved across the frame.

"No," he breathed. It was another drone. A tiny scout.

An eyeblink later, a rocket grenade bounced into view and flew at the missile. Even as Sean registered what had happened, a thunderous explosion ruptured the stairwell from above, the concussion pushing him into the sublevel.

He cursed. He'd failed to take out the mech. And from the red filling his HUD's sit-map, the enemy was closing in on their position from both above and below the surface. Knowing he had only a few minutes at best, he ran off to find another missile.

[27]

Location: Segment 5, Lakshmi Colony_

THE ENEMY'S SUBLEVEL COUNTER-ATTACK PUNCHED THROUGH earlier than expected. It caught Sarah as she emerged from their landing pod on a last-minute run for more medical supplies. First, explosions tore through two nearby doorways. An instant later, the fire suppression system showered the deck with water and foam. Then a spray of bullets and grenade drones poured into the cavernous room.

All about Sarah, others who'd been out in the open poured gunfire into the gap. They instantly started falling over from return bullet strikes. To Sarah's horror, she saw several drones fly among them, exploding against those who'd found concealment.

Too frightened to scream, Sarah dropped to all fours and scampered from the onslaught. Claire said into Sarah's ear, "This way to nearest cover, ma'am." A fat, green arrow pulsed in the HUD. Sarah rose to a crouch, adjusted her course and charged off. As she hunkered away, she slipped and skidded on the newly slicked metal deck.

She crossed ten meters before something struck her pack and

sent her twirling to the ground. An instant later, a slug hit next to her hand. She yelped. She fought off her urge to panic and scanned about for a way to escape. By chance, she'd fallen near what her HUD said was a dead marine. Letting out a whimper, she clawed up to the body and flattened out.

Claire said, "Enemy's on your right! Pivot left for better cover." Another green arrow told her which direction to move. Sarah did as the A.I. suggested, narrowly escaping a smattering of bullets.

For a few seconds, she lay panting and shaking. When she finally looked up, she realized what little concealment the corpse gave her. She knew she couldn't stay there, but the dingy surroundings did not appear to offer anything better nearby.

As smoke filled the compartment, blue icons manifested to mark the scattered Mykonians. Through the streaming beads of water on her helmet, Sarah watched as two marines beside a crate jerked from the impact of machine gun fire. The fresh corpses collapsed, and the white glow of death suffused their forms in her HUD.

Eyes popping further, Sarah cried, "Claire! Which way should I go?"

The A.I. didn't answer.

"Claire!"

"I'm sorry, Lieutenant," the machine finally replied, "but the connection to my server has been interrupted. Last report indicated mechs were fighting Bravo Company units in the next compartment. The mechs seem to be a signal interference source."

Following those words, the information tags above her compatriots dimmed to indicate the information might be out of date. The few friendly drones she could see settled to the ground. Sarah felt ice locking her limbs into place. They were being jammed like on the *Feni*.

The corner of her eye caught sight of a marine crawling from another landing pod's opening. Something flew into him and exploded. The blast cleaved the body at the waist, flinging bits up to smash against the cluster of pipes on the ceiling. Pieces crashed back onto the black metal deck far from their owner. Mouth agape, Sarah stared at the victim's limp torso.

That's going to be me if I don't get out of here!

But she didn't know where to go. She lay in the middle of a mostly barren utility space the size of a sports field. The tension lines holding up a slippery floor offered no cover. Dying fires at the treatment area's cluster of pallets lit the gloom. She thought she saw a few bodies lying about the suffocating flames. She noted the exit signs beyond them but wondered how she would get to any of them without being killed.

Looking forward again, she made out several darkened hatches set in a wall. Flickering light from a firefight in the next compartment silhouetted figures crouched in or about the openings. The suitless enemy soldiers exchanged staccato streams of death with the few living marines laying prone around Sarah.

I'll get through this! she told herself once again. Then, as she blinked away welling tears, three of the hostiles advanced to a pair of squat boxes less than fifty meters from her. The nurse began to hyperventilate as they shot in her direction. A round hit the body she lay behind. This finally prompted Sarah to pull her sidearm, thumb off its safety and return fire.

By luck, she caught one of the nearby men in the chest. He fell to his back, screaming. His companions zeroed in on Sarah as a more urgent threat than the marines behind her. She ducked as bullets hailed about. One pinged off her helmet, denting the anti-ballistic shell.

Sarah screamed, her voice rending the air with its abject desperation. Something about her frightened shriek short-circuited their killing instinct, and they stopped shooting.

Too bad for them, the marines behind Sarah didn't.

Both opponents dropped at the same time, convulsing with repeated hits. Then Sarah glimpsed something as it passed overhead from behind and sailed into one of the doorways in the distance. An incandescent detonation blinded her while a roar assaulted her plugged ears. The next beat, two other doorways blossomed with fire, curtailing the Lakshmian counter-attack.

Sarah had only begun to recover from the shock of the explosions when she felt someone lifting her by the strap of her medical pack.

"Come on!" she heard Sean's tense voice say.

The young woman uttered a small cry of joy, relief, and fear as she pushed herself up. Hand in hand, they skittered away on the wet ground. All around them, marines flowed the other direction to secure the perimeter.

Sarah asked, "Where are we going?" She had no intention of getting lost if they separated.

"Stairs are ahead. Let me just get my…" he broke stride only long enough to pick up a missile he'd dropped to the ground. His attention to the mission brought Sarah's mind back to her role in it.

"I should check for wounded," Sarah said as more explosions rang from behind.

"Not until we have some security down here," Sean said. "Mechs ripped through Bravo Company after we landed. Those Lakshmians down here walked through the gap."

"A lot of mechs?" she asked. The last word came out in a huff as her shoulder slammed into the wall next to a stairwell. She took note of a marine kneeling at the bottom, his weapon ready.

"Enough. Hurry!" Sean urged, pushing Sarah up the first flight ahead of him.

A successive trio of bangs above stopped them both cold. The patter of a chunky rain echoed through the stairwell.

Sarah took a step back. "That sounded like—"

"Mortar shells," Sean finished. A louder bang shook the metal railings. The couple started back down.

Sean said, "There's another way up!"

No sooner had he spoken than a final blast broke the ceiling above them. Cubic meters of soil cascaded down. The dirt spilled into and around the staircase, burying all three people nearby.

Sarah howled as she rode out the flood. When it finished, she found herself encumbered by a mess of earth that the burst sewage pipes and sprinkler system were rapidly turning into mud. Somewhere past the curtain of dust, rain, and smoke, she heard the battle raging.

"Sean!" she yelled. She checked her HUD's displays. No vital systems had been lost, but she still couldn't connect to Claire's servers.

She looked about. A black figure stirred from the rubble below. Sarah's heart pounded faster, hoping it was Sean. She exhaled as the marine who'd been guarding the stairwell emerged.

"I'll catch you, ma'am," he said, reaching up. Sarah took his hand and slid to the deck.

"Where's the lieutenant?" she demanded as the marine helped her get steadied. The man opened his mouth to answer when his forehead exploded onto the inside of his face shield. He toppled onto Sarah, flattening her against the base of the dirt hill. She froze in horror at the gore that dribbled centimeters from her nose. She opened her mouth, but if she screamed, she couldn't hear it. Her whole body felt numb, as if her spinal cord had been pinched by fear.

She listened as marines yelled, "mech" and "fall back." Immediately after, Gatlings growled like juice blenders sawing into soft fruit. People screeched and died.

Over the symphony of slaughter, a *clomp, clomp, clomp* drummed. Sarah's heart pounded with such violence that she felt sure the machine would hear it. Fear marred her face as the mech stepped into view beyond the dead marine's helmet.

The machine stopped and swiveled its upper half with unexpected speed. Sarah gulped as it fired at someone out of sight.

Please, God, she prayed while watching the menacing techno-monster. *Don't let it see me. Don't let me die like Horvath did.*

The mech fired again. Sarah chomped down on her lip in a vain effort to stop herself from shaking. *Just stop!* she thought at the machine. She had little doubt that each cannon blast meant another person had been hurt or killed.

Half a dozen more times, the monster belched death. When it finished, a squad of Lakshmian soldiers ran up behind it, moving out of sight.

As seconds ticked by, Sarah noticed the background chatter of small-caliber gunfire growing distant. She realized they must be fighting in the next compartment.

Shivering violently, Sarah leaned her head left and right to ensure no one had stayed behind. She couldn't make out any people through the gloom. She detected no moans or sounds of movement from survivors.

She took two more shuddering breaths then slowly pushed the dead marine off of her. He rolled to the ground, leaving her gasping. She looked about the body-strewn compartment and realized everyone else must have either died or fled. She didn't dare move into the open to be sure.

Looking back to the rubble pile, she whispered, "Sean?" Since he wore his suit, she knew he was probably still alive. A knot of resolve formed within. She would rescue *someone* today.

Twisting around, Sarah began pushing mud and dirt aside. Over a minute of furious work, she etched a groove where she thought Sean might be buried. All the while, gunshots and a mech's footfall continued to stalk her senses.

She paused to scan the compartment through her mud-streaked helmet, but still saw no one. When she turned back, she paled at how little progress she'd made. At what point should she give up and find a way back to the others?

Her voice squeaked. "Where are you, Sean?" Another rivulet of dirt fell into place, triggering a small sob from the forlorn lieutenant. She pounded her fists into the mound. One of them struck something hard. It turned out to be a length of pipe, which she attacked with resentful fury.

To Sarah's surprise, a few blows dislodged the other end from the dirt. Along with a tangled length of rifle strap. And the wriggling fingers that gripped it.

"Sean!" she cried, clasping his hand to establish a fiber-optic connection. As his medical data transmitted to her HUD, she said, "I'm here! Suit and vitals are okay. You're going to be fine."

He bent up at the waist, shedding muck and debris. He looked shaken, Sarah decided, but not in pain.

"How long was I out?" he asked.

At that, she heard a grenade popping somewhere out of sight. She set to scraping the rest of the dirt from his legs. The gunfire drew steadily closer.

"Never mind that," Sarah said, "we gotta move."

Sean nodded. They grasped each other's wrists, and Sarah planted her feet. Leveraging all of her body weight, she tugged.

He didn't budge. Sarah's eyes widened, and her breathing went shallow. She repositioned herself and tugged again. Still nothing.

A slow clomping signaled the proximity of a mech in the next maintenance partition.

"Sarah," Sean said quietly.

"Let me try again," she whispered. She could see a large pipe poking through the dirt around where his legs must be.

"Sarah," he breathed as she strained.

"Just one more try." The growl of the mech's cannon spilled into their chamber. Sarah found herself on the verge of weeping.

"Sarah!" Sean said, rasping. "I'm pinned! You have to get out of here!"

"No!" she protested, raking clumps of soil out of the way.

"Listen to me," Sean ordered. "I have a plan. I dropped my missile just over there. Hand it to me, and I'll cover you."

"I've almost got you out," she insisted.

"Go to the far end of this wall and up the other stairwell there," Sean told her.

"I'm not going to leave you here to die."

"Sarah Riley," he said. He bent forward to cover her frantic hands with his. She stopped and looked up at him with a tear-streaked face. For a few seconds, they stared into each other's eyes.

"Sarah, you have a job to do. Go."

The clomping resumed.

She dove for the missile beside the rubble pile and gave it to him.

The sound of stomping rose, fell and rose again. Sarah realized that the mech must be passing by the doors to their room. The irregular wall wouldn't hide them for long if and when the mech came through. They had no time left.

Sarah wanted to rail at the world for it. She cared for him! Possibly more than she'd cared for any man before him. But she also understood the pleading in his face: his need for her to survive to help the others. In their final moments, her living was the one gift she could give him. She turned and fled.

Her footfalls echoed as she raced to the compartment's far end. As she reached the stairs, she saw the mech round a corner. It swiveled its turret her way, but too late. A massive explosion from Sean's missile consumed the machine. She had a split-second glimpse of him jerking back as something struck his helmet.

Her slick boots lost their footing in the violence of the detonation. She collapsed to her knees at the stairwell's entrance, screaming Sean's name.

He wasn't moving.

Before Sarah could scramble to her feet, however, an awful cacophony followed up the reverberating explosion. Tension cables holding the floor snapped and twanged. The screech of rending metal vibrated Sarah's helmet.

"No!" she screeched.

She saw that the fighting had severed too many of the support cables. The combined weight of the landing pods and surface debris overwhelmed the floor's tensile strength. In only a few seconds, a massive, jagged hole in the colony's outer shell ripped open.

Sarah caught herself at the stairwell's banister and watched Sean's limp form vanish into the depths.

"No!" she wailed. "No, no, no!"

Crying, she held on against the gale in the stairwell and kicked the door's catch so that it blew shut. As vacuum claimed the other side, she felt her heart suffocating.

She said, "Please, please don't let him be dead. *Please!*"

For several seconds she remained slumped against the hatch, wracked with sobs. She replayed the mental video of Sean falling back into the dirt. Had his helmet been cracked? Was he asphyxiating? Or had his face already been turned into a bloody pulp from whatever had impacted him?

A muffled boom from above intruded on her misery. Thoughts of people being dismembered and mutilated replaced those of Sean dying.

Don't let others feel this way, she told herself.

"I have a job to do," she said, echoing his words. Their caring for one another had led him to save her from being killed on the cold maintenance deck. Now, it was her turn to give something back. She forced herself to her feet and returned to the fight.

Location: Lilith's private estate, Lakshmi Colony_

SATISFACTION TICKLED AT LILITH AS SHE WATCHED A SCOUT drone's camera feed of the battle. The Gatling cannons from her mechs tore into a cluster of marines as they emerged from a sublevel exit. Streams of bloody pulp erupted from the hapless men and women.

Lilith snorted. "Too bad for them they didn't go for the docking bays. Then they could have offloaded something with armor to hide behind. Did they really think they had a chance here?"

Henry shot Lilith a side-long glance. "They're not doing as bad as you'd think," he said. "Or have you not been paying attention to the latest wave they scattered around the segment's far end?"

"Isolated pockets," she said. "What of them?"

"The new arrivals seem to have an awful lot of missiles and drones. They're almost done blowing up the transit corridors out of here. They're isolating us. Look."

He pointed to a live feed from one of the patrolling mechs. It blasted at a distant cluster of objects as they flew toward an airlock between colony segments. The jinking missiles slammed into their target, sending up a rolling ball of orange, yellow and black. "You sure you don't want to relocate while you still can?" he asked.

"And leave the protection of my mechs?" Lilith said with disbelief. "Where on Lakshmi is it safer than here?"

"Just about anywhere if you'll renounce your immunity."

Lilith huffed. "You don't trust Dalip's troops to protect me any more than I do."

"You saw how determined that Captain Paulson is to defeat you. Renounce your immunity, and the Wardens will quit broadcasting your location. That will force the Mykonians to spread out across the colony to find you. They'll be easier to pick off after that."

A series of distant booms made them both look up. For the first time in the assault, Lilith felt a genuine thrill of fear.

"Natrix, what's going on outside?" she demanded.

"Enemy missiles are closing on the estate's grounds."

"Show me."

Another gun camera view appeared on the room's center screen. Bullets burped from the barrel into what resembled a loose flock of gray candles. The heavy caliber rounds tore through the formation. One by one, the missiles burst apart into flaming fragments of metal and electronics. Their warheads never had the chance to detonate. A second later, though, a bang filtered down to the bunker. The screen froze then blanked.

Natrix said, "Unit destroyed by a flanking strike. More missiles are inbound."

The staccato burr of heavy caliber Gatlings outdoors increased in frequency. Then the crack of an explosion somewhere in the house above caused Lilith to jump.

"They're insane!" she said. "If they hurt me, the Wardens will kill their families!"

"It's possible," Henry said with a hint of sarcasm, "that you already did that to some of the people controlling the attack. A lot of dependents lived on Zeus after all."

Lilith's breathing grew shallow. "The Wardens would still punish anyone else they cared about." A distant, thunderous roar pre-empted whatever else she had to say.

Over the rolling explosion, Natrix told them, "Habitat breached near 45th Street and 12th Avenue."

Henry's voice took on a subtle note of alarm. "Holes in the colony will start a panic. We won't be able to get out of the segment by ground for several minutes at least."

More explosions echoed from outside.

Natrix said, "The mechs on the estate are taking heavy casualties from guided mortars, empress."

Henry made a thoughtful noise. "They must be using most of their remote-controlled arsenal for this attack. That would explain why we had such an easy time routing that main body of troops. They were saving the smart bombs for this push."

Another explosion in the house sent Lilith's hands flying to her ears. "How exhilarating! What are you going to do about it?!"

Henry shrugged. "Maybe you should let yourself get hurt a little. Who knows how far up their chain of command the executions would run for that."

Lilith muttered a choice invective.

The Celesian made no apology. "At least the broadcast would distract them until the Wardens finished flaying people alive."

"It would bother the Lakshmians too," Lilith pointed out.

"You're the one who said they aren't being very useful."

Lilith sniffed. She had, in fact, considered blackmailing someone into violating her immunity the way she'd tried with Karen. "I don't feel particularly masochistic today."

A rumble from below made the conspirators look down.

Natrix announced, "There's an incursion directly beneath the compound. Mechs engaging."

Without being asked, the A.I. put an image from the defenders onto the viewer. Two holes had appeared in the darkened maintenance compartment beneath Lilith's estate. The machines showered gunfire into the openings, but nothing emerged.

Lilith grabbed for Henry's arm. "They're insane!"

The Gatling cannon fire continued for several seconds, but nothing tried to escape the holes. Then Lilith felt the gut punch of an epiphany. She realized with stark fear what the Mykonians had in mind. They couldn't attack her directly, but they could leave a trap of sorts for her to trigger. The A.I., however, didn't possess the creativity to see the danger.

"Natrix!" the empress cried, too late.

In a coordinated move, the mechs ceased firing their Gatlings and launched four grenade rockets. One caught a rim and exploded harmlessly, taking its brother with it. The other two dived straight through the other hole.

The anti-personnel bombs shattered against the first things they came into contact with. The rounds had been designed to spread damage within a five-meter radius, piercing light armor and flesh. This made them more than adequate to ignite the pallets of armed mortar shells inside the landing pod.

A fireball pulverized the several meters of dirt and rock that separated the basement of Lilith's home from the outer maintenance level. The floor erupted upward, throwing Henry and Lilith through the ceiling. Since Lilith's forces had incautiously triggered the bombs, the Mykonians bore no blame for her injuries under the immunity rules.

Limbs caught amongst the cables and rafting. This held them fast while debris flurried about. Then, as quickly as the inverted burial took place, the soil and building material rushed away.

As did the air.

[28]

Location: CIC, *MSV Tsunami*_

RAFE COULDN'T HEAR IT THROUGH THE VACUUM, BUT HE SAW people in the CIC cheer when Paulson replayed footage of Lilith's house being demolished. A chunk of the sprawling, two-story mansion crumpled and sank into the maintenance level. Gouts of flame, dust, and smoke spat up from the breach.

Part of Rafe wanted to celebrate with the others. They'd gotten lucky and hit Lilith when she should have been invulnerable. But if she died, he thought with turmoil, it would be tougher to find out what happened to Karen.

"Commander Hastings," Paulson said with restrained enthusiasm, "did we get her?"

"Still waiting on confirmation, ma'am."

He studied the real-time Warden feed on Lilith's whereabouts. Her pulsing red dot hadn't moved from the room they'd targeted. *Does that mean she's hurt?*

He checked the live camera view from James. Flying near the colony's hub, the A.I.'s drone had kept out of the jamming that plagued most of Segment 5's assault force. Movement at the picture's edge caught his attention. Another of Lilith's mechs exploded from a laser-guided missile.

Rafe rechecked the Warden feed and frowned. "Lilith may not be dead, Captain. She hasn't moved, and there's been no official message about her." He noted a squad of heavy Warden vehicles rolling to the estate. "Emergency repair bots are closing on the house. She could still escape if she isn't too injured."

The memory of Commandante Wilkinson directing a Warden flashed in his mind. *And maybe....*

"Claire," the Captain said. "Launch the strike team."

Location: Lilith's private estate, Lakshmi Colony_

AS LILITH STARED INTO DEEP SPACE, SHE SCREAMED WITH PAIN, rage, and terror. The hurricane of venting air made it difficult to breathe. Her cracked ribs didn't help. Neither did her broken arm, although it kept her from falling. It had tangled amidst a bundle of thin fiber-optic cables.

To her left, she saw Henry clasping a rafter. In the corner of what remained of the floor, the enforcer stood motionless.

Show off, she thought, sneering.

Then she gave a small cry as she remembered that Henry had not, after all, spent their one-time Warden help option while chasing down Rafe days before. She called out, "Enforcer! Emergency assist! Authorization Kota17. Get us out of here!"

She doubted the machine would hear her, but knew it could read lips. With impressive speed, the bot fired a cable into the rafters and rode it up. Its manipulator arms grappled the beam and shimmied to Lilith. She heard the high-pitched whirr of a cutting tool, then felt the cables slacken. As she slid toward the Warden, rivulets of pain surged through her broken arm.

The enforcer said, "Both of you, grab onto me."

With her good arm, Lilith reached around the Warden's head. A wild-eyed Henry took hold of its torso. The silver and obsidian machine lowered them to the floor and released its cable. Then, like a metal giant, it tucked the humans to its sides and carried them from the house's wreckage.

Location: CIC, *MSV Tsunami_*

RAFE FELT BILE RISE AS LILITH'S RED DOT SHIFTED LOCATION. "Lilith is moving out of the structure."

The comms tech interrupted Paulson's response. "Incoming vid-sig from a General Parashar on emergency channel 5, secured link. He claims he has executed President Dalip and wishes to arrange for a cease-fire."

Paulson exchanged stunned looks with Rafe.

Rafe said, "He's their highest military officer under the president."

The captain considered this then said, "Claire, route call to my HUD on my mark. Let brigade and intel monitor. Ready, mark."

The image of a white-haired Lakshmian appeared. His angular features, tan complexion, and dire expression suggested to Rafe a person of magisterial poise. He spoke with grave intensity.

"Captain Paulson, thank you for joining us in our fight against Lilith." He glanced over his shoulder and barked, "Hold up his body!"

The camera zoomed out to show two soldiers in camouflaged fatigues supporting the dead weight of President Shaasti Dalip. Twin bloody stains marred his white tunic. The general lifted the head by a clump of hair for Paulson to see.

"So that there is no doubt," Parashar began. He finished by lifting a pistol to the corpse's face and pulling the trigger twice.

After, he let the head loll forward. Blood dribbled out of the wounds and down the president's shirt.

Rafe's lip twitched upward.

"I'll be brief," the general resumed. "We have the codes to an Arbiter and will shortly invoke Unrestricted Warfare with it so you can kill Lilith."

While Paulson absorbed the miraculous tidings, Rafe's mind turned with questions. *How did they get those?* He also wondered why they hadn't deployed the Arbiter yet. His immunity wouldn't have been negated by an Unrestricted Warfare zone while he remained outside of the colony.

When the captain said nothing, the general added, "I trust you can hit her with something that won't destroy Lakshmi?"

"We can." She swallowed. "General, this is welcome news, but I am sure you can guess at my questions."

"The ways and means are best discussed later," Parashar said. "What is important is that we defeat our common enemy."

"Very well. How long before you'll be ready?"

"We're trying to get set before your immunity ends. In the meantime, I'll order our ships and troops to stand down. I regret that I don't control the mechs."

"We'll deal with those," Paulson said. "What about Lilith's A.I., Natrix? You can't win back your colony until she has been purged from each segment's command and control center. From what we saw, mechs are guarding the server bunkers."

"We will deal with *those*," the general said, mirroring Paulson's measured tone.

Rafe quirked an eyebrow. He wondered if the Lakshmians had the means.

If Paulson held the same doubts, she didn't show it. "Then we have an accord."

The general nodded. "It is remarkable that Lilith survived your booby-trap. Filling a landing pod with munitions for her mechs to detonate…" He allowed a small smile. "Too bad Lilith's military advisors didn't prepare her for such a creative attack."

Paulson acknowledged the compliment with a knowing grin. She had one more unpleasant question to ask. "Will Lilith's A.I. or any of her henchmen destroy the colony if the empress is killed?"

"You and I wouldn't be talking if the answer to that question could deter us."

"Point," the captain said. "But to prevent that scenario, we should both keep trying to capture her."

"Agreed," Parashar said. "Good hunting to us."

The captain nodded and cut the signal.

Once the screen blanked, Rafe restrained the urge to pinch his helmet-encased forehead. He didn't know what to wish for. What would happen to his daughter and the colony if Lilith died?

No sense in worrying about that. He told himself to be grateful that the estate was far enough between the radiators to fly to from the outside. *We might take Lilith yet.*

Paulson said, "Tighten up on our primary target please, Commander."

Rafe zoomed the drone's camera to resolve Lilith slumped on the ground against an enforcer. A man in black stood nearby.

Rafe said, "That's Commandante Henry Wilkinson to Lilith's right." He marked the figure for the strike team. "If they stay there for five more minutes, we can have them both."

He noticed movement in the wide-angle view. A twin-bladed sky car was putting down near Lilith's position. *Is that the same one Markem took Karen in?* He panned the high-mag viewer in time to see the car's canopy open. It revealed a single male occupant who disembarked and ran toward Lilith.

Rafe said, "That's Markem!"

Where did you take my daughter? he thought with vitriol.

"Claire," Paulson said, "get me some artillery on that air car, now."

"Unable to connect to brigade, ma'am. There's still too much jamming ground-side, and they lost another laser relay. Attempting to reroute the network."

No! Rafe scanned the tactical map. The commando team hadn't breached the colony yet. His heart quickened. *Lilith is going to get away!*

Claire said, "Movement on the estate grounds." Rafe panned to it, expecting to find another mech. Instead, he saw several figures charging at the sky car. They weren't Mykonians.

"Captain," Rafe said, voice urgent. "I think the Lakshmians have beaten us to Lilith."

Location: Lilith's private estate, Lakshmi Colony_

"MARKEM!" LILITH CRIED AS HER BARREL-CHESTED AIDE scooped her into his arms. She yelped from her broken ribs and humerus but held on. She craned to see Henry hobbling behind with an excruciated grimace. Despite her pain, she hollered, "Hurry Henry!"

A line of sparks danced along the open door, shattering its window. She looked beyond Markem to see a ragged line of charging soldiers. *Lakshmians! How dare they! And how did they get onto the grounds?* She didn't want to believe the logical answer: the swarms of Mykonian missiles had overwhelmed all of her top-side mechs.

As Markem slowed, Lilith screamed, "Don't stop! They're trying to disable the car!"

A bullet whizzed by her head. She spat a curse despite the agonizing breath it cost. Then a round blew through Markem's knee. He toppled forward, spilling Lilith to the grass. The

Empress of Belia landed hard on her mangled arm and rolled twice.

Without hesitation, Henry dived behind the "immune" woman, using her as both a shield and a prop for his pistol.

"Help me up!" she ordered Henry.

Before they could move, however, one of the attacking soldiers shot at the nearby vehicle. His rounds ricocheted off. One pegged Lilith's thigh, penetrating her skin-tight suit-pants. She squealed in renewed agony, clutching the limb with her uninjured arm.

Behind Lilith's party, the watching enforcer's optics registered what had happened. The Warden stormed forward.

"Halt!" it roared. A pair of electrodes blasted from its arm. They struck the offending soldier, dropping him mid-stride. His fellows ground to a stop on seeing the enforcer racing at them.

The mechanoid stomped up to the fallen male and flipped him onto his back. He twitched in a pain-ridden daze. Extending shimmering blades from each of its upper appendages, the enforcer skewered the man's shoulders. The Warden raised its prey off the ground, examining him.

"Reyansh Luthra," the machine said in a synthetic growl. "You have broken the Warden Code by violating a protectorate's immunity. The sentence is torment and execution for you, your parents, your sister, your previous two lovers, the following close friends…"

It listed one person after another. By the third name, the condemned man had regained enough of his senses to begin pleading for someone to kill him. He knew what horrors the enforcer would make him suffer.

None of the soldiers dared help: the price for interference would be to suffer an excruciating death. A few of them, however, attempted to skirt the scene toward Lilith. The enforcer said,

"Stop! You accessories to this violation will stay and witness the price of disobedience!"

A grim smile crept over Lilith's face. Unimpeded, she, Henry and Markem dragged themselves into the air car. Within a minute, they had lifted away.

While Lilith settled back in her seat, the execution proceedings blazed from the dashboard screen. A grid of ten windows depicted a captive Mr. Luthra and his loved ones being accosted by enforcers.

They work fast, Lilith marveled.

When the Wardens informed the doomed of their fates, they wailed in abject terror. While Lilith clamped down on her thigh's flesh wound, she sneered at the Lakshmians.

Serves you right for betraying me. May you all burn in hell.

Location: CIC, *MSV Tsunami_*

SINCE SOMEONE HAD TO MONITOR LILITH, RAFE HAD LITTLE choice but to expose himself to the gruesome executions. The Wardens wouldn't allow the vid-window to be closed or moved off-screen. He could reduce, but not mute the volume. At best, he could shrink the proceedings into a corner of his HUD. He tried to ignore the shrieks as Wardens flayed, eviscerated, stabbed, quartered, gouged, scourged, strangled, burned, chopped, and electrocuted their victims. Through it all stung one thought.

Lilith was still loose.

As if to underscore the setback, an enforcer said, "Humans of Cervantes, learn this lesson well. You must *not* defy us."

The words ate at Rafe's spirit.

How do we break free of those monsters? They've made this misery possible and for what?

In reply, he heard only screams. The minutes rolled by and he found himself fighting off the urge to vomit.

He wondered how Anna was coping with the vid or if Karen was even alive to see it. Helpless, he stared with catatonic intensity at Lilith's pulsing red dot, feeling tense all over.

Then a bit of motion on another screen stirred him. He saw several rocket contrails streaking through the wide-angle camera on James' drone. The comms-hampered brigade hadn't quit fighting, Rafe realized. Shortly after, a cluster of explosions peppered a hexagonal building. He trained the drone's camera on a smoldering hole in the roof.

Rafe overlaid the colony map to identify what they'd hit and keyed his general microphone. "We struck Segment 5's control bunker. It's likely out of action." His delivery lacked enthusiasm. Given the chorus of dying souls playing over the speakers, he doubted anyone would fault him.

Then he noticed Lilith's sky car had flown to within a few hundred meters of the drone. The view zoomed in, revealing a pocked frame. The damage explained why it had taken so long for the thing to climb to altitude.

He realized those soldiers had been bolder than he would dare. But had it won them anything? Figures moved inside the sky car's cabin. Lilith was right there, and all he could do was watch her.

Don't throw away your bullets, he recited, forcing himself back to calm.

A moment later, Claire flashed an urgent text message from General Parashar.

"Arbiter ready. Stand by to attack."

Location: Sky car, Segment 5, Lakshmi Colony_

IT TOOK THE CRIPPLED AIR HOPPER SEVERAL MINUTES TO REACH the relative safety of the colony's hub. Only then did Henry cut the propellers back. When the engine noise diminished enough to talk again, Lilith accessed the comm system.

"Natrix, report!" she yelled.

"Empress!" The machine rattled off something Lilith couldn't hear over the screaming execution victims.

"Say again?"

"I said I'm *so* sorry about what happened."

"Yes, yes," Lilith said with a cough. "I'll decompile you later. Some Lakshmian soldiers attacked me. I want to talk to Dalip."

"General Parashar has killed the president, my Empress."

Lilith pulled her mouth into a thin line. She knew the military generally hated her, but she'd thought the weaponry she'd demonstrated had cowed them. Killing their own president meant they were willing to risk total destruction to get rid of her.

"What else?" she asked.

"I overheard a conversation between the General and Captain Paulson. He claims to have codes for an Arbiter and plans to invoke Unrestricted War soon."

Lilith felt hairs tingle along her neck. That wasn't supposed to be possible. She shot Henry an accusing glare. "What do you know about this?"

Henry focused on the car's controls as he maneuvered them near the colony's central truss. "If I was part of the coup," he called, "you wouldn't be here. You'd be in custody, and Markem would have a bullet in his head instead of his knee."

Markem said, "He makes sense to me, Mistress."

The demoness squinted at Henry. "Dalip's people knew *full well* that any Arbiter I gave them wouldn't let them put Lakshmi into Unrestricted Warfare. So, where did they get one that could screw with my immunity?"

"How should I know? I personally shipped off the ones you sold to Celes." He paused in thought. "We can check if the freighter rendezvoused with—"

"Don't bother. You obviously kept one here. Maybe your government insisted. It doesn't matter. Either way, you *knew*."

Henry cocked his head in annoyance. "What must it be like not to be able to trust anyone you can't blackmail, torture, or kill?"

"Why don't you ask your wife?"

Henry rolled his neck. He caught sight of something through the paneless window. A swarm of rockets, perhaps a kilometer away, raced for some unseen target. Straightening, he said, "We don't have time to argue. You need to start Phase Three. Now."

Lilith stared Henry down for a count of five. She called him an obscenity then gazed out the windshield. For several breaths, she stewed in anger.

Of course, he had a point, as usual. Given the all-out rebellion on Lakshmi, she should cut her losses.

"Natrix," Lilith said, "how many colonies do I still control?"

"Eight, Empress."

Lilith growled and thought, *I suppose eight will have to do for now. That's over twenty million lives to start with. And once the ships I bought from Celes arrive, I can conquer more.*

She wheezed after a severe inhalation, then said, "Authenticate Laila omega four three seven zero. Execute Phase Three."

"Command accepted," the A.I. responded with emotionless efficiency. "Executing."

"Finally," Lilith said. She peered out at the colony around them and imagined the scene of terror about to befall her subjects.

They'll be mine to command, she mused with satisfaction. *All of them.*

"Empress," Natrix said with chagrin. "The Segment 5 servers have been destroyed. Local control has been severely reduced."

Lilith uttered something crass. Losing those servers made using the population in Segment 5 difficult. Turning to Henry, she said, "We had better find a way out of here."

Before Henry could react, Natrix shouted, "Alert! Unrestricted Warfare condition set!"

For a stunned second, Lilith sat in disbelieving silence. Then Henry cursed at her and flipped a series of switches. The sky car tore free of the hub and accelerated away. "We have to get you to an enforcer. They need to release you from immunity tracking."

Lilith grasped for the nearest armrest, more out of sudden fear than from Henry's rapid maneuvers. Against her will, at the thought of her vulnerability, she began to hyperventilate.

Henry spewed more vulgarities and said, "Your constant complaining... You've wasted so much time. You've screwed us, Lilith!"

Location: CIC, *MSV Tsunami_*

"LAKSHMI IS UNDER UNRESTRICTED WAR!" CLAIRE TRUMPETED. "Lilith is vulnerable!"

"Hold fire on the nukes," Paulson said. "Target six Goblins in ripple mode on her and launch."

A second passed. Then another.

Claire said, "Captain, there's a problem. Some new immunity protocol won't let me lock onto Lilith."

Paulson snapped, "Does brigade have any missiles left in Segment 5?"

Claire replied, "HQ element is still under jamming. The peripheral units report zero missiles and mortars remaining. Also, they're outside of any unit's smart-bullet range."

In his HUD, Rafe saw Lilith's sky car release from its perch and veer off.

You're not getting away this time!

He grabbed his console's control stick and punched a key to unlock the drone's clamps. His finger slid the accelerator forward to dive after Lilith.

Paulson asked, "Can you catch her?" Ordinarily, the child-sized drone couldn't match an air car's speed.

Rafe noticed smoke trailing from the left engine and said, "They're hurt. We have a shot."

Second by agonizing second, the car crept closer in Rafe's HUD. He noted the craft descended with frightening speed. Before long, the air rotating with the colony increasingly pushed them spinward.

Rafe checked his altitude. Less than a thousand meters remained. The damaged car's lead fell to only ten meters.

To the dying Reyansh Luthra, Rafe promised, *What you're going through will mean something."*

A tone warbled, and Claire said, "Drone main battery is low."

"Never mind that," Rafe muttered. "Switch collision-avoidance to audio only."

"Done," Claire replied. "Caution, your vehicle will no longer automatically steer to avoid obstacles."

"Fine. Range to target?"

"Sky car is ten meters ahead. Altitude, three hundred meters."

The car loomed in the vid window. Rafe pulled on the joystick, and his quarry dropped from the main viewer. He caught his breath as an eddy from the car's engines bucked the drone.

He tweaked the glide slope until the image smoothed.

Claire said, "You're losing them."

"No, I'm not." He hadn't flown drones for years on dark ops missions to not know what he was doing. He flicked his gaze to the three-sixty camera. As predicted, his quarry was leveling out to land. Rafe, however, had aimed for a point forward of their path.

"Collision course!" Claire shouted over an alarm.

The sky car's own accident-avoidance system banked it away from the drone, but Rafe had planned for that. He nudged the joystick, dropping his nimbler craft in front of the car's intake ducts. The inrushing air sucked the drone straight into one of the thrust and lift turbines.

As his camera glitched out, Rafe said, "Gotcha!"

Location: Sky car, Segment 5, Lakshmi Colony_

LILITH NEVER SAW WHAT HIT THEM. SHE JERKED AT THE ANTI-collision siren, felt the car turn sharply, then heard a metal thunk in one of their engines. An instant later, the master alarm blared.

Henry said, "They got us!" The world outside began to tumble.

From the back, Markem called, "Shut down and use the emergency jets to—"

"I know!" Henry barked. His fingers whipped across the controls. The engine whine lessened.

Sounding like a frightened child, Lilith asked, "Are we going to make it?"

Henry ignored her as he worked the joystick back and forth. "Seventy-five meters!" he called. The air copter wobbled violently. "Fifty!"

Panting, Lilith watched the habitat's inner surface zipping by. "Henry!" she cried.

"Twenty-five!" he said and pressed a big red button. A set of emergency landing jets activated.

Henry yelled, "Hold on to something!"

Lilith screamed as the vehicle slammed into a potato field at a relative one hundred kilometers an hour. The car's landing gear snapped on impact, tilting the tail into the dirt. The cabin's occupants screamed as they cartwheeled across the landscape.

Location: CIC, *MSV Tsunami_*

RAFE FOLLOWED LILITH'S RED INDICATOR WITH UNSHAKABLE intensity as it came to rest. He glared at it for several seconds. It didn't wink out.

"Captain," he said with a twist of dread and hope, "she still isn't dead, but she must be banged up."

"Claire," Paulson said, "tell that crack strike team to get to Lilith before the Lakshmians do."

"Relaying Captain, but there may be a problem."

"What are you talking about?"

"There's unusual Warden activity on Lakshmi. I think you should have a look at some of these SPOT reports."

A beat later and Paulson exclaimed, "What the hell?"

Rafe keyed in on what the captain saw. The text accompanied by live video added another couple of knots to his already twisted bowels. "What are the enforcers doing with the Lakshmians?" he asked.

[29]

Location: Office building, Segment 5, Lakshmi Colony_

I HAVE A JOB TO DO.

Sarah closed a vascular clamp on her sobbing patient's shredded artery—a female office clerk who'd been caught in the fighting.

Let me save another life, the nurse prayed. *Please.*

Her vision blanked to be replaced by a picture of Sean falling into space. *He might not be dead,* she reminded herself. She unwrapped a pressure dressing and placed it in the woman's fist. Guiding the hand to a gouge at the upper arm, Sarah said, "Press hard."

A shout from the office's foyer made the nurse look up. She saw a pair of black-clad marines entering, with one supporting the other. She noted the casualty wouldn't put weight on his left leg.

"Sit him down over there," Sarah ordered. Her finger pointed at the big monitor that she'd shot to pieces when the executions began.

She blew a strand of hair from her forehead and stroked the

battered woman's cheek. "It only looks scary," Sarah said, straining sweetness and calm through a forced smile. "I promise, you're going to be fine."

Another explosion rattled chunks of glass from the busted front windows. The wounded woman yelped. Sarah leaned over to shield her. When the nurse looked back up, she saw marines outside shooting.

The lieutenant yelled, "Are they getting closer?"

"They're leaving!" someone hollered. "They're running away!"

Sarah hoped that didn't mean the Lakshmians were evacuating so they could pound the area with mortars. Or something worse. She wished that she could call up one of the marine's helmet cams, but the jamming hadn't abated.

It unnerved her plenty to hear the victims' terrible screams echoing from speakers elsewhere in the office. She shook herself and rose to tend to the next casualty.

"Hey," another marine called. "What are all those Wardens doing?"

The comment brought Sarah up short. Unease tingled along her scalp. She turned around.

At first, she could only see one enforcer striding down the street. Nothing unusual about that. They sometimes swapped out for maintenance. *Maybe it was damaged by the fighting.*

Then Sarah saw a second and a third. Without realizing it, she'd crept to the shattered window. What she beheld drew her eyelids back. Wardens lined the street.

As one, the mechanical zombies spoke: "All resident humans will assemble at Joyti Park. Non-residents will proceed indoors and make way. Comply immediately, or you will be punished."

Sarah's face paled. *Do they mean the wounded in here too?*

She got her answer as an enforcer turned into the building.

The marines parted for it like fish scattering from a shark. It stopped before the strewn-out patients and said, "All Lakshmians will move as instructed or be executed."

"What?" Sarah breathed. The half-dozen injured locals stirred. Most propped or pulled themselves up in a show of obedience. The office lady whom Sarah had helped, however, uttered a small whimper. She'd lost too much blood to do more than rock in terror. The Warden raised its arm, singling her out.

Pity and horror gripped Sarah's heart. She saw in the woman's supine form the haunting specter of her helpless mother during cancer therapy.

Sarah's inner voice cried to save the person.

Before she could consider the risk to herself, Sarah stepped between the enforcer and her patient. "Please, Warden, these people are too hurt to go anywhere!"

She expected the machine to lash out at her. Doing anything that could be perceived as challenging or disrespecting a Warden usually earned several broken bones, at least. Sarah trembled.

Slowly, the enforcer angled its arm to aim at Sarah's face. She had a close-up view of the gun muzzle attached to its mechanical wrist. Her voice cracked as she said, "Please."

For a cruel stretch, the Warden said nothing. It gave Sarah time to dread, to regret her boldness. Sarah's knees threatened to give way. "Please don't kill any more of us."

Something flashed in the machine's glassy, obsidian face. It lowered its arm. "Intercessor protocols invoked."

Inter-what? Sarah thought with breathless apprehension.

"You will assist these Lakshmians to the distribution point at Joyti Park," the Warden said. "Anyone here who chooses to join you may do so, but delay will not be tolerated."

It took Sarah a whole second to realize she hadn't been sentenced to an awful punishment. Her lungs gusted. While sniffing back the sting of emotion, she said to the marines, "Please, help me get them up."

For a beat, they stared at her. Then their sergeant barked out names to serve as a litter team. They hefted bodies across their backs and marched outside without question. Sarah promised the wounded marines she would return as soon as possible. Afterward, she followed the others into the street.

While she hurried alongside her patients, she tried to intuit why the marines had been so ready to aid her. The Warden had tasked Sarah, not them. They also knew from their pre-mission briefing that Joyti Park lay kilometers away. Sending troops there meant weakening the perimeter in the office plaza.

Amidst the clamor of jostling people, she overheard one marine say to another, "I've never seen anyone do something that ballsy before."

Location, Potato Field, Segment 5, Lakshmi Colony_

LILITH CAME TO IN STAGES. AT FIRST, SHE FELT ONLY PAIN: terrible, stabbing pain across an aching body. Next, she heard a voice speak her name. Her eyes opened to a blur.

What's happened to me?

The world sharpened into focus. A tranquil field lay before her. She looked left and saw a man. He seemed familiar, but she didn't know why.

The man asked, "Can you hear me? Do you know your name?"

His question sparked a painful memory. She recalled a woman once told her, "If you ever use your real name again, we'll beat you. From now on, you are—"

"Lilith," she said. "I'm Lilith." Her eyes quested about. She was in a busted-up sky car. Then she remembered, *Oh, we crashed.* She twisted to look behind her and saw Markem's empty seat.

"Where?" Lilith began.

Henry said, "He didn't have his harness on. His body is somewhere outside."

Lilith looked through the nonexistent windshield. She saw a dark, distant figure running at them.

"Who is that?"

Henry followed Lilith's gaze and straightened. "An enforcer," he said. His arm dropped to his restraints, and they loosened at a click. With sloth-like care, he opened the battered door and climbed out.

"I see Markem behind us," Henry said. "He's not moving." He turned to Lilith. "You didn't happen to be lying about having only one Warden assistance option?"

"No," Lilith said, dazed. She paused for a breath. She gasped. "My chest and legs hurt a lot."

Henry studied the crumpled dashboard covering Lilith's lower half. "Can you move your feet?"

Lilith tried, and daggers of pain pierced her limbs. "I can't move. It hurts too much."

Henry cursed. "We don't have a comm link. So even once Phase Three is fully online, we can't use Natrix to make anyone obey us." He stared off at the approaching enforcer. "You'd better hope we can convince them to help."

Lilith, however, screwed her face in anguished fury and dismay. They'd warned her what would happen if she got herself badly hurt. When the mechanoid trotted to Lilith's side, she addressed it with a groan.

"Enforcer, I—"

"Silence!" it boomed. The machine's faceless head peered down at the Belian crime lord. "You are an embarrassment, Laila Kota."

"But, Warden—" A fit of coughing seized her fractured ribcage. She wheezed and spasmed until tears fell from her eyes.

"You have demonstrated your ineptitude time and again." Its words lashed Lilith with shame. "You have been deemed unfit. Your reign is ended."

Lilith gasped for air. Her mouth gaped to utter a furious, "No," but spat up bloody phlegm instead. The enforcer turned away from her.

"Commandante Wilkinson," it said. "The New Belian Empire is yours."

"Hen—," Lilith tried to say, but the racking coughs wouldn't stop. The Celesian and Warden ignored her.

Stone-faced, Henry said, "You're most gracious. Are there any special conditions I should observe?"

"Succeed where this woman failed. Build your empire. Conquer. Disappoint us, and you will suffer her fate."

"What is her fate?" Henry asked with a quirked brow.

"Our displeasure." The machine turned its head toward Lilith. She shrank in her seat. Her once haughty facade had crumbled into the coarse features of an angry, frightened and hurting woman.

"What are you going to do to her?" Henry asked.

"What would be more appropriate?" the machine responded. "Should she live out her life in a brothel wearing a re-sculpted face? Or shall we leave her here for the Mykonians? They will arrive soon after Phase Three's completion."

Lilith's hands trembled. Her eyes burned. She hiccuped, which shot needles of agony into her broken ribs. "I fought for you!" she shouted. "This isn't right! Your mechs were too stupid to protect me!"

The Warden regarded her with metallic dispassion. "Your enemies will have you, then," it said.

Henry took a half-step forward. "Why not remove us both

from the colony?" The Warden continued to glare at Lilith. Henry huffed. "She knows too many secrets."

"Yes," the Warden said. "She does."

"At least let me kill her," Henry said.

"What!" Lilith cried.

"You will be silent or face greater punishment!" the Warden said to the woman.

"Security failures are why she is in this mess," Henry insisted. "For me to succeed—"

The enforcer whirled on him. "Our decision is final! The Mykonians will have her!"

———

HENRY DIDN'T DARE OBJECT TO LILITH'S SENTENCE FURTHER. "What of me, then?" he asked.

"You will depart Lakshmi in our transport. The situation on this colony is too unstable."

At that, Henry noticed a Warden police wagon trundling toward them from a nearby road. "I appreciate your generosity."

"That is wise."

They waited in silence then, mindful of the soon-to-be captive Lilith. When the truck pulled up, Henry stepped to its open rear door. He stopped at its lip to take one last look at the deposed empress. The quivering, half-dead bag of flesh peered back at him from the sky car. He recalled seeing the same forlorn expression on Karen's face hours before.

As the door shut, Henry muttered, "You had this coming."

He plopped his sore body into a stainless-steel seat. The reality that he had not betrayed Lilith fueled a smirk.

I'll need to have a little discussion with Command about how General Parashar got an unlocked Arbiter. Henry leaned back as the truck bounced over the uneven terrain. *Come to think of it, now that I am Belia's emperor, Command and I will need to talk about a lot of things. But first—*

"Warden," he said to the enforcer who'd joined him, "I need to speak with Natrix, please."

"Link established," the machine said.

The first words out of Natrix's vocal algorithms were, "How may I serve you, my Emperor?"

Location: CIC, *MSV Tsunami_*

RAFE SEETHED.

"What is happening down there?"

Lilith's tracking dot continued to pulse red. News had arrived that the Wardens were gathering the citizenry in all eight of Lilith's colonies. And the executions had been hastened to a merciful end without explanation.

What are those mechanical monsters up to? He felt almost as unnerved by the silence on the net as he had been by the screams. It worried him that the Wardens might help Lilith again before the strike team reached her.

He studied a feed from one of the scouts in Lakshmi. A human mass funneled between the enforcers along a street. Here and there, the machines lashed out at someone moving too slow for their tastes.

It's like they're on a death march, he thought with a chill. *And why would the Wardens be so keen to keep non-residents indoors? Is it for crowd control or do they not want us to see something?* Given that even the ground force's drones had been locked down, Rafe favored the latter, unpleasant possibility.

A change in the immunity map diverted his attention. He blinked. Lilith's red dot had faded out. For a few seconds, he stared to make sure it wouldn't return. When it didn't, the commander spun his chair about.

"Attention in the CIC! Lilith has dropped off the immunity tracker!"

A stunned instant later and most of the crew began clapping their hands. Despite the vacuum, Rafe could have sworn he heard the applause. A lump formed in his throat. They finally got her.

Part of him wanted to cheer, but his conflicted heart held him back.

The captain let her crew bask in their victory for a few beats before saying, "Well done, Commander. Well done all." She cleared her throat. "Scopes. Comms. Keep monitoring for any sign of automated retribution. Claire, I still want a body. Once the Wardens let our people move again, how fast can the strike team reach Lilith's last known position?"

"Captain," the A.I. said with a foreboding tone, "a Warden notice just arrived advising that Lilith has been deposed. The message also says that the Wardens have already installed a successor. The new ruler's name will be announced at a later time."

The smiles fled from the crew. Paulson's face turned ashen. "Keep a close eye on those Lakshmian warships."

The plotting chief snapped to his console. "Aye, ma'am. They're still station-keeping a little outside the ten-thousand-klick line. No change in aspect."

Seems they didn't get orders to back down. He returned his gaze to the ground video and suppressed a shiver. *What are the Wardens going to do with the colonists?*

Location: Joyti Park, Segment 5, Lakshmi Colony_

AFTER ALMOST AN HOUR OF WALKING, SARAH AND HER

companions ambled into their destination. It stiffened the hackles on her neck to find an enormous electric fence circling a field inside the park.

That can't have been here an hour ago. Already it penned in tens of thousands of Lakshmians with more flowing through its gates every second. The enforcers at the park had outfitted themselves with mini-Gatlings, like the ones on Lilith's mechs. Sarah glanced at the pale office worker who lay across a trudging marine's back. *We've taken these poor souls so far and for what?*

Some of the women and children behind her raised a cry. Sarah twisted about.

"They're closing the gates!" she said.

At each of the entrances, the Wardens slid fence pieces together like curtain panels. Only a few, well-guarded gaps remained for stragglers to enter.

Maybe they'll let us leave that way?

Seeking to soothe her fears, Sarah jumped upon a bench and scouted around. A bulldozer stood in the park's center next to a mound of freshly gathered dirt. Behind it stood tree-height poles with white projection screens dangling from cross-beams. More fencing stretched in a line from left to right with dozens of regular gaps that a person could walk through. At each entryway, she saw stacked crates.

The enforcer said this was a distribution point, she thought. *What in heaven's name would they want to distribute?*

No sooner had she stepped down than a cluster of Wardens atop the knoll announced, "All residents will remove their clothing. If you do not comply, you will be punished."

Muted noises of disbelief, outrage, and panic rippled through the crowd, Sarah included.

Someplace where Sarah couldn't see, a brash man said loudly, "Are you serious?"

In response, a muzzle flashed from one of the Wardens on the knoll. The crack set off screams. Their cacophony kept Sarah from hearing anything further for several seconds. When the air quieted, she could discern a single male crying in pain.

"You will comply immediately," the Wardens said.

The rest of the people, either silent or whimpering, shucked their clothes where they stood. Anxiety and sorrow furrowed Sarah's young face.

Remembering her patients, she busied herself with helping them undress. She produced shears and clipped off what the wounded couldn't remove themselves. When she got up from the last of them, she scanned the crowd.

Around her stirred a sea of bare bodies. She glimpsed a child clutching her mother. An elderly man who'd stood tall moments before now hunched over. A sobbing wife huddled against her husband's back. Everywhere, people positioned their arms and hands in a futile effort to assuage their shame.

A live video of those gathered up front appeared on the jumbo projection screens. Sarah gasped as a dozen enforcers pushed into the crowd to pull kids off their parents. Hysterical adults screamed their children's names while the youths squealed. The desperate cries sent Sarah quaking. She experienced a flashback of when, helpless, she'd watched Corporal Horvath die.

The plaintiff shrieking lasted almost a minute. By its end, the Wardens hauled six naked children to the top of the little hill. Their distraught faces shone on the screens: three boys and three girls. Sarah guessed they were primary schoolers, ages five to ten.

An enforcer moved to clutch one child's neck with a claw-like appendage. The boy's legs danced weakly, then stilled. For a terrifying instant, Sarah thought the robot was crushing his throat. When it released the balling child, she saw that the Warden had left a thick, black ring about his neck.

A marine asked, "Is that what it looks like?"

"It must be," Sarah said, mortified. "They're putting slave collars on them!"

Before anyone could speak further, a female voice, very similar to Lilith's, blared from the enforcers' speakers. "Lakshmians, welcome!" it said with incongruous cheer. "I'm Natrix. I'll be your host for these proceedings. In fact, I'll be your close, personal, ever-present A.I. overseer for the rest of your natural lives. Today, you become slaves of the New Belian Empire."

Wails and muffled screams echoed across the park. Sarah instinctively raised a hand to cover her mouth but slapped her helmet bubble instead. She made a quick deduction.

Lilith! She got the Wardens to gather everyone to do this to them! Others in the crowd who'd come to the same conclusion cursed the empress's name.

After the Lakshmians had spent a few seconds assimilating their fate, the A.I. said, "Now, now, I know you're all excited about these new changes, but credit must go where credit is due. First off, Lilith has been replaced as your empress. You have an emperor now, but I must say," and the A.I. lowered her voice to a whisper, "he's very upset that you rebelled."

"Oh no," Sarah breathed, dreading what would happen next.

The A.I. resumed a normal tone, "So, we're going to demonstrate on these children the price of disobedience."

The left screen flipped to a view of the parents reaching out for their children. The anguish in the adults' faces mirrored Sarah's own. She heard one woman begging the machines to let her take her daughter's place.

Sarah wanted to rush forward and tell the Wardens to stop. With Natrix working through the enforcers, however, Sarah knew it would probably be suicide.

The A.I. said, "You'll notice the collars on their necks. Shiny, fashionable. Don't worry, you'll all get one before we're done. Now, if you fail to obey any directive, we have five shock settings with which to reprimand you. We'll start with the child on the left and go up from there."

A hand gripped Sarah's arm and turned her from the obscene drama. Startled, she looked up into the eyes of the corporal who'd led their small detachment.

Amidst the horrid sounds of tortured children, he said, "Ma'am, it's time to leave before they outfit these people and send them after us."

Sarah's lower jaw quivered. *Those babies. My patients. How can I just leave them?*

"Lieutenant," the corporal said, "you've done your job."

Hearing her rank broke through Sarah's mental block. She willed a semblance of composure back into her face. "We have to warn the brigade," she said. "Let's go."

As they moved to the nearest gate, she heard Natrix say, "Of course, if you try to take the collar off without permission, or interfere with it, this will happen."

A sharp crack hushed the masses. It stopped Sarah's heart. She knew without looking that the sixth child's neck had been shredded by a slave collar's explosives. She also knew she would never forget the mother's screams that followed.

Holding back tears, Sarah fled the park with the others. As the weary squad jogged away, she kept praying for the living nightmare to end.

Some minutes later, the "No Signal" symbol on her HUD vanished. The chat icon for Sean glowed green once more.

Sarah slowed her pace, suddenly breathless. Before her eyes, text appeared: "From LT Merrick, Sean: I'm okay. Back on *Tsu*. Are you safe?"

She read the words and noted the time stamp. They'd been sent half an hour before. Then she read them again.

Something inside told her that she should be happy about this news, but she felt nothing. She'd cut off her heart so that the horrors would stop hurting.

I'm in shock, she realized.

Claire said, "Incoming call from Lieutenant Merrick." In a daze, Sarah clicked open the line.

[30]

Location: CIC, *MSV Tsunami_*

"ATTENTION ALL HANDS," CLAIRE SAID. "IMMUNITY EXPIRING IN five minutes."

The order everyone expected from Paulson followed. "Signal the fleet. Secure for separation, and standby to thrust."

Behind her, Sean tightened his shoulder straps and fought to stay relaxed. He'd escaped Lakshmi remarkably unscathed but still felt nauseous after tumbling through space for several minutes. A MAC had been on patrol for emergency-detached pods and ejected personnel such as Sean. Once it had brought him back to the *Tsu*, Paulson had jokingly chided him for abandoning his new assignment.

He consoled himself in having at least taken out a mech.

While waiting for the immunity to end, he found himself worrying about Sarah, and what was happening on the colony. He checked the brigade's comms status for the fiftieth time. Still jammed.

Claire said, "Airlocks sealed. Radiators retracting. Auto-separation sequence start. T-minus sixty seconds and counting."

This would be their most vulnerable moment, Sean reflected. As ships broke away, each would lose Commander Rafe's protection. A hit to any one of them would lob shrapnel into the others. By splitting up early, they hoped Rafe's remaining immunity would discourage an attacker from risking harm to the *Tsu.*

"Captain," the plotter said. "Lakshmian flotilla is thrusting for us. One-third gee."

Paulson responded without delay. "Comms, warn them that we'll fire if they don't withdraw immediately."

The seconds ticked by. Sean shook his head. As before, the vessels ignored all communications attempts. He cursed the Warden rule preventing warships from maneuvering within one hundred kilometers of a habitat unless on docking approach. At their present distance, the colony's bulk provided too little cover to be useful. There would be no hiding from Lilith's nuclear lances.

The plotting chief said, "They're in the engagement sphere."

"Attention, fleet," Paulson announced. "This is BELCOM actual. Break for Delta formation. Weapons free. Firing order Foxtrot Uniform Bravo One."

"Separation initiated," Claire said the next instant. Sean felt the ship pivot. A handful of moments later and the main engine ignited at maximum thrust. Seconds after that, the ships began to disgorge missiles. By the first salvo's end, the fleet had safely dispersed into a diamond-shaped wall with the *Tsunami* at its center. As one, they accelerated to meet the Lakshmians.

Claire said, "Immunity expired."

Sean felt his body surging with adrenaline. *This is it.*

Then the A.I. announced, "Brigade comms re-established."

Sean's heart stopped. His eyes darted to the downlink icon. It had winked green.

"Claire, call Lieutenant Sarah Riley!"

After several rings, the woman's face appeared in a window. Her beautiful blue eyes seemed empty. Vacant.

"Sarah?" he asked with caution.

"Sean," she replied. Her hollow voice sent his heart into a paroxysm of anxiety.

Something's very wrong.

"Are you safe, Sarah?" he asked.

"For now, but do you know what's happened here?"

Sean shook his head. "The Wardens locked the troops down. We've been blind ever since."

Pain flickered in Sarah's eyes. "Sean, they're fitting the Lakshmians with slave collars. That A.I., Natrix, is running them. You have to warn…"

The plotter's voice interrupted Sarah. "Ballistics! Tracking five of them!"

Paulson shouted, "Evasive action!"

Sean's gaze whipped to the tactical map. Blips sped from the Lakshmian ships. He knew that if those were long-range lances, the Mykonians could do nothing to stop them. He also had no doubt that the *Tsunami* would be one of their targets.

Sarah saw alarm spread across his face. "Sean?" she asked, fear lacing her voice.

"I've got to go, Sarah," he said. "Stay alive!" He cut the connection, not wanting her last memory of him to be his death.

They had only begun to get to know one another, and he wanted so much to find out if they might have a future together. He knew now it was not to be.

A handful of heartbeats later, the plotting chief shouted, "Detonations!"

He had time for one last thought.

Goodbye, Sarah.

Then the roiling plasma of several fusion bursts streaked into the Mykonian formation. But not one of them touched the *Tsunami*.

Sean blinked and looked around the CIC.

"Report!" Paulson ordered.

In a panting voice, the man at scopes said, "Direct hits to the *Victory, Implacable, and Summoner*."

The woman at comms tried to keep her voice steady as she added, "We've lost contact with…"

Sean called up an image of the nearby *Victory*. The blast had flattened her hull. Sparkling cherry-red and yellow-glowing debris spun away from the twisting wreck. Behind the horrid realization that a quarter of their fleet had been destroyed, Sean thought, *We should be dead. Why are we still alive?*

He checked the tactical map. All five bombs had exploded, but only three had produced a death ray. The other two, presumably meant for the *Tsunami* and *Sorvino,* had disintegrated. *But why?* he asked. He traced their paths back to a single ship: the *Godavari.*

Before he could explore the puzzle further, Claire announced, "The Wardens have released the ground forces from lock-down, but now there is an inter-ship comms block in place." She paused then added, "And I just lost the colony downlink again."

Sean cursed. *Lilith's surprises keep on coming.* By nixing their communications, the fleet's ability to coordinate fire would be degraded.

The plotter said, "New radar contacts from Lakshmi." A second later he shouted, "Missiles launched!"

The map around Lakshmi erupted with trace lines. Sean's heart ramped again at the sight of several hundred rockets streaking for the fleet's survivors. Whatever had happened to Lilith, it seemed she would have her revenge upon the fleet.

"Counter-fire!" Paulson ordered. "Lasers, prioritize non-standard silhouettes. Quick-turn our bow to the colony and launch reserves as needed!"

Sean clenched his jaw. *They knew exactly when to hit us.*

The *Tsunami* and her consorts unleashed still more of their missiles. While those raced away, laser batteries picked off one threat after another.

Sean caught his breath. He knew Lilith would have been stupid not to hide some lances in that swarm.

Punctuating his fears, the tactical map flagged dozens of icons with flashing boxes.

The plotter said, "Mini-Casabas deploying!"

The defenders aimed their lasers to slag the nuclear threats. As Sean dreaded, the lack of comms resulted in several shots being wasted on the same target.

"Detonations!"

As soon as the word had reached Sean's ears, he knew the *Tsunami* had been spared. At that distance, the nuclear flame would have struck in less than an eyeblink.

"Report," Paulson demanded.

The plotter said, "No damage to the fleet, Captain, but we lost a lot of counter-missiles."

"Fire reserves," Paulson ordered.

They're eroding our strength before we get close to their warships.

The map technician next said, "Enemy ordnance bearing down on us!"

Railguns and laser turrets poured fury into the remaining hoard. Missiles slashed through space to converge and die with one another. Those that survived faced streams of depleted uranium from the point defense cannons. Unfortunately, Sean saw that their uncoordinated defenses were being overwhelmed.

Sean's body jerked as the *Tsunami's* lateral thrusters tried to push the lumbering ship from the path of several hurtling missile fragments.

Paulson ordered, "Shutter main mirror."

Two missile icons flashed orange. Claire shouted, "All hands, brace for impact!" Across the CIC, everyone ducked.

The next instant, the room exploded with silent violence. A brilliant fireball blossomed then wilted in the ship's near-vacuum. At the same time, shrapnel and bodies shot about the cabin like confetti in a snow globe. Chunks pelted Sean, making him flinch and scream.

It took several breaths before the flurry lessened. When Sean dared to look up, he beheld utter devastation. Red emergency lights illuminated a cloud of debris. Through it, Sean saw the CIC's forward half had been scoured of equipment and people. Stars shone through a ragged gash that reached to the deck below. He panted for a few breaths, trying to understand how he'd survived the devastation without so much as a suit breach. He prodded his brain to prioritize what he should do next.

The ship. He had to ensure that the ship was still in the fight.

He stopped a floating metal brace with his hands before it could conk his helmet. Beyond it, he saw the captain sitting motionless in her seat. "Claire," he stammered, "report."

In response, a status of the ship's major systems and most significant damage appeared in Sean's HUD. Almost every weapon system except their missiles blazed red.

Claire said, "Sir, Auxiliary Control suffered a direct hit. I have no contact with the XO there."

A wash of icy fear sent Sean shivering. He was next in line of succession.

Activating his magnetic boots, Sean wove his way through the wreckage to Paulson. He put a hand on her shoulder. Medical data fed through the optical connection. Her suit had been ruptured in several places, but the vitals remained stable.

He keyed a channel. "All hands, this is Lieutenant Merrick. I'm assuming command. Get your wounded to sickbay and report your status to Claire. Damage control teams, focus on restoring propulsion and the main laser."

He was unbuckling the captain when a figure stepped up, startling him. "I've got her," Commander Hastings said on the local net.

Sean nodded. He called out, "Any survivors in the CIC, sound off."

Claire answered for the dead and wounded. "I'm only detecting search and rescue beacons, sir."

Sean shuddered. They'd lost so many: the earnest comms tech, their plotting chief, and over a dozen others.

"Signal the fleet with our running lights," he said. "Let them know our condition."

Claire replied, "Working on it, sir. Most of them look to be in as bad a shape as we are."

While slipping into the captain's undamaged day room, Sean tried to squelch his mounting frustration. Their fleet was wrecked. They had no voice comms. He didn't even have a way of letting Sarah know he was alive.

His eyes widened at his memory of her last words. "Claire, did you get a chance to relay Lieutenant Riley's report about the Wardens putting the Lakshmians into slave collars?"

"I did, sir, but I don't think the fleet's in a position to do much about it."

Sean groaned. He had a sudden premonition of ten thousand civilians charging with clubs held high. A desperate train of thought swept through him. The slave collars should work under the same Warden rules that governed the ones at Celes. Any commands to the collars had to originate from an A.I. server bunker. Destroy the bunkers, and the collars couldn't be used to coerce the people.

Sean came to a terrible conclusion. Even though the Wardens allowed only one bunker per segment, the brigade couldn't hope to knock them all out—not with the whole colony turned against them. That left the task up to the fleet.

Unfortunately, there had been good reasons why Paulson hadn't yet holed the bunkers from space. The Wardens had no obligation to patch any breeches before the air bled out. Who knew if the colonists would survive in the sub level shelters until atmosphere could be restored.

Sean shook his head. He wanted someone else to make this decision.

"Tactical," he ordered. The 3D spatial grid with the *Tsu* at its center appeared. He noted that half of the Mykonian ships coasted without power. Did everyone take a hit? The Lakshmians, with full reaction mass tanks, had chosen to evade the Mykonian missile swarm.

They'll be back to harass us, Sean realized. He also understood that if he struck the colony, the *Tsu* would have far fewer missiles left for defense.

But for all he knew, Natrix could be forcing the colonists to prepare more rockets to finish off the fleet. And more frightening still, she could already have the colonists marching on the brigade. He envisioned Sarah being carried off by a desperate mob.

He made his decision.

"Claire," he said, "target Reapers on the colony's command and control bunkers. Three missiles each site, except for Segment 5."

"That will use up almost all of our conventional warheads, sir. And they can't guarantee a kill."

"I'm not going to risk destroying the colony by using nukes. Advise the fleet of our intentions then fire. And don't bother me with what they have to say about it until after it's done." Come what may, he knew that this was the only way to save Sarah and the ground troops without wiping out the civilians.

Claire signaled her compliance. A minute later, the Reapers lashed out at the colony. A few minutes after that and pinprick explosions dotted the rotating cylinder's length.

Location: Segment 1, Warden courier ship, Lakshmi Colony_

EMPEROR HENRY WILKINSON FROWNED AS NATRIX REPORTED THE destruction of all the server bunkers. *I've lost the colony,* he thought. He couldn't even send a termination order to the population's slave collars.

He also reflected that if the crews of the *Rajput* and *Godavari* hadn't sabotaged their long-range lances, the Mykonian fleet would have already been annihilated. At that moment, the mechs aboard were slaughtering the Lakshmian crews for their treachery. The onboard A.I.'s would have to make do without them.

He sniffed. *Fortunes of war.*

At least he'd knocked out the *Tsunami* with the colony's missile barrage along with at least five other ships. The communications blackout weapon had helped ensure all enemies took severe damage, or so Natrix assured him. His forces should be able to clean up the survivors with little trouble.

"Time to cut our losses," he said. "Natrix, nuclear mission. Once my courier is at a safe distance, demolish the colony."

The A.I. remained silent.

"Natrix, acknowledge."

The Warden enforcer beside him spoke, "Phase Four initiated."

Henry's eyes narrowed. Forgetting himself, he asked, "What are you talking about?"

The Warden mercifully took no offense. Instead, it said, "You have activated Phase Four. All software cache weapons are revoked. The colony's Unrestricted Warfare condition is rescinded. All Arbiters have been locked."

"What! You can't be serious! How am I supposed to conquer without—"

A metal fist caught Henry in the cheek, breaking it in three places and knocking him to the floorboard. Gasping from the pain, he pushed himself up. Emboldened by rage, he stood toe to toe with the Warden.

Henry said, "You could destroy the Mykonians any time you want. Why put us through this charade?"

The monolithic robot regarded the human. "You can always resign. We will find another to replace you."

Henry snarled. "Tell me the truth, Warden. Is it possible for Celes and me to defeat the Mykonians?"

Without hesitation, the enforcer said, "It is, but the time for Phase Two overrides has ended. The phase of arenas and challenges is yet to come. Until then, you fight under standard rules."

This is nothing more than a twisted game. For whose benefit or for what purpose, he didn't know. Maybe the theories about the Wardens only wanting to caretake one hundred million humans were true, and this was their twisted way of culling the population. Whatever the reason, what choice did he have?

He considered his position. After the Lakshmian armada crippled the remaining Mykonian fleet, his seven remaining colonies could consolidate their strength. He could hunker down and wait for the warships Lilith had bought from Celes to arrive. He might even be able to convince the Celesians to send more aid despite the risk of open war with Mykon.

Things could be worse.

"Very well," he decided. "I'll play."

Location: Officer's quarters, *MSV Tsunami_*

At long last, Sean felt that the Mykonians' luck had turned. It began with the restoration of communications. Hearing from brigade that Lakshmi had been liberated lifted everyone's spirits. Sean reveled in the vindication of his strike on the bunkers. He celebrated by exchanging texts with Sarah. Enough to assure him that she was safe.

For over an hour after that, the Lakshmians meandered around the Mykonian missile barrage. This gave the savaged fleet precious time to recover. Though some ships remained out of action, the *Tsunami* restored a laser furnace, the fusion drive, and its spinal laser.

From his makeshift combat information center in the officer's quarters, Sean watched the Lakshmians expend obscene quantities of reaction mass to accelerate back into the engagement zone. They didn't quit before reaching a closing velocity of three kilometers-per-second.

As they crossed the nine-thousand-kilometer mark, Claire said, "Signal from acting flag. *Tsunami* to attack with main gun."

Sean put on a grim smile. *Let's see if they have any big nuclear lances left.* He didn't think so. The time to use them would have been at the battle's start.

"Claire, set laser furnace to hundred-megawatt output, full second beam durations on standard cooling cycle. Lock with the *Godavari* and commence firing."

After Claire confirmed his orders, the *Tsunami's* long-range mirror unshuttered and poured forth ultraviolet wrath. An electronic warble marked the first hit. Although he couldn't see it, a millimeter of armor had been etched out of the *Godavari's* hide across a forty-centimeter-wide area.

Claire reported, "Scopes indicate all targets are rolling."

With vengeful glee, Sean thought, *Surprise.*

Another pulse burst from the *Tsunami's* nose. After so many setbacks, after so many deaths, he dared to believe that their opponent had finally blundered. Every twenty seconds, the battleship pounded the frigate with another shaft of invisible heat.

They had few options to counter his primary weapon. It was a question of physics. The *Tsunami's* fifteen-meter-wide mirror allowed it to dish out direct-energy damage at a much greater range than anything else in the battlespace—except, of course, for a long-range Casaba, but the Lakshmians seemed fresh out of those.

Claire said, "Cruiser *Rajput* is opening her bow-shield."

Sean's smile broadened. The *Rajput* had ten-meter-wide main optics in its nose. At their present range, it had little hope of damaging either the *Tsunami's* armored mirror or its edge-on cooling fins.

"Switch target to the *Rajput's* laser," Sean said. "So long as their mirror is exposed, pound it."

"*Rajput* is firing. They're going for our optics."

Sean recognized the desperate tactic. They hoped that the cumulative damage to the *Tsunami's* modular mirror assembly would degrade it beyond usefulness. Its superior armor mesh, however, almost guaranteed that the *Rajput* would lose its reflector first.

"Continue firing," Sean ordered. Had it been him, he would have focused at the *Tsu's* edge-on radiators, hoping to erode their bumper-like shields enough to punch through.

By the fifth exchange, the *Rajput* closed its nose shield back up before the Mykonian lasers could warp the optics. The battleship returned to punishing the *Godavari.*

Claire advised, "They're increasing acceleration again. Military thrust."

"Figured out that they're screwed, have they?"

The *Tsu's* main laser would make them pay dearly for every klick of space they advanced. Their best choice now was to close the range as quickly as possible so that the *Tsu* couldn't destroy the missiles waiting in their bowels.

Fortunes of war, Sean thought. *Payback time.*

Over the next ten minutes, Sean took shot after shot with impunity, shaving off hunks of the frigate's bow and punching through to its mirror below. Meanwhile, the Lakshmians dumped almost all of their remaining reaction mass to increase their closing speed to five kilometers-per-second.

When the range reached six thousand kilometers, the call arrived. "Missiles launched."

His body tightened again. Claire had already done the math for him. The missiles could add another four klicks per second to the closing velocity. That left the fleet ten minutes to knock down up to three-hundred-fifty inbounds.

"Lasers to anti-missile mode and fire." In response to Sean's orders, the laser switched to a higher rate of fire with shorter pulses. At first, they only burned out the missile guidance systems. As they neared, the explosive ablation to their armor knocked them off axis.

When the missiles closed to three thousand kilometers, the Mykonian destroyer, *Audacious* joined with its main laser cannon. At two thousand kilometers, the frigates *Lewis* and *Branford* added their fire.

Claire said, "*Rajput* is opening its nose cone again."

"Retract radiators," Sean ordered. "Take out that laser."

Before the *Tsunami* wrecked the cruiser's mirror, the enemy's fire jammed one of the *Tsu's* radiators into a half-folded position. Another fin spewed hot coolant until valves pinched the flow off. It finished ducking inside the hull.

Sean said, "Hold onto fin number two." He didn't want to jettison it in case they might be able to repair it after the battle.

They had only one large radiator out of four left—two others had been destroyed in the colony's missile attack.

Sean's eyes moved to their lithium heat sink capacity. They had enough for the job, he thought.

Claire said, "Missiles closing."

Much to Sean's consternation, they needed to lob their last Reapers at the threats. Nuclear hellfire finished off the last of the enemy's ordnance. As the rain of dead missiles passed through the Mykonian formation, Sean wondered at the Lakshmians, "What else have you got?"

Both sides held their fire: their heat sinks nearly full.

A short eternity later and Claire said, "Enemy formation approaching one-thousand-kilometer perigee."

Knife-fighting range.

"Signal from acting flag," Claire said. "All ships, fire lasers."

The opponents tore into each other. The *Tsunami* bore two-centimeter-wide holes through the destroyer *Chennai's* armor, wrecking the enemy's mirror. The frigate *Satpura* lost its optics to shots from the other Mykonian ships. The *Godavari* and *Rajput* had nothing left to fight with.

"Extend radiators," Sean said, feeling like he was floating not in space but in a dream. "Continuous barrage until flag orders cease-fire."

He watched as the enemy warships spurted gouts of hull from the repeated laser strikes. He reeled in his bunk as a profound wave of elation and relief crashed together inside him. It combined to form a tsunami of emotion.

They'd won.

[31]

Location: Battalion aid station, Segment 5, Lakshmi Colony_

SARAH FELT AS THOUGH SHE WALKED IN A DREAM-STATE. THE Lakshmians were free. With the server bunkers destroyed, Natrix couldn't control them. To everyone's relief, the Wardens patched the breaches before the air thinned appreciably.

Meanwhile, the brigade recovered James from his hiding place and installed him as the habitat's new A.I. This allowed him to deactivate the bombs in the slave collars.

Sarah had never seen such joy in people before. They danced in the streets. They jumped. They clapped. They hugged and kissed and ran about.

Anytime the Lakshmians saw a Mykonian, their faces beamed. Children frequently rushed up to embrace Sarah. She and the marines accepted the accolades with saddened smiles. The price had been so high.

Out of a landing force of five thousand, they'd lost seven hundred souls. Over a thousand more had been injured. Uncounted Lakshmians had also died between the fighting and their few hours of enslavement. When Sean called Sarah to let her know he was alive, she silently thanked him for not talking about the fleet's losses.

The Mykonians converted an office building into a makeshift aid-station. Through an effort of great will, Sarah put aside her shock and set to healing the wounded. For over a day she worked until she stumbled about, worn beyond all endurance. At that, it took a doctor's orders to make her sleep.

When she woke up a few hours later, a commander wearing a Fleet Intelligence patch stood over her. Stern-faced, he said they needed her to tend to a special patient. He tried to frighten her with all sorts of threats against her life and career should she talk about whom she would be caring for.

Still exhausted, Sarah couldn't have minded less. She had grown too numb inside. Then he told her who the patient was.

Location: Lakshmian Hospital, Segment 5_

The guard waited outside as Sarah stepped to Lilith's bed. The deposed empress regarded Sarah with a blank expression.

"Are you in any pain?" Sarah asked in a monotone. When Lilith said nothing, Sarah added, "I'm going to check you over."

She set to examining the IV line, catheter, splint, and bandages. She changed a few dressings, but otherwise left the previous caregiver's work alone.

When done, she looked again into Lilith's green eyes. The lids drooped with drug-induced malaise, but Sarah felt certain the woman remained aware. Before she could stop herself, before she could think to turn and flee, Sarah bent over Lilith and let her feelings tumble out.

In a hoarse whisper, Sarah said, "I've never hated anyone before you came along. You've threatened everyone and every-thing I love. I've watched innocent people—*children*—die in terrible ways because of you. Thanks to you, I don't know if I can ever feel safe again."

Lilith's eyes drifted toward the pointed shears in Sarah's hand. The nurse tightened her grip around them.

"Do you know what I'm going to do to you?" Sarah asked, her body trembling. Lilith replied with numb silence.

Sarah took the shears and laid them on the stand beside her. A tear rolled down her cheek.

"Whether you like it or not," she said, choking on a sob, "I'm going to forgive you for what you've done to me." She caught on the urge to cry but worked her voice around it. "I'm going to help heal you because you're a hurting human being like me and it isn't my job anymore to punish.

From deep within, a new determination took hold. She eased Lilith's head up to fluff the pillow. The battered woman exhaled a sour fume. Sarah wafted it away with a hand. She raised a translucent bottle and placed its straw to Lilith's lips.

"Water?" Sarah offered.

Location: Lakshmi Colony_

KAREN HAD LITTLE TO DO BUT WORRY FOR ALMOST A WEEK. Within a minute of arriving at Mumtaz's brothel, Markem had stuffed Karen into a pitch-black room. The girl scratched about the locked cell only to find it completely bare, save for a few splinters. Trapped, she missed out on both the colony's enslavement and liberation.

Occasionally, a muscular young man would open the door long enough to pass her water, food and a bucket with which to relieve herself. He promised to hurt her if she called out. She cried herself to sleep whenever sleep would come. She always woke up screaming from a nightmare.

One day, the young man took Karen out. He blindfolded her, tied both hands behind her back and brought her to a ground car. They drove for hours. All the while, the child sobbed in fear that they intended to take her back to Lilith.

When they stopped, the man pulled the sightless Karen out and walked her off for several paces. Their footfalls made a sharp echo. Then Karen felt the hand on her upper arm vanish, and she heard the man trail away.

For almost a minute, she stood trembling in place. Eventually, she worked up the courage to use a nearby wall to work the blindfold off of her eyes. She saw that the man had abandoned her in an alley. The local police found the frightened girl an hour later.

———

RAFE HAD BEEN INTERVIEWING SURVIVORS OF KAREN'S LIFEBOAT when the word reached him.

Sean Merrick said, "Commander, your daughter's alive. The Segment 3 constabulary have her. I'll have Lieutenant Riley and an escort meet you there."

In shock, Rafe fumbled his words twice when asking James to get him a ride to the police station. Inside, he found the pink-haired nurse waiting for him.

The haggard lady stepped forward and said, "She's asking for you, sir."

Rafe quaked, suddenly more afraid than when he'd faced Markem's fists. *I let this happen to her.*

"How is she?" he asked. "What has she told you?"

Sarah's eyes telegraphed worry. "I don't think they did anything to her beyond roughing her up. When I told her you and Anna were safe, she started crying. She kept saying everything that's happened was her fault."

Sarah searched his face, an unspoken question passing

between them: *Do you blame her too?* The notion took Rafe aback. How often in the last few days had he asked himself, "If only she had listened?" He imagined his wife's spirit urging him. *She doesn't need blame, and you, of all people, have no right to lay any on her.*

Rafe left Sarah with the marines and stepped through the door. He stopped as he saw a figure wrapped in a blue blanket. He hadn't seen his eldest daughter in four months.

The girl peered up from her chair, cheeks slick. She drew a shuddering breath.

"Karen?" he said.

The child's fingers twitched about one another. She whispered, "Oh, daddy. I'm so sorry. I'm so sorry."

Somehow, Rafe hadn't expected this. Wasn't she supposed to say hello and run into his arms? He took a ginger step forward, and in a choking voice, he asked, "Sorry for what, baby?"

Karen's lower lip trembled. "Mom's dead because of me. Anna could have gone through what I did because of me."

The words rent Rafe's heart. He saw in her eyes a shame that he shared. *He* had let his daughter fall into Lilith's hands. The father rushed to his little girl and embraced her. He said, "Anna's safe. Your mother is dead because some very evil people killed her."

Karen's throat tightened. She squeaked out, "I could have protected us. And I didn't. I didn't!"

The words fell on him like a leaden mantle. *I could have protected you. And I didn't.*

He said, "You don't know that Lilith wouldn't have found some other way to hurt us."

"No, no, no," she said. "I deserved what happened to me."

Rafe pulled back so he could peer into his precious child's face. He squeezed her shoulders. "*Nothing* you did can excuse what was done to you or us." He tried to brush her hair back. "I will never blame you." To his surprise, he found that he meant it. "I don't want you to ever blame yourself again for this. What's done is done."

Staring off, Karen said, "I should have—"

"Karen," Rafe said, beating back his emotions. "I love you *so* much. I would die for you, no matter what you do or don't do. The only important thing now is that you're safe again."

"I could have—"

Rafe took his daughter's face in his hands. As his own eyes poured, he felt her tears flow through his fingers. For a time, he watched her face, remembering it as it had once been and would be again.

In a hoarse voice, she said, "I'm so sorry."

Rafe whispered, "You are my daughter, and I love you. Nothing you could possibly do will ever change that. And I want you to know that I am *so proud* of you for taking care of your sister and for surviving."

"But I should have—"

"Shh," Rafe cooed. He pulled his child close again. "You're safe now. I'm here. And we'll get through this together."

EPILOGUE

Location: Liberty Base, Lakshmi Colony_

ADMIRAL PAULSON ARRIVED AT HER OFFICE IN A DISTRACTED state. There was so much to do. Forces were converging on Belia. A Mykonian battlegroup would arrive next week. The Celesian ships that Lilith had purchased would reach the New Belian Empire within a month. Following those flew still more warships flagged under Celes, in violation of treaty. The Celesians insisted, of course, that they intended no hostility.

The liars.

The Belian Imperials held almost half of the region's colonies. The rest had formed an alliance alongside Mykon to oppose them.

We're at war, she thought. *We can only hope it remains a cold one.*

A knock at the door startled Paulson. "Come in," she called, expecting to see her aid. The door swung open to reveal a group of Warden enforcers.

She shot to her feet, heart suddenly pounding, unable to guess what they could've wanted.

They entered with silent efficiency, fanning out to the walls.

From their midst, a single tall male of middle age and trim build entered.

"Good morning, Admiral," the man said in a firm tenor. "My name is Len. We have a lot to talk about."

Within the tight constraints of Cef's rules, Len mesmerized Paulson with details about Cef, himself and the contest for control over human civilization's dying embers. He explained bits about the Reservation Charter governing Cervantes: a document humanity had lost to time and calamity. Paulson listened with increasingly shallow breaths.

After staring dumbfounded at Len for several moments, she asked, "Why? Why do we have to go through this game?"

"In point of fact, you do not. We can make you do nothing to one another. Unfortunately, I believe most will participate out of fear. You have suffered from some of the incentives given to Lilith. There will be others: special weapons obtainable through quests or inside arenas of challenge."

Paulson's head turned a fraction. She peered, transfixed at the being who had flipped her world upside-down. Her list of questions had grown long, but she still didn't fully understand the stakes.

"What will this Cef do if he wins the game?" she asked.

"I... cannot discuss that."

Paulson rubbed a finger along an eyebrow. "Mr. Len, until you walked into my office, I grew up believing Cervantes's civilization had all but wiped itself out at least twice. Are you saying Cef is responsible for all that?"

"The Reservation Charter prevents us from killing unless there has been a violation of the Warden Code. That is all I can say on the matter."

Paulson wanted to slam her fists on the table. "Damn it, we figured that much out on our own. What *can* you tell me? Is the population ceiling theory right? Is this game Cef's way of killing off our excess numbers?"

"A direct answer is not possible," Len answered. "I can share that the Reservation Charter only requires us to support one hundred million of you. I think you can make the right deductions from there."

Paulson groaned. This was like playing charades with words.

"Is Cef the one who came up with this insane contest?" she said.

Len's gaze faltered. He fidgeted. "Please, understand there are many strict rules I must work under. If I overstep them, the penalties are severe. Most violations will cause forfeiture of the game."

Paulson sneered at Len. "Why should I believe you? You could be another part of this sick circus for all I know."

Len gave her an embarrassed, sympathetic smile. He looked to a Warden at his right and nodded. An instant later, Claire interrupted them.

"Admiral," she said.

"Not now," Paulson replied.

"Ma'am, you ordered me to advise you immediately when I had news about Gita Tiwari-Hastings."

The hairs on Paulson's neck stood bolt upright. A twinkle, equal parts hope and sorrow, shone in Len's eyes.

The admiral said, "Go ahead."

"Ma'am, Chief Hastings and fifteen other Zeus residents just appeared outside Gate 12: the one for the Warden shipment that docked this morning. My diagnostic suggests a Warden command was keeping me from seeing them."

Paulson stared at her visitor, eyes narrowed.

Len said, "After Zeus broke apart, there were pockets of survivors: some in the airlocks, others sealed in corridors. We had the Wardens put the people into suspended animation." He paused to let the admiral regain some poise, then added, "I think a personal call to Commander Hastings is in order. He deserves to hear this news first."

Paulson tried to fathom the gift's implications. It argued that Len really wanted to help. He could also be playing a cruel joke. Humanity had clearly been deceived for centuries.

"Why?" Paulson asked. "Why care about us?"

Len's smile faded. His words came heavy with emotion. "Because it is the right thing to do." Paulson opened her mouth to ask for more explanation, but Len held up a hand. "I will advise you when and where I am able. I failed to defend you before. Never again." He looked into Paulson's eyes. "This I swear: no matter how long it takes, I will not stop until you are free."

THANK YOU!

THANK YOU SO MUCH FOR READING *CAPTIVE EMBERS* BY BRIAN Mansur. We hope you enjoyed it as much as we enjoyed bringing it to you. We just wanted to take a moment to encourage you to review the book on Amazon and Goodreads. Every review helps further the author's reach and, ultimately, helps them continue writing fantastic books for us all to enjoy.

IF YOU LIKED THIS BOOK, CHECK OUT THE REST OF OUR CATALOG at www.aethonbooks.com. To sign up to receive updates regarding all new releases, visit www.aethonbooks.com/sign-up.

ABOUT THE AUTHOR

BRIAN MANSUR IS A NERDY SCI-FI geek who resides in the enchanted plains of Iowa with a beautiful Ecuadorian princess, their handsome son and assorted pluppy dogs. When not living the glamorous life of a top-tier customer service agent, he enjoys plotting the destruction of America's enemies as an Army National Guard officer. *Captive Embers* is his debut novel.

You can reach him through brianmansur.author@gmail.com.

ACKNOWLEDGMENTS

I stand on the shoulders of giants. While the inclusion of any organization or person's name here does not imply endorsement of this book, I owe are great debt of thanks to the following:

- Steve Apple, David Kiel and Kelly Starks, who gave me permission to retool a few scenes and characters from their work.

- Winchell Chung's Atomic Rockets website (www.projectrho.com), Rick Robinson's Rocketpunk Manifesto (www.rocketpunk-manifesto.com), Matter Beam's ToughSF Blog (toughsf.blogspot.com) and a fine gentleman named Alex H. These people and their resources helped make this novel scientifically plausible.

There are so many more individuals whose support made this project possible. In addition to those mentioned above, others who provided critical feedback and/or encouragement include:

Steve Beaulieu, Rhett C. Bruno, Matthew Friedman, Eric Langill, David S. de Lis, Vance Mansur, Rob Meier, Michael Schon. Thanks everyone.

SPECIAL THANKS TO:

ADAWIA E. ASAD
BARDE PRESS
CALUM BEAULIEU
BEN
BECKY BEWERSDORF
BHAM
TANNER BLOTTER
ALFRED JOSEPH BOHNE IV
CHAD BOWDEN
ERREL BRAUDE
DAMIEN BROUSSARD
CATHERINE BULLINER
JUSTIN BURGESS
MATT BURNS
BERNIE CINKOSKE
MARTIN COOK
ALISTAIR DILWORTH
JAN DRAKE
BRET DULEY
RAY DUNN
ROB EDWARDS
RICHARD EYRES
MARK FERNANDEZ
CHARLES T FINCHER
SYLVIA FOIL
GAZELLE OF CAERBANNOG
DAVID GEARY
MICHEAL GREEN
BRIAN GRIFFIN

EDDIE HALLAHAN
JOSH HAYES
PAT HAYES
BILL HENDERSON
JEFF HOFFMAN
GODFREY HUEN
JOAN QUERALTÓ IBÁÑEZ
JONATHAN JOHNSON
MARCEL DE JONG
KABRINA
PETRI KANERVA
ROBERT KARALASH
VIKTOR KASPERSSON
TESLAN KIERINHAWK
ALEXANDER KIMBALL
JIM KOSMICKI
FRANKLIN KUZENSKI
MEENAZ LODHI
DAVID MACFARLANE
JAMIE MCFARLANE
HENRY MARIN
CRAIG MARTELLE
THOMAS MARTIN
ALAN D. MCDONALD
JAMES MCGLINCHEY
MICHAEL MCMURRAY
CHRISTIAN MEYER
SEBASTIAN MÜLLER
MARK NEWMAN
JULIAN NORTH

KYLE OATHOUT
LILY OMIDI
TROY OSGOOD
GEOFF PARKER
NICHOLAS (BUZ) PENNEY
JASON PENNOCK
THOMAS PETSCHAUER
JENNIFER PRIESTER
RHEL
JODY ROBERTS
JOHN BEAR ROSS
DONNA SANDERS
FABIAN SARAVIA
TERRY SCHOTT
SCOTT
ALLEN SIMMONS
KEVIN MICHAEL STEPHENS
MICHAEL J. SULLIVAN
PAUL SUMMERHAYES
JOHN TREADWELL
CHRISTOPHER J. VALIN
PHILIP VAN ITALLIE
JAAP VAN POELGEEST
FRANCK VAQUIER
VORTEX
DAVID WALTERS JR
MIKE A. WEBER
PAMELA WICKERT
JON WOODALL
BRUCE YOUNG